# This Nowhere Place

# This Nowhere Place

NATASHA BELL

MICHAEL JOSEPH

MICHAEL JOSEPH

UK | USA | Canada | Ireland | Australia
India | New Zealand | South Africa

Michael Joseph is part of the Penguin Random House group of companies
whose addresses can be found at global.penguinrandomhouse.com

First published by Michael Joseph, 2021

001

Copyright © Natasha Bell, 2021

The moral right of the author has been asserted

Set in 13.5/16 pt Garamond MT Std
Typeset by Jouve (UK), Milton Keynes
Printed and bound in Great Britain by Clays Ltd, Elcograf S.p.A.

The authorized representative in the EEA is Penguin Random House Ireland,
Morrison Chambers, 32 Nassau Street, Dublin D02 YH68

A CIP catalogue record for this book is available from the British Library

HB ISBN: 978-0-241-44888-5
OM PB ISBN: 978-0-718-18754-5

www.greenpenguin.co.uk

For Jamie

There are some things an outsider can never understand. People think that because they've passed through, because they've queued for the ferry, or because they've stayed overnight in a B&B and eaten soggy fish and chips on the beach, that they know this place. That they know what someone like Jude has been through here.

She taps her fingers on the arm of her wheelchair and watches Tarek gesture towards a screen she can't see. They both wait for his colleague to reposition the camera in the corner of her living room. Under different circumstances, she'd have little time for these men. A small voice in her head tries to tell her it's not too late to change her mind.

She dismisses it and clears her throat. 'I want to say something before we go any further.'

Tarek doesn't look up. 'Give us one second.'

Jude takes a breath and tries again. 'What I told the police wasn't strictly true.'

This time Tarek's eyes flick to the scar on her cheek. He waves his fingers at his colleague and a red light appears on the front of the camera. 'Go on.'

'When I woke from my coma and they asked about the girl that was found with me, I – well, I could have told them more.'

'Do you know what happened?' Tarek says, leaning forward.

Jude frowns. 'No. My memory of that night has never returned.'

He sits back in his chair.

'You have to understand,' she says, 'I never asked for any of this.'

'If you don't remember that night, then what did you lie to the police about?'

She digs a fingernail into her palm. *This is the right thing to do*, she reminds herself. 'I told them I didn't know their dead girl.'

'But you did?'

'Cali and I met her at the end of January.'

'Five months before her death?'

Jude nods.

'Okay,' Tarek says, clearly trying to hide his excitement. His response is so predictable it almost makes her laugh. 'Tell me what happened in January 2016.'

She adjusts her weight, wincing at the familiar discomfort in her injured hip. Her dad used to say that if something was going to happen to the rest of the country, it would happen in Dover first. She pictures her father's strong arms and easy smile. It's been two months already and she cannot believe how much she misses him. She'd been thinking about moving to Hastings, starting afresh, but when her dad got sick she realized what this town meant to her. Before he died, he helped her understand it was time to do this; time to stop hiding.

'There was a riot,' she says now. 'Hundreds of people surged through our city to demonstrate against all the things they thought were wrong with the country – namely immigrants and refugees.'

She studies the man across from her. An estimated 2,000 migrants were illegally entering the country every week back then. There were 2 million people living in camps around Europe. But she doesn't need to tell him that, does she? He was one of them. One article called him 'the Syrian Louis Theroux'. He's built a career by casting an acerbic Middle Eastern eye on Western problems. Presumably that's why he's interested in all this in the first place. With the ten-year anniversary coming up, he thinks he can cash in on a quick, sensational story. She wonders if he understands how close it felt for them here, though. On a clear night as a teenager she could almost see the camps. Twenty-one miles across the water. It broke her heart to know that people like him were living and dying in a city of tents.

She takes a sip from the glass of water on the table and wonders how far she can steer him. 'It's hard to understand unless you're from here, but Dover is the sort of town that's anchored to its history. To the whole country's history, in fact. There are ancient boats buried beneath roundabouts, Roman remains under swing sets. Every step you take in this town is on top of someone's blood, someone's bones, some-one's tragedy.'

'What does—'

She cuts him off. 'Chalk absorbs water faster than it releases it. Julius Caesar said this part of the coast was impenetrable, so he sailed on to start his invasion around the coast at Thanet. But what Caesar didn't understand was that when the temperature drops, the saturated cliffs freeze, the water expands, and the chalk cracks and crumbles into the sea. The cliffs are just as vulnerable as they are tough.'

Tarek looks as if he's about to say something, but she hurries on.

'I have a theory that the cliffs are like the people here. They crack and crumble, but somehow they stand tough and impenetrable, guardians of the centuries.'

That was good, she thinks. He'd better put that in.

'What happened on the day of the riot, Jude?'

His dark eyes remind her of Cali's. She looks away. 'I hurried into town. I didn't know how, but I needed to help.'

Jude remembers standing at the end of Effingham Street, by the roundabout, as the rioters stomped by. She felt like spitting, throwing a punch, doing something. But, in truth, she was frightened too. She was fifteen and any one of those men could easily have overpowered her. She imagined bumping into them later, on her way home or on another day. She imagined how their rage might manifest one-to-one.

'I went to Cali's house afterwards,' she says to the camera.

*You should have been there*, Jude said, standing in Cali's bedroom doorway. *It was intense.* Foot up on the nightstand, Cali continued painting her toenails in silence. Jude sat down and stroked the cat.

'Cali was upset by the violence, so I suggested we get out of the way, go up to the cliffs.'

Ever since they were little, the cliffs had been their place.

'Just before we got to the old sound mirror, the heavens opened, so we ran to shelter in it.'

Jude pauses. Should she tell him what a sound mirror is? He's not from around here.

'They were a forerunner of radar. Big concrete dishes that gave early warnings of incoming enemy aircraft.'

Tarek nods.

'We often sat up there. We hadn't seen anyone else on the paths, which was how we liked it. We were starting to get cold, though. Sometimes when it was like that, Cali would be fine and chatting right up until she started shivering uncontrollably. She hadn't even started out chatty that day, so I kept glancing at her, trying to work out how long we had before I'd need to get her inside and to a hot chocolate and a radiator.'

4

*You want to talk about what's up?* Jude said. *I'm here if you need—*
*Drop it, will you?*

Jude tucks her hair behind her ear. It's been a long time since she's deliberately remembered these events. She takes another sip of water and gives a small smile to the camera. 'Her sister, Rose, was staying and I said it had been nice to see her again, but Cali didn't reply. I asked what was wrong and told her not to shut me out, but she kept messing around with her phone. After a while she placed her hands on the concrete lip and pushed herself out of the mirror. Then she turned back to face me, this hard look in her eye. She lifted her head and shouted into the curve – I'll never forget what she shouted: "I wish I'd died! I wish they'd let me die!"'

Jude swallows.

Cali's cry was deadened by the wind and the rain. Jude looked at her best friend standing there getting wet. Until that moment it hadn't sunk in how close she'd come to losing her, how awful it would have been if she had.

She shakes her head for the camera. 'Cali grinned and asked if I thought anyone had heard that out to sea. I didn't know if she was serious or not, I didn't know how to respond. But then a small, clear voice startled us. "I heard you," someone said. We turned and there was this girl.'

Tarek leans forward again. 'This was the first time you saw her?'

Jude narrows her eyes. There were three Dover Girls, she'd like to remind him; this is as much her and Cali's story as it is this girl's. She's fed up of people forgetting that.

She takes a breath and tries to calm down. His interest is natural. After all, this is the part she hasn't told before. When the police questioned her after she woke from her coma, she gave their dead girl a name but told them she'd been Cali's friend, not hers, that she'd met her at a party once but had no idea why they'd been found together on the night of Cali's funeral. Her parents closed ranks. They asked the authorities and the reporters to respect their daughter's privacy, to let her concentrate on her recovery. She was a victim too, they reminded them.

'She was tiny,' Jude says now. 'There was almost nothing to her. She looked like she'd wrapped herself in all the clothes she owned. Her tatty woollen scarf was whipping so fiercely in the wind that I was scared she might blow away. She had dark eyes and a mole on her cheek. I had no idea where she was from, but you could tell it wasn't Dover. There was water dripping from her nose and eyelashes and she was shivering even more than Cali. She stared at us until Cali sat back down and gestured for her to join us.'

Jude pauses, reliving the memory. She looks around the room, comforted by her things. It is okay, she tells herself. She has built a good life. Still, it's hard not to recognize that things could be completely different right now. If they'd never taken shelter in the sound mirror that day, her best friend might still be alive.

Jude closes her eyes.

*Who are you?* Cali said.

*Will you help me?* the girl replied in thickly accented English. *My name is Mo.*

# Dover Girls

**94% Match**   2026   15   1 Season   **HD**

## Episode List

| | | |
|---|---|---|
| 1 | **The Girls** | 9 |
| 2 | **The Town** | 61 |
| 3 | **The Riot** | 105 |
| 4 | **The Party** | 145 |
| 5 | **The Fire** | 181 |
| 6 | **The Fall** | 231 |
| 7 | **The Search** | 269 |
| 8 | **The Funeral** | 299 |
| 9 | **The Grand Shaft** | 329 |
| 10 | **The Truth** | 357 |

# The Girls

## CONFERENCE ROOM – BEST WESTERN HOTEL

Woman with short hair looks around before leaning back in chair.

> ROSE
>
> I don't know what you're hoping to find out here, but what happened to my sister was a tragedy.

**SCREEN TITLE: ROSE WALKER, CALI'S SISTER**

> (scratches behind ear.)
>
> No family should have to go through what mine did.

CUT TO.

## MODERN FLAT – LIVING ROOM

Woman in wheelchair drums her fingers on the arm.

> JUDE
>
> You want me to introduce myself?

**SCREEN TITLE: JUDE CAMPBELL**

> Fine, well, hello, I'm Jude – Judith Campbell – and I'm one of the Dover Girls.

The one that survived.

CUT TO.

## AERIAL ESTABLISHING SHOT

White cliffs. Harbour. Ferries. Port.

VOICEOVER

In the summer of 2016, in the quiet port town of Dover, by all accounts a 'nowhere place', two teenagers died and one was left with life-changing injuries.

CUT TO.

## ARCHIVE FOOTAGE: CHANNEL 4 NEWS

Journalists stand in front of iron gates crossed with police tape.

REPORTER

An as-yet unidentified teenager has fallen to her death in Dover on the day of the funeral of sixteen-year-old Cali Walker, who herself was found at the bottom of Shakespeare Cliff just two weeks ago. A third – local girl Jude Campbell – remains in a critical condition after the incident. Rumours have been spreading about a suicide pact, but the discovery of £500 in cash at the site of the second death has sparked further police enquiries.

# NEWSNIGHT

Presenter in the studio with panel.

### PANELLIST 1

The suicide rates for teens across the country are at an all-time high—

### SCREEN TITLE: PSYCHOLOGIST & REPRESENTATIVE OF CHILD AND ADOLESCENT MENTAL HEALTH SERVICES (CAMHS)

—and what happened in Dover is the final wake-up call. We need this government to take immediate action.

### PANELLIST 2

I agree.

### SCREEN TITLE: MP FOR HACKNEY NORTH

The hijacking of this incident by a small number of right-wing agitators intent on pushing their immigration agenda is despicable. Young people in our country are dying right now because—

### PANELLIST 3

I'm sorry, but I have to stop you there.

There is no actual evidence this was a suicide pact. That's something the liberal elite are bringing in to muddy the issue. Because what we do know is that one of the girls found at the bottom of the Shaft was *not* a British citizen. She came to this country illegally. She—

CUT TO.

JUDE

I was fifteen at the time. I was taking my GCSEs, about to start college. I had my whole life ahead of me, just like Cali.

INTERVIEWER
(off-screen)

And Mo?

JUDE

Absolutely. Just like Mo too. Like both of them.

(pauses.)

I want to make it clear that *I* never blamed Mo for what happened. She was our friend – mine and Cali's. We didn't care where she was from, how she'd got here. None of that mattered to us.

CUT TO.

ROSE

My sister was nice to people – too nice if you ask me, which is why I think she got mixed up with what she did.

I didn't know anything about that girl Mo until after it was all over, but I'm not surprised my sister befriended her. That's the kind of thing she would do. And if she thought Mo was in trouble, if she felt like she hadn't been able to keep her safe—

Well, Cali wouldn't have been able to handle that.

CUT TO.

## SCHOOL PHOTOGRAPH

Young girl with brown hair and dark eyes grins at the camera.

JUDE

(off-screen)

Cali Walker was my best friend. My best friend for, well, forever really.

CUT TO.

ROSE

Cali had no problem making friends, but it was finding ones that understood her that was the problem.

(looks away.)

There's not a day that goes by that I don't miss her.

CUT TO.

JUDE

Rose and Cali weren't full sisters, okay? They had different dads, and there was six years between them, so they weren't close.

Cali's dad left when she was really young. Her mum met him in South America while she was travelling. She'd abandoned Rose with her parents and disappeared to see the world. Then she turned up pregnant again and they all moved to Dover. Cali's dad left after a couple of years, then they had a step-dad around for a bit, but mostly it was just the three of them. Then, when Rose left, just Cali and her mum.

INTERVIEWER

(off-screen)

When did you meet Cali?

JUDE

(laughs.)

In toddler group, apparently. Though I can't remember that. Supposedly Cali raised her hand to be my pair as soon as my mum set me down.

From that day, every day, we drank our juice side by side, held hands during story-time and napped with our heads touching. If one of us was upset, the other threw a tantrum in solidarity.

(takes tissue.)

Excuse me.

(wipes eyes.)

It's not what you say about friends, I suppose, but I really think it was like love at first sight. Best-friend love. Even when we were tiny, we just instinctively knew everything about each other. We were one and the same. As close as two people could be.

CUT TO.

ROSE

You're not sisters, people used to tell us. Like we were stupid children who must be confused. How could this pale, pudgy tomboy be related to the beautiful, olive-skinned, half-Brazilian girl?

(scratches neck.)

I used to make up excuses to cross from the junior to the infant playground to check up on her. Other kids fell over and burst into tears, or sulked because they were the slowest in races and got left

out of games. But I never saw Cali cry at school.
She kept it all inside.

CUT TO.

JUDE

(sobbing.)

You think as time passes things will stop hurting,
but they don't.

CUT TO.

ROSE

(frowns.)

I don't think any of us understood what Cali was
going through.

CUT TO.

JUDE

(wipes eyes.)

The day Cali left for Reception, my mum told me
I screamed so loudly and so incessantly that she
had to be called to come and pick me up.

(faces camera.)

I suppose, in a way, that was the first time I lost
Cali.

ROSE

I promised her I'd always be there for her. But when she needed me most, I failed.

# THEN

Rose smiled at the woman on the opposite bar stool. This was her second date of the day, but it seemed she would still be going home alone.

'Two in one day!' her housemate, Jax, had said that morning, raising his hands to his mouth.

'Scandalous,' his partner, Sean, had said, punching her in the arm.

You had to be open to possibilities. That was her rule. You literally never knew who you were going to walk into a bar and meet. She wasn't a monster. She wanted to find the real thing as much as the next person. She'd grown up listening to songs and watching films about true love. Even if they were all grossly heterosexual, she wasn't immune to their messages. But she was practical too. Nothing in her life so far had indicated any of those fairy-tale endings might apply to her.

Initially she might have signed up to the app hoping to find something real, but when she did finally meet up with someone for the first time, the woman bought her one drink then asked if she wanted to do a line and fuck. Rose had had a split second to adapt her expectations, to decide whether to go home alone or to see where life took her. Within a year she'd become the one asking those sorts of questions and watching how her dates' features changed, how their eyes bulged or their cheeks coloured while she tried to make a quick assessment about what sort of women they were. Some would turn up wearing their hearts on their sleeves and she was never a twat to them, never took advantage. But if they were up for a good time, then so was she. Why not? Nobody got hurt.

The woman opposite her tonight was Australian. She worked in publishing and her profile picture had shown her flexing into an improbable-looking yoga position on top of a climbing frame. Rose had been expecting someone easy-going and adventurous. All this woman had talked about so far, however, was that she wanted to settle down and have children but also thought she might be in love with her therapist. Rose was on the rebound from the one proper relationship she'd ever had and not feeling all that picky, but even she could tell there was no spark here. Grace had dumped her on New Year's Day and made some pretty reductive comments about Rose acting like a man just because she was butch, but they'd at least had chemistry. Even when she was complaining that Rose didn't tell her enough about herself, or that she must have more of an answer than 'nothing' when she said 'What are you think-ing?', five minutes later they'd be panting and sweating and none of it would matter.

The Australian was still talking, so Rose drained her beer and signalled to the barman for another. Her mind wandered to her sister. She'd missed a call from Cali yes-terday. When she'd tried to call back in her break at work, her piece-of-shit phone had decided the 24 per cent of battery it supposedly had was in fact a big fat zero. Cali hadn't been picking up since, and the single grey ticks beside Rose's last five messages said they hadn't even been delivered.

'Do you think I'm emotionally unavailable?' she'd asked Cali when they'd last spoken. Rose had been standing out-side Grace's flat, wondering what had just happened.

'This girl's basic, stop thinking about her,' Cali had replied.

Rose had laughed and nodded at a bank of recycling bins. If they'd been in the same city, she'd thought, she could have sacked off work and taken Cali to a pub. They could have drunk with the New Year's Day crowds and it would have felt good and a little weird because her kid sister was basically an adult now. Sweet sixteen. Rose had been dreaming about asking Cali to join her in London after her GCSEs. She imagined them living together while Cali sat her A-levels, maybe even went to university; helping her sister build a proper, stable life. In reality, Rose was barely able to look after herself: she lived as a lodger, worked in a coffee shop, and spent too many nights in grubby gay bars to ever be responsible for a teenager. But the idea helped ease some of her guilt for abandoning Cali in Dover.

The following day Cali had posted a picture of a dead squirrel with the words:

THE WORST IS NOT, SO LONG
AS WE CAN SAY 'THIS IS THE WORST'

Rose had shot off a DM asking if Cali was okay and got an equally cryptic:

We two alone will sing like birds i' th'
cage

*You're mad*, Rose had typed back. Cali's reply was immediate:

O! Let me not be mad, not mad,
sweet heaven!

Seriously, what are you on?

King Lear, you idiot. I get my mock
results on Monday.

Shit. Good luck.

Rose's message window had filled with a laughing and crying emoji and a bunch of kisses. She'd sent some kisses back and gone to work, easily forgetting about both her sister and Shakespeare. That was the last she'd heard from Cali until the missed phone call yesterday. She really needed to phone her back.

'I've got a breakfast meeting tomorrow,' Rose's date said finally, leaving a pause. 'You coming to the tube?'

Rose glanced at her empty glass. 'I might stay for another.' She noticed a flicker of judgement pass across her date's features. *Fuck you*, she thought.

Once the other woman had left, Rose messaged her colleague to ask if he fancied a drink.

Already out, chica. Come join!

Twenty minutes later, she met Diego outside a pub in Vauxhall. 'Let's go somewhere we can party!' he said, kissing her on the cheek.

Rose hesitated, wondering if her bank balance could survive a proper night out.

'Come on,' Diego said. 'You are sad and depressed and you need cheering up. I read this article that said MDMA can cure things like PTSD. There have been trials and everything. *Es terapéutico!*'

Rose laughed. 'You're a doctor now then, are you?'

Diego grinned and led her towards the Tavern, ducking first into an alleyway so he could wrap them each a bomb.

'Thanks,' Rose said.

'*De nada.*'

Ten minutes after they'd got through the queue and inside the club, Diego buggered off as she knew he would to chat up some sequin-clad guy. She started with beer, then moved on to whisky, her thoughts thudding with the beat as she came up. Thursdays were normally decent in this place, but tonight was quiet. She glanced at Diego and his victim. She ordered two shots and checked the app in case someone new had replied. She knew it was a bad idea to come out wanting to pick up. At the beginning of the night you set your sights high, then they started to drop, until it was an any-port-in-a-storm kind of situation. But Rose needed a release. She moved through the thin crowd, thinking of ports and storms and ferries on the Channel. She closed her eyes as she danced, imagining herself a fishing boat stuck out at sea, the bodies around her gulls diving for scraps. There used to be these sea-men, the Cinque Port Pilots, who were paid to guide the larger ships into shore. Funny what she remembered from school.

She felt an elbow in her back as someone pushed past, then a hand on her shoulder. 'Steady!' someone said as she staggered into them.

'I'm fine,' she murmured, searching for the beat again. Those men knew all the sandbanks and rocks around Dover, all the currents. They steered their little boats with great ocean liners following, pulling them safely into port.

Rose lurched forwards. She felt the room spinning. Her vision began to flicker and she laughed, realizing she was fucked. She wished she could call up a Cinque Port Pilot and tell him to steer her little sister to her, to guide them both home.

'Are you okay?' someone asked. It was a woman's voice, deep and sexy. She sounded Eastern European. Rose looked up, ready to smile, feeling slightly dizzy.

'You were calling for someone called Cali,' the woman said. 'Want me to get her?'

That's when it registered Rose was sitting in the bogs. On the damn floor. She'd been sick in the sink. Fuck. What was she playing at?

'What's your name?' she asked, wading through her heavy thoughts to wonder if she still had a chance. 'Where are you from?'

The woman laughed. 'I am not going home with you.'

Rose stuck out her bottom lip. She could see her trying not to, but the woman smiled.

'Poland. My name is Kassia.'

'Can't knock a girl for trying,' Rose said, giving her a wink.

'Even with vomit on her shirt.'

'Shit.' Rose looked down and, yes, she did have vomit on her shirt. She fumbled to zip up her jacket.

Kassia laughed again. It was loud and confident, a bark of unapologetic amusement.

'Don't laugh at me.'

'Why not?' Kassia was still smiling, her almond eyes creased at the sides, her teeth thrust forward over her bottom lip. Washing pots at work the next day, Rose found she could remember her perfectly. She only remembered snippets of the night, but she could see Kassia in HD clarity. She had pale skin and dark hair, thick eyebrows. She didn't look like most of the people in the club. She was older too, Rose guessed. Her hair was chin length, thin and tightly moulded to her head, making her ears and eyes seem enormous. No boobs to speak of, but an amazing arse.

'If you are okay, I am going to leave you,' Kassia had said, turning so Rose could admire the vintage 501s hanging low on that arse.

'Wait.'

Kassia looked back. 'Not tonight.' And she pushed the door and left. Rose ran the tap, half-heartedly trying to clean up her mess. Rinsed her mouth, splashed water on her face. Her cheeks were flushed, but she looked okay still. She made her way out of the loos and into the club, looked around the bar, the dance floor, the seats up at the top, but Kassia was gone.

By Sunday, Rose still hadn't heard from Cali. She tried to tell herself Cali must have dropped her phone in the loo or trodden on her charger, but she looked at the list of undelivered messages and admitted it was time to take the plunge.

'Rose?'

She heard the surprise in her mother's voice. They'd graduated from the zero contact they'd had after Rose first ran away to the odd *how are you?* and *happy birthday* text, but as a rule they did not speak on the phone. Rose hadn't been back in person for almost two years.

'Where's Cali?' Rose said.

'At Jude's, I think.'

'You think?'

Her mother sighed. 'She's a teenager, she's never home.'

Rose could picture her mum under a duvet in their stuffy living room, the curtains drawn. A scene that hadn't changed in years.

'She hasn't answered her phone in days. When did you last see her?'

'The girls were here last night. What's with the third degree?'

Rose pushed her lip stud back and forth with her tongue. 'I don't know. I'm worried about her. Is she okay?'

'She's fine.'

'Will you ask her to call me?'

She heard her mother yawn.

'Mum?'

'Sure. I'll pass on the message. Anything else?'

'Uh, no.'

'Well, it's nice of you to call. Nice of you to ask how I am, wish me a happy new year, keep me updated about your life.'

'Mum—'

'I know you think everything's my fault and that I'm this terrible mother who can't be trusted to look after your precious sister, but you're not exactly the world's best daughter.'

'I know.'

'Jasper died.'

'Cali told me.'

'And you didn't think to get in touch, see how I was doing?'

'Cali said you didn't get out of bed for days.'

'Of course I didn't! I loved that dog. I was heartbroken.'

Rose took a breath. 'How are you now, Mum?'

She made a noise like she was blowing a raspberry. 'Fine.'

'What does the doctor say?'

'I've got a new one. I think she's got my prescription wrong.'

'You're taking it, though?'

'You don't have to treat me like a child.'

'Are you working?'

'Yes, actually. I have a shift tonight.'

'Good.'

Rose stared at a spot on her wall. She'd spent the first seventeen years of her life trying to understand her mother's actions and moods. It was selfish, but Rose's life was much simpler when she tried not to think about her.

After they'd hung up, Rose got out of bed. She was still worried about Cali, but maybe she didn't need to be. Maybe she was projecting her own strange frame of mind onto her sister.

She rang Diego and a few hours later they were back in his favourite shit club. Rose's head was spinning and she was dancing with a woman with pigtails that she wasn't sure were ironic. Once she'd fuzzed the edges of her thoughts with lager and sambuca, though, she hoped it wouldn't matter. The logical solution to the dread she knew she'd feel when she woke up tomorrow and realized there was another day to be endured before she could drink and numb herself again seemed to be to make sure she woke up next to someone. Anyone really.

Then she saw Kassia standing behind the bar.

*This is it*, Rose thought through her stupor. She slithered away from pigtails.

'You work here?'

'Obviously.' Kassia pointed at Rose's beer. 'Last time was free, but I'm not cleaning you up again.'

Rose blinked, embarrassed. 'I'm fine tonight.'

'We all think we are fine until we are not.'

Rose nodded. It was the truest thing she'd ever heard. She wanted to lean across the bar and smash her lips against this woman's.

Kassia tilted her head, amused.

'What's funny?'

'You.'

'I don't mean to be.'

'I assume not.'

'When do you finish?' Rose said, floundering.

'Soon.'

'Are you staying out?'

'Until I go.'

'Do you want to go?' This was as close as Rose could get

to asking outright. She was normally in control, but with this woman she was not. It frightened and excited her.

'With you?' Kassia said, their eyes locked.

Rose broke their gaze, sipped her beer.

'You want to go home with me,' Kassia continued. It was a statement, not a question.

Rose nodded, glancing at the row of bottles behind Kassia's shoulder, feeling as if she was admitting she'd done something wrong to a teacher.

'Why?' Kassia said.

'Why does anyone want to go home with anyone?' Rose said, too fast, too flippant. Not cool.

'So go home with anyone.' Kassia gestured to the dance floor.

There was a pause. Rose said too quietly to be heard over the music, 'I want you.'

'Excuse me?'

Rose looked up. Kassia was pressing for eye contact. She wetted her lips with the tip of a pink tongue. 'I want to go home with you,' Rose shouted.

After she'd signed out, Kassia guided Rose to a bus stop, onto the top deck, then down again, through an empty car park, past a closed-up TK Maxx and along terraced streets. She settled on a house in the middle of a row.

'You have housemates?'

Kassia shook her head. 'Not tonight. One dropped out, the other is at home for the week.'

'Are you a student?' Rose asked, confused. She'd thought she was older.

'PhD.'

'Smart, then.'

Kassia cocked her head. Rose didn't know what to say, so glanced around the hallway.

'So,' Kassia said.

'So,' Rose said.

'Come here.'

Afterwards, they listened to Rose's heavy breaths, her heart-beat slowing, her sex in their nostrils. Kassia lay back against the pillows. She was still in her clothes. Rose rolled over and reached for Kassia's fly.

'It's okay,' she said.

'I want to.'

'I know you do. But it is okay.'

Rose frowned. She didn't get it. She didn't want to be in her debt.

'Can I at least see you?' she said after a while.

'Why?'

'I've been thinking about your arse for days.'

That laugh again, only now Rose felt included. Kassia rolled off the bed and, standing in front of the curtains, pulled her trousers off. 'Happy?' she said, lying down, still in her shirt.

Rose slept curled inside her, waking to pee and lap water from the tap. She lay awake, her head already pounding. Her phone was dead, she didn't know the time. Kassia switched on the light and reached for a strip of ibuprofen from the nightstand, handed it to her.

'Thanks,' Rose said, touched. Kassia turned off the light and they fell back to sleep.

Kassia brought her a cup of coffee in the morning. Rose reached to pull her onto the bed and she didn't resist. She walked home feeling invincible. Then she plugged her phone in to charge and it pinged with a voicemail from Dover hospital.

Cali had tried to kill herself.

# 2026

Tarek presses pause, freezing the frame on Jude's face. He stares at the pale scar dissecting her right cheek. It was hard not to keep looking at it while filming with her. Scars, physical and mental, are the topic of much of his most celebrated work, but in front of Jude he felt like some curious child, sure his flickering eyes betrayed the thoughts in his head. Could she tell he didn't trust her?

He jumps back to a section near the beginning and presses play.

'—it's a simple fact that unless you spend some time actually in this chair, looking like I do, you have literally no understanding of what it's like. I'm the first to admit that before the accident I was completely ignorant. I was one of those people who might hold a door for someone like me, but still secretly resent it if they blocked my view at the cinema. It's human nature that we struggle to empathize with things we have no personal experience of, things we see as distant. That's why I set up my charity, The Cali Walker Foundation. We pair mentors with at-risk and vulnerable teenagers, to try to help them through the difficulties of circumstance they face so they can reach their full potential. Cali was the most caring, compassionate person I've ever met, but from a really young age she was let down by both the system and those around her. I set it up in her name so that every day I'd be reminded of why I'm doing this.'

Tarek rubs his face and leans back in the hard hotel chair. All this will get cut. The revelation that she lied to the police about knowing Mo was interesting, but too much of the footage they shot with Jude consisted of virtuous waffle like this. He's not an idiot; he knows it's why she agreed to do this – to take control of her public image. He was surprised when she changed her mind about participating, but then she mentioned running for mayor and things began to make sense. Politicians, though, even of the small-town variety, rarely make good interviewees. Especially not ones as burnt by the media as Jude. His instinct tells him there's still more to this story; Jude was too careful and composed throughout filming not to be hiding something else.

He opens the file with the new footage they shot today. He scrolls forward and makes a note of the time stamp, then presses play.

'Thanks,' Rose says on-screen. 'Should I go on?'

Tarek hears his own voice, then watches Rose cross and uncross her legs, clearly considering how to continue her narrative. He spent all morning observing her, trying to work out how to get her to open up. Frustratingly, the most honest moment they had today was off-screen, during one of the breaks.

'I saw online that you're having a baby,' Rose said, dropping down beside him on the bench outside the hotel.

Tarek had been checking his email and hurried to put his phone away.

'My partner and I are trying. She's wanted a family for ages.'

'Congratulations,' Tarek said.

Rose stared at the boats bobbing in the harbour. 'She doesn't want me to talk to you, you know? By the time she finds out, I'm hoping . . .' She trailed off. 'I want to make her happy, but it's a lot – the money, time, everything.'

Tarek studied Rose's profile, wondering where this was going.

'I keep thinking I don't know what a normal family looks like. I wake up in the night worrying I won't know how to do it. What if everything that happened means I shouldn't be a parent? What if I don't deserve a family?' She turned to Tarek. 'Do you ever feel like that?'

Tarek didn't know what to say. He was glad Rose was opening up to him. The more comfortable she feels with him off-camera, the more she's likely to reveal on-camera. But he felt a spark of anger too, a stab of loyalty for her partner. He wanted to call her up and tell her what Rose had just said. Because surely nobody would want a child with someone who wasn't sure. After Helen's second miscarriage, Tarek had almost given up hope. Rose's worries make no sense to him. Having lost his family the way he did is the very reason he wants to create one. It's precisely because of what he's been through that he's sure he'll do anything to protect Helen and their child. Anything at all.

'I know you don't talk about your life much,' Rose said, 'that your whole thing is telling the stories of others. But I read that you came through the camps, that you lost everything. I know it's a strange thing to say, but learning that made me feel like you'd do this right. Like you'd understand something deeper about the questions you're asking. I don't know. Maybe that's stupid. What you went through must have been awful and I know it's not the same or anything. But still. Sometimes when I'm talking to people, I feel like I have to split them into two types: those who have been through something big, and those who haven't.'

Tarek nodded. Years of doing this job have taught him to keep silent, to allow people to talk. Everything she was saying would have been better on camera, but it was useful nonetheless.

'And I don't mean like those who've been in a car crash or

had cancer or something when they're so clearly a blameless victim that all you can feel is sympathy. I mean like addicts, like me. People who've experienced something that's fundamentally changed who they are and how they look at themselves. People who've had to come face-to-face with the darkest parts of themselves and find a way to keep going. People who understand the kind of loss and guilt that never goes away.'

Rose pulled a packet of cigarettes from her jacket. Tarek reached into his own pocket and offered the lighter he carries despite never having smoked.

'Thanks,' Rose said as she exhaled. She glanced at the cliff to her right. 'I read about your awards and I watched your film on mental health in detention centres. Your work's kind of, I don't know, sensitive. And honest. I like that.'

Tarek crouches now to retrieve a Coke from the minibar. Rose is still talking from the screen. He perches on the edge of the bed to watch. She's leaning back in the conference chair, left ankle crossed over right knee, shirtsleeves rolled up to reveal arms almost black with tattoos. Her manner in front of the camera isn't as open as it was on the bench.

'The thing is,' she's saying, 'I wasn't exactly in the best place at the time of all this. I'd been spinning on my axis for a while, telling myself I was taking control of my life when probably I was doing the exact opposite. It's something you see again and again in meetings: people don't realize how out of their depth they are until after they've made it back to shore. *If* they make it back.'

Tarek learnt a long time ago that there are two types of interviewees: the ones hungry for attention, and the ones scared of it. Jude was the former. As long as he let her rattle on about her charity and the council, he didn't have a problem getting her to talk. Even if what she actually had to say, in the end, amounted to very little.

Rose is different. It took him several lengthy phone calls to convince her to talk to him. He'd laid it on pretty thick that this was her chance to tell Cali's story, to reach out and help other families suffering the effects of depression and mental illness. But he's under no illusion that it was the £5,000 fee he offered out of his own pocket that swayed things. She's more talkative than he imagined, but he can tell she's already decided what she does and doesn't want to speak about.

He fast-forwards, watching her move jerkily around on the padded chair in the corner of the hotel conference room. He'd have preferred to film her at home, but she refused. This place has seen better days, but they've been good about accommodating him. The staff seem excited to have filming going on here, even if few of them are old enough to remember the events it's about. Tomorrow, he'll see if Rose is up for a change of location. He'd like to take her up to the cliffs, see how she remembers Cali in the place that she died, but he'll need to tread carefully.

He pauses and clicks back to Jude. What he needs to find are some nuggets from each of these testimonies to pull to the front of the feature, dangle as promises of what's to come. He won't be able to construct a full narrative until he finishes filming with Rose, but his mind is already racing towards the copy he'll need to write for the press release, the voiceover he imagines gently guiding the narrative. His producer has run a couple of names past him. Martin is a long shot, but might work. Tarek's been wondering about a female voice, though. It seems more fitting for the story. He already feels uneasy that it's him and a male cameraman conducting these interviews. He's all too aware of the potential criticism that they'll give this story a male gaze. There *are* ways around such things, though. It has to be done sensitively, that's all. Which is always the case. Filming in Dover is no different from filming in Lagos or Zaatari. And besides, Tarek does have his reasons for feeling this is his story to tell.

His blood ran cold when he first came across the name Mo in an archived news story four months ago. After an initial flurry of social media chatter, several outlets had reported that the girl found with Jude at the bottom of the Shaft might have been known as 'Ellie'. When Jude regained consciousness, however, Kent Online reported that she'd referred to her as 'Mo'. Both names remained unconfirmed and most reporters seemed to prefer the splashier 'undocumented immigrant', so though Tarek had been aware of the incident when it happened, it wasn't until he stumbled across the article earlier this year that he made any kind of connection. He tried to tell himself it was nothing, a tiny coincidence not worth getting his hopes up about. It didn't work. Absurd as it was, he felt an inexplicable certainty that finally, after all this time, he was on the right track. That this was the girl he'd been looking for.

'What's the angle?' Tarek's boss, Olga, asked when he pitched it. 'Who's going to care?' Those were her normal challenges to any new pitch and Tarek had come prepared with information about the continually climbing rates of teenage depression and with viewing figures for similar cold-case documentaries screened in the past eighteen months. Still, he felt his palms sweating. He's never used his professional resources for a personal investigation before. That the ten-year anniversary is coming up worked in his favour, but he still had to push hard to get Olga to sign off on the modest budget he needed. Two British Journalism Awards, an Amnesty Media prize and a BAFTA are not enough to give him carte blanche. She wants to send him back to Nigeria for a follow-up to his 2022 documentary. She's also been suggesting for a while that he consider returning to Aleppo to do a piece about his former home. Tarek saw her eyes light up when he mentioned Dover, thinking he was about to pitch her something along those lines: a backwards journey across the Channel, through the desecrated camps, retracing his trauma across land and sea. He wasn't able to tell her why he thinks this story is linked to that trauma, why it's so important he investigate it now.

'It's very British,' she said finally. 'You've made your name as an intrepid investigator. Your viewers expect you to go places they wouldn't dare.'

'It's because it's so British that this piece has legs,' Tarek argued. 'And who better to investigate something so insular, something so small-town, than an outsider?'

Tarek jots a sentence on the back of a hotel envelope, then scribbles it out. This story is as much about the place as the characters, but he wonders if it's the depth of history here that's allowed these events to go so unnoticed. He searches through Jude's footage for a section he remembers.

Despite her insistence on answering the question she wished he'd asked rather than the one he actually had, Tarek did warm to Jude when she started talking about her town. His father was a history professor, so he too grew up feeling the streets he walked upon held more than the present. Unlike Jude, though, the history of his upbringing is lost. Even if he wanted to, he has nothing to return to.

He closes his eyes and tries to push it away, but already the image is surfacing. The one he's been trying not to see since it landed in his inbox. The blue lips and blood-crusted hair. The hollow cheeks and far too pale skin. The woman should never have sent it to him. When he first got through to her, Tarek thought she was going to be as unhelpful as everyone else he'd spoken to. She repeated what he'd heard before: if he wanted to access a nine-year-old file of a case with an unidentified body then he needed to apply to the Missing Persons Unit with an official request. If his application was accepted, he'd be offered an appointment to attend a supervised file viewing. If he wanted to copy any of the documents to take away or to access any forensic or DNA samples, he would need to apply separately for a licence, stating what he intended to use them for. Tarek growled on the other end of the line that this was an absurd amount of bureaucracy for a single Jane Doe file. The woman apologized and explained once again that changes in the law meant they had to be much more careful about data protection. She agreed with him that the situation was problematic.

'We used to put the whole database online,' she said, 'even some of the photographs. That kind of large-scale public identification appeal is unthinkable now, but it used to mean people could take an active role in searching for their lost loved ones. Now there's none of that. Even if you told me you thought you were related to this individual, I couldn't offer you any more help. The sad fact is that ninety per cent of these files will never be opened again.'

'Is there no other way?'

'You could try the original investigating force—'

Tarek cut her off. 'It was Kent Police that referred me to you.'

'Look,' she said, 'I know it's frustrating and I can see on the record that this is the fifth time you've rung. I can't make any promises, okay, but if you start the ball rolling with the paperwork, I'll make a note of your details and see if there's anything I can do to speed things up.'

Three days later, she sent him an email.

**To:** zayattarek@tnnmedia.co.uk
**From:** dyardley@nationalcrimeagency.org
**Date:** Mar 3, 2026, 9.32AM
**Subject:** Bureau Reference Number: 16-679368 – CONTENT WARNING

Dear Mr Zayat
I'm sorry they're so disturbing, but I know how desperate you are to identify this one. I hope it helps your research.
Best wishes
Deborah

'It's not her,' Tarek said aloud after he'd opened the first attachment. Relief flooded his limbs. He'd prepared himself for the worst. Even though it meant he would need to start his search from scratch, the fact that this wasn't the girl he was searching for brought him a renewed sense of hope. He was almost smiling as he clicked on the second attachment and watched the profile load on his screen. Then his face fell. From this new angle, he could see a mole just above the jawline. He stared at it for a long time, wanting to rub it off. Everything else, he thought, he could justify away. The hair was too long, the skin too pale, the eyes too tired. But really, there was only one answer to the spot the difference he was playing with his memory: the girl in the picture was dead.

Tarek opens his eyes. He breathes slowly and tells himself to get a grip. He's seen bodies before. He's witnessed loss. Besides, he still doesn't know for sure. He won't be able to see the rest of the file until his paperwork and licences are approved. Even with the mole and the coincidence of the name, he can't be 100 per cent sure this is her. He knows about false positives and confirmation bias. After searching for so long, it would be entirely feasible for his subconscious to be so set on the answer he wants to find that it wilfully ignores indicators to the contrary.

And even if it is her, he already knows that the police file won't tell him what happened. No part of him believes these stories about blackmail and attempted murder. Or the ones about suicide. Something else occurred that night, and if he wants to know the truth, he needs to see this documentary through.

He gets up to retrieve another Coke and settles back in the desk chair. He trims a section and adds a transition, then drops an image from his archive into the reel. He rewinds a few minutes to play it back. Jude's voice echoes in his ears as Cali's Year 10 school photo fills the screen. Tarek tries to concentrate, but the image blurs and morphs before him. He knows his mind is playing tricks on him, he knows he's over-tired. But still his mouth falls open as his vision fills with a tangle of blood-crusted hair, blue lips twisted into a silent scream and that accusatory pair of cold, dead eyes.

# THEN

The last time Jude had set foot in the hospital was when she and Cali were made to come to apologize to Vicky Redcar after the incident at the swimming pool. She thought about that ice-cold outdoor pool as she waited for the lift up to Cali's ward. Hitting the water was always such a shock. Once she scrambled to kick her legs and flail her arms, though, Jude always experienced a second of euphoria. It felt like she could feel every cell of her skin, even the folds between her toes and the crinkles of her knees. Afterwards, they'd finish lengths and have to stand shivering in their suits while the pervy PE teacher picked them one at a time to dive for a weight or show their backstroke or whatever it was that got him off.

That day, Jude had been standing in line chatting with Cali, holding her arms over her nipples and feeling horribly self-conscious. Cali had filled out in all the right places, and it seemed everyone else's acne and puppy fat had miraculously vanished, while Jude's body had been on a single-minded mission to embarrass her. She'd cut her ponytail off in an attempt to feel sophisticated and edgy, but it had only made her aware of the exposed back of her neck. She'd touched her hand there, feeling the chill of her chlorine-soaked fingertips.

Then Vicky Redcar had turned around from in front of them and spat, 'Lesbians!'

In the length of time it took for the word to leave Vicky's cold-sore lips and reach Jude's water-clogged ears, Cali had screamed, 'Bitch!', Vicky's mouth had dropped into a perfectly shocked 'O', and Jude had found herself releasing her hands from her armpits and stepping forwards. Without thinking about it, she'd shoved Vicky along the tiles on the edge of the pool. That second of surprise as she watched Vicky's head bash the side and her pink blood flower in the water had felt to Jude like diving into the freezing pool. The sounds of the sports field and the roar of the road beyond the hedge had fallen away. Her cells had felt the paralysing shock, followed by an instant rush of adrenalin.

Vicky's cut was tiny, but an ambulance had been called in case she had concussion. Cali had got in first to tell Mr Peterson they'd all been messing around and Vicky must have slipped. Nobody contradicted her, not even Vicky, but Mr Peterson had insisted on driving Cali and Jude here after school to apologize for their part in it all.

This time it was Cali, not Vicky, lying in a hospital bed and Jude felt her stomach twist in fear and a touch of excitement at the drama of it all. Cali looked small against the sheets, a smudge of dark hair and drained skin. Jude sat in the visitor's chair and chewed her fingernails, wondering what she would tell people at school. She imagined narrating how she'd held Cali while she cried, encouraging her to let it all out.

'Do you want me to get anything?' she asked. 'A magazine? Chocolate? Sweets?'

Cali said no and they fell back into silence. Jude stared at a piece of tinsel still stuck above the nurses' station and wondered what else she could do, how to live up to her role as Cali's truest friend. It was awful, she thought, that Jackie had gone home. It just went to show, really, how much Cali needed her. Who else did she have? She watched Cali playing with her phone. She was lucky, that's what the nurse had said.

Lucky that her mum had left her shift early and found her daughter, lucky that the ambulance had come so quickly, lucky to have had her stomach pumped.

'Give us a minute,' Cali said.

Jude looked up and saw Rose standing at the edge of the curtains, her hands thrust into the pockets of an enormous coat. She hadn't spent any time with Rose since they'd visited her in Margate in Year 8, not long after the swimming pool incident. Rose had been living there for a bit more than a year by then. She'd mussed up Jude's hair when they arrived. 'Not many kids your age would be brave enough to go that short,' she'd said admiringly.

'Get a room,' Cali had said, rolling her eyes.

They'd walked along the front and Rose had paid for them to go on a couple of the beach rides. They'd watched the town dip and rise from the seats of the miniature Ferris wheel, played the arcades and eaten ice creams on the sand.

'Uh, hey,' Jude said now, getting to her feet. 'How are you? D'you want this seat?'

Rose had put on weight and got at least three new piercings. 'Thanks,' she said, barely glancing in Jude's direction. Jude felt a stab of disappointment.

As they'd walked back towards Margate station that day, they'd seen a group of men with shaved heads, cherry boots and green bomber jackets on a corner outside a pub.

'Let's cross the street,' Rose had said, and she and Jude had stopped at the zebra crossing.

'I'll catch you up,' Cali had said, adjusting her skirt to show an extra inch of thigh and strutting towards the skinheads.

Jude had followed Rose across the road, neither of them taking their eyes off Cali. As she passed the men, a couple of faces turned in her direction, mouths moving. Cali must have said something back, because one of them cracked a smile and moved his lips again.

Jude's gaze had drifted from Cali's back to the weird wave-like art museum. There was a piece of glowing neon art outside that they'd passed earlier. It said *I Never Stopped Loving You.*

'You all right?' Rose had said after Cali was safely past the men. 'My sister's just being a prat.'

'I know.'

'She doesn't understand those guys can be dangerous. She doesn't understand what it's like for us.'

Jude hadn't replied. It was strange and slightly thrilling to realize that something as simple as cutting her hair and not prancing around like Cali could make Rose assume she belonged to an 'us'. Did she think Jude was gay?

That was years ago and they'd barely crossed paths since. Jude fingered the hoop in her left ear and looked around the ward. It was good Rose had come, she supposed, but where had she been all this time? Did she think she could just walk back into Cali's life and everything would be fine? It was Jude who had been here, Jude who knew everything Cali was going through.

Cali caught her eye. 'Get us some tea, yeah?'

Jude looked at Rose, who stared back with a blank expression. After a moment, she raised her eyebrows and said, 'Milk, one sugar.'

*

Rose watched Jude's back as she made her way to the lift. 'Where's Mum?' she said, aware of the thin curtains separating them from the families around.

'Went home to get some rest.'

Rose looked at her pale sister. She imagined rubbing the outrage and attitude back into her cheeks, shaking her until she swore. 'What were you—'

Cali turned her head away. 'Do we have to do this? You and me, do we have to have the same conversation I'm having with everyone else?'

Rose bit down on the back of her lip stud, the metal comfortingly solid between her teeth.

Cali sighed and turned back to face her. 'Yes, I know how stupid it was. No, I'm not going to do it again. No, it wasn't anything to do with you.'

Rose pulled her fist inside her sleeve and wiped it roughly over both eyes. Cali reached to take Rose's hand from inside the soggy fabric.

'But I am sorry,' she added quietly.

'I don't know what I'd have done.'

'I know.'

Rose looked at Cali's hand squeezing her own. She was meant to be here looking after her sister and instead she was the one being comforted.

'Miss Walker?'

They looked up to see a woman wearing a lab coat over a dark blue dress.

'Which one?' Cali said, laughing weakly.

The doctor smiled back at her. 'I'll be back to check on you, but I was hoping for a word with your sister.' She turned to Rose. 'I'm Dr Parker. Cali's friend told me you were here. Would you mind if I spoke to you in private for a moment?'

Cali rolled her eyes and let go of Rose's hand.

Rose followed Dr Parker out of the ward and along a corridor to a small room. She indicated for her to take a seat and closed the door.

'I wanted to ask a few questions about your family history.'

'Didn't you talk to my mum?'

'I did.' Dr Parker hesitated. 'Understandably, she was quite disorientated, so I was hoping you could fill in some blanks.'

Rose pushed her lip stud out and sucked it back in. 'Okay.'

'We know it was your mother's medication that Cali took. I was wondering if you could tell us if there's anything we should be aware of about your family, any problems at home or previous attempts at self-harm?'

'Self-harm?' Rose repeated.

The doctor crossed her legs and leant forwards slightly. 'I've spoken to your sister this morning, and I do not think she truly meant to do herself damage last night. What I think Cali suffers from – which is not uncommon in someone her age – is a lot of anxiety and difficulty controlling her emotions. She's experiencing a great deal inside and when she can't cope it sounds like her instinct is to look outside for an act that others will notice.'

'You think she's just attention seeking?'

Dr Parker shook her head. 'Please don't misunderstand me. There is no "just" in these situations. Your mum's mood stabilizers are strong, but thankfully the dosage Cali took did not put her at risk of permanent damage. I don't think your sister actually wanted to hurt herself or even imagined she'd end up in hospital, but what she did is still incredibly serious. And what worries me about this kind of—' She paused and glanced at the neat rows of leaflets on the low coffee table. '—well, this kind of *provocative* thinking, is that it can lead an individual to act in a way that has consequences they didn't intend.'

Rose studied Dr Parker in silence.

'Everything you tell me is strictly in order for us to

provide your sister with the best possible care. I want to help Cali. We've referred her for psychological assessment and we've spoken to her school, so there will be extra support there, but we'd like to know if we need to put any other measures in place or if specific avenues of testing might be beneficial.'

Rose sighed, resigned to where this was going. She liked how separate her life in London was from all this. She liked not having to be the girl she'd been growing up. 'You want to know about my mum?'

'I know this is difficult.'

Rose pinched the top of her nose, wishing she was somewhere else. How to explain without sounding like every twenty-two-year-old with a family-shaped chip on her shoulder? How to describe what it's like when you're eight or twelve or fourteen and your mum waits for you at the school gates with this look in her eye that you know means you're about to get a shit ton of sweets or ice cream or whatever you want, but you might also be getting on a train to Cornwall and missing the next week of school, or taking a £200 taxi to a spa hotel you know she can't afford, or spending six hours in B&Q buying the equipment to build a treehouse? Those planks sat rotting in the garden for six months until a skinny Welsh guy knocked and asked to buy them. Jackie had been asleep, so Rose had said yes and pocketed the money to buy an iPod.

'She has mental health problems,' Rose said, submitting to the easy way out, though she'd grown to hate that description. It felt like an excuse. It presented her mum as the only sufferer and left little room for Rose and Cali's experiences. Jackie did have mental health problems, yes, a variety of diagnoses and various bottles of pills, but what Rose wanted to ask Dr Parker was: did that really let her off? Did that make it okay that she'd dumped Rose on her grandparents and set off around the world? That she'd only come back because she got pregnant again? That she'd found them a so-called father figure who couldn't stand having a stepdaughter who wanted to play football and dress like the boys? That somehow last night she'd allowed Cali to swallow half a dozen lithium tablets?

'Okay,' Dr Parker said, making a note on her pad. She asked some more questions, filling in boxes on her form, her face twisted in sympathy. 'I'm going to recommend we keep your sister in for a few days. Make sure there are supports in place before she returns home. Are you able to stay in Dover for a while?'

'I—' Rose stumbled. All the way down she'd been concentrating on Cali, thinking about getting to her, being with her, supporting her; but somehow she'd failed to consider the reality of that meaning she'd need to stay here. She watched the flicker of confusion on Dr Parker's face, imagined the woman's judgement. 'I'll try.'

*

To Jude's dismay, as she came out of the café holding three teas, she bumped into Cali's boyfriend, Goofy, clutching a box of Celebrations. She had to ride the lift back up to the ward with him and watch Cali smile and let him kiss her on the lips and say how nice those completely inappropriate chocolates were. They all had to listen to him give a little speech about how worried he was and how he'd got there as fast as he could and he was sorry if there was anything about him that made her feel unhappy.

Jude stared at Cali's hands, willing him to leave. She'd spent years studying the topography of her friend's nails.

49

Cali started chipping polish off as soon as it dried, picking the skin around her fingertips, then pulling the paint off in strips and flecks. Jude would find little pieces of colour on her carpet after they'd hung out. Cali painted right over whatever was left, each nail becoming a landscape of valleys and mountains, sedimentary layers of green upon yellow upon black upon red.

To Jude's horror, Goofy started crying. She watched Cali put her hand on his arm. He'd given her that blue, she remembered. The bottle had a picture of Minnie Mouse on it. Jude had told Cali she thought it was creepy. Not that anything about a twenty-year-old going out with a sixteen-year-old wasn't creepy, but it was that he was always giving her these stupid childish gifts that really freaked Jude out. Like sheets of transfer tattoos with Tinkerbell on them. Cali told her he called her Tinkerbell sometimes, so she thought it was sweet. She told Jude she liked that he was kind and made her laugh and didn't keep asking her what she wanted to do with her life.

He once gave her a Pez and had to explain what a Pez was because Cali had never seen one before. 'Why's Goofy only got one weird foot?' she said, turning the plastic sweet dispenser upside down. They laughed so hard after he left. That's when Jude started calling him Goofy. Another time he'd turned up with a small jewellery box. Inside were two keyrings, each in the shape of half a broken heart. When held together, the heart was complete and the writing on them read *BEST BITCHES*. 'It made me think of you two,' he said. Jude assumed he meant it as an insult, but for once she'd kind of liked the gift. When Goofy had gone, she and Cali clipped the keyrings to their backpacks and made up a stupid rhyme to go with them that they filmed and posted to their feeds.

'That's the famous Kev then,' Rose said after he'd dried his tears and left for work. Jude caught her eye and finally they had a moment of connection over what a loser Cali's boyfriend was.

'Shut up,' Cali said. 'How's *your* love life?'

'Point taken.' Rose grinned. 'You got a boyfriend too, Jude? A nice, goateed older man like our Cali here?'

'Fuck off,' Cali said, almost falling out of bed as she reached to thump Rose on the arm. It was good to see them fooling around and for a moment Jude almost felt grateful to Goofy for bringing them all together.

'Or a girlfriend?' Rose added, arching one eyebrow.

'No,' Jude said, feeling her cheeks growing hot. She thought about that moment in Margate and pushing Vicky Redcar into the pool. She hated how black and white everyone expected things to be, how simple people like Rose and her parents and even Cali sometimes wanted to make things.

'Jude's not gay,' Cali said, swiping open an app. 'She's asexual.'

'Yeah?'

Jude sighed. When she and Cali were younger, they'd mapped out their lives, dreaming of mansions in far-away places with butlers delivering snacks while they collaborated on chart-topping albums. Jude knew those were childish fantasies, but she'd always thought that whatever they actually ended up doing, it would be together. None of those dreams had involved boyfriends or husbands, and she hadn't been prepared for the obsession with romance and dating that infected all of her peers as soon as they moved to secondary school. Even now, she didn't understand why everything had to be about who you fancied.

'I just haven't met anyone I like,' she said. 'I don't see the point.'

'Good for you,' Rose said. 'Concentrate on your studies, keep your head down.'

'*Concentrate on your studies, keep your head down*,' parroted a talking slice of toast from an app on Cali's phone and they all laughed.

A little while later a porter came around with a dinner tray. 'You're probably dying to get back to Mum and Dad and some home cooking,' he said as he set it down. Jude caught Cali's eye and had to bite the inside of her cheek. Rose looked like she wanted to throw up.

# 2026

Tarek's phone makes a noise as it skids across the ledge in front of the television. He leans against the arm of the chair to reach it, tipping onto the two left legs and knocking a stack of papers off the desk as he does so.

'Shit.'

He swipes at the phone. It's his cameraman, Gary, asking if he fancies a drink downstairs. Tarek types back an apology, then looks at the time. He should have phoned Helen by now. She told him she was fine with him making this documentary, even after filming was moved to a month before her due date. 'If it's something you have to do, then it's something you have to do,' she said sweetly. She's always sweet. Always supportive. She says she understands. She's an artist too, after all. Tarek feels strange when she calls him an artist, though he does like the idea that they're connected in that way. That whatever invisible, intangible thing gives her the inspirations for her poems is similar to the drive he feels to find a story. Most people hate journalists, but Helen sees something noble in what he does. Even when he leaves her home alone and eight months pregnant.

*Sorry for not being in touch*, he types. *Are you still up?*

He waits to see if she comes online. His message has been delivered but remains unread. Tarek feels a pang of guilt and longing and wonders why any of this ever seemed worth being away from Helen so close to the birth of their child. He tries to picture her lying in their bed, curled around her enormous stomach.

He crouches to retrieve the littered scraps from the floor, muddling voiceover scripts with storyboards, notes about contrast cuts with receipts and half-filled coffee stamp-cards. Helen is constantly buying him notebooks and pleading with him to sort the messy boxes in the attic. It horrifies her that he doesn't organize and file his work, archive his old projects and keep a proper paper trail of how his ideas develop. He's tried to explain that making tidy lists in neat notebooks feels stifling and too like the tedious grammar exercises he was subjected to by the English tutor he used to share with his little sister, Inji. His filing system is in his head. He jots things down to record them there. And when he does need to find a scrap of an idea he's scribbled on an envelope in the middle of the night or on the back of a sandwich wrapper in a jeep crossing a military checkpoint, he more often than not can. If the thought is important enough, it will find its way back to him. If it isn't, the note was written to be lost in the first place. Like the ones he and Inji used to write and slip under doorways or between books. Their parents were always finding them and frowning at the words they didn't understand. Tarek and Inji thought they were so clever, writing their secrets in the English their parents were paying for them to learn, unaware that language was only the beginning of the things that would separate them.

He replaces the papers and turns to the small window to look at the moon shining above the harbour. If he adds up the trips, he's spent probably four or five weeks along this coast in the past few months, staring at this stretch of the Channel. It hasn't got any easier. He almost had to leave the room when Jude started lecturing on the topic.

'The French and British governments may have succeeded in moving the problem away from Calais,' she said to the camera, 'but the crisis has been growing steadily worse year on year. There may be no Jungle – not as you remember it – but there are smaller, unofficial and much less equipped camps in almost every town along the French coast.'

Gary caught Tarek's eye with a small frown, but Jude seemed oblivious to any irony. She went on and on, as if he of all people needed her to tell him that hundreds of people have died trying to cross this stretch of water, and that instead of making any provisions here, the UK government keeps paying to increase security spending, desperate to avoid having to deal with the problem on British soil. Her grand finale was to pronounce this the main reason she wanted to do the documentary, to make it clear that she does not agree – and never has – with any of the rhetoric that uses her name to call for tighter security and less sympathy. That she herself never blamed Mo for what happened, and all she ever wanted – all she still wants – is to help and welcome people like her. Finally, she stopped and blinked at them, waiting, Tarek almost thought, for a round of applause. It was all he could do to lower his gaze and pretend to make some notes.

He draws the curtains, shutting himself in the tired hotel room. He looks around at the mess of his things. *You're a slob, brother,* Inji used to tell him, jumping on his bed, sending his clothes and textbooks flying. *When I grow up I will not be like you.*

He stretches with a wince. He's noticed his friends have begun to nod at him lately, grumbling over their pints about their own ailments. He can't decide if it's a good thing or not that even his physical pain has been assimilated, that those who know nothing about his past can sip their beers and sympathize with a casual, 'We're not young any more, are we?'

He thinks about taking a pill, but there's no point trying

to sleep yet. He rarely sleeps well when he's away from Helen. Lonely hotel rooms, wherever in the world they happen to be, however plush or otherwise, offer him little comfort from the crevices of his mind.

He slides his feet into the brightly coloured trainers Helen mocked him for buying and leaves the room. The corridor is still. The patterned carpet runs past identical doors, plastic hangers dangling their occupants' requests not to be disturbed. Tarek's always liked hotels at night. When he's had to stay for long periods in one place, like for the Lagos shoot and the piece in Berlin, he's formed oddly intimate relationships with the night staff. Porters and receptionists have grown used to seeing him, known to make his sweet tea before he asks and advised him on where is safe to stroll at strange hours.

He's not an unsociable person, but days like this take it out of him. He loves his job but has never got used to its extremes: long, solitary months of preparation, research and editing, interspersed with intense, hyper-social and hectic periods of shooting. Even as a boy, Tarek needed time to recharge. With two older brothers and a younger sister, it wasn't always possible at home, but he found ways. It wasn't until he was an adult that he properly understood the necessity of his parents each having a study – a door that could be shut against curious or begging children, even against each other.

Tarek and his siblings never wanted for love, but they were not spoilt with the kind of attention he sees his friends devoting to their offspring. They spend an afternoon together and all it seems they talk about are the children running around their feet. If the conversation is allowed to stray to Tarek's filming or Helen's upcoming collection, it's invariably interrupted by Mollie or Bertie tugging on an arm to beg for juice or cartoons. The adult sentences hang there, unfinished, never to be picked up. Helen has promised they won't be like that, but Tarek wonders how she can know. It feels like a bad omen to worry about such things after everything they've been through. Tarek blamed himself for Helen's miscarriages, taking them as punishment for the critical eye he'd been casting on the way their friends parented, for the lingering thoughts he'd been having about his own childhood. When she got pregnant again, he promised to be nothing but positive, nothing but grateful.

He still is, he thinks, but at some point they will have to face the practicalities. He wants his child to feel protected but also brave. To be independent and self-sufficient, but to always know where home is. He wants them to be proud of their heritage but not conflicted by it. To have all the privileges of his British friends' children – to want for nothing and to feel like they deserve their place in the world – but also never to forget who they are. The child of a refugee. The grandchild of two fighters.

*That* is why it's worth being away from Helen right now. It's why he's here and why he must press Rose for answers tomorrow. For his child to have a real family, Tarek needs to find out what happened to his own.

# 2026

Rose sits on the edge of the bath staring at the bottle in her hand. What is she doing? Her sponsor always makes a joke that if he's ever going to fall off the wagon then it'll be with some seriously good whisky. 'The kind they age for half a century in a hand-whittled cask made from fairy wings,' he says. Yet here she is sitting in her bathroom with a £15 bottle of Captain Morgan's Spiced Rum. When she walked out of the hotel earlier, though, and into the corner shop to pick up a pack of cigarettes, her eyes landed on the amber bottle and it felt like the proud, mustachioed captain was calling out to all of her anxieties.

She knew as soon as Tarek got in touch what the risks were, what she had to lose. She knew he'd be asking Jude as well and that little good could come from the two of them raking over the past. But even before he offered the money, his talk about giving her the opportunity to tell Cali's story, about giving her sister a voice, had wormed its way into Rose's thoughts. She'd lain awake wondering if this was a chance to move on. Perhaps by talking about it again, by saying as much as it was safe to say, she might be able to dislodge the anchor of guilt she's been living with. Even if it only shifted a few centimetres, that would be something, wouldn't it?

She's not sure if that's exactly what today achieved, but it did feel nice to talk to Tarek. She's grown so used to blocking off all thoughts of that time that allowing her mind to return freely to those memories did, in fact, feel like a release.

As soon as Gary turned the camera off, however, doubt began to creep in.

'That was great,' Tarek said, noticing her worried expression. 'I know it's hard to go back to these events and remember what happened, but your story is powerful, Rose. The way you tried to be there for your sister and the price you paid – are still paying – for not succeeding, that's going to have real resonance for a viewer. You made the right decision, you know? You're doing the right thing.'

Looking at his wide, trusting smile, she felt sick. If she'd been capable of doing the right thing in the first place, they wouldn't need to be here. And if he knew how wrong the decisions she made back then really were, there was no way he'd treat her this kindly.

She rubs her thumb over the label, then up to the bottle's neck, feeling the gentle ridges of the foil seal. She is stronger than this, she knows she is. She closes her eyes. She's not a believer, but she does like the simplicity of the prayer. 'Grant me the serenity,' she murmurs to the toilet and the towel rail.

After a while she opens her eyes and gets to her feet. Whatever else she's feeling, £5,000 means another chance. It'll pay for another round of IVF, another shot at a family. All she has to do is spend two more days in front of Tarek's camera. She places the bottle in the waste basket by the sink, lifts the liner out of the basket and ties the handles together. The bag swings by her thigh as she unlocks the bathroom door and makes her way to the outside bin. She lifts the brick holding down the lid and thrusts the bag to the bottom, making sure it's covered by the rest of the rubbish. Just two more days.

# THE TOWN

## THE WHITE CLIFFS

The iconic chalk face on an overcast day. Lone walker on footpath.

> JUDE
> (off-screen)
> What can I say? I'm a diehard Dovorian! I love this place.

CUT TO.

## DOVER HIGH STREET

Market Square on a Saturday. Mixture of chain stores and boarded-up shopfronts. Shoppers hurry by a charity collector. Middle-aged man with a pint standing outside Weatherspoon's stares directly into the camera.

> ROSE
> (off-screen)
> This town is a dump.

CUT TO.

## WEST HARBOUR

Jude sits on a bench overlooking the marina. Behind her, a park stretches in front of a new development of shops and houses.

JUDE

(smiles.)

I'm running for mayor because I truly believe in the future of Dover.

CUT TO.

## FERRY PORT

Rose stands in front of the East Harbour, a large ferry blocking the horizon behind her.

ROSE

Things are getting better, the papers say, but they're not looking at Dover. Our roads are still gridlocked, our air is some of the most polluted in the country, our town centre is dead—

(laughs.)

You know they tried to put in a cable car? Look around, is that really what this town needs? We're consistently voted in the top ten worst places to live in the country. Our house prices have plummeted. Our average income is two thirds of the national average. Our cliffs have been turned into barricades . . . But yeah, shove a cable car in and I'm sure that'll help.

CUT TO.

JUDE

The thing about Dover is it's where real, honest, hard-working people live. We might not have all the fancy things they have elsewhere, but we have soul.

INTERVIEWER
(off-screen)
Did you like growing up here?

JUDE

What child wouldn't? You've got the sea and the cliffs, and all this history.

CUT TO.

ROSE

I hated growing up here, couldn't wait to leave. I went to Margate first, but that wasn't much better. On my nineteenth birthday I packed my bag again and got on another train, watched as Herne Bay and Whitstable and Gillingham flew by until finally I was out of Kent.

(laughs.)

When a teacher used to ask us what county we lived in, we'd always dare each other to say 'Cunt'. They never cottoned on, maybe they thought we were too young to know the word. Bye Cunt, hello London, I thought that day.

(sucks bottom lip.)

But I ended up back here all the same.

CUT TO.

JUDE

We're not called the Gateway to England for nothing; we have thousands of years of history and a role in every major epoch. There's nowhere I'd rather be.

CUT TO.

ROSE

(leans forward.)

Do you know what it's like living somewhere where all anyone talks about is how old and important everything is? What about the present, huh? What about the people living in this shit, divided town right now? What about the racism and homophobia? What use is an ancient castle and some famous chalk when if you're any kind of minority you're scared to walk home at night?

CUT TO.

JUDE

Coming out of Dover to the west, there's this enormous cliff that I used to think looked like a mountain reaching right into the sky. I'd never thought about why it was called Shakespeare Cliff until we got to secondary school and our English teacher made us read *King Lear.*

(blinks away tears.)

Cali loved that play.

CUT TO.

ROSE

Cali hated Dover too. She used to call it a 'nowhere place'. She said the only people who ever came here were heading somewhere else.

CUT TO.

JUDE

(touches cheek.)

I preferred *Othello.*

CUT TO.

ROSE

I wouldn't have come back if it wasn't for my mum. If I'd had my way, I'd never have set foot in this town again. But that's life, isn't it? Sometimes you don't get to make those choices.

# THEN

*I should never have left*, Rose thought, standing in Cali's doorway staring at the soiled bedsheets and the mess left by the paramedics. She'd convinced a nurse to let her stay with Cali for the past two nights, but she was being discharged tomorrow and Rose had finally admitted she had no choice but to return to the house.

She'd looked in the kitchen first, noting the remnants of hard and unidentifiable food stuck to the dishes stacked in the sink, the load of washing mouldering in the bottom of the drum and the out-of-date ready meals in the fridge. She'd have liked to have been able to chalk these things up to signs of immediate distress, indicators that her mother's routine had been upset by her youngest daughter's hospitalization. But, honestly, this was pretty much how Rose remembered the place, and the fact that Jackie hadn't returned to the hospital since Cali's admittance didn't suggest an especially deep level of concern. Rose had taken one of the yoga breaths Sean was always telling her to and approached the living room.

There was a period, when Cali was a baby and her dad, Gabe, was still around, where Jackie spoke almost exclusively in old Portuguese proverbs. Some had stuck and become cryptic family sayings. *Beware the door with too many keys*, Rose remembered as she knocked. There was no answer, so she turned the handle.

Inside, she found the curtains drawn and the TV silently flickering with an old episode of *Two and a Half Men*. Jackie was sitting up in the corner of the folded-out couch, tucked against the arm and with her knees curled up to her like a child. Her eyes were open, staring at the silent TV, but Rose had the sense she wasn't seeing it at all. She'd looked from her mum to Charlie Sheen and back again. Jackie hadn't moved, hadn't acknowledged her, hadn't registered anything. Rose had left the room without either of them saying a word.

She stared now at the nail varnishes on Cali's bedside table, willing herself not to cry. The more time that had passed, and the more miles she'd put between herself and her guilt at leaving, the easier it had become to both feel and not feel it. Guilt was simply a presence in her day: a comforting reminder that whatever she was doing with her life, deep down, she was really just a fuck-up. With that in the back of her head, it had become easier to say yes to that fourth pint, to take a dab from a stranger's pouch, to see where life took her. At work, when a customer complained, even if it was over something stupid or she knew they were only trying it on to get a free drink, there was a *Just Say Yes* policy. It was company-wide: a decision made in some boardroom that it wasn't worth the effort to argue. About anything. The customer was always right. Employees must always say yes. Rose liked the policy so much she carried it out of work. Just saying yes to things became easier than considering them, weighing the pros and cons, wondering if something was a good or a bad idea. It got her in trouble sometimes. It pissed people off sometimes. But if *Just Say Yes* was her policy, she could divorce herself from the consequences. *She* hadn't made the decision, the company above her head had. The bosses and the bosses' bosses. She was simply a pawn being moved through the game. And as a pawn she had no responsibilities. As a pawn, it was okay for her to fuck up, to let people down, to forget to call a girl back, to use the last of the loo roll, to steal Jax's soya milk, to abandon her family.

To prove to herself how not good she was, that afternoon – that first afternoon back in her childhood home – instead of worrying about what Cali was feeling lying in that hospital bed or if she'd be okay, Rose found and smoked the weed hidden in her sister's sock drawer, drained a six-pack and thought about women. She also went to the shop, tidied Cali's room and the kitchen, reset the washing machine for a new cycle, and shoved two chicken kievs in the oven, but after that, she sat on her old childhood bed and opened the app. Miss Australia had messaged to ask if Rose wanted to go to a gig on Friday. Even though she didn't like her, Rose was annoyed that she was going to have to say no and wondered who she would take instead and whether they'd have a good time. Then she wondered what Kassia was doing and if she'd want to see her again. She thought briefly about sending a friendly hello, but couldn't find the courage. Instead, out of curiosity, she clicked the search button and started swiping, intrigued to see what her possibilities might be in her home town.

Her settings were only set to 2km – she was lazy, even in London – so she scrolled through the queer and lonely population of Dover in all of about four minutes. There at the end was Megan Sutcliffe, whom she remembered from a couple of years below her at school. Her big brother had been in Rose's class and she'd played clarinet at the end-of-year assemblies. Rose flicked through Megan's photos, thinking of all the godawful lessons she'd sat through at that school staring at the back of Eliza Sawyer's head, sweating through the summer term but never wanting to take her oversized jumper off, crying in the loos because her period had come again.

Rose hated this town and she'd hated school. In the time she'd been gone she felt like she'd reclaimed a part of herself. She still had her blue days and still encountered her fair share of arseholes in London, but she was beginning to feel okay. In

71

beds all around the city, she'd started to learn to love her body, to appreciate what it could do, what *she* could do. And with this knowledge came a certain confidence, one that meant even if she didn't look like a supermodel, even if she was more of a poor-man's Ellen than any of the cast of *Orange is the New Black*, if she got Megan Sutcliffe out of the skinny jeans she was wearing in her profile picture, she knew what she could make her feel. So with her mum zombied out in the living room and Cali lying on a ward, Rose, total twat that she knew she was, touched herself thinking about a girl from her secondary school and another she'd been on one date with and another whose bed she'd woken up in a few mornings ago.

Later that evening, when she'd run out of beers, she walked across the rec with her hood up, looking at the rusted swings and ageing zipline they used to play on. Jude's house backed on to the other side of the rec, one of a row of six detached houses, invisible behind their electric gates and anti-vandalism coated walls. The posh houses is what they'd called them when they were little, scaling the climbing frame to peek into their gardens and windows. Cali grew cross with Rose for saying that once. She said it wasn't Jude's fault her parents had proper jobs and they shouldn't be judgemental.

Rose climbed the porch and rang the bell, wondering how many years it had been since she'd last stood there. Jude's mum answered.

'Hello?'

'Hi,' Rose said, suddenly awkward. 'I'm Cali's sister.'

'Rose?' Mrs Campbell said. 'Wow, I didn't recognize you. You've grown up.'

Rose sucked the ball of her lip stud. Grown up was a euphemism she'd been hearing since she hit puberty. Grown up meant a whole range of things from cutting her hair to putting on weight, piercing her face, switching from football tracksuits to band T-shirts and baggy jeans, trainers to Docs. When most women got told they'd grown up it meant they'd turned from the curly-haired, gingham-wearing little darlings they were remembered as to the graceful young women they were always expected to be. For Rose, it meant she'd subverted those expectations, transformed from slightly rough tomboy to fully fledged dyke, padded out those expected curves and moulded her hair into a mohawk to leave no room for doubt.

'Come in,' Mrs Campbell said. 'How is Cali? She's being discharged tomorrow, isn't she?'

Rose nodded, feeling sorry for disturbing her tranquil life like this. 'We're picking her up in the morning.'

'Well, if there's anything we can do.'

'I was hoping to talk to Jude.'

'She's upstairs. You want to go on up? Do you want a cup of tea? Do you remember where it is?'

Her darting questions made Rose feel tipsier than she was. She smiled politely and told her she was fine for tea and that she thought Jude's room must be on the left.

'Thanks, Mrs Campbell.'

'Sandra, please. I've known you since you were a child. Do you mind taking off your shoes?'

Rose's feet sank into the thick carpet. There were flowers on the windowsill halfway up the stairs and no dead woodlice or piles of pet hair in the corners. She wondered if they had a cleaner. She couldn't imagine Sandra bending down once a week to hoover each stair.

She heard music coming from behind Jude's door. A crosstrainer stood at the end of the landing, looking out over a glass door leading to a balcony. A balcony. Who had a balcony? What was the point of a balcony? When she saw her tomorrow she was going to lay into Cali for ever criticizing her for calling these the posh houses. They were fucking palaces.

Rose knocked and the music went off. Another second and Jude opened the door. She was wearing a pair of leggings and a large jumper. The dishevelled look suited her better than the self-conscious, mascara-caked version she left the house in. Like this, Rose noticed she too was beginning to look 'all grown up', though in a more predictable sense. Even her short hair somehow made her seem more rather than less feminine. If she was surprised to see Rose standing on her landing, she didn't show it.

'What's up?' Jude said.

'I wondered if we could have a word about Cali.'

'Sure. You want to sit?'

Rose followed her into the room and took the plastic desk chair. Jude shut the door and sat on the bed.

'I wanted to ask a favour.' Rose had never been quite sure if Cali's friend was an awkward misfit she felt sorry for, or a total suck-up. The past couple of days at the hospital she'd definitely been getting on Rose's nerves, but she didn't know who else to turn to. 'I have to go back to work next week and I was wondering if you could keep an eye on Cali for me. I don't know how much you know about my mum . . .'

Jude cocked her head in sympathy. 'Cali said she's sleeping a lot again.'

'Right.'

'She's okay, though, right?'

'Sort of. Look, I don't think Cali's going to do anything. I mean, the doctor said she didn't think—but I still don't feel great leaving her.'

'She can stay over here!' Jude said. 'Or I'll sleep at yours.'

'Uh—'

74

'Seriously, it will be fine. Don't worry, I can look after Cali.'

'I'm not asking you to spy on her or anything, but just, let me know if there's anything I should worry about.'

'Of course.'

'And don't tell Cali I asked. She'd hate it if she knew we were discussing her.'

Jude pinched her thumb and forefinger together and mimed pulling a zip across her lips.

Rose got up to go.

'Can I show you something?' Jude said, looking nervous. 'I told Cali I wouldn't tell anyone, but after what she did . . .'

'What?'

Jude turned to her computer and pulled up a website called Blue Mondays. She scooted to the left so Rose could see. It described itself as a *pro-life, peer-to-peer support forum for those wishing to discuss feelings of despair.* A notice on the home page warned that this forum was monitored for content and was intended as an aid for help and to show people they were not alone. Anyone found posting goodbye messages or behaving either aggressively or persuasively to another forum member would be removed.

'What is this?'

'Cali left it open on my computer once last summer.'

Rose sat back down. She clicked on a thread titled *I want to die.* It was written by a thirty-two-year-old woman whose toddler had recently been taken from her. She said she got to see her son for only three hours a week and it was breaking her heart. She'd started using drugs again, which she'd stopped when she found out she was pregnant, and was considering taking an overdose because at least then her family might think it was accidental. She said she could only think of two people who would be affected by her death and presumably they would eventually get over it and realize the world was a better place without her.

The replies beneath were sympathetic and supportive. They gave her the numbers of helplines and told her she was not alone. One user had posted:

It doesn't matter how you do it, because all suicides are accidents. Nobody purposefully intends to find themselves in so much pain that they'd rather die than wake up. The fact that your life is like this and that you feel this way is the culmination of a series of accidents.

Another had written:

Have you thought about the possibility that those two people might NEVER get over it? Why should they? YOU can't. What if your son grows up to feel the same as you? What if he needs you?

Rose turned to Jude. 'Did Cali post on here?'

Jude twisted the ring on her right middle finger. Rose wondered if she was deliberately drawing out the moment, enjoying the drama. 'I don't know,' she said finally, her eyes wide and full of concern.

Rose's thoughts raced as she walked back across the rec. At the hospital, she had somehow been able to convince herself that what Cali had done wasn't such a big deal, that it was scary and dangerous, but over. Back in the house, though, the walls felt like they were pressing in. Her little sister had been thinking about this for months. She was sixteen and it was possible she'd actually wanted to die. Rose thought back to the last few times they'd spoken on the phone. Cali had sounded fine. She'd made Rose laugh taking the piss out of Grace, and talked excitedly about an art project she wanted to do. While tidying her room earlier, Rose had found three university brochures stuffed between the bed and the wall: Loughborough, Leeds and Newcastle. Cali had folded the corners of some of the pages. A properly suicidal person wouldn't have done that, would they?

Rose stuck her head into the living room and found Jackie sitting in pretty much the same position as she'd left her. She'd eaten the chicken kiev, though.

'Thank you,' she said as Rose bent to retrieve the plate.

'She speaks!'

Rose saw the hurt in her mother's face and regretted her tone. For all the ways she hated this woman for tapping out on them, for giving them this fucked-up family, for allowing Cali to get to where she was, she was still her mum.

'Rose,' Jackie said, her voice hoarse. For a moment Rose had an image of her returning from her night shift to find Cali passed out. What if she'd panicked and failed to call an ambulance? What if she'd gone straight to bed and not found her until the morning?

'I'm here,' Rose said. She looked for a place to sit. The chair was pushed up against the window, too far away not to be a solid statement that she didn't want to be near her. She perched on the side of the folded-out sofa bed and twisted her torso so they were facing each other.

'Cali's coming out tomorrow?'

Rose nodded. 'You gonna pick her up with me?'

Jackie stared at the duvet.

'What happened, Mum? Did you know something was wrong? Why didn't you tell me?'

Jackie glanced at the drawn curtains, as if the answers might be somewhere outside. 'I didn't know,' she whispered.

77

Rose took a breath, teetering on the edge. This woman hadn't known her own daughter was so depressed that for months she'd been sitting upstairs reading a suicide forum.

'They've referred her for counselling,' Rose said after a while, 'and got the school involved.'

Jackie's cheek twitched. Their encounters with local authorities had rarely been positive. From a young age Rose had learnt to distrust the middle-aged women who turned up with a smile and ate their biscuits while asking how they all were. They had different faces over the years, but arrived like clockwork after Rose got busted smoking weed up on the Western Heights, after Cali ran away and was found on someone's boat in the harbour, and after the neighbours called the police because Jackie was playing loud music at 4 a.m. 'Fucking pigs,' Jackie had said that time and turned it down long enough for the patrol car to leave, then rocked it back up again. She'd laughed at Mrs Fry who'd come out to her front gate to shake her fist at them. 'Let's dance, babies,' Jackie had said and twirled Rose and Cali around the living room, their hearts beating with excitement to have such a dazzling and intense moment with their mother, even if they knew it meant she'd spend the next forty-eight hours in bed, letting the dog eat the slices of toast they left beside her pillow.

'I'm worried,' Jackie said, still staring at the curtains.

Rose shook her head. She hated her mother right then, with all of the frustration she'd felt at Cali's age, for all of the ways she'd misunderstood her. Jackie had dumped this family here, with no thought what it would be like to grow up gay or butch or just different in this godawful town. She'd left them to fend for themselves, tapping out of life for days or weeks on end. She'd blamed Rose when John left, unable to face the fact she'd fallen for a cheating scumbag. Then she'd kicked her out two weeks before her A-level exams, fucking up her daughter's chances like she'd fucked up her own.

All the things Rose had buried for the past six years were bubbling to the surface, threatening to erupt along with her anger about Cali. But then she saw Jackie as she was, squashed into the corner of an ancient sofa bed. She looked small and vulnerable. Rose tried to fit the shape before her into the mould of the glamorous mother she'd been so excited to see on the doorstep at six years old. She tried to imagine this woman as a defiant pregnant teenager, then a lone female traveller, her hair whipping behind her as she sat on the back of Gabe's motorbike. She tried to see the woman who'd bundled her into a taxi and told her grandparents to fuck off after they screamed at her for getting knocked up again, the woman who'd dried her and Cali's tears when Gabe left, the woman who'd removed her satin shoes on her wedding day to spin them on the dance floor, laughing that finally they'd be a proper family. None of those women matched the grey-faced creature before her. Just as none of her memories of her little sister matched the Cali that must have trawled through that website thinking about ways to end her life.

'Me too, Mum,' she said eventually.

Jackie pulled her gaze from the curtains and focused on Rose. Her eyes welled with tears. Rose had always thought of her mother as young and relatively beautiful – the pale version of Cali. She wasn't even forty yet. But as she watched Jackie's face crumple, Rose realized for the first time that her mother looked old. She shifted her weight and crawled up the mattress. At the top, she reached her arms around her mother and settled her head under her chin, listening to the heart beating beneath her ribs.

# 2026

Tarek is standing in a pool of light spilling from the lobby, wondering which way to walk, when Helen replies.

> There you are. I fell asleep on the
> sofa waiting for you to call.

Within seconds her voice is in his ear. He takes a few steps towards the promenade as he listens to her laugh about how long it took to get out of the bath.

'Wait,' he says, 'did you have an appointment today? How did it go?'

'It was fine,' she says, though he can hear a hesitation in her tone.

'What is it? What's wrong?'

Helen sighs. 'Nothing's wrong. The baby's fine. Only—'

'What?'

'The midwife was concerned about the baby's growth so he sent me up for a scan. It was just a precaution and everything is fine, but—'

'What?'

'I know we said we didn't want to find out, but you weren't there and the sonographer asked and I just, I wanted to know everything I could—'

Tarek smiles, relief flooding through him.

'I'm sorry, I feel awful.'

'It's fine.'

'Do you want to know?'

'If you want to tell me.'

'I don't like knowing when you don't.'

'Then tell me.'

There's a silence on the line and Tarek wonders if they've been disconnected, but finally Helen says, 'We're having a boy.'

When they decided not to find out, Tarek thought it wouldn't matter to him. He'd always thought it silly to pin your hopes and expectations for a child on something as arbitrary as its sex. For years he's been sharing posts criticizing gender reveal parties and signing petitions calling for better support for trans children. It would have been hypocritical to have suddenly decided it mattered for his own child.

It's hard to remember those arguments in the moment Helen tells him he's having a son, though. Something far more instinctive kicks in. He is going to be a father to a little boy, he realizes. He is going to raise a man.

'Say something,' Helen says. 'Are you pleased?'

'Very.'

'I cried when she told me.'

'It feels . . .'

'Right?' Helen says.

'Yes.'

Tarek looks at the blackened harbour and the elegant shadows of the new marina buildings where Jude lives. Is it because of this project that he feels like this? Are the strange and tragic lives of the three teenage girls he's investigating responsible for the relief he feels to be having a son?

'I should go,' Helen says, stifling a yawn.

After they've hung up, Tarek sends a string of hearts and a blue baby carriage followed by an exclamation mark. Helen sends back a smiley face and a lipstick kiss. He watches to see if she'll write anything more, but her avatar registers offline.

*Gross!* he remembers Inji saying in an exaggerated American accent when she found out about his first girlfriend. His school friend had recently taught him about BitTorrent and they'd been watching American sitcoms after their parents went to bed each night. *First comes kissing, then comes marriage, then comes Tarek with a baby carriage!* she said, pulling a face. *I never want to get married, I'm going to travel the world.* He begged her not to tell their parents, promising her unlimited use of his computer. She spun around in delight, then ran out of the room shouting, *Smell ya later, man!*

Little reflective dots glint out to sea, warning buoys marking the border defences preventing unauthorized access to the harbour. Tarek's thoughts begin to scatter as he hears the familiar siren call of grief. He thrusts his hands in his pockets and walks the other way along the front, instinctively drawn to the scruffier old town rather than the gentrified and overprotected waterside developments.

He's been thinking about his father lately, about what the transition from son to parent will involve and what difference it makes if you haven't been a son for most of your adult life. It's his mother, though, that comes to him now. He pictures her walking beside him. He owns no photographs of either of them, will have nothing to share with his child but memories. Memories that feel at once crystal clear and entirely fuzzy. If he looks straight ahead at the tall, thin streetlamps and the lights on the horizon, he can imagine his mother in perfect detail. But if he tries to turn to her, to say something or to place her feet solidly on the earth of this country she never saw, she vanishes, dissolving back to the faraway land of his childhood.

Tarek has told Olga it would be difficult for him to return to Syria, potentially dangerous even. He doesn't know if she believes him. Plenty have returned. There have been incentives to do so. Global economies rely on those who do. But there are also enough like him who haven't for it not to seem so out of the ordinary. Return versus integration. Tarek appeared on a Channel 4 debate about that very thing, having to argue his case against a red-faced politician set on sending him back. 'I'm not denying everything you've done for Britain, but the fact is your country needs journalists too. Your country needs skills like yours to rebuild itself. Have you no national pride?'

Tarek made his case that England was his home, pointed out that he had a wife and friends here, that this was the country in which he voted, paid taxes, signed petitions and hoped one day to raise his children. He came off well, according to the reviews, but he left the studio shaking. Of course he had pride. Of course he cared about the future of Syria. But how could he explain to a man who knew nothing but pubs and horse racing, business class and offshore havens, that the idea of returning at the age of thirty to the place your brothers and your parents and all of your friends lost their lives, the place you saw devastated by bombs, was like Peter Pan knocking on your window and asking if you wanted to fly to a Neverland you knew didn't exist?

*What is past is dead*, his mother used to say when he injured himself or cried that someone had broken something of his. *Keep moving and don't look back*, she told him the last time he saw her.

*Come with us*, he said. *Let us stay together.*

His father might have agreed, even though to leave Aleppo would have broken his heart. But his mother shook her head. *I have work to do here.* She was not wrong. The city was in need of doctors, more and more so as the hospitals were bombed and the aid agencies moved their people further out. Tarek followed the news whenever he could, searching for the locations of the strikes, the descriptions of the injured. When he got hold of phones, he called and called, getting through once every ten or twenty times. *We're fine*, his mother assured him, patient as ever with her youngest son. They'd moved all medical care underground, set up makeshift hospitals. His mother was teaching others basic surgical skills, trying to spread her knowledge. His father was going out after every strike to record and photograph the damage, making logs to aid future restoration projects.

*Come now*, Tarek said into plastic handsets from Greece and from Macedonia, from Austria and from France.

*I can't*, his mother replied. *You understand.*

*I don't!* he wanted to shout like he had when he was seven or eight and shut outside her study. *I need you!* he'd screamed back then and felt like screaming again. He didn't care whose lives she was saving or what larger cause she was fighting. He was her child and he needed her with him. He needed to know she was safe.

If his parents had listened to him, if they'd been less self-sacrificing, less caring and virtuous, they might now be preparing to meet their grandson. They might have continued to teach him what a family was. They might have saved their own children before other people's.

Tarek looks up. The floodlit castle floats above the town, a solemn Disneyland. He glances towards the underpass that leads to the high street and feels his shoulders tense. There's something eerier about this deserted port town than many of the other places he's walked at night. He heads along the main road, which is still backed up with HGVs crawling towards the ferry terminals, and presses the button for the crossing. On the other side is the strange new-build with the one original wall. Facing outwards on that painstakingly preserved wall is the faded mural of a man on a ladder chipping away one of twelve yellow stars. Tarek remembers the lengthy court case, not long after the artist funded a migrant rescue boat, where the family who owned the building attempted to sell the painted-over mural. They lost and were forced to restore and develop around the three-storey piece of art.

Tarek's eyes wander to the graffiti at the bottom of the man's ladder.

BEST DECISION EVER
#notinmyname
we still ♥ EU
FUCK OFF FOREIGN SCUM!

Tarek walks on. It used to bother him, knowing how many of those he encountered must have voted in favour of the mess they were living through. 'It's not that 52 per cent of the population is racist,' his friend Akpene told him one day in their digital journalism class, 'but the racists now feel like they've got the support of 52 per cent of the population.' Tarek found it harder to make that distinction, but over the years he taught himself not to think about it, not to dwell on how many of his colleagues, friends and in-laws were afraid of people like him. He couldn't expect his boss or Helen's parents or her childhood best friend, he realized, to understand how personal their marks on a ballot paper felt to him. How devastating it was to wake up in his tent that Friday morning ten years ago and hear the news spread around the camp. The people had voted, the prime minister had resigned, and the place they were all waiting to get to – desperate to build new lives in – had effectively closed and bolted its doors.

He takes a right and loops around to the deserted high street, peering in shop and café windows. He passes a man curled in a sleeping bag and feels a pang of guilt at the thought of his empty hotel bed, of all the beds he's rested his head on since he last slept in a doorway.

'Survivor's guilt,' the therapist for his detention centre documentary told the camera, 'is the perfectly common response to having survived a traumatic situation that others have not. The sense of: "Why me and not them?" But it can also manifest in other ways, in feelings of inadequacy at one's own experiences of suffering and a desire to swap places with anyone one perceives as in a worse-off state. At its basic level, this is a form of emotional self-harm. You are constantly telling yourself you do not deserve what you have.'

Tarek leaves a five-pound note tucked under the man's sleeping bag and hurries back towards the harbour front. Back in his room, he grabs another Coke and settles before his computer. If he's not going to sleep, he might as well get some more work done. He needs to focus on Rose and Jude and Cali, on the secrets of this strange town and how they relate to his own.

# THEN

Rose heard the music from halfway along the street. She'd stopped at a pub on the way up from the station, eking out as much time as she could before arriving at the house. It was freezing, but Jackie had all of the windows open and was playing a selection of early nineties hits at full volume. Cali had been out of hospital for almost two weeks now. Rose had stayed for most of the first, then returned to London to work as many back-to-back shifts as she could. Her manager, Claire, had been a bit of a dick about it, but finally agreed to let Rose use the holiday she'd been saving, so here she was back in Dover for a solid ten days.

She stood in the hallway listening to banging from the kitchen, then climbed the stairs and poked her head in Cali's room. All the furniture had been pushed towards the window and there was newspaper laid out on the floor. She opened the door to her own room and found Cali curled on the bed.

'What's going on?'

Cali didn't look up from her phone. 'Mum's redecorating.'

It had been a long time since Rose had witnessed one of her mum's highs. She'd come back to look out for her sister, to spend some time with her and try to make up for being so absent. But maybe there was something more useful she could offer Cali: a break.

'Why don't you go stay with Jude?' she said. 'I'll take care of Mum.'

Cali looked up. 'You sure? What if you fight?'

Rose didn't reply.

'Rose—'

'What?'

'Be nice.'

Rose's tactic when her mother was like this had always been to avoid her as much as possible while still maintaining a loose supervisory role. On the first day she kicked around the rec with Jude and Cali, and on the second they went to the cinema with Cali's awkward boyfriend, but mostly, as she had when she was Cali's age, Rose retreated to her room. With Jackie swirling in her own vortex and Cali safely with Jude, it was easy to get away with drinking through most of the day. She made regular trips to the newsagents and hid the empty cans beneath her bed. This was her holiday, she reasoned, so it was perfectly acceptable to be tipsy by midday.

On the third day, sometime after her fifth beer, she ventured into Cali's room and borrowed her ancient laptop. The password was the same as it always had been: Jasper2010. The browser took an age to load, more than enough time for Rose to question what she was doing and ask herself why she didn't feel capable of confronting her sister directly. Nevertheless, once it did, she opened Cali's History and stared at the repeated *Blue Mondays*.

The most recent thread on the site was by a student who claimed nothing was wrong and that life was fine, but he couldn't stop thinking about ending it. He said he couldn't think of a reason not to, especially if he planned it out in meticulous detail and simply followed it through like it was inevitable. Rose read the responses, all telling him he wasn't alone and directing him to places he could seek help. She tried to imagine Cali writing something like this, reading replies from strangers like these. Cali didn't seem to have any login details saved, but Rose clicked to the navigation page and scrolled back to July. Jude had said Cali used this site over the summer. Had she posted? Would Rose recognize her words if she had?

She sat up half the night reading, engrossed by people's willingness to lay themselves bare. She was horrified by how frequently people referred to previous attempts, some five or six years ago, or back in their childhoods. She'd been an idiot, she realized, to have listened to that doctor and been seeking Cali's smiles and laughter as signs that she felt better. What if all the doctors and counselling could do was press pause? What if months or years later Cali found herself back in the same place?

Rose scanned quickly through the replies, recognizing the avatars of the moderators who gave identical responses each time. Their concern seemed less genuine when she read it on every thread. *Please know you are loved. Please seek help. These are the numbers you can call to talk to someone. What you say is confidential.*

There were a few regular forum users who obviously weren't moderators. They wrote things like: *Those of us with suicidal thoughts are not searching for a way to die, we are simply seeking a way to make the pain stop,* and *I've been there brother, hang on.* These users had tried, but come back from the brink. Rose wondered how far they'd truly come, though, if they were still hanging around on the site. What sort of person scrolled through this much pain for fun? What sort of person sat around reading one stranger after another tell you they wanted to die?

Rose's phone vibrated in her pocket and she wriggled to get it out without tipping the computer or spilling her beer. She felt a surge of happiness to see Kassia's name.

> I am going to assume you lost my
> number . . .

> Sorry! Things have been crazy.

Take me out tomorrow and I will
forgive you.

                              I'm out of town.

☹
Where are you?

                    Dover. With my family.

Are you close?

Rose looked at the ancient *xx* poster on the back of her closed door. Behind it, she could hear the wails of her mother's music pumping from downstairs and the thumps of her footsteps as she hurried between rooms, intent on missions only she understood.

*Sort of,* she typed. *I'm not sure.*

Ok . . .

                         It's complicated.

What are you doing now?

              Sitting in bed reading some seriously
              depressing crap on the internet. You?

Out with friends. Are you okay?

Rose took a long sip of beer and stared at her phone screen.

Rose?

                              Not really.

No?

My sister tried to kill herself.

Oh my god. Is she all right?

I guess.

I don't know what to say.

Me neither.

How are you?
What I mean is are you looking after
yourself as well as her? What do
your parents say?

It's just my mum. She's got her own
issues.

Rose, I cannot imagine what you are
going through. I wish I could help.

Sorry, I don't mean to dump on you.
We hardly know each other.

Do not be sorry. I want to get to
know you.

Rose leant back against the pillows, trying to picture
Kassia's skin and face and smile. Sleeping in her old bedroom night after night, it was getting harder and harder to
remember the life she'd built elsewhere.

She fell asleep with the computer still on her lap and a
half-full can of lager balanced precariously between the edge
of the bed and the wall. She woke with a crick in her neck
and moved the can to the windowsill. The computer screen
woke with the site still loaded. A flag at the top of the page
said there was a new post.

Guys, I'm going to do it. I know I've said that before, but this
time it's different. I can't keep living like this. I have hydrogen
sulphide. I'm going to take it as soon as I've hit send. Maybe a
couple of you will read this before it gets taken down for
'forbidden content' or whatever. Maybe not. I don't suppose it
matters either way. See some of you on the other side.

---

PilotBoy

Rose looked at the clock in the corner of the screen. Four
minutes since it had been posted. Her heart pounded in her
chest. She should do something, but what? All she knew
about this guy was his avatar. What else could she tell from
this message? Would the moderators have more information? Would they be able to send an ambulance to his address?
She watched the minutes tick by, wondering where this man
was. She pictured him in a bathroom, empty bottles of
chemicals beside him. For all she knew he could be living
next door. He could be in Dover or Denmark, London or
Los Angeles. She'd read last night that someone committed
suicide somewhere around the world every forty seconds.
All around her people could be feeling like this man, contemplating what he was doing. How many people had she
passed on the tube or served at work who had been thinking
about it, who had actually gone home and done it?

She rang Cali.

'Are you okay?'

'Yeah.'

'I mean really, are you actually—'

'You sound weird.'

'I need to know you're okay. I love you, you know?'

'I'm fine. What's going on?'

Rose hesitated. 'I know about Blue Mondays.'

Cali didn't respond.

'Cal?'

'I just read it a couple of times, that's all.'

Rose took a breath, willing herself not to cry. 'You can be honest with me. I just want to know.'

'Christ, I'm telling the truth, all right?' Cali snapped. 'I came across it when I was searching for stuff, that's all. It's not that big a deal. How did you even find out?'

Rose looked at the post on the screen in front of her. 'You know you can come to me? You don't need to use something like this.'

Cali sighed. 'I know.'

'I love you.'

'You already said that.'

In spite of herself, Rose let out a laugh.

'How's Mum?' Cali said, which was when Rose realized that, for the first time in four days, the house was silent. Jackie's music had been a constant, day and night. She'd hardly slept and Rose had grown used to hearing her clattering around at all hours. But that morning it was quiet. Rose's first thought was panic. If her mother had left in the night she'd have to find her. She told Cali she'd call her back.

Jackie was in the living room. Conked out. Tumbling down from her cloud nine. Rose looked at her mother's sleeping face and felt sorry for her. She would feel terrible when she woke up, but for Rose it was a relief to know it was over. She draped a blanket on her and tiptoed back to the kitchen. She made herself a strong coffee to shake her hangover and set about trying to sort out the house. She put everything back in the kitchen cupboards and cleaned the work surfaces. Once the rest of the house was done, she ventured into Cali's room. It was a bomb site, two of the walls half done, paint dripped on the carpet and skirting boards.

Rose found some old clothes in her room and did what she could to tidy up her mother's redecoration job. It wasn't until the afternoon that she remembered PilotBoy and the forum. She booted up Cali's laptop again, but couldn't find the post. As he'd predicted, it had been taken down.

Cali moved back in the next day and she and Rose made dinner together and drank two bottles of wine while making plans to hang out in London over the summer. Rose woke on Saturday morning to her phone buzzing against the bedside table. It was Kassia again.

How are you feeling?

Horrendous.

Hungover?

Definitely.

Well I might be able to help with
that. I am at the station.

What?

I am in Dover, if you want a
distraction.

You're here?

I thought you might need someone
to talk to. Someone other than your
family.

So you came to Dover?

I have never been before. I wanted
to look around.

94

On a freezing cold day in January?

It is okay if you don't want to see
me. I know it is a bit weird, but I am
here if you want. If not I will go to the
castle and have a day out.

If you wanted a day out you should
have gone to Brighton or Whitstable.

In fact, I can think of forty better
places you should have gone.

You should ask my advice before you
take a day trip next time – you have
terrible taste.

It doesn't seem too bad so far. A
man called me darling and offered
me his bag of crisps.

Did you take it?

No.

Sensible girl. Probably laced with
rohypnol.

Can you put rohypnol in a bag of
crisps?

Questions one only asks in Dover.

So do you want to meet me or
what?

I think I do.

Rose draws her dressing gown tighter and presses her weight into the kitchen counter, waiting for the kettle to boil.

'Where were you today?' Kassia repeats.

Rose reaches for the jar of chamomile and places a bag in each mug, keeping her back to her wife.

'I went to surprise you at work. Lucy said you've taken the week off and left her in charge.'

The kettle finishes boiling and Rose pours the water. 'I was filming.'

'Excuse me?'

Rose turns and offers Kassia a mug. Her mouth is drawn and there's a crease between her brows, but even in moments like this Rose sees the same almond eyes and pale, freckled skin she first fell for. 'The documentary,' she says, bracing for Kassia's response.

Her wife stares at her, ignoring the tea. 'Are you serious? You went behind my back?'

Rose places both mugs on the scratched table they inherited from the previous tenants. It's late and she wants to go to bed, but she sits.

'I didn't want you to worry.'

'This is exactly what makes me worry!'

Kassia begins pacing around the small kitchen. 'Oh my God, I do *not* need this, not today.' She stops abruptly and fishes in her handbag for something. 'Do you see this? Left all over my waiting room again.'

Rose takes the piece of paper from Kassia's outstretched

hand. It is a flyer for the New Nationalist Action Alliance, a small local group with a reputation for stirring up violence. On the front is a large red and white flag, reading:

BORN IN ENGLAND, LIVE IN ENGLAND,
DIE IN ENGLAND.

'It's the third time this year.'

'Kash, I'm so sorry.'

Kassia returns the flyer to her handbag, which Rose guesses contains more. She wishes Kassia would throw them out like the trash they are, but she says it's important to keep a record. Today's pile will join the rest in the drawer upstairs.

Kassia groans. 'And now I get home and you tell me this. What are you thinking, Rose? You can't talk to this man. Our lives are hard enough without you—'

'I've got it under control,' Rose says, trying to hold her wife's gaze. 'I know the risks.'

Kassia steps towards her. 'Do you?'

Rose looks away and Kassia lets out a frustrated sigh.

'It's not just about you, is it? It's about that untrustworthy little weasel, Jude. If she's doing this too then—'

'Kash, it's okay. Really. In all these years, Jude hasn't remembered anything. Why would she now?'

Kassia shakes her head. 'What about me? What about your mother? What do you think it will do to her if the truth comes out?'

Rose holds up her palm. 'It won't.'

'You're playing with fire, Rose.'

'This is something I need to do. For Mum, for us. We need the money, don't we?'

'Not this much.'

Rose sighs. 'It's not only that.' She clenches and unclenches her fist. She should tell Kassia about the bottle in the bin outside, she knows she should. Or at least call her sponsor. She looks into her wife's face. 'I don't know how to explain it, but it feels important to go back through these things, to think about what I did.' Her eyes drift to the fertility calendar on the pinboard. 'Especially now.'

Kassia takes Rose's wrist. They both watch as her fingers trace the inky swirls on Rose's forearm, lingering briefly on the thick Helvetica letters reading: *This is the worst*.

'I promise I'm being careful,' Rose says. 'I won't say anything I shouldn't, but what I can say, well, it feels like an opportunity to confess. To what I can, at least. Wipe the slate clean before we start a family.'

Kassia holds Rose's palm between her hands. 'You are a good person, Rose. You didn't do anything wrong.'

Rose nods, listening to the words for the thousandth time but still not allowing them to penetrate. Kassia lets go of her hand and folds Rose into her chest, stroking her back. Rose's nostrils fill with the remnants of Kassia's perfume, but her mind is retreating. From their kitchen and their home, from this life they've built that sometimes feels solid beneath her feet and sometimes doesn't.

'What did you tell him today?' Kassia says into her hair.

'Nothing much.'

Kassia's hand pauses on Rose's shoulder blade.

'Did he ask about the Shaft?'

'Not yet.'

# 2026

Tarek scrolls up and down the familiar grid of images. He's been studying these photos for weeks, searching for clues in the washed-out filters and comments beneath. Before he even arrived in Dover, he felt familiar with the place from Cali's memorialized page. He'd pored over shots of ironically scratched-out road signs, boat tarpaulins billowing in the wind, cliffs rising over turbulent seas, seagulls diving for fish and chip wrappers, and that one distant, moody silhouette labelled *Mo*.

Cali had an eye for photography, but also one for humour. Amongst these landscapes are dozens of goofier snaps. Cali and Jude pirouette on a bandstand, then press fish-lip faces together. What looks like an early prototype of the Rose he met today glares out of the screen with a rainbow halo and kitten ears, and a gaunt young man with a goatee grins beneath a hat made of digital French fries. Tarek scrolls through images of a scruffy border collie and a sleek black tomcat, then returns to the silhouette. The figure takes up less than a tenth of the square frame and is little more than a few smudged pixels, but he feels himself falling into her. When he thinks he can bear it no more, he clicks on and she is replaced by a picture of an ornate road sign. Beneath an elaborate coat of arms, it reads:

Welcome to
DOVER
Please D i e Slowly

The comments under this horribly prophetic image read *stfu* and *rofl*, *ikr* and *call me bb*. Hastily typed sentiments from acquaintances long grown, preserved forever in this microscopic corner of the internet. There are laws in place now to deal with digital legacies, especially for minors, but Cali died before all that. To remove this image or the whole profile, someone would need her original username and password. Teenagers today know better than to document their lives like this; they want transience, not posterity. That too, though, is risky. Tarek knows of at least two investigations currently being conducted into this and another leading site. His colleague, Livia, is consulting with one of them, hoping to get a scoop.

'It's all very well this push towards ephemerality,' she told him at the Christmas party, 'posts that disappear after a few hours. But do you know what happens to all this "deleted" media?'

Tarek shook his head.

'Well, the idea that it's gone is bullshit,' Livia slurred, spilling wine on the cuff of her blouse.

Tarek smiled politely and scanned the room for Helen, who he knew didn't want to be there. He's never been a fan of social media, so he paid little thought to Livia's warning that night, but an idea comes to him now. Cali could have posted more, could have left other traces of the girl on the cliff. He taps out a message to Livia and presses send. He doesn't know if what he's asking is possible. If it is, it's unlikely to be legal, but for the first time in his professional career, he's willing to pay any price.

He collects his empty Coke cans and throws them in the bathroom bin. Back in the bedroom, he unbuttons his shirt and lays it gently over the back of the chair. He removes his trousers and hangs them on an arm, balls his socks and shoves them in a corner of the messy case spilling onto the floor. From the dresser, he picks up his wallet, digs his finger deep inside the inner pocket and slips out the ancient photocopied photo. He returns Inji's serious stare, remembering his little sister's excitement the day they went to get passport images taken. Inji protested furiously as their mother adjusted the hijab she hated wearing and instructed her not to blink, not to pull a face, not to smile. *Yes, Mother*, Inji said, winking at Tarek as she stepped in front of the photographer. It took ten minutes of their mother and the photographer growing increasingly incensed before Inji had run through her comic routine and they managed to get this shot.

It was only Tarek and Inji getting their pictures taken that day. They were the youngest of the siblings, although with almost nine years apart Tarek always objected to being lumped together as the babies of the family. To Inji he was a big brother, just like Adnan and Khalid, only without the wives and children that made them so dull. She looked up to Tarek. She asked about his studies and what was going on at the university, about the protests and what it was like when they held him at the checkpoint. Tarek loved all of his family, but there was something special about Inji, the only girl, the baby he had held and fed and swaddled and cooed at. When she was tiny he had told her a story that they were twins, split in egg form and kept apart for nine years, but now reunited. They would go on adventures together, tackle monsters and evil rulers, cross deserts and mountains in faraway lands.

Later, he found her a pain. He complained to his father that he couldn't cope with a kid running around while he tried to study. His father chuckled and shut his door. Inji and her best friend were always begging Tarek to look at their drawings, read their stories, judge their competitions. He sat under the stairs with his books to avoid them, or snuck out and walked to the public park. He'd like to think he wouldn't have been so impatient if he'd known what would happen. For a second, he is transported: looking up from his desk at two pairs of eyes spying through the doorjamb. Inji's best friend was Amena, a tomboy with strict parents. She changed her clothes as soon as she left her house and asked everyone she wasn't related to to call her by her brother's name: Mohammad. Mo, as she became known in their house, was goofy and funny. Despite Tarek's annoyance at always being interrupted by a couple of giggling kids, he was almost as fond of her as his sister. More often than not he would relent and succumb to their games, scrape back his chair and dart after them. If he tries, he can still hear both of their voices, shrieking as he chased them through the house.

He runs his thumb over Inji's serious, thirteen-year-old face. What happened to the other photographs taken that day? Within six months of Inji posing for this, both Adnan and Khalid were killed and smiles became a rare thing in the Zayat household. What are the chances that shots of Inji pretending to fall off the stool and twisting her mouth into ridiculous grimaces still exist somewhere? That they were stored on a hard drive and not crushed by rubble? Tarek remembers standing with tears of laughter in his eyes as he watched his sister mess around. He remembers his mother turning pink with anger, unaware of what lay ahead for her family but certain nonetheless that it was important to get passports, to prepare for the worst. How could she have imagined what the worst would be? That more than a decade later, this photograph would be all Tarek has left of his family?

He places it on the desk, clicks off the main light and lies back against the plump pillows. If memories were as simple as footage, he could cut and edit them, streamline the narrative of his life into a more palatable, pre-watershed version. Would he do it? His memories haunt, but also sustain him.

Inji comes to him now, seven years old and grinning with Mo by her side. *What have you done?* Tarek says, narrowing his eyes. *Nothing*, she sing-songs. He runs to his room, inspects his desk and his bed, the wardrobe and the window. Nothing seems to have been moved. *You're paranoid, big brother!* The two of them run off, laughter echoing through the house. He searches and searches, but can't find their mischief. A week later he notices it: their names written on the inside cover of every book he owns.

*Inji & Mo*
*Inji & Mo*
*Inji & Mo*
*Inji & Mo*
*Inji & Mo*
*Inji & Mo*
*Inji & Mo*

As if they feared the contents might allow him to escape. As if they needed him always to remember them.

# THE RIOT

## BIGGIN STREET

Protestors wearing black hoods and carrying England flags march towards a Sports Direct sign. Single taxi stuck in the middle of a crowd outside Boots.

CROWD
(chanting)

Refugees, go home!

Refugees, go home!

CUT TO.

## EFFINGHAM STREET

Three lines of police officers block the road in front of another crowd.

VOICEOVER

On Saturday, 30th January 2016, the streets of Dover became the scene of a violent and chaotic clash between far-right anti-immigration protestors and their anti-fascist opponents.

CROWD
(chanting)

Off our streets!

Nazi scum!

Off our streets!

Nazi scum!

CUT TO.

## MONTAGE. CAMERAPHONE FOOTAGE.

Men covering their faces surge towards a police barrier. Purple smoke rises from the middle of a crowd. Four officers escort a man in a Union Jack hat to a waiting van.

VOICEOVER

Approximately 200 anti-immigration protestors, including representatives from the English Defence League and the National Front, travelled from around the country to take part in the demonstration organized by the East Kent Alliance. Meanwhile, Unite Against Fascism and Kent Anti-Racism Network held a counter rally with speakers including Labour MP and shadow cabinet member Diane Abbott.

Grey-haired woman holds sign reading #hopenothate. Sirens wail as riot police prepare to engage.

VOICEOVER

Violence erupted when the two groups met, and protestors, police and bystanders were all injured in the clash.

Three men stand on a wall waving a National Front flag. The two sides meet outside Dover Discovery Centre. A glass panel is smashed with a baseball bat. Woman shields herself using a vegetable box. Man with bloodied face gives Nazi salute. EU flag burns on pavement.

CROWD
(singing)
You're not English any more!

CUT TO.

## JUDE'S LIVING ROOM

Jude sits with arms folded.

JUDE
That's when everything started.

CUT TO.

## CONFERENCE ROOM

Rose shifts uncomfortably in her chair.

ROSE
Yeah, I was in Dover for the riot. Kassia too. She'd come to surprise me.

CUT TO.

JUDE

Cali was upset by the violence, so I suggested we get out of the way, go up to the cliffs.

(shakes head.)

I had no idea who we were about to find up there.

# THEN

Kassia sat on the pebbles facing the sea. As Rose approached, she noticed a small star tattoo beneath her hairline, the edges soft and blurred by the years and an inexpert tattooist. She wondered suddenly what Kassia had been like as a teenager. What had led her into a tattoo parlour and Cali to their mum's medicine cabinet?

Kassia's shoulders stiffened and she turned her head. 'Hey,' she called out, her expression bright. Rose picked her way across the remaining pebbles and dropped down next to her.

'Is it weird that I came? All the way here I've been thinking I am not sure, perhaps Rose will think I'm a stalker.'

Rose smiled. 'Yeah, it's pretty weird,' she said, waiting a moment to tease her. 'But nice.'

'Good. Because I promise I am not a stalker. But I was sitting at home thinking about you and I didn't know what to do with my day, then I thought if I could cheer you up even a little bit maybe it would have meaning.'

Rose nodded. It *was* strange that Kassia was here. This girl had seemed cool and self-assured when they'd first met. Now she'd followed her across counties.

'What's she like?' Kassia said. 'Your sister?'

Rose closed one eye and squinted with the other at a ferry beyond the harbour. The bruised sky above it promised a miserable afternoon. 'She's great,' she said slowly. 'Complicated, I guess, but sweet too.'

'I would like to meet her.'

Rose was quiet. They'd slept together once; they definitely weren't at the meeting the family stage.

'What should we do?' Kassia said. 'You want to show me your town?'

They wandered along the front, snaking towards the noisy and industrial Western Harbour. Kassia pointed at the boats and workmen, asking questions Rose couldn't answer. They climbed a barrier and looped away from the water around to Snargate Street, where the traffic crawled towards the port. They stopped in front of the big iron fences at the entrance to the Grand Shaft. The main gates were propped open and a poster told them today was the first day of an open weekend.

'Should we go in?' Kassia said.

Rose followed her along a strip-lit tunnel leading into the cliff. A faded notice told them the building of the Shaft began in 1806 to assist with the movement of troops between the castle on the east cliff and the defences up on the Western Heights. The triple-helix staircase had been designed to enable pedestrian access from the harbour straight up through the cliff to the barracks at the top.

At the far end of the tunnel, they reached the central light shaft in the middle of the staircases. White bricks and barred windows circled up to a grated skylight.

'It's like being at the bottom of a well,' Kassia said.

'Race you to the top?' Rose said, standing at the foot of one of the staircases. Kassia's face lit up and she darted towards the gate to her left, stealing a head start.

Halfway up the tight spiral, Rose met a family making their descent. She moved to the inside wall to let them pass, her boots not quite fitting on the narrower edge of each step. She peered through the bars of a window, trying to work out where Kassia's staircase was in relation to hers. At the top, she stepped out onto a circular platform. On her right, a long, straight set of concrete steps led further up the cliff, towards the Western Heights. On her left, a brick wall held back the bracken and blocked the view of the harbour and the sea.

'It is nice to visit your home,' Kassia said, leaning against the wall. She didn't even seem to be out of breath. When Rose didn't reply, she said, 'It doesn't feel like home? That is sad.'

Rose made a face and looked at her feet. She felt oddly naked in front of this woman. 'I spent so long wanting to get out of Dover,' she said, kicking a stone, 'that I don't know what that word means any more.' She looked up and shrugged. 'I feel as much for this place here as I do for the house I'll sleep in tonight.'

Kassia smiled. 'So your home can be the great Grand Shaft.'

'Sounds pretty phallic.'

Kassia's eyes crinkled when she laughed. 'How come we are surrounded by all these penis-like buildings, but when they dig a hole in the ground it also had to be named after men?'

Rose nodded. 'It should be the Grand Gash.'

Kassia shrieked. Then she leant forward and pressed her lips to Rose's cheek. Rose wanted to pull her into a proper kiss, but Kassia had already turned back towards the staircases. By the time they reached the bottom, it had started to rain. Kassia pulled her hood over her head, then laced her fingers into Rose's.

'Tell me some more about your sister.'

Rose thought about how happy Cali had seemed when she was little. How happy she'd wanted everyone else to be. *Where does he live?* she'd ask as they passed someone asking for change, *Who looks after him?*

'Cali cares too much,' Rose said now. 'About everything. If she thinks someone's unhappy, she'll carry that around with her all day.'

'She sounds kind.'

'People don't always get that. They see the girl from the broken home with the older boyfriend and—'

Rose couldn't finish. Kassia reached her hand out to touch her shoulder. They stopped walking and stood letting the rain soak them. Rose bowed her head and tried to shield her eyes, but Kassia folded her into a hug. 'It's okay,' she said, her breath against Rose's neck.

'I'm sorry. I don't usually do this.'

'I understand.'

*Do you?* Rose wondered.

After a while she wiped her face with her sleeve. Kassia promised she didn't look awful or puffy and they continued. Rose wondered if she should ask Kassia to stay. Her mum and Cali probably wouldn't care, but she couldn't picture Kassia in the house. They turned the corner towards Market Square and stopped.

Up ahead stood a line of yellow-jacketed police officers. Behind them, a mass of jostling bodies.

'What the fuck?' Rose said.

Kassia reached for her hand as a cry rose up from the crowd behind the officers. There was a surge forward and the line of yellow broke briefly, allowing through two men with shaved heads and bandanas around their faces. Several officers tackled them to the ground while the rest regrouped to close the gap. Rose caught a glimpse of the letters NF rippling in the centre of a flag and felt a shiver run up her spine. Something flew into the air and fell with a smash.

'I think we should get out of here.'

She pulled Kassia back down the street they'd come along,

garbled chants following them. Rose heard the words 'Go home,' and tightened her grip on Kassia's hand.

'What's happening?'

Rose didn't reply. She was struggling to breathe again. Everything felt linked. Kassia wasn't meant to be here; Rose's lives were not meant to meet. 'I'm sorry,' she said as they dived into the shelter of the train station and Kassia shook off her hood.

'It's not your fault.'

'Are you okay?'

Kassia nodded, causing a raindrop to drip from her nose. 'What about you? Are you worried about your sister?'

Rose hadn't thought about Cali until now. 'Where are you?' she asked as soon as she picked up.

'On the cliffs with Jude.'

Rose told Cali to stay up there, not to go into town. She could picture her rolling her eyes, thinking her sister overbearing, but she didn't care. She didn't want Cali anywhere near those men.

They hung up, and Rose and Kassia climbed over the railway bridge and onto the platform. They stood next to each other, shivering as they stared at the departures board. 'Are you going to be okay on the train?'

'It's good to leave while it's still going on, I think.'

'Maybe.'

'You're back in London next week?' Kassia said, attempting a smile.

'I think so,' Rose said, suddenly aware of the other people on the platform. She felt torn between wanting to reach for Kassia and not wanting to do anything to draw attention.

'I would like to see you,' Kassia said.

'Me too.'

Rose fiddled with the buttons of her jacket. She was used

to being in control of situations with women. To not giving a fuck what anyone around her thought.

Kassia reached her hand out and brushed her chilly fingertips over Rose's knuckles. 'I am glad I came. I've had a nice afternoon.'

Rose laughed. 'Yeah, the thugs in the street were a real highlight.'

Kassia leant forwards to kiss her and Rose felt a rising of desire. She should have asked her to stay, she thought. But the train was pulling up and Kassia was leaning away, a smile on her lips. Rose watched her walk through the carriage and find a seat, willing her to look out of the window. They'd spent the whole afternoon together, but suddenly it wasn't enough. She watched Kassia shrug off her coat and root in her bag to pull out a bottle of water and a book. Kassia looked out the opposite window, then up as a man placed his luggage in the overhead rack and settled opposite her. The announcement blared on the platform and the doors bleeped. Rose cursed herself for standing there like a desperate rain-drenched idiot, but just as she was about to turn away, Kassia looked through the smeary window across the aisle. Her face split into a smile, and Rose wondered if all that had been a test to see if she would wait. Kassia was laughing. At Rose or herself, it wasn't clear. But she waved as the train pulled away, and Rose waved back, feeling a surge of something like happiness.

\*

A few miles away, along the muddy cliff paths, Jude sat shivering on the concrete lip of the sound mirror.

'Help you?' she said.

The girl stepped forward slightly, water dripping from her

nose and cheekbones. 'The fighting, in the town,' she said. 'I am scared. I do not know where to go.'

'Shit, you're freezing,' Cali said, moving towards her. She ushered the girl into the sound mirror, elbowing Jude to get her to move up. 'Mo, right? I'm Cali, this is Jude.'

'Can you help me?' Mo repeated. 'I am trying to get to Calais.'

Jude frowned. 'I thought everyone there wanted to come here.'

Cali shot her a look that told her to shut up. 'Ignore her, Mo.'

Jude bounced her trainers against the concrete. It was typical for Cali not to question things. But where was this girl from? How had she got here? Where were her family? She was sitting on the top of their cliffs begging them for help. Jude felt for her, obviously, but that didn't mean she automatically trusted her. Who was to say Mo was even her real name?

'Where's your stuff?' Cali asked.

Mo lifted her backpack.

'That's it?'

'Don't you have a tent?' Jude said. 'A sleeping bag?' She'd seen footage of the camps on the news, and before Christmas she'd helped her mother organize a collection of donations to be sent over with a charity.

Mo shook her head. 'I find shelter there.' She gestured back along the headland.

'The lookouts?' Cali said, wrinkling her nose.

Jude chewed the inside of her cheek. She'd always felt a sense of ownership over the buildings on the cliffs. Whenever they came up here, she scoured the walls for fresh graffiti, annoyed by new names and recent dates. But Mo nodded.

'You'll freeze,' Cali said.

'I need blankets. Can you help?'

Jude knew exactly what was coming next, but she was still pissed off when Cali said it.

'We can bring you things. Can't we, Jude? You have sleeping bags in your garage, right? And other things. We can bring you a stove and food and anything else you need.'

'It is true?'

Cali nodded and smiled at Mo, completely ignoring Jude – as if she hadn't just agreed on her behalf that they'd steal from her parents and help this strange girl who they knew absolutely nothing about.

# 2026

Jude yawns and leans back against the armchair while the screen in her lap loads the next video. The title sequence of an old breakfast show she never watched plays before cutting to a cookery segment. Tarek, along with an actress whose face Jude vaguely recognizes, stands behind a counter trying to follow a celebrity chef's instructions while two perky presenters bat questions at them. The clip is dated 15 June 2021, just after the release of the detention centre film that made Tarek's name.

'The thing is, there are a million ways to tell a story,' he says, frowning as he whisks a bowl of egg yolks over a pan of simmering water, 'and a million different stories inside each one you're trying to tell.'

'Keep going, don't let them curdle,' the chef says, reaching past him to turn the heat down.

Jude sighs and closes the tab. She's been sitting here for hours, watching and re-watching these pointless clips, failing to quell the panic rising within her. What's done is done, she's been trying to tell herself. She said what she wanted to say last week; all she can do now is trust that this man knows what he's doing.

She stares at her reflection in the darkened balcony door. The estate agent who sold her the flat thought she was crazy choosing one on this side of the development. 'You could have a south-west-facing balcony and views of the harbour and cliffs,' the woman began, then stopped, realizing what she'd said, who Jude was. 'I'm sorry,' she stuttered, 'I didn't think. Of course you don't want to be reminded every time you look at the cliffs—' She continued to talk as she fished out the keys for the units still available on the east side of the marina, feeling the need to tell Jude she thought it was terrible *they* were still being let in. Jude gave her usual look of pained patience, but nevertheless fell in love with the flat.

She pinches a small section of her tongue between her teeth and glances at the mustard-yellow appliances on the access-adjusted kitchen counter. It amazes even her sometimes how, against all odds, she's turned her life around. There have been moments, like graduating with a first or winning the funding bid to set up her charity, where her achievements have felt solid and tangible. But it is in everyday living, her dad always used to tell her, that true success lies.

'No good ever came from running away,' he said when she told him of her plan to move to Hastings. She'd come home after university and struggled to settle back in. She'd decided a new start was what she needed. But three weeks after her announcement, her father was diagnosed with inoperable pancreatic cancer. The doctors gave him months, but her tough old dad lasted just over a year. That year was a gift, she recognizes now. They'd always been close, but in his final months she felt like her father saw her in a way no one ever had. While her mum was at work, Jude and her dad talked for hours. Sometimes she could see him growing tired or struggling with the pain, but he'd continue asking questions, pressing her to think about what she wanted out of life. Everything she has now, is down to him. He encouraged her to join the council, to apply for the bid, to move into her own place.

She looks around. She's always found pleasure in the

confluence of form and function, which is why everything in this room is both aesthetically pleasing and fit for purpose. If things go to plan, that's exactly what Tarek's documentary will be too.

She returns her attention to the screen and types her own name.

---

| jude campbell | 🎤   🔍 |
|---|---|

✅ **Dover Girls – Wikipedia**
https://en.wikipedia.org/wiki/Dover_Girls
The deaths of two teenage girls and the life-changing injuries of a third in the port town of Dover sparked controversy and political tension in the run-up to the 2016 . . .

**Deaths:** 2     **Date:** 15 May – 3 June 2016
Cali Walker – **Jude Campbell** – The Grand Shaft – Brexit

✅ **'What Is Happening to Our Children?'**
https://www.theguardian.com/opinion/dover-girls
05 Jun 2016 – Several mental health charities have called on the government to increase funding to youth support services following the possible suicide pact of **Jude Campbell** and . . .

✅ **Unidentified Dover Girl Believed to Be Undocumented Immigrant**
https://www.mirror.co.uk/uk-news/unidentified-dover-girl . . .
20 Jun 2016 – Kent Police have released a statement saying they suspect the teenage girl found dead in Dover alongside **Jude Campbell** entered the country illegally . . .

✅ **Illegal Immigrant Blackmailing Innocent Teen!**
https://www.englishdefenceleague.org.uk/dover-girls
Brutal attack of fifteen-year-old **Jude Campbell** was part of complex blackmail scam run by migrant gang. Time to take action . . .

When Jude first woke up, she was horrified to discover what was being said. She thought anyone sensible must be able to see that both the blackmail and the suicide pact theories were insane. But her story had been seized upon by parts of the media. She found herself a poster child for both national pride and liberal blame. Strangers contacted her to say it was her fault that people had voted the way they did, that they hoped her injuries had left her sterile. Others offered their condolences and said she was the reason they were fighting to close the borders. All over the country, people were using her name – sending her threats, sending her praise. If she wasn't being told it was her fault foreigners were being beaten up in the street, then she was being blamed for a mental health crisis, for copycat attempts.

It died down eventually, but it's never gone away. There's always someone like that estate agent to remind her of what happened and the symbol of fear and anger it turned her into. Some flick her sympathetic looks as she does her shopping, their gaze lingering on her wheelchair. Others avoid her eye altogether, or mutter things under their breath as she passes. She's learnt to live with it. Her policy from the beginning was to avoid journalists and publicity, to try to keep her head down and stay out of the conflicts people wanted to drag her into. That's why she said no when Tarek first got in touch at the beginning of the year. Her dad was deteriorating and things were busy at the charity; the last thing she needed was someone excavating ancient history. Her dad had been telling her to stop punishing herself, to move on. They'd talked about almost everything by then. 'Cali would want you to live your life,' he said. 'You need to put what happened behind you. You were a great friend to her and you did everything you could. Now it's time to do something for yourself.'

'Dad, there's something I need to tell you,' she said on March 7th, pushing open the door to the living room they'd converted into a bedroom. The previous day he'd placed a shaky hand on top of hers and told her he was proud of her. 'Cali would be too,' he'd added. Jude had gone home to her new flat thinking about her best friend, wondering if there was any way that could be true. If it wasn't but her dad thought it was, then didn't that cast doubt on his pride too? She wondered if she'd ever be able to achieve the things he wanted her to achieve, be the person he believed her to be, without telling him what she'd done. So she'd woken up determined to confess, to take the burdens she'd lived with for the past decade to the man she knew loved her most in the world. To ask for his forgiveness.

But, instead of hearing her dad's friendly hello as she entered the room that morning, it was her mum that replied.

'Jude, darling,' she said, standing by the window with tears streaking her face. 'He's gone.'

Helping her mum pack up his things, Jude discovered her dad had been writing her a letter. A long, rambling and cringingly sentimental pouring out of love that he never got a chance to finish. *Don't run away from things*, he repeated four or five times. Then towards the end: *Hold your head high. Face your demons.*

That afternoon she got back in touch with Tarek and told him she would do his documentary. Even in her grief she wasn't stupid enough to think that confessing to him would be a sensible substitute for confessing to her dad. But the past is undoubtedly Jude's biggest demon and following her father's advice is the best tribute she will ever be able to pay him.

She sets the laptop aside and transfers out of the armchair. The uncanny thing is that now it seems, even without knowing the truth, her father understood exactly what was best for her. With the surge in media attention for her charity and the possibility of her becoming mayor, finally laying the rumours to rest is undeniably in Jude's interest right now.

She makes her way to the study and flicks on the light. It's late but she wants to go through her speech again before tomorrow. She catches herself biting the nail on her ring finger and stops. There's no reason to be nervous. Two thirds of the councillors have promised her their votes. She's served with them for almost a year now, proving her worth even to those who questioned her initial appointment. All her life, it seems, she's been fighting to be seen as more than the labels others have given her – whether to do with her age, her class, her gender, her disability or, most infuriatingly, what happened on a single night ten years ago.

Well, this coming year is going to be her chance to prove people wrong. Pretending she didn't know Mo and trying to stay neutral was a mistake. She realizes that now. The mystery and her silence have only made things worse. From now on, she'll answer people's questions, show that she understands their concerns.

Tarek's documentary is a risk, of course. It's not just her

own testimony that she has to worry about. She knows he must be in touch with Rose. He's not wrong about there being different ways to tell each story; hers and Rose's are unlikely to agree. But Jude is not the only one with something to lose here. And, done right, it has the potential to release her from these narrow boxes she's been put in. If things go her way tomorrow evening, she'll spend a year as the right honourable Mayor of Dover, cutting ribbons in front of shops, posing at school fetes and chairing council meetings. Hopefully that kind of local exposure, along with the honesty she's shown to Tarek, will begin to encourage people to think of her as something more than one of the Dover Girls. If she can be set free from that label, then she'll finally be able to fight for the things she believes in. For tolerance, fairness, forgiveness. Founding a charity in Cali's name was a start, but there's so much more she wants to do, so many ways she hopes to live up to her father's pride.

On the corner of the desk, where she placed it in preparation for last week's filming, is the framed photograph of ten-year-old Cali smiling on top of Shakespeare Cliff. Jude reaches for it. *When can we go up there by ourselves?* she used to ask her mum over and over. *When you're ten*, her mum finally snapped. She remembers thinking ten was forever away. She remembers wishing she had Cali's mum.

It wasn't that Jackie didn't care, but she had too much on her plate to worry about every last movement of two little girls. She worked nights at the ferry dock, so during the day she'd slip around the house in her dressing gown. After Cali's stepdad, John, left, she lost the job at the docks, but her sleep pattern never changed. Sometimes whole weeks would go by where Cali and Rose had to raid the freezer for the last fish fingers and pool their change to buy a loaf of bread. The kitchen floor was always bumpy with spilled cat litter pellets, the cat always darting into the bathroom to drink from the toilet bowl. It almost makes Jude want to cry now, the memory of how Cali's house used to be, but it didn't feel sad back then, only exciting. There were no rules in Cali's house. Even when John was there, he was mostly at work or the pub, so the only person in charge was Rose, and she didn't care. Jude's house was different. If they took the bikes out of the shed, they had to say exactly where they were going and promise to use the pedestrian crossings. They had to shout and come straight back if anyone tried to talk to them. Ten came and her mum still wasn't happy. *Why don't you start by going to the shop for me? That's a grown-up thing to do.*

*You promised we could walk the cliffs*, Jude remembers wailing for a week.

Then Cali had a brainwave. *My sister will come.*

Rose had shaved her head earlier that year and she looked like a fuzzy alien as it grew back. Jude had heard John say she looked like a freak. She had big eyes, though, like Cali's, only blue-green rather than dark brown, which meant she could pull off short hair. Jude had spent hours in front of the mirror stretching her eyelids as wide as they would go, trying to emulate Cali's innocent doe-eyed look. Somehow those eyes made both Cali and her sister look friendly no matter how much they scowled.

They ran ahead of Rose on that first walk, puffing themselves out on the steep paths and pressing their cheeks together at every kissing gate. *It's bad luck not to kiss at a kissing gate*, Cali said as Rose banged through behind them. Rose laughed and sucked on her cigarette, eyeing them like strange creatures that had climbed over the chalky edge.

Jude can't go up there any more, and maybe she wouldn't even if she could. She closes her eyes, remembering how the path took you inland to get past the docks and under the

road, then through a tree-covered archway next to the allotments where the butterflies hung out. After that, you realized
you were already halfway up Shakespeare Cliff and the bent
metal fence to your left was the only thing protecting you
from the sheer drop. When it opened out to let you see the
thick sky beyond the fence, you were further out than most
of the town. That was Jude's favourite place to watch the ferries from, but Cali always had to place her hand up against
her face. Sometimes Jude walked beside her like a human
shield, imagining she was a brave knight ready to sacrifice
herself if the cliff crumbled. She'd be hanging from the edge
with one hand and Cali would be sobbing. Jude would tell
her it was okay, she was happy to die a noble death, protecting her delicate lady. Over and over, Jude imagined their last
words to each other before she dropped to her peril. Never
once did she consider Cali might be the sacrifice and her the
one left abandoned and alone.

The summer they climbed the cliffs with Rose had been
full of dry, cloudy days that filled Jude with an energy she
couldn't dispel. A pinkish glow sat like a halo on the horizon
that afternoon. She ran ahead and jumped on a block of concrete poking from the cliff. *Look, I'm a sergeant!* she cried,
spraying bullets from an invisible machine gun. A little further on, they reached a row of four flat-topped structures
with panoramic cut-out windows looking out to the sea. Jude
thought they looked like robots poking their heads up from
the grass to study the planet they'd secretly colonized. Like
something out of *Doctor Who*.

*The prime minister came here,* Rose said, *and got annoyed that
enemy ships were pissing around out there like fuck you, so he put a
bunch of guns up here. Soldiers had to sit in these lookouts for like twelve
hours at a time. If they fell asleep, the whole country could be taken.*

Jude eyed Rose, unsure if she was taking the piss. She'd

never seen her show an interest in anything and couldn't picture her sitting in a classroom paying attention.

*You want to go in?*

*Rose, come on*, Cali said. *It's not safe.*

Rose stepped over the weeds towards the cliff edge. Jude followed, careful to tread where she did.

*You're going to die!* Cali said, crossing her arms and planting herself firmly on the path.

*We'll just be a sec*, Jude said, hoping Cali wouldn't sulk at her. She and Rose made their way round to the narrow jut of grass in front of the first robot's single eye. The railway tracks and the grassy reclaimed banks of Samphire Hoe lay a hundred feet below. Rose ducked her bald head beneath a rusty beam that read DANGER KEEP OUT and swung her legs through the opening. She jumped onto the concrete floor with a thud. Jude never told Cali, but heights made her just as scared, only the thing that locked Cali's knees and made her whimper made Jude want to inch forward, even jump. Taking the ferry with her parents, she would stand on deck leaning against the railing and imagine diving overboard, crashing down into the churned sea. She would wonder what it would be like to fall. To sail in the air like a seagull, feel the rush of the wind. Standing on the cliffs, she'd imagine her fragile bones bashing against the white chalk, bouncing onto the reclaimed parkland below.

Jude lifts her hand to her cheek to trace the uneven landscape of her scar, disturbed by the memory. It's terrifying to think how prescient some of those thoughts were.

Oblivious of what was to come, that day she swung her ten-year-old legs onto the ledge and jumped down. She and Rose stood in a rectangular enclosure, the walls marked by damp and graffiti. *I haven't been here for years*, Rose said. She pointed to the small knee-height opening on the back wall. *There are tunnels too.*

Jude knows now, of course, that the government tried to tidy the cliffs of eyesores in the seventies, levelling the magazine buildings and blowing up the entrance tunnels. They tried again, after what happened to Cali. In a way she's glad she can't get up there now, that her memories can remain pure. She's heard they've made a right mess of it.

*You should bring a torch if you want to explore,* Rose said that first time. *There's a trapdoor in one of the fields, but I could never open it on my own, which is why I came up here. Most people are too scared.*

Jude smiled, proud to have proved herself brave. Beyond the concrete, the sea stretched to the horizon. She had to stand on tiptoes to see out. Half a century and more had passed since men stood to attention there, watching out for the nation's enemies. *It's so cool,* she said, running her hand over the back wall. *But do you mind? I mean, can I come here?*

Rose laughed. *All yours.*

Jude clears her throat. She has more important things to do right now than get lost in old memories. She spins away from the desk and heads towards the door. In the bedroom, she folds herself over to reach for the box beneath the bed. She lifts the lid and places Cali's photograph face down between a crumpled envelope and a tin of old nail-polishes. She glances briefly at the other items in the box – a pink fluffy pencil topper, a plastic sweet dispenser, a keyring and an old Android handset – before replacing the lid and shoving it back in its place.

She turns, ready to return to the study, to her speech, to her future. She catches sight, though, of her bulky wheelchair in the mirror on the wardrobe door and hesitates. She remembers the feel of Rose's hand on her shin as she gave her a leg-up to climb back out, the stretch of her now-wasted muscles as she shimmied over the wall and stood up straight on the thin patch of grass between the building and the drop. Again, Jude's stomach flipped at the thought of sailing down, but in two short steps, with Rose's arm held out to balance her, she was back on solid ground.

Cali was making patterns in the dust with the toe of her trainer on the path. *Finafuckingly*, she said. She and Rose were the only people Jude knew at that age who swore. It made the hairs on her neck stand up.

*I'm bored*, Rose said. *Let's go back.*

*Fuck's sake. I just waited like an hour for you two. I want to walk over there.* Cali waved her hand at the horizon.

*Why?* Rose said.

Cali shrugged.

*It's cool in there*, Jude said. *You should come next time.*

Cali made a face. *It's none of my business if you two wanna kill yourselves, but I'm happy being alive, thanks.*

Jude locks eyes with her reflection and reminds herself it was not her fault. This is a mantra she has been repeating for almost ten years, both a source of comfort and a drive for life. Everything she's done, everything she's doing, everything she hopes to achieve, is in Cali's name. Because deep down Jude knows it has never been her father's, or Tarek's, or anyone else's forgiveness she needs. Only Cali's.

# THEN

'What are you doing?' Jude said once she and Cali were out of earshot. They'd agreed to meet Mo back at the lookouts in a few hours, but she couldn't hold her tongue any longer.

'What?' Cali said.

'We can't just let her live up on the cliffs.' The storm had passed, but the paths were slick with mud and they were struggling not to slip on the steep bits. 'We need to tell someone she's here.'

Cali stopped dead. 'What are you talking about? Who?'

Jude paused a couple of feet below her. 'The police? Our parents?'

'Jude, you saw what happened in town today. You saw how scared she was. She's obviously come here illegally. You tell the police and they'll put her in a detention centre and send her back.'

'She wants to go back!'

'She's confused. She's probably traumatized. She doesn't know what she wants.'

'Exactly. She needs proper help. What if she has family somewhere? What if someone's looking for her?'

Cali set off again, her trainers sliding as she overtook Jude. 'Why are you being such a dick about this?'

Jude followed, tears pricking her eyes. She'd been rehearsing this conversation in her head for the past hour, but this was not how it was supposed to go. She couldn't stand arguing with Cali.

'Seriously,' Cali said, 'if you don't want to help, then don't.

I'll find a sleeping bag another way, but I can't believe you're being like this. How can you live in your big fucking house and not want to help someone with nothing?'

'That's not what I said. I do want to help.'

'You sure?'

Jude sniffed. 'What if someone finds out?'

'We'll be careful.'

Jude hated the idea of Cali being angry with her. And she didn't know what they were supposed to do really. The migrants she'd heard about were always male, always hidden under trucks and packed in between goods, desperate and ready to lash out. They definitely didn't want to go back.

Jude's parents were out, so they let themselves in and grabbed two large IKEA bags to fill with things. They rooted through the garage, packing two sleeping bags, blankets, pillows, the camping stove and fuel canisters. They filled a picnic bag with tins from the back of the cupboards, the end of the loaf from the bread bin and three leftover doughnuts. Jude didn't want to take more in case her mum got suspicious. 'We'll go to the supermarket tomorrow,' she said. At least no one would notice the missing camping things in winter.

'One sec,' Jude said when they were almost done. She ran up to her room and pulled down the strings of battery-pack fairy lights she'd draped over her bed and mirror. She looked around for what else she could take. She found a blue notebook with white stars on it that she'd been given for Christmas and hadn't yet used, a vanilla-scented candle and a stuffed bear. Would Mo think that was childish? Would Cali? She packed it anyway.

It was evening by the time they got back to the lookouts, sweating and out of breath from climbing up the muddy paths with all that stuff. They found Mo sitting in the dark, her clothes still damp, shivering.

'Shit,' Cali said, 'we should have brought you clothes. Here.' She pulled out a blanket from the bag. 'You need to take those off. I'll give you my hoodie and you can wrap this around your legs. Jude, what can you spare?'

Jude hesitated. She thought about the bear in her bag and felt foolish. 'Um, she can have my hat and scarf.'

'Great.' Cali took Mo into one of the back rooms and Jude heard them murmuring as she helped her undress. Jude didn't know what to do with herself, so she started unpacking the things they'd brought. She laid one of the sleeping bags on the ground and realized how horrible it was going to be for Mo lying straight on the concrete. Tomorrow she'd bring the blow-up mattress. It was on top of her parents' wardrobe because they'd used it over Christmas when her uncle and cousins came to stay, but it wouldn't be missed until they next had guests. For now, she used some of the blankets to try to make a more inviting bed. She pulled out the stove and set it up, arranging the tins of spaghetti and sweetcorn so Mo could see her choices.

She heard Cali laugh. Mo said something too low to be heard. Jude pulled out the fairy lights and arranged them around the space. There was a nail in one of the concrete walls and she managed to anchor another end with a brick on the ledge of the wide window. She stared at the sea, wondering what Mo had been doing and thinking while they were gone.

'Oh my God,' Cali said when they re-emerged from the back room. 'This place looks great.'

Jude turned and smiled, pleased to have done something right.

Mo smiled back, her mouth twisting at the edge. She was wearing Cali's blue hoodie, the oversized sleeves rolled up around her wrists. 'It is very nice. Thank you.'

'What if someone comes up here?' Jude said.

'They won't,' Cali said.

Mo looked between the two of them.

'What if they do?'

Cali glared at Jude. She bent to rummage in her bag, then walked back towards the entrance. Jude and Mo followed. They watched Cali write on the wall in large Sharpie letters: *ENTER AT OWN RISK*. Beneath, she drew a cartoon grim reaper. 'There,' she said and the subject was dropped.

Mo insisted they eat with her. Jude showed her how to use the camping stove and the pan to heat the spaghetti. They dipped the bread in and scooped sweetcorn straight from the tin. Afterwards, Mo took the doughnuts and a plastic plate into a corner. A few moments later, she returned with them arranged into a face. Cali laughed and took a picture.

'We'll need to bring water for you to wash up,' Jude said. Her mind was racing with more and more things Mo was going to need. 'Extra fuel for the stove.'

'And something to block out the draught from the windows,' Cali added.

'You are both kind,' Mo said.

'It's nothing,' Cali said.

'I do not like to ask you for more, but there is one thing I really need.'

'Tell us.'

'A phone. To contact my parents. Mine is taken. They say it is further payment.' She paused and looked out to the sea. 'That we have no choice.'

'That's awful,' Cali said.

'I need to find my family. We are meant to meet, but it doesn't happen and now I do not know.'

'That's why you need to get back to Calais?'

Mo nodded.

'I have an old phone,' Jude said. They both looked at her. 'I mean, the battery's not great, but I can bring my charging block too. We'll need to get you a SIM. We can do that tomorrow, right?'

Cali nodded. Jude still wasn't sure if this was the right way to be handling the situation, but it felt good to be helping someone, and good to be doing it with Cali.

The next day she packed the phone, the blow-up mattress and the foot-pump into her backpack. She met Cali in town to buy the SIM card and food. Police tape cordoned off part of Market Square and Jude noticed shards of broken glass in the gutters, but other than that Dover seemed to be continuing as normal.

As they walked around the supermarket, Jude realized they hadn't asked what Mo liked or if there was anything she couldn't eat. This whole thing was ridiculous, she thought; they didn't know anything about this girl. They settled on tins of soup, more spaghetti, bread, a block of cheese, biscuits and a bag of oranges. They also lugged two large bottles of water to the checkout. 'We can take these home with us each time and refill them,' Cali said.

The walk was slow carrying everything. The weather had improved and the weak sun felt nice on Jude's face. 'This is good practice for our walk,' she shouted back as she crested the steepest hill.

'Sure,' Cali panted, a few paces behind.

Last summer, after a long, sticky walk all the way to Hythe, they'd been staring out at the blocky chimneys at the end of the Dungeness peninsula when Cali asked if Jude wanted to keep going. It was too far, Jude had reasoned, they had to get back. Cali had looked disappointed, though, so Jude had suggested they come back another day, stay overnight in a hotel perhaps and continue from there. Over the next week or two, the idea had spiralled into a plan to walk the whole south coast once they finished their GCSEs. Maybe even further. They hadn't told anyone yet, but Jude had bought a map and begun to plot the route.

They found Mo sitting on top of the fourth lookout with a blanket around her shoulders, writing in the notebook Jude had given her. She waved when she saw them and put the book in her backpack. Jude was curious what else she had in there. She wondered what she would pack if she had to leave home with no more than she could fit in her school bag.

'We brought more food,' Cali said. 'And a phone.'

Mo's face lit up. 'Thank you!'

She'd moved the sleeping bags into one of the back rooms and made a little nest, leaving the camping stove and other things in the main area, like a kind of living room. 'You like my pad?' she said in a nasal American accent, her face splitting into a grin.

Jude wondered what her parents would say if they found out what they were doing. They'd almost certainly tell them to go to the police. But perhaps Cali was right. Mo was on her own, she was vulnerable. She must have been through so much already.

'Awe-some,' Mo said when Jude pulled out the mattress and started pumping it up. Once done, Mo sat on the end and bobbed up and down, pretending to bounce herself off in every direction.

Jude smiled, looking at the concrete around them. Cali and she were planning to carry tents and camp along the way for their walk, but suddenly the idea of sleeping up here like Mo seemed utterly depressing.

'Do you need more clothes?' Cali said. 'Or anything else. Were you okay last night? Did you feel safe?'

Mo nodded. 'I am okay.'

*She's been through worse*, Jude thought.

They spent the afternoon with her. It was cold but clear, so Cali suggested they go for a walk. She wanted to show Mo their favourite places. Jude tried not to but she felt annoyed. She liked Mo, but they didn't know her and she didn't see why they had to share everything with her. Nevertheless, they climbed onto the old railway vent that Cali liked. It was set back from the edge, so not as scary as the lookouts.

'Why does everyone want to come here so bad anyway?' Cali said, leaning on the railing and looking at the smudged horizon. 'There's nothing here!'

Jude laughed, then stopped. She shifted her weight back and forth against the railing. After a while, Mo said, 'The one thing a person needs is hope. Over there, we have no hope.'

'Sorry,' Cali said. 'I didn't mean—'

'It is okay,' Mo said, reaching her hand out to touch Cali. Jude looked at Mo's fingers on her friend's arm. Something about the gesture made her uncomfortable. She wanted to talk to Cali about what they were doing, ask her what the actual plan was, how long they were going to help this girl.

Jude coughed. 'When we were younger,' she said, 'the jungle used to mean the warren on the outskirts of Folkestone.'

Mo removed her hand and Cali gave Jude a look like she didn't know what she was talking about.

'Remember? That bit below the café. We used to call it the jungle.'

'I guess,' Cali said, turning back to the sea.

Jude was hurt. She couldn't believe Cali would dismiss the memory like that. Most people stayed on the top of the cliffs, but she and Cali used to drop down from the café and snake into the woods. This was back when they were eleven or twelve and she used to tell her mum Rose still came on their walks. Jude always felt bad for lying, but she knew Cali needed to escape. Jackie had started sleeping all the time and the tension between her and Rose was bad. *We need to walk*, Cali would message, and Jude would know it was urgent.

When they got to the top of the jungle, they had to go single file down the steep, muddy steps. Jude would go first, beating back the brambles from the underused path. When Cali got stung by nettles and cried out, Jude would hunt for dock leaves while she sat on a log and moaned. 'Don't scratch,' Jude would say, kneeling to rub the waxy leaf on Cali's skinny legs. One day, Jude felt not the soft, light hairs but a prickly stubble. Cali must've seen her face because she snatched the leaf and said, 'I'll do it.' Jude said she wanted a razor that weekend and her mum laughed for a whole minute.

Hardly any walkers were adventurous enough to come via their jungle. If the girls heard voices, they'd hide in the trees and make animal noises. Then they'd run up to the clearing with the mouldy rope swing and shriek with laughter. Sometimes Cali wrapped the swing around her neck and pretended to hang herself. Jude would rush up and hold her legs, untangle her neck and lay her on the ground to check for breathing. She'd tell her it was okay, everything would be okay, until Cali pretended to choke back to life and they looked at each other seriously.

Jude didn't know why, but she wanted Mo to know all of this, to understand what was between her and Cali. Whatever she'd been through, she couldn't just turn up, sleep on their cliffs, place her hand on Cali's arm like that, and think it was in any way equivalent to a lifetime of friendship.

She studied Mo as Cali helped her off the vent. Swamped inside Cali's blue hoodie, she looked like a lost child. Mo was a refugee, Jude reminded herself. She'd lost everything and all she was asking for was a little kindness. The Jungle – the real one, not their warren – was no playground. The newspapers said that several thousand people were now camped there, all desperate to make their way here.

She watched Cali hook her arm into Mo's and lead her along the path. Neither looked back to check Jude was coming. She ground her heel into the soft earth and waited for them to notice. The further they got from her, the closer their two bodies seemed to grow, until if she squinted they looked like a single blurry unit escaping across the clifftop.

# 2026

Tarek's arms and legs and back ache. His eyelids droop as the cars whip by. He knows somehow that it's six in the morning and he's safe in a hotel in a country he's allowed to be in, in a life he's worked hard to deserve. But as he tosses and turns, dreams trickle into memory and it is also the end of January 2016 and he's a stateless citizen once again: undocumented, undesired, disregarded and displaced. They've been here every night for the past week, shivering on the side of the motorway. Jabir complained earlier that he didn't feel well and wanted to take tonight off. He thinks he might have swallowed some of the tear gas they were sprayed with a couple of days ago.

*Brother, we need to try*, Tarek said, though he too saw the appeal of a night's rest. The past seven nights they've come here, only to return to the camp before daybreak. Tonight will no doubt be the same.

*We go tomorrow,* Jabir said. *Sleep tonight.*

But when Tarek crawled into his tent, he found himself shivering so much he couldn't sleep. All he could do was listen to the chatter and cries, the sobbing and prayers around him. He thought of his parents, stuck underground. He pictured Inji, spending another night alone somewhere. She wasn't answering his calls. He made a silent prayer that she was safe. That everyone in his heart was. He couldn't bring himself to think of all the ways they might not be. He unzipped himself and climbed back out to the tarpaulin city. He urinated, then made his way to Jabir's tent.

*Brother*, he whispered. *I am going to try. If I get my good chance, I will see you over there.*

He heard Jabir groan. *Wait*, he said groggily. His face appeared in the broken flap where the zip for his tent should have been. His hair – which Tarek had cut the day before, sitting Jabir on a chair in the middle of a clearing, gently laying a threadbare towel around his friend's shoulders and rolling out his father's barber kit with the same careful grace he'd been taught to do at home – was spiked and messed up with sleep. *I come.*

Tarek glances back to see his friend walking behind him. He's fifteen, only a year older than Inji, but already he looks worn. His shoulders sag and Tarek knows he's tired, but Jabir's head whips back and forth as he scans the lanes of traffic. They need a truck travelling slowly enough that they can run beside it and grab on. Tarek's seen it happen; he knows it's possible. Still, he's scared. On their third or fourth day of trying there was one. A whole gang of them ran after it, shouting and jostling each other to get there. Tarek saw first one, then two, then three of his new friends make the leap, cheers of success following them as they clung to the doors. Tarek felt a pang of jealousy, even while he shouted for joy. *Why them?* he asked silently. He was ready, he thought. He knew what to do after jumping on. How to check the lock to see if it was possible to hide inside, or how to climb beneath the truck bed, cling to the wheel arch and hold himself up. He knew to wait until he felt the sway of the water, the confirmation that he'd made it onto the ferry, before releasing his breath, before taking his phone and sending his final goodbyes, then discarding the battery and SIM card that might be used to trace where he was from. All of that had felt so close when he saw his friends waving from the back of that truck, so achievable even though Tarek's feet remained firmly on the tarmac.

Then Mattheus jumped too, his hand reaching out for the pole. His feet landed on the lip of the bumper, but his worn-out sneakers slipped. His grip on the pole wasn't tight enough and he fell, tumbling hard on the tarmac, rolling over and over as the ground ripped the skin from his face and arms and shins. The car behind swerved with a long honk of its horn as Mattheus came to a stop in the middle of the lane. Tarek, Jabir and the others stopped running. They pulled Mattheus from the road and carried him back to the camp. A young blonde woman and a tall man with floppy hair came out of the medical tent to help. They asked questions in English. Tarek translated the answers. They told the boys to go back to their tents, to talk to the legal volunteers about their reunification applications, to stay away from the motorway.

Tarek watches a truck whizz by in the far lane. The drivers know they're here and speed up along this bit, making it harder for them, making it more dangerous. In his heart, he knows they won't make it tonight. They'll give it another hour. By then he'll be exhausted enough to sleep through the cold. He hopes Inji is warm.

Tarek is ripped from his thoughts by the rumble of a large engine coming up in the near lane. This could be their chance. He turns to look behind him, his mouth already open to shout to Jabir to get ready. But the words never leave his lips. The truck is going too fast, the driver's foot pressed to the pedal. Tarek watches the passenger-side grill slam into his friend. He sees Jabir's face as his limbs judder. Then he's gone. The truck speeds on, Jabir trapped beneath it.

Tarek breaks into a run. He howls Jabir's name, his voice lost in the whip of the wind and the burr of the traffic. Up ahead he sees a dark mound. He slows as he approaches it, wanting to turn and flee. This does not look like his friend. It is not a teenage boy. Tarek doesn't think of his grandparents or his brothers in that moment, whose bodies he helped bathe and shroud. He doesn't think of his mother's hospital or of the medical tents run by university graduates back at the camp. He thinks of animals, slaughtered and abandoned. He thinks of meat. Nobody mourns the cow in the abattoir. Nobody cries over roadkill.

He wants to turn back. Back to the camp, back in time, back on his decision to bring them out here tonight. But his feet carry him forward until he reaches the mound of blood and flesh that both is and isn't his friend.

Tarek bolts awake, a film of sweat clinging to his skin. He turns on the light and looks around the messy hotel room. It is more than a year since he's seen those images in his sleep. He touches the fingers of his right hand to the space beneath his heart, feels it drumming through his shirt.

An image comes to him of his former therapist, sitting with her ankles crossed in her book-lined room overlooking Russell Square. He spent session after session talking about that night. He told her how he fainted and a passing driver called an ambulance for them both. How after that he stopped chasing the trucks and went back to the legal volunteers, the ones who recommended him as a translator when the BBC journalist came asking. He had no way of knowing then, but that contact proved invaluable when he was wading through the tar-like bureaucracy of detention. She campaigned for him, visited him, and kept him going at some of his lowest moments. The day he found out she'd secured him a place on a London university scheme to help refugees train as journalists, Tarek wept. He wept because he was getting out and would have the opportunity to study again, to apply for papers and try to build a life. But he also wept for those he'd lost, for everyone who hadn't made it as far as him.

Once, his therapist asked him why, amongst all the horrors he'd seen on his journey from Syria, out of all of the tragedies in his life – Adnan, Khalid, his parents, Inji, Mo – Jabir's death was the one that haunted him most. Tarek stopped going shortly after that. They'd been having sessions for three years, ever since he started earning enough to justify the expense. He'd told her everything about himself, everything he'd seen and everything he'd done. But when she questioned why Jabir's death affected him so, he realized that she was a stranger. That she would never understand.

Tarek rubs his left eye and hauls himself out of bed. He reaches instinctively for his computer, swipes it awake and finds Rose paused mid-sentence. He stares at her frozen features. She thinks they are similar, she and him, that they have both been changed by the lives they've led. Would she say that if she knew the truth? Could she cope with his conscience?

He turns towards the bathroom, but something catches his eye. A piece of paper lies on the carpet in front of the door. He feels a chill down his spine. It wasn't there when he went to bed, he is certain. But who has reason to slip a note under his door in the middle of the night? Gary would message. Could it be from reception? Something from the management about tomorrow's room booking?

Inexplicably, Tarek opens the door and peers along the empty corridor, as if the sender might be there, waiting for him. He sighs and reaches for the note. Standing in his boxer shorts and T-shirt, with the door still open, he unfolds the paper and reads:

REFUGEE, GO HOME.

# THE PARTY

## JUDE'S FLAT

Jude smooths the arm of her chair.

                    JUDE

In the middle of March, Cali had this idea to take
Mo to a party. She wanted to dress her up and
pretend she was new at our school. I wasn't convinced but I went along with it.

                                        CUT TO.


## CONFERENCE ROOM

Rose picks at a hole in her jeans.

                    ROSE

I used to look at everything Cali posted online.
Watching those little story things as I brushed my
teeth each night made me feel like I knew what
was going on in her life.

    (shakes head.)

But I should have been paying more attention. I
should have known what Cali was up to and who
she was hanging out with.

                                        CUT TO.

Cali gave Mo this false name for the party. Hardly anyone paid attention to her, but I guess a couple of people remembered the name later on.

Cali thought the whole thing was hilarious. She kept saying we should go out again. I wasn't sure. I thought what we were trying to do was help Mo get home, not integrate her with Dover's party scene.

CUT TO.

ROSE

I'd gone back to London at the beginning of February and was trying to make an effort to call, but it was hard to get time off work to visit. I didn't have two days off together for about six weeks. I needed the money, so I couldn't say no.

(rubs face.)

That sounds like an excuse. The truth is it was easier to get swallowed back into my life than it was to worry about something far away. I was drinking a lot. Sometimes with Diego, sometimes on my own, then more and more with Kassia. 'One more, no more!' we told each other at three, then four, then five a.m. Every time I reached for my phone it was to see if she'd messaged me. One morning I realized we'd spent every night together for a week.

It's awful, I know, but in the middle of everything my sister was going through, I was falling in love.

CUT TO.

JUDE

I stayed the night at the party and went home the next day. I assumed Cali took Mo back to the cliffs, then went to her boyfriend's. It didn't feel like my business to ask. If I'd known what was to come, I wouldn't have let her out of my sight.

# THEN

The last thing Jude wanted was go to a dumb house party at Goofy's dumb mate's house. But Cali had said she had a plan and that she needed Jude's help. And at least a party meant some time away from Mo. They'd been going up to see her every day for six weeks now, no matter the weather, no matter what else was going on. Cali still got scared on the bit by Shakespeare Cliff, so every evening Jude had to walk on her outside edge and make sure the torch shone only on the path, never on the railing or into the void of the drop. Jude wasn't afraid of falling so much as of meeting someone. She'd been thinking about how strange it was that Mo was on her own. According to her dad, several thousand people were entering the UK illegally every month. What if there were more of them up on the cliffs somewhere?

They hadn't encountered anyone yet, which was lucky because even if it was just a dog walker they might have had trouble explaining what they were doing. Not least because Jude herself wasn't especially clear on that. 'We're trying to help!' Cali said over and over, but as the weeks passed Jude had started to worry there might be no end to the extent of help Mo was going to need.

Last weekend, for instance, when Cali had convinced Jude to spend the night up there, Mo had managed to drop another bombshell. They'd packed a ton of snacks and a bottle of wine that Cali had asked Goofy to buy for her and headed up for a sleepover. Jude didn't like wine much, so she'd pretended to sip. She'd watched Mo lift the bottle briefly to her mouth, unsure if she was doing the same. It didn't seem to have occurred to Cali that Mo might not drink, that they didn't have a clue what she believed or how she might be judging them. Cali had drunk long gulps, her lips and teeth turning purple in the weak light.

'Thank you for being my company,' Mo said.

'We want to be here – right, Jude?'

Jude nodded. They'd tidied up the crisp packets and beer cans, draped blankets and towels over the window and door openings, and pinched a 'Danger: Unstable Rock' sign from further along the cliff to discourage nosy walkers from venturing off the path. Mo had hung the fairy lights over the airbed in the back room and stacked the magazines and books they'd brought next to her pillow. It felt almost cosy now.

'We can look at the stars?' Mo said, gesturing towards the staircase.

'Sure,' Cali said. Jude followed as they shuffled out of the doorway and up the steps to stand on the grassy roof. It was cloudy, but the moon was big and low and ships twinkled on the black sea. Cali let out a giggle and Jude turned, but whatever the joke was, she'd missed it.

'You tell me about your family?' Mo said, still smirking.

*How about you tell us something about yours first*, Jude wanted to reply.

'It's me, my mum and my sister,' Cali said, 'though Rose is in London.'

'She is successful then,' Mo said, stroking one palm on top of the other like a rapper making it rain. She'd told them she and a friend had practised their English through illegally streamed MTV. She looked ridiculous, Jude thought.

Cali laughed. 'Not exactly. She works in a coffee shop in London Bridge.'

'And you, Jude?'

'She's an only child. No siblings.'

Mo made a noise in her throat. 'I think you are lonely then.'

Even with a language barrier, Jude thought that was rude. 'Not really.'

'Have you heard from *your* family?' Cali said. 'Did you get through on the phone yet?' She'd told them she was trying every day, but no one ever picked up.

'I need to get to them.'

'How?' Jude said.

'I need money.'

The words hung in the night before them. Jude didn't know what Cali was thinking, but the whole situation was making her increasingly uncomfortable. They'd done so much for Mo already, given her all of the stuff in that lookout, helped her stay warm and fed. Jude wasn't waiting for a thank you or anything, but it felt like nothing they were doing would ever be enough.

'How much?'

Jude tried to catch Cali's eye, but she looked away.

'Five hundred euros.'

'Fucking hell.'

'Jude!'

'Is it for smugglers?'

'Obviously,' Cali said.

'I mean, aren't there other ways? Legal ways?'

'No other way,' Mo said.

'There wouldn't be this massive mess if the legal system worked, would there?' Cali snapped. 'It's not as though people like Mo risk their lives for the fun of it.'

'Sorry,' Jude said. 'I—'

'Whatever. I'm cold, I'm going back inside.'

'How are you going to get the money?' Jude asked as they followed Cali back in.

'I do not know.'

They reached the lamplight and Jude saw Mo's face was twisted in sadness.

She insisted Cali and Jude take the airbed. She said they were her guests and made herself a mattress of blankets on the floor. Cali's mood improved as she finished the bottle of wine. They played music through their phones and told Mo about the boys in their class. Around two, they zipped up their sleeping bags. The blow-up mattress squeaked as Jude and Cali tried to get comfortable. Jude rolled onto her side and stared at the dark shadow of the back of Cali's head. She listened to Mo breathing beside them until she drifted into a dream about guns and boats and betrayal.

Mo had still been asleep when they woke. They'd left a note saying they'd come back later and climbed down the dewy path. They'd snuck into Cali's house through the back door, kicked their trainers off and climbed under Cali's duvet. 'We should help Mo get the money,' Cali had said, rolling to the edge of the mattress and turning her back to Jude.

Whatever this plan of Cali's was tonight, Jude assumed it must be about that. She didn't see how going to a party was going to help them get 500 Euros, but at least it meant a night of acting like normal teenagers. A night without Mo.

She walked across the soggy park at half past six, expecting to find Cali listening to music and trying to decide what to wear. Nobody answered her knock, which wasn't unusual, so she tried the handle and walked in. The living-room door was closed as normal. She made her way up the stairs to Cali's room. Again she knocked, but there was no answer. She opened the door and there in front of her stood not just Cali but Mo too.

She'd been stripped of the tatty clothes she'd arrived in and of the hoodies and tracksuits they'd carted up the cliffs to keep her warm. Her hair had been washed and teased out, and she wore a pair of Cali's skinny jeans and a top that clung to her ribs. 'Hello,' she said with a lipstick smile.

Jude stood in the doorway, dumb with surprise.

'Close the door, will you?' Cali said. 'I don't want my mum to know she's here.'

'What's she doing here?'

'I brought her down for a shower.'

Jude looked at Mo's outfit. She was clearly not going back up to the cliffs in that.

'Cali says there is a party.' Mo moved her elbows and hips in a ridiculous little dance.

'You're coming?' Jude said, wondering how long they'd been here hanging out without her. All afternoon perhaps. 'Isn't that risky?'

Cali groaned. 'Only if we tell the truth. No one's going to care if we say she's a girl from school.'

Mo twisted her hands together. 'I do not come if you do not want, Jude.'

'What?' Jude said, her face growing hot. 'No. I want you to come, obviously. I just didn't know, and I'm worried about you.'

'Yes. I can tell.'

'Chill out, Jude,' Cali said. 'It's one night and it's only Kev's mates. It'll be fine. Mo deserves to have some fun.'

Jude let Cali do her make-up and swap the top she'd arrived in for one of hers. When Mo was in the bathroom, she asked Cali what she was playing at.

'I've got a plan,' she said with a grin. 'To help her get the money.'

'What?'

'I think Kev will help. I just need to ask him in the right way.'

Jude frowned. 'Does he even have that much? What are you going to say it's for?'

'To go see my sister. That I want to surprise her.'

'And you think he'll give it to you?'

'Why not?'

Jude looked at a dried paint drip on the wall by the light switch. She didn't like Cali's boyfriend, but even so she wasn't sure how she felt about conning him out of cash. 'Perhaps you should tell him the truth.'

Cali snorted.

'Or ask Rose?'

Cali shook her head. 'She's skint, and anyway she'll think I'm in trouble if I start asking her for money.'

They heard the honk of Goofy's horn in the street outside. He'd watched too many films, Jude thought. 'So why does Mo need to be here for this plan?'

'She doesn't,' Cali said, applying a final layer of mascara. 'But it'll be fun.'

Cali gave Goofy a kiss over the handbrake as they piled into his car. 'This is my mate, Ellie,' she said, leaning back. Jude could hear the nervous excitement in her voice. Goofy was their first test.

'All right, Ellie?' he said, then put the car into gear.

It wasn't something she had ever thought consciously about, but Jude was used to being the one with the big house. Her family wasn't rich or posh, and it drove her mad when someone said they were, but she knew she was lucky. When her mum had decided to move back to Dover in the nineties, house prices were cheap. She'd stuck it out in London for a couple of years after finishing her social work degree and bought a crappy flat on the end of the Jubilee Line where nobody in their right mind wanted to live at the time. She'd met Jude's dad and convinced him to come back to the coast with her. She'd got a job with the council and Jude's dad had switched from a private firm to port security. They'd sold her mum's flat and bought their house in Dover for next to nothing because it was in such bad shape. Jude's mum had taught herself to decorate, while her dad had got his uncle down from Inverness to help with the plumbing.

So it wasn't like she was born with a silver spoon in her mouth. Her parents had worked for their house, for their life. They'd worked to give her the childhood she'd had, which she would forever be grateful for. Jude knew the world was unfair and she always gave a quid to the guy who slept rough outside the church when she could spare it. She always made eye contact and said sorry when she couldn't. She knew she had certain privileges and was keen to help those who didn't. But she never considered herself part of the problem. She wasn't like the boarding school kids they made fun of or the families in the mansions out in the villages. She didn't covet other people's lives or take what she had for granted. She was a good person, an ally.

When they arrived at the party that night, though, and Jude walked through the thick doors into an arched hallway with a sweeping staircase, she felt pure jealousy. It shocked her. She had no need to envy these people, whoever they were, but their massive fireplaces, fingerprintless mirrors and swallow-you couches screamed such a sense of smugness that she immediately wanted to break something.

Cali walked in with Goofy, leaving Jude and Mo to trail behind. Jude curled her arm into Mo's and tried to take charge. She could feel the heat of Mo's skin beneath Cali's top. She wanted to ask if she wore clothes like this at home,

157

if her parents would approve. Was this the England she'd dreamed of?

They stuck close to Cali and wove their way through the house to the kitchen. Goofy introduced them to Bobby, the man-boy whose parents' house it was. Goofy winked at Jude, which made her throat constrict. Cali was right, nobody paid Mo much attention. Jude kept staring at people's faces as they sipped their drinks. She felt like shaking them. 'Can't you see who's here?' she wanted to shout. 'Can't you see what's right in front of your face?' Even dolled up like Cali, she thought it was obvious Mo didn't belong. It occurred to Jude that they didn't even know how old she was.

Goofy and Bobby talked about a video game, then moved on to how much they'd drunk the other week. Listening to these conversations with an awareness of an outsider's ears, Jude realized how ridiculous it all was. Bobby seemed like a nice enough guy, she supposed, but that only made her anger at him, at his house, at how oblivious he was to Mo's situation, worse. If her parents were this rich, she thought, she and Cali could properly help Mo. They could give her the money and she could go back to wherever it was she was going. Then, she thought, things could return to normal; Cali and she could get on with their lives.

Someone handed Jude a beer. Someone else asked if she'd ever tried Petrone. She was so far in her head that drinking their alcohol and eating their crisps seemed like the best way to get back at these people. She wandered through the rooms, watching Goofy's friends dance and chat and kiss. She lost track of Mo, but she wasn't worried. Cali was right, these people weren't threats, not in the immediate sense.

She stepped outside and heard Cali's voice from around the corner. She moved a little closer to listen. Cali was doing it, asking Goofy for the money. He was talking all strange and deep, like he imagined an authority figure might. Jude could picture his hands on Cali's shoulders, an adult explaining things to a little girl. He was saying no. He didn't have that kind of cash. Couldn't she get Rose to help? He sympathized, but he was broke. Why didn't she get a job? He sounded so patronizing that Jude almost stepped around the corner and threw her drink over him. She didn't know how Cali didn't scream at him. But Cali was playing to his performance, talking like a child, whining and pleading and saying she understood, but she'd really appreciate it if he could help, even just a little bit. Jude felt embarrassed for her friend. He'd already said no, he wasn't going to change his mind. She returned inside, looking for Mo. She grabbed another drink on the way, then wondered if she needed to sit down.

By 11 o'clock she was spewing in Bobby's fancy legged bathtub while Mo rubbed her back. She listened to Cali talking to Goofy in the doorway, saying there was no way they could take her home in this state, that her mum would flip.

'I don't trust her in my car anyway,' he said. 'I'll ask Bobby if there's somewhere she can crash.'

He disappeared and Cali said something soothing while Jude retched again.

'Don't leave me.'

'I have to get Mo back, don't I?'

Cali handed Jude a bottle of mouthwash and someone else's toothbrush. Goofy popped his head round the door to say Bobby had offered the spare room at the end of the hall. Cali pulled Jude's trousers and top off, and tucked her into the bed. She told her there was a washing-up bowl on the floor if she felt ill again and that she and Goofy would be back in the morning. Jude turned and saw Mo standing in the doorway, waiting. Once more she asked Cali not to go, but she did.

Jude woke in the night with someone's skin against hers, fingers fiddling with the clasp of her bra. 'What the—' she said, her words thick and slurred.

'Sorry.'

Bobby's voice. Hot breath against her neck.

He removed his hand. 'Can I sleep here? There are no beds left.'

She shuffled away from him, tucked her knees up to her chest and made a non-committal grunt. It was his house and she was there alone. She didn't fancy lifting her head off the pillow, let alone walking back to Dover. In a tight, foetal ball, she listened until she heard his light snores. Eventually, she allowed her limbs to relax and fell back to sleep.

Again, she woke with Bobby's hands on her. His fingers were inside her bra this time, his index finger and thumb roughly pinching her nipple. She felt the sticky heat of his body pressed against her back and the top of his thigh pushing to make a gap between her legs.

'Get off,' she said, clearly this time, and his body immediately went slack. He removed his hand and flopped back against the mattress. How long had he been touching her?

'I'm sorry,' he said again. She could smell the rum on his breath as he rolled back towards her and murmured that he couldn't help himself. Every muscle in her body stiffened as he ran his fingers through her hair. 'I don't normally fancy girls with short hair, but it really suits you.'

Jude stared at the greeny-yellow hands of the glow-in-the-dark alarm clock on the bedside table and kept entirely still. After a while, Bobby moved to the other side of the bed. Jude shuffled to the very edge of the mattress and buried her face in the pillow. She thought about crying. She thought about screaming. Instead, she reached her arm out of the duvet and fumbled on the floor until she found her top, the stupid strappy thing Cali had convinced her to wear because it showed her cleavage. 'What cleavage?' she'd said, looking down. Now she wished she was entirely flat-chested and wearing a full-length smock. She pulled the top under the covers and wriggled around to get into it.

'You don't need to do that,' Bobby said sleepily.

He didn't touch her again, but neither did she sleep. As soon as it was light, she prised herself out of the bed and showered in the marble monstrosity next to the bathtub she'd puked in. She scrubbed and scrubbed her skin, imagining Bobby's prints seared into her flesh. She tried not to think how vulnerable she'd made herself, how easily he could have done more than he did. A little corner of her brain wondered what it would be like to step out of the shower and back into the room, to peel back the covers and lower her dripping body onto him. That was really fucked up, she realized. She closed her eyes and tipped her head under the water, thinking about Mo and all the things she may or may not have been through.

There was a dark red flannel hanging from a hook beneath the shelf of shampoos. Jude ripped it off the hook and stuffed it into her mouth, then allowed herself to cry.

Rose glances from the lens to the horizon, trying to keep pace with Gary's backwards steps. Tarek walks with one hand on Gary's shoulder to guide him, his focus darting between Rose and the path. His questions have been simple enough so far this morning, but the more she tries to think of answers, the more her own press for attention.

She woke at five this morning and found the bed empty. Kassia must have gone for an early walk, something she does when stressed or upset. Rose felt the duvet of guilt that follows an evening of disagreement. By the time Kassia returned, she'd laid the table for breakfast, cut bananas and strawberries for their cereal, even poured the milk out of the carton and into a jug.

'What's this?' Kassia said.

'I'm trying to say sorry.'

Kassia didn't point out that if Rose was really sorry then she would have called Tarek and told him she was pulling out. Kassia didn't say much in fact as they ate their breakfast and scrolled individually through the news. It was only after she'd laced her shoes and checked she had everything in her bag that she came to kiss Rose goodbye and addressed the elephant in the room.

'Ask yourself, why does this Zayat man care?' Kassia said. 'It's not because he wants to help us pay for IVF or to help you clear your conscience. He wants to tell a story, that is all. And the more sensational the better. It doesn't matter to him if you, or me, or anyone else in this town has to pay the price.'

'Can you talk about what it was like moving back here?' Tarek prompts, bringing Rose back to the here and now. He too seems distracted this morning. He asked Rose while they were setting up if she ever felt unsafe in Dover. She thought about the flyers left at Kassia's practice and the graffiti she passes on her way to work, but shrugged and tried to make a joke about keeping enemies close. Tarek didn't smile.

She sucks her lip now, annoyed that Kassia's caution has stuck in her head, that the hope she felt yesterday that this might be a positive thing, a way to move on, has been tarnished by her wife's suspicions. She likes Tarek and she wants to trust him. She wasn't stupid, she reminds herself; she did her research, read the contract, watched his other programmes.

'When I first moved back,' she says slowly, trying to banish Kassia's warning, 'it was unbearable. I felt Cali everywhere. I was twenty-three, but this town made me feel permanently fifteen.'

'And what about now?'

Rose stops walking. 'I've built a life here, haven't I? So it's different.' She looks at the shingle beach ahead, remembering staring at Kassia's tattoo all those years ago. 'Sometimes, though, it feels like the thing that's more real than time is place. Like the past and the future are just decorations pinned to this town. Underneath there's something else, something broken.'

By midday they've shot footage of the beach, the harbour, the high street, the close where Rose and Cali grew up, and the park behind their house.

'You want to join us for lunch?' Tarek asks as Gary unclips the mic from Rose's collar.

She hesitates.

'Or we can meet back at the hotel at one thirty.'

Rose nods. Maybe she should have lunch with them, learn a little more about Tarek's plans for the finished documentary so she can put Kassia's mind at ease. But she's been talking all morning and she needs time to collect her thoughts. She gives them directions to the good fish and chip shop, then takes a more circuitous route back into town to avoid walking the same way. She buys a sandwich and a drink and makes her way to Pencester Gardens. Once she's eaten, she still has forty-five minutes. It's enough. She throws her rubbish in the overflowing bin and walks out of the park via the snicket leading to Castle Road. It takes her twelve minutes, striding at a decent pace, to get to the Retreat. She signs in with Felicity on reception and asks how her husband is doing after his hip replacement.

'That was months ago, luvvie, he was back on his feet in six weeks,' Felicity says with a laugh.

Rose makes her way to the large lounge. Jackie sits by the far window, a jigsaw puzzle abandoned before her, her eyes fixed to the silent television.

'Hi Mum,' Rose says, pulling up a seat. 'How are you?'

Jackie turns, her eyes large and watery, but she doesn't say anything.

'I'm sorry I haven't visited lately.'

Rose takes her mother's hand. Her fingertips are cold against Rose's walk-warmed skin. Jackie's attention returns to the muted television and Rose looks around. She's never got used to this place, or to the clumsiness of one-sided conversations.

'I'm doing this thing,' she says after a while. 'For TV actually, you might see it.'

Jackie doesn't respond.

Rose sucks her lip. 'It's about Cali. Well, her and everything that happened.'

Jackie removes her hand from Rose's palm and reaches for a puzzle piece. Her tongue pokes from the corner of her mouth as she places it against the top edge of sky. Rose remembers dancing around the living room with this woman in the middle of the night. Her mother was never entirely healthy, she knows, but she didn't used to be like this. It was the weight of the events of 2016 that put her here, the weight of failing her child. If Rose is going to be a parent, then she cannot risk the same.

'Kash thinks it's a bad idea,' she says, twisting the edge of her sleeve.

Jackie places another piece and sits back. Rose follows her gaze to the screen. The local news is playing. Rose recognizes the outside of the town hall and her breath catches as the camera pans to a woman wearing a dark blue suit, her elbows resting on the arms of her wheelchair. The subtitles scroll along the bottom of the screen.

*— not interested in pointing fingers. What we need is to move forward. Dover needs a fresh start. If I'm elected mayor, I promise to —*

'I-I have to do this,' Rose says, staring at the scar on Jude's cheek. 'I have to face up to what I've done.'

There's a clatter as a man on the other side of the room drops a plastic bowl. Rose watches a nurse hurry over to tidy up the mess, then turns to her mum.

'I have to explain,' she says more firmly. 'Not everything, but what I can. I'm worried about what it will do to me if I don't.'

Jackie places one more puzzle piece and pushes the pile of odd ones away from her. She rests her head lightly on Rose's shoulder. The news item finishes and the programme moves on. They sit in silence, staring at the flickering images.

'I love you,' Rose says as she gets up to leave. 'I'm sorry I didn't always let you know.'

She places a kiss on her mother's forehead. Jackie reaches out and touches Rose's wrist, turning it to place a puzzle piece in her hand. Rose lifts it to look. It is part of a door, a faint line of wood grain bisecting the right-hand side, and on the left, the top circle and beginning flare of a black keyhole. She swallows. 'Beware the door with too many keys?'

Jackie nods.

'I'm being careful, Mum. I promise.'

# THEN

Jude sat naked on Bobby's plush bathmat staring at her phone. Cali's message said Goofy would pick her up in a bit. She wanted Cali to come. She needed her friend. But it was hard to type those words, hard to admit to that vulnerability. And what if she brought Mo? Jude could hardly complain about what had happened with Bobby in front of a girl who there was every chance had been through a whole lot worse.

Nobody else was up. After getting dressed, Jude wandered through the rooms, touching objects, tempted to knock them to the floor or hide them in her bag. Her head throbbed and she felt on the verge of throwing up again. She opened drawers and read letters taped to pinboards. In the study, she ran her fingers along the spines of books, wondering if they were first editions. She sat on the green leather chair and placed her feet upon the desk. She found a piece of gum in her pocket and chewed it until it was soft enough to stick to the top of the monitor. She tried the drawers and rifled through receipts and old bits of paper. In the bottom one, she found an envelope addressed to Bobby, a line and a kiss beneath his name. It felt like a card. She jammed her finger beneath the flap and opened it. There was a frog on the front with a speech bubble reading, *Have a ribbitulous birthday!* As she lifted it up, a flurry of crisp pink notes floated from inside. Jude laughed, picking one up and holding it to the light. She'd only ever held a fifty-pound note once before, at her summer job at the fish restaurant on the harbour. She counted them. Ten. Five hundred pounds.

She didn't for a moment think about putting them back. From the second it fell from the card that money felt like hers. Or Mo's. This was what she needed, what she'd asked them for. And – the thought crept in before Jude could help it – it would get her out of their lives. Jude smiled. This felt like fate. That Goofy had turned Cali down and Bobby had been such a shit to her all seemed to make perfect sense now that she had five hundred pounds stuffed into her jeans pocket.

She heard a honk from the street and climbed in the front of Goofy's car feeling calm. Bobby obviously hadn't been given the card yet, so nobody would notice the money was gone until his parents got back, by which time it would be too late to guess who'd taken it. Maybe Bobby would have to fess up to having had a party and get in trouble himself. Jude smiled at the thought. It was a victimless crime as far as she was concerned.

Goofy was trying to tease her about not handling her drink. She interrupted to ask where Cali was.

'Home, I think. She took that girl Ellie back last night, just messaged me this morning to come get you. Nice taxi service, eh?'

She got him to drop her at Cali's, but there was no answer to her knocks and for once the door was locked. *Where r u?* she typed. *I need to tell you something.*

She wandered to the rec and sat on a swing, but the gentle swaying made her want to hurl. Would Cali have gone up to see Mo already? She could feel the money against her thigh and was struggling to think of anything else. She considered going up and giving it directly to Mo, but she wanted to talk it through with Cali first, make sure it was the right thing to do. How exactly was Mo going to get back across the Channel? And what was she going to do after that? The more she thought about it, the less Mo's story seemed to make sense. People wanted to come here, not go back there. And how was she even sure she'd be able to find her family? On the other hand, if they gave her the money and she disappeared, maybe none of that would be Jude's problem any more.

She got up and pulled her coat around her. All she had beneath was Cali's strappy top. She could have gone home to find warmer clothes and better shoes, but she knew that if she walked into her house she'd start having second thoughts. If she had to face her mum or dad, lie about having had a good night, sleeping at Cali's and nothing out of the ordinary having happened, she knew she'd start to feel guilty.

She walked across town towards the cliff path. It was one of those sunny misty days where smoggy pollution hung over the port like a layer of grime. She was halfway up by the allotments and it was almost two o'clock when she heard back from Cali.

> Sorry babes, slept all day. Getting
> up now, want 2 meet at mine in an
> hour?

Jude felt relieved. So Cali was home. She must have been asleep when Jude knocked, that was all.

An hour wasn't long enough to get up to Mo and back down to Cali's, but something told Jude to keep going. She wanted to check Mo was there, to make sure Cali had taken her back. Jude did want to help Mo – obviously she did because she'd taken the money, hadn't she? – but that didn't mean she wanted her coming to their parties, staying in their houses, invading their lives.

She heard voices as she approached the wooded section and stepped into the trees to hide. Between the branches, she saw Mo and Cali, arm in arm. Cali was laughing hysterically, as if Mo had said something utterly hilarious. Jude bit the edge of her thumb to keep quiet. Cali wasn't home and she hadn't slept all day. Had she even slept in her own bed? What if she and Mo had camped in the lookout just the two of them, talking all night about what a drag Jude was?

Cali unhooked her arm and threw it around Mo's shoulders, making them both stumble. Mo giggled and pretended to push Cali away, then pulled her back. Jude watched as they carried on walking, heads leant together. She thought about Bobby and how scared she'd felt. All she'd wanted was for her best friend to make everything okay. Instead, Cali had been up here laughing about her with a girl they barely knew.

She watched through the branches until they reached the bend by the allotments. Was Mo going to switch sides and shield Cali from the edge, she wondered, wiping her eyes. Would she do everything Jude would for her?

Once they were out of view, she stepped back onto the path and continued the way she'd been heading. She was panting by the time she reached Mo's lookout, and she stormed down the stairs, yanking down the blanket they'd nailed across the doorway. Without hesitating, she headed straight for the back room and grabbed Mo's backpack. She carried it into the main room and emptied it onto the floor. A thick brown envelope fell out, along with some scraps of paper, the charging block, a book, a small stuffed monkey, and the blue and white starred notebook Jude had given her. Jude picked up the envelope and shuffled through half a dozen photographs paper-clipped to a bunch of documents written in what she presumed was Arabic. The book and the scraps of paper were in the same script. She reached for the notebook and flipped to the first page, but it was just as indecipherable. She threw it across the floor. Then she noticed a bulge in one of the side pockets of Mo's back-pack. Jude slipped her hand in and discovered the old Android phone she'd stopped using when her parents gave her an upgrade last Christmas.

She held down the button on the side and watched the screen illuminate with the familiar green robot. When prompted, she entered her own 4-digit PIN. She let out a laugh when it worked. She'd had to tell it to Mo when they inserted the new SIM card back in January and the stupid girl hadn't even bothered to change it. The homepage loaded with a background picture of Cali pulling a face and more squiggly Arabic script that Jude couldn't understand. She recognized the green and white speech bubble icon, though, and clicked to open it. Mo's chats were listed on the right rather than the left-hand side of the screen, but it took less than a second for Jude to spot the only two in English: the group chat between the three of them titled 'Super Robot Monkey Team', and a private one with Cali.

Jude clicked on Cali's name. The last messages they'd exchanged were yesterday morning. Cali had sent Mo a list of reasons to come to the party and a string of praying emojis, until Mo finally replied, *Ok you convince me.* Jude scrolled up, reading the things they'd sent each other during school hours and in the middle of the night. Their jokes and questions were banal enough, but it was the frequency rather than the content that made the backs of Jude's eyes prickle. The group chat between all three of them contained mostly practical things: times when she and Cali would arrive, questions about what Mo needed, updates on her food and water levels. Meanwhile, it seemed, Cali and Mo had been messaging doz-ens of times a day, picking up on conversations they'd started as a group, keeping each other company when neither of them could sleep, sharing their hopes and fears. The more

Jude read, the more hurt she felt. Cali and Mo had been getting to know one another without her.

Jude stopped scrolling, her thumb hovering over a GIF Cali had sent. It showed a baby repeatedly flopping face-first into a sofa cushion. Mo had replied, *LOL, What is that?*

> Me when Jude bangs on about what A-levels she wants to do and where she wants to go to uni.

Oh.

> I mean, here I am just trying to get through the day without throwing myself out the fucking window!

What is wrong?

> Nothing. Just the usual. Sorry, feeling stressed and J is NOT helping.

She does not understand how you feel.

> Nope. I'm so glad I have you to talk to, J drives me crazy sometimes.

She sticks to you like glue.

> I know, right?

I think she has an obsession. She is lovesick.

> Ha, that'd be funny. Nah, we've just known each other for ages.

I am serious. I think she is in love with you.

Lol.

It is why she does not like me.

> That's not true. Look, I gotta go to
> Maths, but I'll see you later, right?

> And don't worry, Jude's all right,
> she's just a bit weird sometimes.

Be careful. Some people seem
sweet on the outside but inside they
are sour.

Jude kicked the empty backpack at her feet. She bent down and picked up the star-patterned notebook she'd given Mo. She opened it and began tearing out the pages. She didn't know what Mo had written in there, but if that was the sort of thing she was saying about her to Cali then who knew what she was putting in a diary. Jude tore out every page with writing on, then sat on the cold concrete floor amid the debris. She looked around at the home she'd helped build for this back-stabbing, judgemental creature who seemed to think she knew her best friend better than she did. She thought about Mo's face as she'd stood in the doorway last night, waiting for Cali to leave her there in Bobby's house. She thought about the feeling of his hands on her skin, the smell of rum on his breath. Tears and snot streamed down Jude's face and her breath hiccoughed in her throat, until her eyes landed on the camping stove.

She stared at the box of matches lying next to it. She crawled over, twisted the knob to open the valve, and struck a match to light it. She gazed at the flickering blue flame. After a while, she stood up and yanked one of the old towels Cali had hung as a draught excluder from its nails. Still

173

crying, she held its tatty edge over the stove. Once alight, she dropped the towel on the floor and fetched another.

When she had a small fire going in the centre of the room, Jude fed Mo's documents into the flames. She watched the papers curl, feeling a rush of power, as if burning her identity might erase the girl herself. She was about to burn the photographs too, but looked at the three faces smiling up at her from the top one and hesitated. A seven- or eight-year-old Mo stood between two adults, their arms around her shoulders, a beach in the background. Jude remembered the money in her pocket. She remembered the drowned rat of a girl they'd found on the cliffs in January. Jude had tried to help her, she really had. But where had that got her? She and Cali couldn't keep doing this. Mo couldn't stay here.

Jude looked around, taking in the candles and the fairy lights and the stuffed bear she'd given Mo that first night. She remembered how hard it had been to lug all this stuff up here and how much she'd wanted to tell her parents or a teacher or the police. She remembered Cali promising over and over that they were doing the right thing, that Mo *needed* their help. Then she remembered Bobby moaning that he couldn't help himself. She saw herself sitting in his bathroom, messaging her best friend. She saw Mo leaning her head into Cali's as the two of them walked away from her.

With fresh tears in her eyes, Jude picked up one of the spare gas canisters and carried it into Mo's bedroom. She unscrewed the valve and poured fuel over the bed, the blanket covering the window and the clothes, magazines and books piled in the corner. She opened the other canister and knocked it over in the doorway. Then she picked up the matches, wiped her face with her jacket and set light to it all.

# 2026

Tarek leaves Gary in the pub next to the fish and chip shop, intending to head back to the hotel, but finds himself lured into a garish high street card shop on the way. He stands before the display of blue and pink offerings, realizing he cannot send Helen any of these, even ironically. As he turns to leave, his eyes land on a plain photographic card featuring three penguins waddling flipper to flipper towards the camera. He picks it up and heads to the counter.

'It's polite in this country to queue,' a woman snaps behind him. Tarek turns and realizes his mistake. He steps back, catching the eye of another woman with a dark, greying bob standing near the entrance. She gives him a sympathetic smile, but it cannot undo the effect of the first woman's tone. All morning he's been trying not to think about the note under his door, telling himself he refuses to be messed with by anyone too cowardly to say what they think to his face, but his hands tremble now as he waits his turn. The woman cuts her eyes at him as she leaves with her purchases and it is all Tarek can do not to spit one of the retorts racing through his mind. The young white shopkeeper smiles as if nothing has happened and waits for Tarek to pay.

Outside, he pulls out his phone, tempted to rage to Helen or a friend. He has a new email, though, and is distracted by it as he walks. It's from his colleague, Livia.

**To:** zayattarek@tnnmedia.co.uk
**From:** walkerl@tnnmedia.co.uk
**Date:** May 6, 2026, 1.14PM
**Subject:** Re: query

I just want to check I'm clear – you want access to all the
temporary stories of a dead account? From what I understand,
that's technically possible, but I'm sure I don't need to tell you it's
ethically rather dubious. I can pass the request on to my contact,
but you know you won't be able to use any of it as material, right?
Even if you had permission from any living relatives, those files
technically belong to the host company and it's not in their interest
to publicize that they've kept them.
Let me know if you want to go ahead.
Lx

Tarek types out a reply as he enters the hotel. So far both
Cali and Mo are knowable to him only through the eyes of
others, so if Livia can get him anything, it will help. He's desperate to dig deeper, to discover more about their friendship,
to see Mo as Cali saw her.

Back in the conference room, he fishes through his notes
for a number. He has to make selections from two menus
before he's put through to the correct department.

'Unidentified Cases, Stewart speaking.'

'I'd like to enquire about the status of an application.'

'Do you have your reference number?'

Stewart sounds bored, or busy, though Tarek finds it hard
to believe there's much to do in a department that seems to
have basically shut up shop. 'I can't see anything on the system,' he says after Tarek has repeated his number. 'And I
can't give you an update until we've started processing it and
it's on the system.'

'And when is that going to be?'

'Right now it looks like we're processing applications received up to 21st February. You said you sent it nine weeks ago? It might still be another two or three weeks until you're on the system.'

'Are you joking?'

'No, sir.'

'Can I talk to your supervisor?'

'I am the supervisor today, sir.'

'Well, your manager then. Someone who can actually do something.' Tarek's tempted to ask for Deborah, the woman who sent him the photos, but he knows she's done more than she should for him already and he doesn't want to get her into trouble.

'I can give you a complaints address if you'd like,' Stewart says brightly.

'I would like,' Tarek spits. They hang up and he types out a furious message. He cannot wait another two or three weeks. Helen is due, Olga won't extend his deadline and he – he needs answers. He *has* to see that file.

He rocks on the back legs of the chair, trying to calm down. There must be another way. He should press Rose further, find out what she knows about the fire and where Mo went afterwards. He's getting close to what he's here for, he can feel it, and he can't let it slip away. He leans a little too far back and his chair tips. As he's steadying himself, he notices something poking out of his rucksack. A small white envelope. He looks around the empty room. He's had his bag on his back all day, while they filmed all over town. How long has this been there?

Inside the envelope he finds a folded A5 leaflet. An image of the British Isles in the bright colours of the Union Jack sits above the black smear of the rest of Europe and the blood-red outlines of Turkey, Syria, Iraq and Iran. Beneath, it reads:

TAKE BACK CONTROL IF YOU
BE*LEAVE* IN BRITAIN.

Tarek saw an art installation a few years ago where a to-scale model of central London was pasted in flyers like this, then gradually flattened by the bounce of a dozen beach balls featuring the faces of politicians. Someone told him afterwards that you could still order the literature online, get T-shirts and mugs printed up with their slogans, to commemorate what was achieved.

He opens the leaflet and finds a slip of paper with a black and white logo featuring the initials *NNAA*. On the other side, someone has written:

YOU DON'T BELONG HERE.
THIS IS NOT YOUR STORY.

Tarek stares at the neat biro letters. He thinks of the woman who snapped at him in the card shop and the shopkeeper who did nothing. There were a bunch of loud teenagers in the fish and chip shop, and plenty of pale old men who turned their heads when he and Gary walked into the pub earlier. Whoever it was, Tarek imagines reaching for the person who wrote this, feeling them tremble in his grip. They couldn't be more wrong. This is the *only* story his family has left, and he will not let a couple of cowardly threats take it from him.

A single chime interrupts his thoughts and he turns back to his computer. Still holding the note, he navigates to his messages. Livia has sent him a link, no text or explanation. He clicks and his screen goes black.

'Shit,' he says. What has he done? The computer returns to life with a download bar. Before he can cancel it, a folder titled CaliGR8 opens. It contains 7,613 files, each named with a 10-digit number. Apprehensively, Tarek opens one. A pair of dark brown eyes fills his screen. The lashes bat as the camera pans out to reveal a nose and puckered mouth. Then the lips split into a smile and Cali laughs. 'Happy V-Day, bitches!' Piano keys play as the camera zooms in on her throat and tiny hearts fall like rose petals on a small gold Tinkerbell.

Tarek reads the file name: 14-02-16-19:36. It's a timestamp. Below it, there's a smaller file titled 14-02-16-19:36-responses. He clicks back to the parent folder and scrolls up and down. He looks between his screen and the note, feeling almost euphoric. Before him is every temporary social media story Cali Walker posted and every reply she received between 2014 and 14th May 2016 – the day before her death.

# THE FIRE

## CLIFFTOP. DAY.

Hazard tape flaps in the wind as the camera pans a utilitarian structure overlooking the sea.

On March 20th emergency services were alerted to a blaze in one of the World War Two defence buildings on the cliffs above Samphire Hoe. Three fire engines and one ambulance attended the scene. A teenage girl was found outside the building, suffering from third-degree burns and smoke inhalation. Forensic investigation after the event determined the fire started sometime between 2 and 3 p.m. The initial cause was uncertain, but canisters of camping fuel were present in the structure and encouraged the fire to spread. In the charred remains, other items, including sleeping bags, clothing, cans of food and a teddy bear were found. Officials could not rule out arson, but no arrests were made.

CUT TO.

## CONFERENCE ROOM

ROSE

Nobody could tell us what Cali was doing up there, why she'd run into a fire.

CUT TO.

# JUDE'S FLAT

I hadn't been anywhere near the cliffs that day, and I hadn't heard from Cali since the party the night before. She wasn't replying to my messages and I had no idea where she was.

(touches cheek.)

I walked around town in the afternoon, looking in the shops. Eventually I headed home.

INTERVIEWER
(off-screen)

What time?

JUDE

Um. Five maybe. I'm not sure.

INTERVIEWER
(off-screen)

So Cali had already been taken to hospital?

JUDE

(nods.)

My dad was home, pulling his hair out. Where have you been? he said. I just stood there thinking this couldn't be happening again.

CUT TO.

ROSE

By the time I got to the hospital, the police were crawling along the corridors, waiting almost as eagerly as we were for her to get out of surgery. She was their only witness.

CUT TO.

JUDE

I'm still uncertain what happened. Or what to think. Did Mo start the fire? By accident? On purpose? Or was Cali trying to hurt herself again? I honestly don't know.

CUT TO.

ROSE

I asked Jude if she knew what had happened, but she said she hadn't seen Cali since the day before. She looked pale and as worried as I was.

CUT TO.

JUDE

The doctor came to tell us Cali was out of surgery. They'd taken skin grafts from her thighs for the burns on her arm and shoulder.

CUT TO.

ROSE

Later that evening we were allowed in. Cali had bandages all over her left side. She would be scarred for life, we'd been told, but I guess the idea hadn't really penetrated until I saw her like that.

I asked her what happened, but my mum hissed at me not to harass her. We'd barely said three words to each other since I'd arrived. How could she have let Cali get hurt again? I thought.

CUT TO.

JUDE

It was only family allowed that first day. I sat outside worried sick.

CUT TO.

ROSE

After the bandages came off, we tried to pretend we weren't staring, but all we could see were the scars. The main thing was that Cali was healthy, that her lungs hadn't filled with smoke, that her skin was responding to the graft and that she'd be able to come home soon, but I felt something like grief for my sister. For the loss of her perfect beauty. How many times as a child had I resented her for it, wanted her to know what it was like to stand out and not fit in?

CUT TO.

## JUDE

Hospitals are weird places. You either never go or you're there all the time. Growing up I'd only ever been once, after a school friend slipped and banged her head on the side of a swimming pool. But 2016 was the year of hospitals. It was so frightening, sitting there again, feeling like I'd almost lost my best friend for the second time in a few months.

CUT TO.

## ROSE

Once Cali was less groggy I told her she could trust me. I told her it didn't matter what she'd been doing up there. But she wouldn't say anything. I asked who'd called 999 and she said she couldn't tell me. I asked why not and she said she'd made a promise. I was getting pretty frustrated with her to be honest. I asked if she was in trouble and she shook her head. That was all I could get out of her. Whoever she was protecting, she was not going to betray them, even to me.

# THEN

'Mo dragged me out of the fire,' Cali whispered after she came out of her second surgery. 'Is she okay?'

Jude squeezed Cali's good hand and told her not to worry. 'What were you doing up there? Why would you go in?'

'Her stuff was in there,' Cali murmured, 'everything she owned. You should have seen her. I thought she was going to run in there. The only way I could think to stop her was to do it myself.'

For a split second Jude wanted to ask if Cali would have done the same for her. She bit her cheek. 'Don't worry. It's going to be okay.'

She waited until Cali was out of hospital to tell her Mo was gone.

'What do you mean?' Cali shouted. 'Where the fuck is she?'

Jude glanced at Cali's bedroom door. Jackie and Rose were downstairs. 'I'm not sure.'

'You told me she was okay.'

'I told you not to worry. I wanted you to concentrate on getting better.'

Cali tried to get out of bed.

'What are you doing?'

'We have to find her.'

'She's gone. Maybe she found a way to get to Calais.'

'She needed money. She needed our help.'

'Cali, let it go. We did what we could.'

Cali stared at Jude. 'How can you be like this?'

'I'm trying to look out for you.'

'Get out!'

'What?'

'Seriously, Jude. Fuck off. I don't want you here.'

Jude spent three weeks watching the ticks beside her messages turn from grey to blue but never receiving a reply. She sat on top of the zipline platform in the park so she could watch the back of Cali's house, noting the movement of the curtains in Cali's room, trying to catch a glimpse of her. She could tell by the washing that remained hanging in the overgrown garden and the bins that weren't put out when Rose must have returned to London. Jude went to her classes and to her volunteering shifts, she replied to the questions her parents asked her and smiled and said of course when people at school told her to wish Cali well. Inside, though, she felt numb. She didn't know what to do without her best friend.

Finally, one Sunday morning, Cali replied: *You can come over if you want.*

'I'm sorry,' Jude said, standing in the doorway. She'd been rehearsing what to say for weeks, but now she found herself stumbling over the words. 'I wanted you to get better – I was trying to be a good friend – I was scared for you.'

Cali was slumped against her pillows, scrolling through her phone.

'Please, Cal. I'll do anything to make it up to you.'

Cali put down her phone and began picking at her fingers. Jude watched her peel a strip of pink polish from her thumbnail. Now the bandages were off it was hard not to stare at Cali's left arm. In a way, it wasn't as bad as Jude had feared. The skin graft was red, but smooth. The swelling would go down, they'd been told at the hospital. The less severe burns on her face and shoulder were almost healed already. She'd been lucky, everyone said.

Finally, Cali spoke. 'I can't believe she's gone. She saved my life.'

Jude swallowed. She knew she should proceed with caution, but couldn't help blurting, 'What were you even doing up there? We were meant to meet at yours.'

Cali sighed. 'We were coming down to meet you, then Mo realized she'd forgotten her phone.'

Jude stared at the logo of a compact of blusher abandoned on the floor. Mo's phone was currently in her desk drawer with the envelope and photos. She'd turned it on once, seen there were sixteen notifications from Cali, all asking where she was, if she was okay, then turned it back off and shoved it away.

'We'd been trying to think of ways to get the money,' Cali said.

Jude felt a lurch in her chest. She'd hidden the £500 in her bookshelf. It wasn't her fault she hadn't had a chance to give it to Mo, she told herself. It wasn't *her* that had messed things up and gone back to the lookout.

'What are we going to do?' Cali said.

Jude frowned. 'What do you mean?' Without a phone, unless Mo came back, there was no way of getting in touch with her. Jude felt almost cheered by this, until she remembered what Mo had said about her to Cali.

'We can't pretend like she didn't exist. We need to do something.'

Jude didn't know what to say. She couldn't tell Cali that that was all she wanted: to pretend Mo didn't exist. That she was sorry for what she'd done, sorry for hurting Cali, sorry for making her angry, but not in any way sorry that it had got rid of Mo. 'Maybe she'll come back,' she said quietly. 'Find us when she's settled.'

She visited Cali every day after school, bringing her revision sheets from their teachers and messages from their class-mates. Cali had her Art and English books out most days, but wasn't interested in anything else. The doctors were pleased with her progress, but Jude wondered what Cali felt when she looked in the mirror. She remembered a stupid game they'd once played, asking each other if they'd rather have scars all over their face or be really dumb.

'How dumb?'

'Like Laura Myers dumb.'

'You're so mean!' Cali had said, punching Jude's arm.

'Well, what would you choose?'

'Dumb,' she'd said.

'Really?'

'Not like I think I'm hot shit, but I like having guys look at me. I like feeling sexy.'

'I suppose,' Jude had said. She'd chosen the scars, thinking that even if she was lonely at least she'd be able to entertain herself.

Now that felt like the worst conversation they'd ever had. Jude vowed never to be so callous again. She vowed to make up for all of her mistakes. She did everything she could for Cali in those weeks, brought her all the presents she could think of, looked for topics of conversation to take her mind off things, and posed and pulled stupid faces with even stu-pider filters in an attempt to make Cali laugh.

By the end of April it seemed like it wasn't just Cali's skin that was healing. She started cracking little jokes again, gos-siping about boys, and not looking entirely vacant when Jude brought up their walk. Goofy came to visit and the shit presents he brought piled up beside the bed. One day, Cali told Jude that he'd said Bobby was asking after her.

'We should go on a double date!'

The idea made the backs of Jude's knees sweat, but she nodded and said maybe. Even the memory of Bobby's unwanted hands couldn't dampen the relief she felt to finally have her best friend back and all to herself.

# 2026

Tarek struggles to maintain Rose's eye contact. All afternoon he's heard Cali's laugh in the back of his mind, seen the bat of her eyelashes and the flip of her hair. He should not have looked at those images, he knows. They were private, meant for deletion. Cali put them into the world thinking they would disappear. But ten years after her death, 7,613 files sit on his device. He's aware he's been more economical with the truth for this documentary than in his entire career, but somehow sitting before Rose this feels like his most illicit secret. What would he give to hear Inji's voice once more? To watch her smile and laugh, hear her and Mo joke around and get lost in the trivialities of their days? If those files belong to anyone, it's Rose.

They wrap at four, earlier than Tarek intended. He knows when to stop pushing, though, and in truth, despite his guilt, all he's been able to think about this afternoon is reopening that folder. He helps Gary pack up and carry the equipment to the lift, and they part with a plan to meet later for dinner. Back in his room, Tarek feels like a voyeur peering through a window in the middle of the night, but nonetheless scrolls to the bottom of the folder and clicks on the last story. What loads is an 'am-listening' link to Taylor Swift's 'Bad Blood', followed by a teary apology. Tarek frowns, not understanding the context. He scrolls up through the folder, back to January 30th, the day Jude said they first met Mo.

A shot of Shakespeare Cliff shrouded in a black raincloud is followed by a drenched selfie, a few looped seconds of water streaming down concrete, a superzoom into the centre of the sound mirror, and finally a Sharpied stickman carrying a scythe and the words *ENTER AT OWN RISK*.

Tarek is disappointed. He moves forward in time, selecting stories at random. He watches a clip of Cali dancing, a loop of a dog chasing its tail, a picture of an election sign with a vomiting caterpillar dancing on top, a series of ironwork tools in glass cases with flashing hashtags *#History* and *#SchoolTrip*, an earnest conversation with herself in a bathroom mirror, two poll questions asking *Fish Fingers or Chicken Nuggets?* and *Team Taylor or Team Katy?*, a tub of hospital jelly with the caption *living my best life*, a puddle of bandages on the floor, and a strip of caution tape flapping back and forth in the wind, but not a single glimpse of the face he is looking for.

Tarek sighs. Did he really think he'd find her here? That after being so careful, so protective, Cali would just post her friend's face for the world to see? He clicks back to the school-trip story and watches the camera pan around a room of objects. 'This shit is *old*,' Cali's voiceover whispers. This stuff would mean the world to Rose, he knows, but to him? How would he feel if someone else resurrected his sister like this?

He shuts his computer and looks at his watch. Cali has put an idea in his head, at least, and he should still have time before the museum closes. His phone vibrates against his thigh as he's leaving the hotel. It's a form message from the Missing Persons Unit saying they've received his enquiry and will respond within forty-eight hours. 'Wankers,' Tarek says aloud and feels a little better.

'We're closing in half an hour,' says the woman as she issues his ticket.

'I won't be long.'

He makes his way up the stairs to the centerpiece attraction. He has been meaning to come since he first got here, though if he's honest with himself he's also been avoiding it. The lights are low in the temperature-controlled gallery. In the centre of the room, in a large glass case, is a wooden object only partially resembling a boat. It is the oldest known sea-going vessel in the world. At 3,500 years old, Tarek has read, it is older than the Roman Empire and Tutankhamun. It was one of the first things that caught his attention in his initial research survey of Dover. He closes his eyes now and tries to imagine what his father would make of this. As a child, when Tarek accompanied him to museums, he looked not at the objects but at how his father inspected them. He would press as close as he could to the glass and squint through his spectacles, his lips moving with murmured thoughts.

One time, his father made him study a small white cylinder. *See the Mesopotamian sun god?* he said. Only eight or nine, Tarek strained to make out the engravings, struggling to understand what was so impressive about something smaller than the size of his finger. *This seal is four thousand years old*, his father said, staring expectantly at his son, and suddenly Tarek saw not what his father was hoping he would see, but what beauty there was in a man who saw wonder in the world. Tarek tried to hold on to that memory as he started his career, to honour his father in the way he approached his subjects. His openness and willingness to question everything, not simply to rest on prejudice or assumption, but to find the core of humanity and passion at the heart of even the most divisive topics served him well for the first few years.

Tarek opens his eyes. It feels like a long time since he's managed to channel his father's uncontaminated curiosity and reverence for every artefact regardless of its flaws. He sighs. The only impressive thing about this hunk of wood is that it has survived. That is literally all that distinguishes it from every other boat that sailed alongside it. He pinches the bridge of his nose, trying to hold back tears. For that's all that distinguishes him, too; he survived and those he sailed alongside didn't.

He told his parents Inji was too young to make the journey to England, too young for him to keep safe. They told him it was his duty to do what was best for his sister. The truth was he was afraid to take her. He'd been knocking on Inji's door, trying to comfort her. Always he found her curled in a ball, staring straight ahead. Once upon a time he'd been proud of the fact that his sister never cried. He'd thought her tougher than other little girls. At fourteen, though, having seen an explosion rip through her school, having buried seven of her classmates, he found her lack of tears unnerving. This girl was not the sister he'd grown up with; she was something new, something broken. She said little and ate even less. Mo had stopped coming round, which can't have helped. Tarek assumed her family must have left, like almost all their neighbours had. When his mother started making preparations for him, she insisted. Inji had been through too much, she said. She couldn't stay. Tarek tried to argue. He pleaded with his parents to come too, to let them go as a family, but it was useless. Within weeks, he and Inji were crouching with three dozen others in a forest next to the water on the Turkish border, clutching life jackets and each other, as they waited for the signal to board the dinghies.

He remembers how pale Inji was that night, staring at the water through the trees, contemplating – he assumed – the crossing ahead.

'Hey,' he said, trying to snap her out of it. 'Have you heard from Mo?' Perhaps her family had taken this same route, he thought. Perhaps she could tell them it was safe, that the life jackets they'd purchased would protect them, that what was on the other side was worth it. All the things Tarek was struggling to tell himself.

Inji peeled her eyes away from the sea, but the look she gave him was so distant, so disconnected from the trees and the dirt and the huddling families around them, that suddenly Tarek too felt petrified.

He wipes his face and turns away from the boat. There's a temporary exhibition on old children's toys in the room opposite.

'Five minutes until we close,' an attendant tells him, hovering by the door. He's the only visitor left.

'I'll be two seconds.'

Tarek hears her exhale, but steps up to an old Victorian zoetrope. He crouches to look through the slit and spins the wheel to make the pictures inside turn. A tiny pony gallops around and around the circumference of the toy. Tarek is fascinated by the illusion of action, the lack of progress.

The attendant clears her throat. 'Sir, I have a home to go to.'

Tarek removes his eye from the toy. 'Lucky you,' he murmurs as he leaves.

# THEN

Rose pinned her nametag to her apron and tapped out a message to Kassia to say she'd see her at the ticket barrier, then climbed the stairs to the café floor.

'Coffee caramel ice for Julie, double shot latte for Tom,' she called, feeling the familiarity of the complicated, inconsequential routine. It was good when she got a rhythm going, when she could get ten or twenty drinks out in a row without someone interrupting to tell her they'd asked for no whip, or wasn't that one meant to be soya. Blake, the barista, kept fucking up the cup markings, though. Rose caught a couple of mistakes before they got to the customer, making a skinny wet latte even though the cup said soya, and double-checking with Wendy that she definitely wanted a flat white and not her normal white Americano.

'Thanks,' Wendy said, giving Rose a wink.

Rose smiled, but even with the extra work being created, her mind was wandering. It was May already, a month since she'd last visited Cali, six weeks since the fire. Kassia had been the one to suggest they go this weekend. As soon as she'd mentioned it, Rose had been obliged to say yes. Both because her girlfriend wanted to meet her family and because she'd done exactly what she'd promised herself she wouldn't and reverted to the role of shitty, absent sister.

*Girlfriend.* She wasn't quite used to that word yet. Things had been going well for a few months now, and Kassia had been amazingly supportive during the weeks after the fire, but that didn't mean Rose had felt ready when Kassia put her knife and fork down a couple of weekends ago and asked what they were doing. At first Rose had thought it was a joke. She hadn't been worrying about labels and it hadn't occurred to her that Kassia might have been. She'd eaten a last bite of scrambled egg on toast and shrugged.

'I am not trying to force you, but I need to know.'

Kassia looked so serious and hurt that Rose didn't know what to say. 'We're having fun, right?'

Kassia stood up and carried her plate to the sink. Rose stared at her profile as she ran the tap and started scrubbing the egg pan.

She hadn't felt ready for the conversation, but that didn't mean Rose hadn't been paying attention to Kassia. She'd learnt she was writing her PhD on trauma and the formation of false memory in survivors of domestic abuse, that she was behind and stressed and needed three cups of coffee before she could bear to open the document each morning. She'd learnt Kassia enjoyed moments of submission but hated feeling out of control; that she was self-conscious of her body and more likely to have an orgasm if she still had some clothes on. One morning Rose had asked about the scratches on the tops of her arms, and Kassia had buried her head in her pillow and murmured that she'd been stupid when she was younger. 'I was hoping you wouldn't notice.' Rose had kissed the crappy star on Kassia's neck and traced the curve of her spine. She'd asked Kassia about growing up in Kraków, why she'd wanted to study in England and what she hoped to do after she finished her doctorate. They'd talked about the TV shows they'd watched and the bands they liked, about how neither of them was very good at keeping up with current affairs but it was strange and worrying to think about the calls for them to leave the EU and a reality star running in the primaries. They'd talked about Cali and their child-hoods, and feeling like outsiders. They'd spent whole days in bed, telling themselves they were about to get up, then watching the light die through the window. All that had been more than fun and Rose knew it, but she didn't know if she was ready to define it. She didn't know how to admit to herself what she was starting to feel, let alone offer Kassia the answer she wanted.

Kassia twisted the tap off and turned to her. 'Is this only fun to you?'

Rose remembered Grace confronting her on New Year's Day, telling her she was cold and unemotional. 'I don't know.'

Kassia laughed. 'Well, Rose Walker, Mysterious Queen of her Emotions, I like having fun with you and I would like to keep having fun with you and nobody else.'

Kassia wasn't Grace, Rose reminded herself. She'd felt more optimism over the past months than she had in the past six years. Her eyes flicked to Sean's *Shantay, You Stay* magnet on the fridge behind Kassia's head and she said, 'Okay.'

'This is okay you agree, or okay you want to run away?'

'Okay I agree.'

'You get what I mean?' Kassia had said, sitting back at the table. 'I am too old to be wondering if I am competing with someone or worrying if I should get tested.'

'I get it,' Rose had said. 'I don't want that either.'

'And I would like to know you properly.'

'You do.'

'All of you.'

So tonight Kassia would meet her sister and her mother. Rose's two lives would collide.

She picked up a cup and started making a hot chocolate.

She poked her head around the espresso machine to make eye contact with the young girl who was waiting. 'You want whipped cream?'

The girl nodded and stepped around the counter to watch Rose make the drink. Sometimes Rose felt like an actor, flitting between parts as barista, housemate, sister, daughter, and now girlfriend. She didn't dislike any of the roles, but she often felt on the verge of forgetting her lines. As much as she wanted to make Kassia happy, Rose was scared she couldn't trust herself. What was stopping her walking out of a shift and calling Diego, placing a pill upon her tongue and following someone else home? She didn't know if anything had actually changed inside her, if the things Grace had said at the beginning of the year weren't in fact true. What if she was fundamentally incapable of the kind of relationship she was trying to have? What if all of this was as pretend as the smile she was about to direct at this girl waiting for her hot chocolate and staring like she'd never seen a butch lesbian before?

'Medium hot chocolate for Mo,' Rose called out, reading the Sharpied name on the cup. The girl's fingers brushed hers as she reached for it. 'Have a nice day,' she said, making eye contact as she'd been taught.

'Thank you,' the girl said softly.

Rose turned to the next drink. She noticed the girl a while later, standing at the condiment bar, still staring. *What's her problem?* she wondered. She was wearing jeans and a blue hoodie, like one Rose had seen Cali in before. Everything she wore looked like it needed a good wash. Rose wondered where she'd got the money for the hot chocolate.

Blake got to the end of the queue and Rose made the final drinks. The girl was still there. Rose had some milk left in her jug, so she grabbed a new cup from the stack and pumped four squirts of chocolate syrup into it.

'Medium hot chocolate for Mo,' she shouted again and placed the cup on the pass.

The girl jumped and Rose suppressed a smile. It was a small gesture and nothing really, she knew, but it was what she could do.

'Thank you,' the girl said again, a little louder this time. Her voice was thick with an accent Rose couldn't place. 'You are kind.'

'It's nothing.'

'It is not.'

Rose laughed. 'All right then.'

The girl frowned. 'There are some people who are kind and some people who are dangerous. It is not always easy to see which.'

Rose gave a polite smile. She was starting to wish she hadn't bothered.

'I think you come from a kind family.'

Rose couldn't tell if this was meant to be a question or a statement. She shifted uncomfortably. 'Sure, why not?'

The girl nodded at Rose's name badge. 'Protect your family, Rose. Look after them. They are the only thing that is important.'

Rose looked at the girl with her grubby clothes and serious expression, wondering how she herself would survive on the streets of a strange country, then how Cali might. 'Look,' she said, checking Blake was clearing tables. 'Do you need some food?'

The girl's face split into a smile as Rose opened the pastry fridge and used the tongs to pluck two muffins into a paper bag.

'They're getting chucked out in an hour anyway. Sorry if they're already stale—'

'Thank you, Rose. I do not forget this.'

At 7.45, Rose hurried through the crowds, still thinking about the girl, wondering where she'd found to sleep and if anyone was looking out for her.

'I bought gins for the train,' Kassia said, holding out an M&S bag.

'Angel,' Rose said, kissing Kassia's cheek and feeling the gradual pull of her own small universe. They found a table seat in a middle carriage and sat opposite each other. Rose drummed her knee as they pulled out of London, thoughts of the girl replaced by her creeping anxiety about the weekend to come.

'Relax,' Kassia said, reaching for Rose's hand. 'I promise I will take them as they are.'

# 2026

Rose stands at the entrance to the rec, staring at the kids playing on the new climbing frame and slide. This morning Tarek asked when she'd last been here and she struggled to remember. Packing up her mum's house when they moved her into the Retreat, she thinks now. That was after Cali. After Jude woke from her coma. After Jackie slipped further than she ever had before, and Rose and Kassia had to admit they couldn't care for her alone. She remembers Jude's mum seeing them loading up the rental car and walking across the rec to say hello. Rose stiffened at the sight of her and almost cried out when Sandra folded her into her arms and made her promise to keep in touch. *That woman should be scratching my eyes out, not hugging me,* she said as Sandra walked away.

There's a bench where the roundabout used to be, and Rose sits at the opposite end to a woman with a pram. From this angle, she can see both the backs of the terraces and, in the other direction, the tall rear security gates of the posh houses. There's a small, round trampoline with a net around it in the garden of her old house. She wonders what the child who lives there is like, how he or she gets on at school, and if both parents live at home. Who sleeps in the room where Cali took those pills? What have they done with the dent in the doorframe from the time John lost his temper?

Rose rubs her eyes. She doesn't need to torture herself like this. When she and Kassia first moved back to Dover, the streets felt full of ghosts. She'd stared at school gates and bus shelters, the old youth club and every shop that had closed down, letting the past flood the present. It seemed impossible then that she could build a new life on top of the old one, but like most things it had just taken time. With Kassia's help, Rose managed to carve out a new identity. The melancholic significance of each street and building faded until finally she saw them for what they were. The specifics of her and Kassia's life settled like sediment: her job at the restaurant, Kassia's clinic above the card shop, the gym they used, the cinema they went to, the fish and chips they ate and the supermarket they shopped at all forming a solid layer on top of the jagged flint of the past.

Until Tarek got in touch in February, Rose had been managing to feel almost whole. She'd managed to convince herself she'd done her AA steps and come out the other side. Sitting here, though, she feels the pull of her former selves. She can't deny the threads that link her to the chubby child that learnt to ride a bike in this playground, the sad teenager who smoked beneath the zipline platform, or the nervous twenty-something who had no idea what she was messing Kassia up in when she brought her home for the first time.

The woman at the other end of the bench casts a furtive glance at Rose, her eyes lingering on the flowers in her lap, then returns her attention to something in the bottom of her buggy. Rose was planning to go home and surprise Kassia after work, cook her a meal and find a way to make up. But she wonders now what exactly she thought she was able to apologize for. Flowers will never be enough to make up for everything she's put her wife through.

The woman glances at her again and Rose stands. She walks to the edge of the rec and shoves the flowers in the dog bin. A whirring mechanical sound makes her turn. The gates to one of the posh houses are opening.

Rose counts along the row to make sure. She only ever

entered from the front, but she's certain it's that one. Jude now lives in the marina development. It's never been mentioned aloud, but it's one of the reasons she and Kassia haven't tried the restaurants there. There were enough calls to boycott the area in protest at the council wasting money during a recession when it first opened that neither of them had to acknowledge their true reasoning. In a similar way, they've never had to discuss why they prefer the out-of-town supermarket, why Rose goes to meetings in Folkestone and why Kassia pays to use a hotel rather than the public pool. Avoiding someone in a town this size is difficult, but not impossible.

The gap in the gate widens and a large drive comes into view, revealing two women talking beside a red Vauxhall. Rose steps forward, her breath catching. She watches Sandra hug her daughter and help her into the driver's seat. Jude is wearing another trouser suit and her hair is glossy and freshly styled. Her mother folds her wheelchair and loads it behind the driver's seat, then closes the door and says something through the window. Jude reverses out of the drive and the gates whirr back into action, swallowing Sandra from view.

When Jude stops at the end of the track to check the road, her gaze drifts towards the rec. Rose isn't quick enough to turn away. Jude's face registers surprise and confusion, then her lips curl and she raises her hand to the window. She's smiling and waving as if she and Rose are great friends, as if it hasn't been two or three years since they last had a stilted conversation in Market Square, as if they have never been anything more sinister to each other than childhood neighbours.

Jude stops moving her hand but continues to smile. Rose feels a wave of nausea and silently begs her not to drive over. She cannot talk about their mothers or the weather or what's happening in the area. She tries to imagine what Kassia would tell her to do. Kassia would instruct her to go along with whatever Jude wants, to keep the peace. With difficulty, Rose raises her hand and returns Jude's wave. She stretches her mouth not exactly into a smile, but something approximating one.

Jude is satisfied. She widens her grin and waves once more. Then she gives a single nod and drives off, leaving Rose standing on the edge of the playground, her heart pounding in her chest.

# 2026

At the first set of lights, Jude reaches for her earpiece and swipes at the screen on the dash. The light changes and she pulls away, listening to the dial tone. She really doesn't need this today. The point of visiting her mum before the election meeting was to calm her nerves, but now she feels anything but calm. She should be thinking about her speech, about how to present herself and arrange her face if she wins.

The ringing stops. 'Hello?'

'What's going on with Rose?'

There's no reply.

Jude clenches her teeth. Sometimes she truly hates this woman. 'Kassia, seriously, it's not like I have any desire to talk to you either. But this is important.'

She hears the sound of movement on the other end of the line. Footsteps, then a door shutting. Finally, Kassia speaks.

'What is it you want?' she says in a clipped, superior sounding tone.

Jude digs her fingernails into the soft leather of the steering wheel. She's trying not to panic, trying to remember the look on her father's face when he told her she deserved her dreams. 'I've just seen Rose up by my mum's. What the hell was she doing there?'

'Did she see you?'

'*Yes,*' Jude all but shouts.

'Shit.'

'I assume she's doing this documentary.'

There's a pause. 'Are you?'

Jude sucks her cheek. She doesn't see why Rose and Kassia ever had to move back here, why they couldn't have stayed in London and left her alone. They'd all be happier that way, wouldn't they? 'We have a deal,' she says. 'Remember?'

'I remember.'

'Nothing I'm doing is breaking our agreement, but if Rose—'

Kassia cuts her off. 'Rose isn't going to say anything either.'

'How can you be sure? Are you there for the interviews? I've got a lot going on right now and I don't have time to worry about her fucking things up.'

'Then don't,' Kassia says curtly. 'Let me handle it. For the record, I'm not happy about either of you talking to this man, but if you insist on taking the risk I'll do what I can to protect you both.'

Jude glances at the clock on the dash. 'I don't need this. I've got the mayoral election in an hour—'

Kassia gives a short laugh. 'I will hold my thumbs for you.'

Jude frowns and throws her earpiece on the passenger seat. She pulls into a parking bay and fumbles angrily as she transfers into her chair. She's worked hard for this moment and she deserves it. For years, she's held her tongue, keeping her own as well as other people's secrets, and she will not let an imbecile with a drug-addled brain or her stuck-up wife ruin things now. Rose never understood Cali, and she never deserved the sympathy she received. She's never realized how lucky she is to have gotten away with everything.

To have gotten off scot-free for putting her in this wheelchair.

# THEN

Jude stared at the rings looped through the top of Rose's ear as they walked along the river path. She watched her hunch her shoulders and run a nail-bitten hand over the shaved bit of her head when Cali leant in to whisper, 'Kassia's nice.'

They'd been to Flick's Deli to see Jackie at her new job. It had been busy with the Saturday brunch crowd, but Jackie had introduced them to her colleagues and grinned as she brought over their teas and bacon and egg sandwiches.

'Mum seems pretty good,' Rose had said when she'd returned behind the counter.

'You said she's got a new doctor, right?' Jude had tried to chip in, but Rose had given her a cold look, like it was none of her business. *It's not like you're ever here*, Jude had felt like saying. She probably knew more about what was going on in Cali's house than Rose did. Did she have any idea what Cali was still dealing with?

'You're allowed to be happy, you know?' Cali said now, elbowing her sister in the ribs.

Jude stepped around them as they stopped in a half-hug, half-wrestle. They really didn't look anything like sisters, she thought. And they had nothing in common.

She quickened her pace to catch up with Kassia, trying to think of a topic of conversation. She noticed Kassia looking at a *Vote Leave* sign stuck on a wooden pole in one of the gardens on the other side of the river. 'Sorry it's not more welcoming here,' she said, falling into pace.

Kassia turned to her with a blank smile. 'I like Dover a lot.'

'What you talking about?' Cali said, as she and Rose caught up.

Jude pointed at the sign. 'I was saying I'm sorry it's not more welcoming for Kassia. It's shit, isn't it? I mean, what even happens if we do leave? Do you get to stay? I guess you and Rose could get married—'

'Woah!' Rose said, holding her hands up and laughing. 'Slow the fuck down, will you?'

Jude glanced at Kassia. She was smiling, but didn't say anything.

They looped back into town, then up to the park behind their houses.

'Rose says you're an artist,' Kassia said, sitting on the edge of the roundabout.

'Not really,' Cali said, plopping on the grass.

'She's doing this cool picture of a child on a beach,' Jude said. 'Based on that migrant story.'

Cali shot Jude a look, but Kassia said, 'Wow, that's a heavy topic. It's great to be so engaged at your age.'

'It's necessary, isn't it?' Jude said, trying to remember the things she'd heard her parents say. 'I mean, it's just ridiculous what's happening around the world right now—'

'Oh my God, shut up,' Cali said, dropping her head dramatically into her lap. 'Nobody wants to talk about that.'

Rose and Kassia laughed.

'Is that what you want to study at university then?' Kassia said as Cali sat up.

'I dunno.'

'There are some great art schools in London.'

Jude felt stung. She tried to think of something else to say. Rose was sitting next to Cali on the ground. If Jude sat there too it'd be like they were interviewing Kassia, but if she sat on the next seat of the roundabout she'd be facing in the wrong direction.

'You should,' Rose said. 'Your stuff's great.'

'I told Cali she should come and volunteer with me,' Jude blurted, leaning on one leg, trying to look casual. 'It'll look great on her UCAS application.'

'When have you seen my stuff?' Cali said.

Rose hesitated. 'I saw some of your sketchbook when I was back in January.'

'You went snooping in my room?'

Jude froze, wondering what would happen. Then Cali laughed. 'I knew you had because I noticed something was missing.' She gave Rose a pointed look.

'Yeah, sorry, I guess I owe you a couple of joints.'

Jude didn't know what was going on. She'd felt relaxed and included earlier, like the four of them made a good team. She'd even wondered about suggesting she and Cali take the train up to London one day so they could all hang out again. But now she felt left out. She looked at Kassia, but she was sitting on the roundabout and smiling like this was the most normal and comfortable situation she'd ever been in.

'I should get home,' Jude found herself saying. As soon as she had, she hoped Cali would ask her to stay. But within minutes she was walking across the park to her house. She kicked the grinning monkey face painted to the side of the spring seesaw by the gate. It jerked towards the ground, then wobbled back into place, still smiling. She kicked it a second and a third time, then glanced back, worried they might be watching. They weren't, which was somehow worse. Jude growled in frustration. Why, when Mo was finally a distant memory and she and Cali were getting close again, did Rose and her annoyingly bland girlfriend have to come and push Jude away?

'What are you looking at?' she said to the determinedly cheerful monkey.

\*

'What you looking at?' Rose said a couple of hours later, standing in Cali's doorway. Kassia was in the bathroom, brushing her teeth.

'Just a forum.'

Rose felt her stomach constrict. Cali had seemed so healthy and animated that it was hard to remember what she'd done just a few months ago. Rose wondered if she was still using the Blue Mondays site, but didn't know how to ask. 'How's your arm?' she said instead.

'Want to see it?' Cali said, rolling up her sleeve.

'Does it hurt?'

Cali's smile dropped. 'A bit. I don't know. Sometimes I forget about it, then . . .' She pulled a face.

'Are you still seeing your counsellor?'

Cali nodded.

'What do you talk about?'

'You can't ask that.'

'Sorry, I just want to know how you are. I know I'm not very good at being here, but I worry and . . .' Rose trailed off and leant against the doorframe.

Cali studied her. 'Do you ever just look at the world and think, fuck, what can I do? How can I even live without doing more damage?'

'What damage are you doing? You're the kindest person I know.'

Cali shook her head. 'I tried to help someone and I think I might have just made things worse.'

'Who were you trying to help?'

Cali returned her attention to her phone. 'It doesn't matter.'

Rose wanted to press her, but was afraid of pushing Cali away. She looked around. 'I'm sure that's not true.'

Cali sighed. 'I don't even know what the point is sometimes.'

Rose scratched the back of her hand. 'I found your university brochures. Why do you have them hidden?'

Cali wrinkled her nose. 'I dunno if it's what I want.'

'I'm proud of you, you know? For being who you are. For everything.'

Cali pulled her sleeve back down. 'Even if it is what I want, I don't want to say it is and have everyone looking at me like they're disappointed if I don't get in. Or worse, looking at me beforehand like they *know* I won't get in.'

'It can't help having a friend like Jude.'

'What?'

'She seems to have everything, right? Do you ever wonder what it would have been like to have a childhood like hers? To have everything come easy?'

'That's not what her life's like. Everyone has their shit.'

'You're way too nice, you know that?'

'It was lovely to meet you,' Jackie said the next morning, giving Kassia a hug. 'Come back any time.'

Kassia laced her fingers between Rose's as they walked towards the station. 'It's nice, feeling like a part of your life.'

'You *are* part of my life,' Rose said, squeezing her hand.

Two figures turned onto the path ahead and they fell into single file to let them pass.

'Rose?' one of them said, stopping at her elbow.

Rose looked up and realized it was Sandra. Next to her stood a stocky, bearded man she vaguely recognized as Jude's dad.

'Hi.'

'Back again?' Sandra said. 'Craig, you remember Cali's sister? You girls staying long? How's Cali?'

Rose's head spun with her questions. 'Uh, she's all right. This is my friend Kassia.' She should have said girlfriend, she realized immediately. Kassia would be hurt that she hadn't.

'Nice to meet you, Kassia,' Craig said, holding out his hand.

'You too,' Kassia said, her voice light. Maybe she hadn't noticed.

'Great day for it,' Sandra said. 'We're heading up to the castle.'

Rose smiled.

'Well, it's lovely to see you again.'

'Jude has the perfect family,' Rose said when they'd found their platform and settled into their seats. 'Cali spent like half her childhood over at their house.'

'No family is perfect,' Kassia replied.

Rose looked out the window as they pulled out of Dover. They'd finally reopened the Folkestone line. It was a nice little stretch, coming out of the town towards the sea. You went past the old railway buildings and along the seafront, then into a tunnel through Shakespeare Cliff.

'Look,' Kassia said. 'I have a text welcoming me to France. My phone thinks we are over there.'

'That happens,' Rose said, checking her own. She was apparently still in Britain.

Kassia frowned. 'This is weird, with everything going on right now.'

Rose nodded.

'I was thinking about what Jude said. I might have to go home if I don't finish writing up my thesis on time.'

'Yeah?' Rose said. 'That sucks.'

'Yes, it sucks,' Kassia said, a little too loudly.

Rose nodded, wondering if she should have asked Cali outright if she was back on the Blue Mondays forum.

'I have one year left. It's not long.'

'You'll be fine. You work really hard.'

'I am not sure how possible it feels, and it's not helping not knowing what will happen. I don't want to lose my life here.'

'What's the worst that would happen? You have to go back for a bit to keep writing, then you come back to do your viva, yeah?'

'Vi-va,' Kassia said, correcting Rose's pronunciation.

'Whatever.'

Kassia turned to face her. 'No, not whatever. What is wrong with you? I am telling you I am worried I might have to leave London and your response is to say it doesn't matter? Would you even miss me?'

Rose turned too, confused. 'Of course I'd miss you. What's this about?'

'Never mind.'

Rose put her hand on Kassia's knee and squeezed it. She craned her neck as they emerged onto Samphire Hoe, trying to see the lookouts towering above. She could hardly bear to think about how close she'd come to losing her sister, twice now.

At Ashford, Rose noticed Kassia still hadn't taken her book out of her bag. She watched her hands moving in her lap. Kassia was pressing her nails into the skin on her wrists, one at a time, creating bracelets of half-moon indentations. The rest of her was still and seemingly calm, but the force with which she was pressing into the skin frightened Rose. She circled Kassia's wrist with her thumb and forefinger, covering the red marks.

'Stop it.'

Kassia pulled her hands away, blinking. Rose wondered if she'd even realized what she was doing.

'What's wrong?'

Kassia looked out the opposite window as they pulled out of the station.

'Kassia, are you okay?'

She shook her head and Rose saw tears welling in her eyes. Kassia tried to blink them away, but one rolled down her cheek into the collar of her dress.

Conscious of the family settling in the four-seater in front of them and the girl with the backpack across the aisle, Rose said, 'What's going on?'

Kassia broke eye contact to study the pattern on the back of the seats. 'I feel like I am not important to you.'

Rose let out a breath she hadn't known she was holding. For a moment she'd thought something was really wrong.

'I am convenient to have around, but not a priority.'

'What are you talking about? I just took you to meet my family.'

'You introduced me as your friend. You do not care if I have to leave.'

Rose swallowed. 'Obviously I care. But what can I do about it?'

'You can have an emotional reaction.'

Rose glanced around. She felt lost. 'I'm sorry for calling you my friend.'

'It is not only that. I know it is only little things, but they add up. Like laughing when Jude said we might have to get married.'

Rose snorted. 'Come on, we've only known each other a few months!'

'That is not the point. You treated even the idea like a complete joke. You made me feel stupid.'

Rose pinched the top of her nose. 'I didn't mean to.'

Kassia sighed. 'I don't want to marry you, Rose, but I told you before I do want more than someone to have fun with.'

'Me too.'

'Are you sure?'

'Of course,' Rose said. She meant it, she thought, but there was something scary about the intensity with which Kassia was looking at her. She wanted to tell her to calm down, not to worry, not to make them have this conversation right now. She didn't know how to tell her that this was as sure as she'd ever felt, but that she'd never taken anyone home before, never held hands with someone in front of her sister, never cared so much about what other people saw when they looked at them together.

'It is like I am swimming in the deep end while you have only dipped one toe in the shallow pool.' Kassia's pupils darted between Rose's as she spoke. 'I do not need you to dive straight in with me, but I do need you to get in the water. I need to know you want to reach the deep end one day. If all you want is a relationship in the shallow end, then I wish you would be honest.'

They were drawing in to London Bridge. Rose handed Kassia her bag from the overhead luggage rack. She tried to take her hand on the platform, but Kassia pulled away.

'I want to go home alone.'

'Kash, don't be like this.'

'I value love, Rose. It is important to me. Maybe the most important thing there is. Perhaps that means I am some hopeless romantic, but this is how I am.'

Rose scratched the back of her hand. They hadn't mentioned the word before.

'The way you treat me sometimes, it is like you do not have space for a girlfriend. And I have to ask whether that is

219

about you not wanting to let anyone in or just not wanting to let me in.'

'It's not you.'

'I deserve to be with someone who wants to call me her girlfriend.'

'I'll get better. I promise.'

Kassia shook her head.

'Kash, I'm sorry. I'm going through something at the moment. I'm worried about Cali—'

'Rose, I know Cali's been through a lot, but caring for one person does not have to mean you close everyone else out. She's got your mum, she's got Jude. You need to worry about yourself sometimes too.'

Rose knew what she was meant to do. She was meant to go home and figure out a way to convince Kassia she was serious. She was meant to buy flowers and send a long email expressing her honest feelings. Almost as soon as they said goodbye, though, she felt like a weight had been lifted from her chest. The air felt heavy in her lungs when she thought about Kassia and all the ways she was disappointing her. It was easier not to think about her at all. Easier to step across the platform onto her train and pull out her phone. Easier to call her sister, hoping for a laugh and a chat; and when that didn't work, when Cali's phone rang and rang until it went to voicemail, it was easier to send Diego a message and head out for a drink.

# 2026

'The great majority of councillors have voted in favour and therefore, on 6th May 2026, I declare Councillor Judith Campbell duly elected the Town Mayor of Dover.'

The crowd claps politely and Tarek finds himself rising to watch Jude receive a fur-trimmed robe and a weighty chain of office. He almost laughed when she told him she was running for mayor. It sounded like such an antiquated role. His picture of a mayor was a fat old man wearing a shiny necklace, not someone like Jude. When he looked it up, though, he discovered that while the position of mayor is chiefly a representative role, he or she is also the chairman of the town council. He didn't have to spend four days with Jude to realize how ambitious she is, so he can see how this might be part of a larger plan.

She's asked to read a declaration, then begins a gushing thank-you speech. The other thing he learnt when he looked it up was that both Dover Council and the mayorship have spent the past few years trying to rebuild their reputation after a series of scandals involving drugs, blackmail and questionable spending. He forwarded that article to his boss, citing it as proof that the biggest secrets lie in the sleepiest of places.

He looks around now. The audience is mostly white, mostly middle-aged, and Jude has their rapt attention.

'Should get the green light on reopening the detention centre now, at least,' whispers a woman to Tarek's left as Jude wraps up.

Her neighbour hums in agreement. 'About bloody time.'

There's more clapping and music and the crowd is invited to join the council for a reception in another room. A hand on Tarek's shoulder makes him jump. He turns to see the woman from the card shop, the one with the greying bob who smiled in sympathy earlier, holding out his jacket.

'It slipped off the chair,' she says with a smile.

'Thanks,' Tarek says, taking it from her.

'She won then?' Gary says when Tarek joins him in the pub. He places his drink on a cardboard coaster and sits down. The wall next to their table is scrawled with marker pen, writing sweeping up to the ceiling, engulfing every surface.

'Everyone that's swum the Channel,' Gary says, seeing him look. 'I had to ask the barmaid. See this?' He points to a scrawl near the light fitting that reads: *Eva Lombardi – female world record holder. 6 hours, 59 minutes, 18th August 2023.*

'Right,' Tarek says, glancing between the walls and the ruddy-faced drinkers around them. He thinks about the difference between swimming the Channel to be greeted by a pint, and wading out of the Mediterranean – dehydrated, exhausted, scared beyond your wildest nightmares – only to be told you're not welcome. He takes a sip of his Coke and tries to shift his thoughts to something more suited to dinner with his colleague.

After they've eaten Gary asks him to stay for a nightcap, but Tarek makes his excuses and heads outside to call Helen. She picks up after one ring. Tarek smiles at the sound of her voice. His entire life he's suffered from anxiety. Even as a teenager, he found his heart racing and his breath catching in the middle of a seemingly normal day. *You have an overactive imagination*, his father told him. *You think too much*, his first girlfriend laughed. In the first few months of dating

Helen, though, he noticed a sensation he'd never felt before. When he was with her, his thoughts slowed to a normal pace. He stopped waking in the night worrying about what he had to do or needing to make lists of things to check.

He tries to tell her about the bar, about the records on the walls and what they made him think.

'Are you wondering if there's a narrative in there? Something to pitch?'

Tarek presses the button for the pedestrian crossing. 'I don't know. It's strange being here. I keep thinking . . .' He trails off.

'That's natural, darling. I'm not surprised.'

The cars and lorries stop and he crosses the road. It's natural, she thinks, because of what he's been through, because of who he is. Would she think it were natural if she knew why he was really here? If she knew the choices he's made?

'Give yourself a break,' Helen is saying. 'You're human, remember? My best human, but human nonetheless.'

They hang up as Tarek reaches the hotel. He's about to go in, but changes his mind.

*This is stupid*, he thinks half an hour later, shining the torch from his phone along the steep path. He follows it up and around the jut of the cliff, wary of the rusty-looking fence and the drop below. It levels out as he reaches the top and he takes a moment to catch his breath. He swings the light around, taking in the metal barriers cutting off the stretch of grass leading to the edge. Barbed wire is coiled on top, an extra deterrent, though Tarek certainly has no desire to explore closer to the edge. He rests the beam on the large sign reading: SHAKESPEARE CLIFF. Beneath, red letters tell him to keep out, and a crude picture of a falling stickman illustrates the message.

He continues along the trampled track, through a small wooded patch and back out to open grass. The ugly barbed-wire fence continues all the way down and up the steep climb of the next cliff. He isn't prone to fatalistic imaginings, but he wonders what would happen if he tumbled to his death here. How long would it be before someone found him? Gary would miss him in the morning and Helen would worry at some point, but how would they know where to look? He takes a couple of steps inland. He should be in his hotel room going through today's footage, thinking of how to structure tomorrow's filming. He should be taking a shower and getting a decent night's sleep. He should be thinking about how to spoil Helen when he gets back, how to prepare himself for fatherhood.

The light from his phone is trained at his feet, but the glow of the moon is enough to pick out the silhouettes of the first lookouts against the sky. Tarek quickens his pace. He isn't thinking of Helen any more, or their unborn son, of Rose and Jude or Gary and Olga. He thinks only of the lost and frightened teenage girl who walked along this path ten years ago. The girl who sought refuge here.

The barbed wire blocking the staircase of the fourth look-out is thick, but a single coil. These barricades were erected in a hurry, and a fair while ago if the rubbish and weeds are anything to go by. Tarek removes his jacket and wraps it around his hand. He tests his grip against a section of wire and feels a faint pressure against his palm, but no pain. Parts of the wire are wrapped into the weeds growing from the wall and they rip away as he drags the coil noisily up the staircase. He picks his way over the remaining debris and into the structure.

A breeze blows from the long, wide window at the front. He steps into the large central room and walks around, reading the graffiti on the walls. Much is faded, the dates long gone, but he finds a couple from this decade. Someone has been here. Teenagers, perhaps. Local kids, unaware of what happened. He can imagine wanting to explore a place like this. He never told his parents, but after one of the early airstrikes, he and his friends crossed town to see what had happened. They picked their way over the rubble, fascinated by the skeletons of desecrated buildings, too young to comprehend what they meant about their own mortality.

He makes his way to one of the back rooms and tries to imagine making a shelter here. He slept in worse places back then, for sure. This room is shielded from the breeze, especially in the corner there. With Jude's camping equipment, it mightn't have been so bad. Did she sit here at night reading books and listening to podcasts? he wonders. Was she afraid?

*Don't trust anyone,* he told Inji as he pressed her body to his for the final time.

He was meant to be right behind her, a few days at most. He hadn't told her that he'd used all their money to get her on that truck. She knew the price of the normal fee, knew they were short of the amount for two. But he'd told her he only needed to find another couple of hundred euros, that he'd call their parents and get them to send it, that he'd join her as soon as it arrived. The truth was he needed almost two thousand, and even if their parents had that kind of money, Tarek could not admit why he needed it. They'd never forgive him for sending Inji alone, never understand the difficulty of the decision he was faced with. To stay together, in a camp that was falling apart and being threatened with demolition, where kids were going missing, girls were heard screaming and the authorities were more likely to confiscate your phone and your shoes than do anything to help. Or to chance the journey separately.

225

Inji refused to leave him to stay in Salam, the protected area for women and children, so they'd found a spot in the main camp, where almost all of the faces they saw were male. The few women who were there kept out of sight. A week ago, a young Eritrean man had run screaming through their section of the camp, pulling at people's clothes, beating his breast. When finally someone had managed to translate, Tarek learnt the man's wife had disappeared, that she'd been seen being pushed into a car with several other women and driven off. The next morning, Inji told him one of the friends she'd made had a bandaged arm from where the police had beaten her. This was no place for a teenage girl, he realized.

He knew it was risky, that was why he'd spent the rest of their money paying another passenger for Inji's protection. He'd heard stories about girls her age making the journey alone. He knew not to trust the smugglers. He'd watched the crowd as it assembled before midnight and picked out a man with his arm around his wife. While Inji had fiddled with her backpack, checking she had her documents and their father's cousin's address, he'd stepped over to the couple and spoken rapidly in Arabic. The man was a doctor, he learnt. His wife was pregnant. Tarek was pleased with his instincts. *Help my sister,* he pleaded. *Keep her safe, get her to England.* Then he thrust all the euros he had left into the man's palm.

*Inji,* he called, beckoning his sister over. *This is Nizar and his wife Sara. They're from Atarib. Stick with them, yeah?*

His sister gave him a look, but smiled at the strangers.

*Don't show anyone your papers,* he whispered as they embraced. They'd managed to avoid being registered in any of the countries they'd passed through. Their only chance of claiming asylum in England rested on nobody being able to prove they'd already entered Europe somewhere else. He'd heard stories of people getting across the Channel only to be discreetly shipped back to Calais. *Don't tell anyone who you are or where you're from. Not until you get there, okay?*

*Don't let her go!* he heard his father's voice in his head.

*I have to, baba. I have to.*

'I had to,' he says on top of the cliff now. He'd talked to everyone he could. No one could give him a price from Calais to England for the both of them that he could afford, and there was no way he was going to let Inji risk her life on the motorway. As long as he could make sure she got there safely, he was sure he could find a way to follow.

He looks around the small concrete room. 'I did what I thought was right,' he murmurs to the grime-covered walls.

Inji's face comes to him. *Brother,* she said as they sat waiting in the car park, her cheeks glistening in the moonlight. She was crying, he realized. *Do you believe in Paradise?*

Inji never spoke like this. Their parents had encouraged each of their children to find their own way. Adnan and Khalid had, but Tarek and Inji had grown up on YouTube. They'd learnt to question things. Tarek was not an atheist, but he wasn't sure yet what place religion had in his life.

Inji's knees were curled up to her chest. Tarek moved towards her. She shook beneath his touch. He wished their mother was there. He wished he knew what to do.

*I saw her die,* Inji said.

He frowned. *Who?*

She looked up at him, tears streaming down her face. *Mo.*

Tarek felt a pebble drop from his throat to his stomach. The explosion at the school had happened while he was being held for protesting, and all his mother had told him when he was released was that seven of Inji's classmates had been killed. Inji herself hadn't wanted to talk. Their entire journey together, she hadn't mentioned anything to do with home. He'd chalked it up to shock. He'd assumed Mo and her family had also left, found a way out through Turkey or Lebanon, heading for Macedonia or Greece. It hadn't occurred to him that she could have been one of the seven. His mother hadn't told him his sister had watched her best friend die. Rage bubbled suddenly at both of his parents. How could they have sent their daughter away like this?

Tarek rubbed Inji's back as she cried. He looked at the men and women around them. Sara was laid out on the tarmac, her head resting on a bag, one arm placed protectively over her stomach. Nizar smiled at Tarek. He looked nervous.

The crowd began to move. Someone was telling them to get up. *Hurry!* shouted one of the organizers.

Inji lifted her head. Her face was red and swollen. *I want to stay*, she whispered.

Tarek looked around. *Come on.*

*Don't make me go*, she said, a little louder.

*Inji*, he pleaded. Nizar was helping Sara to her feet. The message was going around that the truck was on its way. There was no time. He pulled Inji up.

*Please. Let us go together.*

*It's for the best,* Tarek said. He couldn't look her in the face. He waved to Nizar and started towards him, dragging Inji by the wrist.

*No!* she shouted. *I don't want to leave.*

Heads turned in their direction. *Keep quiet*, Tarek said, afraid the smugglers would refuse to take her.

Inji planted her feet and pulled back against his grip. *I won't go without you.*

Tarek spun round to face his sister. *Grow up*, he hissed. Before he'd thought about it, he'd grabbed her shoulders and shaken her back and forth. Those around them carried on collecting their things. They were being ushered to the edge of the car park.

He locked eyes with Inji, trying not to see the fear on her face. He had to make her understand. *You are not a child any more*, he said. *This is not a game. You need to go with these people. You need to pay attention to what's happening and you need to get to Manchester. Understand me?*

Inji let out a sob.

*Stop being a baby. Everyone here has lost someone. What do you think makes you so special?*

She twisted from his grip and picked up her bag.

*I hate you*, she said as she turned to follow the others. *I will never forgive you for this.* Tarek watched her catch up with Nizar and Sara. He wanted to run after her. He wanted to tell her to come back, that they'd find another way. He'd spent weeks trying to find another way, though. This was the only option. He'd fix everything when they both got to Manchester. For now, he had to let her go.

Tarek leans against the wall and sinks to the floor. He presses his palms to the cold concrete. He sent Inji across the Channel all on her own, knowing she was grieving for her best friend. He told her not to tell anyone who she was. The truck she was on was meant to go to Birmingham, but he's spent years searching and there's no trace of her there. Jude said they found Mo on the cliffs at the end of January, which means the dates match up. If for some reason Inji got off in Dover, if she ran away from a riot in the town and met two girls who wanted to help, if she gave the first name that came to her head, then that means his sister spent a month and a half living in this shelter.

Tarek lets out a sob. She spent a month and a half up here, and the worst part is he can imagine this might have felt like the safest part of her journey. For Inji, this might have felt like home.

# THE FALL

# GREEN CERTIFICATE ON WOODEN TABLE

Pan from left to right.

| DATE | NAME | SEX | AGE | OCCUPATION | CAUSE OF DEATH |
|---|---|---|---|---|---|
| *Fifteenth day of May, 2016* | *Cali Jennifer Walker* | *Female* | *16 years* | *Student. (Minor)* | *Subdural haematoma. Cranial trauma.* |

ZOOM OUT TO.

Royal Coat of Arms, encircled by text:

**CERTIFIED COPY**
**GENERAL REGISTER OFFICE. ENGLAND.**

CUT TO.

# JUDE'S FLAT

Jude stares out of the window, tears in her eyes.

CUT TO.

# CONFERENCE ROOM

Rose blows her nose.

(off-screen)

Would you like a break?

ROSE

(shakes head.)

I'm okay.

INTERVIEWER
(off-screen)

Are you sure?

ROSE

(nods.)

I remember the 15th May because I rang Kassia that morning.

(scratches the side of her head.)

We hadn't spoken in weeks. I didn't know what to say. Except sorry. And that I missed her.

CUT TO.

JUDE

I stayed at Cali's the night before.

(touches cheek.)

We were revising for our exams.

CUT TO.

ROSE

We talked for almost two hours. I told her the last thing I wanted to do was hurt her. I told her I wanted to get better at this.

When I think about what my sister was going through while I—

(looks away.)

CUT TO.

JUDE

(sobbing.)

I'm sorry. It's just so painful. I don't know if I can talk about this.

CUT TO.

ROSE

I thought things were going well, but then I said this thing. I told Kassia I didn't want to make her feel bad but that sometimes everything felt like too much.

Too much? she said and I could hear the hurt. I was getting it wrong again.

(nostrils flare.)

I had no idea then what too much was. No clue at all.

# THEN

'Let's go meet the boys,' Cali said. She was lying on Jude's bed, her phone in the air.

Jude looked up from her book, remembering the feel of Bobby's hands on her skin. 'Our first exam's on Tuesday,' she said. They'd been on study leave since the beginning of the week and all Cali had wanted to look at so far was English and Art, so they really did need to revise.

Cali pulled a face. 'How sharper than a serpent's tooth it is to have a thankless child.'

Jude rolled her eyes. 'Nothing can come of nothing, though, right?' she said, returning to her Biology revision guide and leaning back against the wardrobe. 'Okay, by which two processes does glucose enter cells in the human body?'

'Fuck's sake, how does it even matter?'

Cali stood up and began to pace around the room, picking things up and putting them down.

'It matters until Tuesday morning, that's all. Then we can forget about it forever.'

Cali flicked the pages of Jude's copy of *King Lear* then threw it to the floor. 'I don't care about Biology, I don't care about *any* of this. What's the point when Mo—'

'We need snacks!' Jude said, getting to her feet. Cali had been in a foul mood all week, moping about and murmuring that she couldn't stop worrying about Mo. Jude was getting sick of it. Downstairs she pressed two lemonade cans between her arm and her stomach, and picked up two bags of crisps and a packet of biscuits. She carried her haul upstairs and placed it on the carpet. Cali was fiddling with something on the bookshelf.

'What's this?'

'What?'

'This,' Cali said, turning around. She held a blue notebook in her hand. Jude looked at the pattern of stars on the front. The spine was cracked and the cover sagged where she'd torn out Mo's entries.

'Nothing,' she said. 'An old notebook.'

'Like the one you gave Mo.'

Jude felt a tightness in her chest. 'Is it? Yeah, I got given two for Christmas. That's why I gave her the spare.'

Cali studied her. 'What about this?' She fanned the notebook's remaining pages, revealing the fifty-pound notes Jude had slid between the sheets. Two fell out and fluttered to the floor.

'My savings,' Jude said as levelly as she could.

'Your savings?'

'From work.'

'You did not get paid in fifties for waitressing last summer. And how the fuck do you have so much?'

'I got it changed.'

Cali raised her eyebrows. 'You're a shit liar. Where the fuck did you get all this money?'

Jude tried to match Cali's stare. 'All right, but you have to promise not to tell anyone.'

Cali waited.

'I found it.'

'You what?'

'Basically.'

'Where?'

Jude swallowed. 'At Bobby's house.'

'You stole this from Bobby? Fuck. He said he got in major shit after the party. Is this why?'

Jude's cheeks were burning. She felt out of control, but also strangely exhilarated. She'd hated keeping all this from Cali.

'You little thief!' Cali said.

Jude couldn't tell if she was angry or impressed. She took a breath. 'There's something I didn't tell you about that night.'

'How much is here?' Cali said, pulling the notes out and counting. 'There must be—'

'Five hundred. I—'

Cali looked up. 'That's basically what Mo needed.'

'That's why I took it,' Jude said honestly.

'But you didn't give it to her.'

'I-I didn't get the chance.'

Cali narrowed her eyes. 'What are you going to do with it now?'

'I was thinking I should donate it. Like to a refugee charity or something. Then I thought it would be useful for our walk. We could split it and give some to charity and—'

'Maybe you should give it back to Bobby.'

Jude blinked. 'You wouldn't say that if you knew.'

'Knew what?'

'The night of the party . . .' Jude began but trailed off, unsure how to describe what had happened.

'What?'

'Bobby, he tried to—'

Cali folded her arms. 'Tried to what?'

'Don't look at me like that.'

'Like what? I'm not looking at you like anything. But you were pretty drunk, you know? He said you tried to kiss him when he was going to sleep and he had to push you off.'

Jude stared at Cali. She couldn't believe she was taking Bobby's side. 'I didn't.'

Cali shrugged. 'You might just not remember. I was so wasted this one time with Kev that I woke up and freaked out that we hadn't used a condom. I made him get it out of the bin and show me. It was gross, but I had literally no recollection.'

Cali sat on the floor and took a bag of crisps. Jude watched as she pulled it open and began to crunch loudly. After a while, Jude sat too and reopened the Biology book. She flipped to the end of the next module and tried to concentrate on questions about stem cells and plant reproduction rather than the sick feeling simmering in her stomach.

Cali finished her crisps, then kicked Jude's foot. 'Want to sleep up on the cliffs again this weekend?'

They hadn't been up there since the fire. Jude had missed their walks, but she'd been trying to be sensitive to Cali's needs. 'Why now?' she said.

Cali was tucking the fifty-pound notes back into the half-ripped notebook. She stood up and put it back on the shelf. 'We need to practise for the summer, don't we?'

'I suppose.'

Cali turned around to face Jude. 'You scared?'

'Of course not. What's there to be scared of?'


As she approached the lookouts on Saturday evening, Jude began to worry Cali might have invited the boys. She'd wanted to walk together, but Cali had insisted they meet up there. What if she thought she could stage an intervention and get Jude and Bobby to make up? What if they all stood there telling her she'd imagined what he did?

An old piece of police tape flapped in the breeze beside the first lookout with an A4 notice taped to it:

Kent Police are aware of illegal activities taking place in this area and are conducting regular patrols.

Jude narrowed her eyes. That better not be true. Her parents would kill her if they found out she was spending the night up here.

She checked the first three lookouts, but found them empty. Her dad had told her the council was talking about pulling the fourth one down because the fire had damaged the structure and they were worried it might collapse and fall on the railway tracks below. His position – as representative at the meeting for the Grand Shaft Preservation Society, for which he was Volunteer Coordinator – was that such a thing would be a tragedy. The situation had reignited the larger debate about what to do with all the clifftop buildings. The National Trust had weighed in that the sites had historic value and needed to be protected, but plenty of others saw them as dangerous eyesores and were using the fire as proof that they encouraged illicit behaviour.

Whether or not it was structurally sound, Jude wasn't especially keen to re-enter Mo's former home. 'Cal?' she shouted from the top step.

There was no answer. Reluctantly, she ducked under the caution tape and descended the stairs. She hesitated at the door and touched her hand to the charred wall, rubbing at the brick until she uncovered Cali's grim reaper.

Inside, the smell hit her first. She was surprised it could have lingered in a place so open to the elements. She looked at the black walls of the main room and wondered what it must have been like for Cali running into the flames. She felt a wave of nausea. A circular chunk of metal was all that was left of the camping stove.

The scent of burnt rubber and plastic was worse in the

back room. Where the sleeping bags and airbed had been was now a mess of shrivelled black and orange lumps. The rest of the room was littered with burnt objects, things she could and couldn't identify. She kicked her feet through the debris, marvelling at how actual things could disappear into ash and air. She still hadn't figured out what she'd do when her parents noticed the things missing from the garage. She had time to figure it out, she kept telling herself.

Something glinting by the window caught her eye. She bent to pick it up, recognizing its shape immediately. In her hand she held half a heart. The loop where it should have been connected to its keyring was twisted and bent. Jude rubbed her finger over the back of it, thinking there was something magical about this being the one thing to have survived the fire. She didn't even mind that Cali had lost it.

But she turned it over and felt her skin prickle. She slid her backpack from her shoulder and fumbled to reach the side zip, but all she found was the empty chain of the keyring. The heart in her hand was hers.

'What you got there?' Cali said, making Jude jump.

'Nothing.' She turned around and slipped it into her pocket, trying to remember when she'd last noticed it on her bag. It could have fallen off anytime, she reasoned, it wasn't necessarily the day of the fire. Nevertheless, her cheeks felt warm under Cali's gaze. 'It's pretty grim in here,' she said as lightly as she could.

Cali shrugged. 'More pleasant than my last visit.'

Jude tried to return Cali's smile, but there was something about the way she was standing that made her uneasy.

'What did you just put in your pocket?'

'Nothing.'

'Seriously, what was it?'

'It doesn't matter.'

'Then it doesn't matter to tell me.'

Cali made a lunge for Jude's pocket. Jude stepped back, tripping over a lump of shrivelled plastic and causing a cloud of ash to rise. She coughed. She was standing in the very centre of the small room and the smell was overwhelming. She tried to step forwards, but Cali blocked the door.

'Let me out.'

Cali didn't budge. 'I thought you loved these buildings.'

'Come on, Cal.'

Cali folded her arms. 'You know what I realized we haven't done in a while?' Jude watched as she reached around to her own backpack and unclipped her keyring from the strap. 'What do you say, Best Bitch?'

Jude opened her mouth, but no sound came out.

Cali smiled. 'It's on your bag, isn't it? Get it out. How does the rhyme go? We're like sisters, we're like twins, we do everything together . . .' Cali nodded for Jude to continue. 'Go on!'

Jude's tongue felt sandpaper dry. 'I, uh, promise you . . .'

'My best friend . . .'

'We'll stay—'

'Bitches forever!' Cali shouted. 'Come on, Jude, where's your keyring?'

Jude swallowed. 'I lost it.'

'Really? When? Where?'

'I'm not sure.'

'You're lying. I know it's in your pocket.'

Jude felt the shock of being caught out, but recovered quickly. 'Why the fuck are you grilling me then? I lost it here one time when we were visiting Mo, obviously. I just found—' Suddenly it occurred to her that she hadn't even had her bag with her the day of the fire. She'd come straight from Bobby's house and she hadn't gone home. Her shoulders relaxed.

'So why did you hide it? Why do you look so guilty?'

Jude shrugged. 'I don't.'

Cali shook her head. 'You didn't lose it.'

'It was on the floor.'

'I know,' Cali said slowly. 'I put it there.'

Jude frowned.

'I took it off your bag the other day and I put it on the floor tonight.'

Jude felt the prickle of sweat around her collar and under her armpits. 'Why?'

'To see what you'd do.'

Jude tried to laugh. 'You're crazy.'

'I'm actually starting to think you are.'

'Come on, Cal,' Jude said, working to keep her voice light. 'What's going on? Let's get out of here.'

Cali stood in the doorway, the keyring still dangling from her hand. 'I had this thought when we were revising in your room and it scared me because I thought there was no way what I was thinking could be true. You're my best friend and if it was, that would mean—' She paused, shaking her head. 'I couldn't even think about what it would mean. But you know how something gets stuck in your head and it won't go away? So I thought I should check.'

'Check what?' Jude said slowly. 'What are you on about?'

'Check what you did if you found something of yours here.' Cali raised her eyebrows. 'Something you might have dropped when you started the fire.'

Jude's mouth fell open. 'I—'

'You gonna deny it?'

'Of course I am,' Jude said. 'How can you say something like that?'

Cali took a step into the room. 'I went to your house tonight and told your mum I'd left my Biology book in your room. She let me run up there to find it. You've got literally no idea how nice your family is, do you? How much I used to wish I could be part of it.'

Jude's chest tightened. She backed up until her rucksack bumped against the wall. Her knees felt weak.

'I didn't know what I was looking for. Maybe the money was all you were hiding, I told myself. But maybe it wasn't.'

'Cal,' Jude said.

'What?'

'I can—'

'Explain?' Cali laughed. 'Yeah, I'm sure you can.' She reached into her bag and pulled out the brown envelope containing Mo's photographs and phone. 'I'm sure you've got a perfectly worked out excuse as to why all this was in your desk drawer.'

Jude heard a rushing in her ears. She sank to the floor.

'I know the truth, Jude. You stole Mo's stuff and started the fire.'

The smell of burnt plastic made Jude want to hurl. 'How can you believe that?' she said weakly.

Cali rolled up her left sleeve. 'This is your fault, you know?'

Jude stared up at her friend, searching for the words to make her understand. The silence was unbearable. 'I didn't mean for you to get hurt.'

Cali took a step back. 'What about Mo?'

Jude shook her head. 'I just wanted her to leave.'

Cali dropped her bag to the ground. 'What is *wrong* with you? Mo needed us. She had nothing, and everything she did have you fucking took from her.' She started pacing, the envelope still in her hand.

Jude followed her back and forth with her eyes. 'All I wanted was to scare her, give her a reason to move on. I didn't realize—How could I have known you were on your way back? That you would—'

'It's ridiculous,' Cali said, cutting her off. 'You were jealous of a girl with nothing.'

Jude sniffed. 'What did I have to be jealous of?'

'Exactly. A girl who lost her home, her family, her friends. Everything. We were trying to give her a little bit of comfort – a sleeping bag and a fucking airbed, as if that was in some way going to make anything better. But you couldn't even let her have that.'

'I *wasn't* jealous,' Jude said.

Cali stopped pacing and planted her feet in front of her. 'Then why did you do it? Why were you *so* desperate to get rid of her?'

When Jude failed to answer, Cali picked up her bag and walked into the main room. Jude scrambled to her feet to follow. She watched Cali pull her cigarettes and a lighter from her pocket. She lit one and inhaled, long and slow, then turned back and blew a cloud of smoke between them.

'Mo thought you fancied me.'

Jude tried to laugh. 'That's crazy.'

Cali's face was in shadow, but the whites of her eyes glowed.

'I don't,' Jude said.

'You sure?' Cali moved forwards, close enough that Jude could smell the smoke and the wine on her breath.

Then she leant in and kissed her.

Jude stepped back. 'I'm not gay!'

'Then what are you? And what do you want from me?'

Cali wiped her mouth and leant to retrieve a half-drunk bottle of red from her bag. It clinked against another.

'I'm your best friend.'

'Wrong!' Cali threw her arms around the blackened room, spilling wine onto the concrete. 'Look what you did here.'

Jude reached out for her. 'I need you. We need each other.'

Cali pulled away.

'We're going to walk the coast.'

'As *if*,' Cali said, shaking her head. 'That was never going to happen. You like planning adventures because they make you feel exciting. But the truth is when something real happens in your life – when someone who actually needed our help turned up, you got all chicken-shit that you might have to make some real sacrifices.'

'That's not true.'

'It's why you think you need me, to prove you're not just exactly who you are: perfect, boring Jude who's going to have a perfectly boring, perfectly perfect life. You have no idea what it's like to feel trapped, to feel like you need to escape.'

'Cal, I'm your friend.'

Cali shook her head. 'Have you noticed you want to be my friend most when my life is falling apart? The worse everything is for me, the better a friend you get to feel.'

'How can you say that?'

'I think that's why you went along with things with Mo to begin with. Because her life was so shitty you could feed on her drama. But when you realized it wasn't *you* she needed, *you* she was confiding in, then you couldn't stand it, could you?'

Cali drained the rest of the wine. 'Don't look like that. I'm not gonna shop you to the police or anything, am I? Even if it's what you deserve. A nice little arson conviction on your record would really help with those university applications, wouldn't it? To think I defended you. Every time my sister called you a spoilt brat, I told her she was wrong, that she couldn't see the real you. But it was me that was blind, wasn't it?'

'Please—' Jude reached for Cali's hand, but she yanked it away.

'I've had enough, Jude. You need to forget about me. Go to college, go to university, meet a nice boy. Or girl, I don't care. Just get it out of your head that either Mo or I or anyone ever wanted you to step in and save us.'

'You can't throw away everything we've been through. I won't let you.'

Cali hurled the wine bottle at the floor, making Jude jump. 'Fuck off telling me what I can and can't do!'

Jude sank to the ground. She was on her knees, reaching for Cali's feet. 'I need you.'

Cali stepped away. 'You gave me third-degree burns, you psycho.'

'Please,' Jude said. She looked around, her eyes blurred with tears. Her gaze fell on a long shard of the broken bottle. She picked it up and pressed it into her palm, welcoming the pain. 'I'll make it up to you,' she said, holding it up to her cheek.

'What the fuck are you doing?'

Jude stared at Cali, unblinking. 'I'm sorry. About your arm, about everything. I didn't mean it. I'll prove to you how sorry I am.' She drew the glass across her face and a dark line appeared against her pale skin. Blood trickled down her chin and neck, soaking her shirt. 'A scar for a scar.'

'You're crazy,' Cali whispered.

'Forgive me, Cali. I need you to forgive me.'

Cali shook her head and turned towards the stairs. 'You don't need to be like this, Jude. There's nothing in your life to make you like this.'

'Wait!'

'No,' Cali said, looking back. 'Don't follow me. I'm sick of you following me. I'm sick of everyone and everything. Just let me go.'

# 2026

A pale light illuminates a triangle of concrete beyond Tarek's freezing feet. He reaches for his phone to check the time. Somehow he dozed off up here.

With difficulty, he stretches out his legs and pushes himself off the ground. His joints crack and his back screams out in pain as he steps into the main room. Beyond the slit-like window, the sun is beginning to rise to his left, a slender golden crescent glittering against the water. Tarek stares, drowsily awed by the quiet majesty of this daily occurrence.

On the concrete ledge in front of him is a small slug. Tarek watches its antennae bob as it makes its slow way forward. Inji once woke him in the night because of a slug. He jumped out of his sleeping bag, his heart racing. He didn't know whether to laugh or to shout at her when he realized the object of her terror. After everything they'd gone through, everything they'd survived, she was afraid of a creature the size of her little finger.

Tarek picked it off the tent and pretended to throw it at her. She took a step back, swearing at him in Arabic then English. The noise woke a neighbour and they were told to calm down.

*Don't kill it*, Inji said, taking a cautious step forward. *Let's set it free over there. Maybe it will find a home.*

That was less than a week before he put her on the truck. He called her phone five times a day, every day, though she never picked up. He asked others to look out for her, to send him a message if they got their good chance and spotted her once they reached England. But hope is hard to cling to when everything is taken from you. A week after she'd gone, Jabir died and so did his plan to follow her via the motorway. The following evening, he returned to his tent, his mind blank, his soul crushed. He emptied his pockets and pulled on the layers which would keep him warm as he slept. He stumbled along the paths to the toilet, past the darkened and glowing tents, hearing the hushed murmurs of the people inside. He was only gone five minutes, but as he stepped back onto the path, he saw a shadow. Someone was in his tent. He broke into a run, shouting something that sounded obscene in the otherwise still suburb. The shadow flinched. A boy – definitely no more than a boy – emerged from the flaps of Tarek's tent. He looked Tarek straight in the eye, then sprinted the other way. Tarek ran after him, darting between tents and alongside makeshift buildings, but the boy was fast. He knew the off-path routes, ducking through tiny openings and jumping obstacles as if they were hurdles. Tarek stumbled and bumped into people queueing for a tap. He'd lost him.

Cursing, he picked his way back to his tent. His sleeping bag was ruffled and pulled inside out. Tarek had known not to keep anything in the bottom, the thief hadn't had it that easy. Except he had. Tarek's phone and wallet had been lying abandoned beneath his jeans. Why hadn't he taken them to the toilet? How could he have been so stupid?

He clicked off the light and crawled out of the tent. He checked no one was around, made his way to the back left corner and lifted the fabric. In the dark, he felt around for the piece of wood he'd placed there and thrust his hand into the hole beneath. Relief flooded through him as his fingers closed over the plastic bag. Back inside the tent, he removed the envelope. There was a list of phone numbers and addresses written on the back. Within, at his mother's insistence, he'd placed photocopies of their passports. He'd also tucked in exactly half of his remaining money. At least the thief hadn't taken everything.

Tarek scanned the list of numbers, trying not to panic. Inji would not be able to contact him now, but she had this same list. He would use some of the money to buy a new phone and leave his number with anyone she might call. Someone would be able to hook him up with something cheap.

He struggled to sleep, haunted by images of Jabir on the asphalt and thoughts that he had done the wrong thing. *I had to, I had to*, he murmured, but saw his parents shaking their heads, horrified by his actions.

He bought a phone the next day and copied out the numbers he needed before returning the envelope to its hiding place. He called his parents, resigned to the fact that he was going to have to admit what he'd done. There was no answer, but he left messages asking them to call. He stared at the children playing in the dust opposite. He tried the other numbers he had. He got through to a university friend, who told him they were struggling to get through from Jordan as well. That evening, his friend called back. He'd spoken to a nurse who worked with Tarek's mother. There had been another barrel bomb attack. Thirteen dead. More injured. He could take comfort, the nurse had told him to tell Tarek, that his mother and father had been together when they died. They'd been trying to help others out of the rubble when another bomb dropped.

Tarek sat rocking in the middle of the path until a volunteer with a nose piercing and a charity T-shirt came and put her arm around him. Was he okay? Did he need help? Why didn't he come with her and have a cup of tea, get some food? She said she wanted to help. Everyone here *wanted* to help, Tarek thought. He followed her, fizzing with anger. Who were these people who travelled here to help? What were they actually doing? Had they helped him keep his family safe? Had they helped him protect his parents? His sister? Had they helped save his home? He sat in their shelter with a mug of their tea in his hands and hated them. He hated everyone in this stinking camp: the Syrians and the Somalis, the Iraqis and the Pakistanis. He hated the children who ran around screaming as if life was a game and the adults whose sobs he heard at night. He hated Jabir for getting hit by that truck, the kid who had stolen his phone, and the adults who had no doubt told him to. He wanted to burn the place. To see all those tents go up in smoke. Then he wanted to lie down in the middle of the flames and burn too. For what was Tarek Zayat's life worth? Absolutely nothing. That's what all this was telling him. What Europe and the UN and all the presidents and prime ministers who didn't want people like him in their countries were telling him. They'd rather he was dead. Better he'd drowned in the Mediterranean than made his way to Calais to pollute this patch of ground.

*We're here if you need someone to talk to,* a woman said, crouching to meet his eye. *We have a couple of counsellors. Would you like me to book you an appointment?*

*Fuck you,* he said. Then louder. *Fuck you! Fuck you! Fuck you!* He threw his mug against the ground, smashing tea on the tarpaulin floor. The woman was knocked back over her heels as he stood up.

*You are not helping! Nobody is helping!* Tarek shouted as he tried to make his way out of the shelter.

Another volunteer stepped in, a man this time. He reached for Tarek's arm, but Tarek shrugged him off. He lashed out, his knuckles connecting with the man's face. He shouted, but Tarek didn't look back. He ran from the volunteers, ran all the way to the edge of the camp, to the wall they'd built to keep them in. Like animals, Tarek thought. He felt like an animal. He felt like tearing flesh from bone, like hunting and howling and destroying anything in his path. But even this fury was about to abandon him. He couldn't hold on to it. Tarek was not a lion, not a hunter or a predator. He was small and worthless and alone. He was a mouse, scurrying unwanted on this earth. A pest. Vermin. To be ignored if he was lucky, exterminated if not. He dropped to his knees and fell forwards. He might have been in prayer if he'd known which way he was facing, if he could have summoned an ounce of faith.

Tarek looks at the slug still inching its way across the ledge, the force of the memory making his legs tremble. Olga has never understood why he won't tell his own story, why he uses his voice only for others. But of everything he's been through, of all the horrors and traumas he's either experienced or witnessed, that day remains his darkest. He didn't need to see bodies or feel blows. It was the realization of the futility that broke him. The futility of trying to travel to safety. The futility of his parents staying to help. The futility of thinking any of them might deserve better. How is he supposed to communicate that? What message can be found there?

He picks his way out of the lookout and heads back along the dewy cliff-path. He uses the last of his phone battery to scroll to the bottom of Cali's folder, to her last post. He watched it earlier, but its significance didn't register. Cali looks out at him now from the dark screen, her face moving up and down as she walks.

'If you're out there,' she says, her voice broken with tears,

'I'm sorry. I failed you. I wanted to help but I got it wrong. I didn't even get to say goodbye.'

Tarek feels dizzy. He kneels on the dewy grass and plays the clip again, then bends forward and places his head between his knees. How many times has he wanted to say those words? How many times has he wished Inji could hear them?

He straightens up and looks at the pink sky. 'Please forgive me,' he says to the sun and the ships bobbing beyond the dock, a half-hearted Fajr prayer. He gets to his feet, ready to make his way back to the hotel. 'Please let today bring me peace.'

'Excuse me,' the night receptionist says sleepily as he passes her desk. 'Are you in room 314?'

He nods, reluctant to enter into conversation. He's impatient to get to his room, to try to get an hour or two's sleep. If he can't he'll have a shower and a coffee, do his best to prepare for the day ahead.

'You left your key in the door,' she says, sliding a white plastic card across the counter. 'Another guest handed it in.'

Tarek reaches into his jacket pocket, but it is empty. 'Thank you,' he says, taking the keycard. He rides the lift up to his floor, puzzled as to how he could have been so absent-minded. He wonders if it was Gary who handed it in and, if so, where he thought Tarek was when he stumbled in from the pub to find him still out.

The lift doors open and Tarek turns left down the corridor towards his room. Then he stops. His door is ajar. He stares at the metal number, a chill tracing his spine.

He taps the bottom of the door with the toe of his trainer and it swings open. He glances in the bathroom, then takes the two steps past the wardrobe into the main room. The faceless figure of his imagination is nowhere to be seen, but his relief is short-lived. Before him is chaos. The TV and chairs are on their sides. The duvet and pillows have been slashed, scattering feathers. Tarek's papers and clothes are strewn over the desk and floor. His suitcase sits end-up on the bed, the contents of the waste-paper bin dumped beside it.

Pulling himself from paralysis, Tarek makes his way to the desk. He roots through the mess until his fingers close around his hard drive and computer. He releases a breath, then turns to look at the room. If not something worth stealing, then what was the person who did this looking for?

# 2026

Rose listens to the whirr of Kassia's electric toothbrush, followed by the splash of water in the sink and the flush of the toilet. She hears the clicks of the bathroom door and the light being turned off. A moment later she feels the tug of the duvet as Kassia gets into bed beside her. It's hours since she messaged to say she was working late. After replying that that was fine, Rose turned off the oven but continued laying the table. They would just eat late, she thought. By ten o'clock, she started to feel stupid. Kassia was clearly avoiding a continuation of their argument. *You okay?* Rose typed out. *Don't wait up*, came Kassia's reply.

She listens for Kassia's breaths to even out, then opens her eyes. Rolling carefully off the edge of the bed, she reaches for her robe and tiptoes out of the room. She doesn't mind the lonely quiet of the early hours, and getting up is better than the alternative. The battle with sleep is one of her least favourite things about being sober.

She makes her way to the bathroom, turns on the taps and pours Kassia's salts into the tub. She glances at the waste basket beside the sink and for a second her thoughts drift to the bottle of rum in the bin outside, but she removes her robe and gets in the bath. She hugs her knees to her chest as the water rises around her ink-stained limbs.

She never wanted tattoos when she was younger, was never drawn to that particular form of rebellion. It's true what they say, though, about it being addictive. Her first sleeve was full in less than a year.

She turns off the taps and lies back. She must have seemed so clueless walking into Castle Tattoos with her virgin skin the day after Cali's funeral. The old man with the rat-tail showed no sign of curiosity when she asked how much it would cost for the words: 'This is the worst.' He instructed her to hold still but said nothing about the tears that rolled down her cheeks as he worked the needle.

Next week it will be ten years since Cali's death. Maybe it's time for a new one. She imagines the scratch and sting, that moment of agonizing, cathartic surrender.

There's a gentle knock and Kassia opens the door. Rose sits up, sending waves towards the taps. Kassia hugs her arms around herself, shivering.

'You want to get in?'

They shuffle their legs and hips until they fit, snugly facing one another in the small bath. Kassia presses her lips together. She looks like she's about to cry. Rose takes her hand and holds it under the water.

Kassia rubs her thumb against Rose's palm. 'I went to the council meeting,' she says. 'Jude's our new mayor.'

Rose frowns, remembering Jude's eerie smile as she waved earlier.

'I spoke to her,' Kassia continues. 'We don't need to worry about what she's said to Tarek. All she's after is a bit of publicity.'

'You didn't have to do that,' Rose says.

Kassia looks up. 'I did, actually. Jude might not be a threat, but that doesn't mean he's not. I'm telling you, baby, Tarek Zayat's not what he seems.'

'How can you know that?'

Kassia looks away. 'You need to trust me on this.'

Rose leans forwards, making the water slosh as she catches

Kassia in an awkward embrace. 'I'm sorry, baby, I hate fighting. Look, why don't you come today?'

'What?'

'Come and watch us filming. You'll meet Tarek, see that he's friendly, that I'm in control.'

There's a flicker of something in Kassia's expression, then it's gone. 'You have no idea what it is like,' she says, cupping Rose's face in her palm. 'How much I would give to keep you safe.'

# THEN

Jude lifted her hand to her cheek. It was cold and wet, but the blood was beginning to thicken. With difficulty she pushed herself up from the concrete. She wasn't sure how long she'd been sitting there, how long since Cali had left. She picked up her backpack and the envelope of Mo's things and made her way out of the lookout. It was darker now, the stars and moon obscured by clouds. She reached in her pocket for her phone and felt the blunt point of the broken keyring. She closed her eyes. A steady rhythm pulsed through her cheek and she was beginning to feel feverish. On the backs of her eyelids suddenly she saw the balloons from Cali's fifth birthday party. She heard a teacher shout for her across their primary school playground, saw Cali's hand etching their names onto a toilet door. She opened her eyes and began walking. The sky felt close, like a blanket wrapped around her cliffs. She searched through teary eyes for the path, her thoughts darting. How could Cali have said those things? How dare she leave like that?

A chime and two short vibrations against her palm told her Cali had posted a story. Jude clicked on the notification. It was a blathering apology. Not to her of course, but Mo. What the actual fuck? What about saying sorry to Jude? What about fourteen years of friendship?

She touched a box at the bottom of the screen and a keyboard appeared, inviting her to type a private reply. She pictured the faces of the skinheads in Margate, heard Bobby's snores as he slept beside her. She remembered the smell of Cali's dog shitting itself in the hallway and the feeling like she was going to be sick after sharing a whole bowl of cake mix. She thought of the pictures on Cali's bedroom wall, and their conversations about Devon and Cornwall and clifftops far away. How could Cali dismiss all of that?

Once she'd finished typing, Jude stumbled forwards. She climbed down and up the steep paths, thinking about the Huguenots and the Vikings, the Romans and the Germans. She felt the violence of history swirling within her as she crested the brow of Shakespeare Cliff.

Then she stopped, freezing in the middle of the path next to the broken sign reading:

WARN
CLIF
EDG

Out on the edge, silhouetted against the glow of the sea, was a figure.

Jude thought of the way Cali clutched her arm every time they walked up the bit by the railings. She'd never seen her so close to the edge before. Cali must have been there for a while, she realized, to have allowed her to catch up. Doing what, she wondered, her thoughts fragmenting. She listened to the wind and her heartbeat, waiting to see what her best friend would do. Cali stood perfectly still. She looked calm, Jude thought. *How dare she be calm after saying all that?* Jude thought about shouting, making her turn, having it out again. Maybe it was her turn to say some things, Cali's turn to listen. But the sight of her best friend frozen on the edge was hypnotic, and Jude found her limbs and her tongue frozen as well.

How long she stood there, she'd always struggle to

remember. When Cali did it, it wasn't with a jump or even a step. It was more like she simply toppled over. Like that baby in the GIF Jude had seen on Mo's phone, the one Cali had sent to make fun of her.

Jude blinked, half expecting to see Cali do it again, and again, on a loop.

Finally, she cried out.

'Cali!' she screamed, every cell in her body waking at once. She darted forwards, past the sign, towards the edge. Cali had stood here just moments ago. Now the clifftop was empty.

'Cal?' Jude said, more softly. Maybe there was a ledge. Maybe Cali was playing a joke, trying to teach her a lesson. 'Stop messing around!'

The clouds moved across the sky and the wind rustled the trees behind Jude. She paused several feet from the edge, scared to go further, scared to look. A minute, two minutes, maybe five minutes passed.

'Come on, Cal,' Jude pleaded. She was shivering, her teeth chattering. She dropped slowly to her knees, placing her palms on the soft ground. A rich, grassy smell filled her nostrils as she lowered herself onto her front and began to inch forwards.

Looking ahead rather than down, she shuffled into position. For all her bravado, she had never looked over the edge of the cliff before, even as a daylight dare. The sea was black before her, only the odd angry breaker glittering against its oily surface. She heard the rhythmic crash of waves hitting the rocks below. She took a deep breath and looked down.

The milky chalk-face glowed in the moonlight. It tumbled rather than fell away, the Bard's pregnant cliff standing proud at the edge of its careless empire. There was no ledge. No grinning Cali waiting to shout 'Boo!' Jude's gaze followed the bracken and uneven rock to the rubble at the base. At first she couldn't see anything. Maybe she'd imagined the whole thing. Her cheek felt numb now in the icy wind, but how much blood had she lost? Could she be delirious? Could Cali be home already, tucked up and alive and still cursing Jude?

No. Because there in the shadows, against the crumbled white boulders, she saw something. A dark leg, the torso hidden from view, but twisted at such an angle that however Jude's mind tried to arrange the rest of Cali's limbs it failed.

Jude thrust herself back, away from the edge. She needed to get off this cliff, she realized. She knelt, then stood up, frantically trying to brush the mud from her clothes. It wouldn't come off. Her chest felt tight and her face throbbed. She needed to clean herself up and inspect the damage to her cheek. She needed to get home.

She turned and placed one foot in front of the other until she was back on the path. She was meant to be staying at Cali's house tonight, she remembered. She'd go there now and wash up, borrow some of Cali's clothes. The back door would likely be open, and if not she could climb on the bin and get in Cali's window like they did that time Jackie locked them out. Tomorrow she'd tell her parents she'd tripped. Over Cali's cat. With a glass in her hand. Yes. She'd tumbled down the stairs, the glass smashing and slicing her face. She pictured the scene over and over as she walked back into Dover, not allowing her brain to stray on to anything else. She heard the smash, felt the bruises. It had happened in the night and she hadn't thought it that bad, so she and Cali had gone to sleep. The cat was fine, a little shaken maybe. She'd cleaned up the mess before Jackie could see. Not that her parents would ask Jackie, they knew what she was like. She'd say it had started hurting in the morning, so she'd decided to come home, that she hadn't wanted to wake Cali. No, Cali hadn't been there when she woke up. Maybe she hadn't been able to sleep and she'd gone to meet Goofy. She'd done that once before when Jude was staying over. They'd had an argument about it. Jude had thought it was rude, but Cali had just shrugged and complained she'd been snoring. That didn't matter now. What mattered was that Jude didn't know where Cali was. She hadn't seen her since last night. She didn't know what mood she was in. She had no idea why Cali might have gone up to the cliffs.

Jude's pulse was almost back to normal by the time she reached the main road. Her mum was going to freak out about her face, she realized as she made her way through the sleeping town. What if she needed stitches? She was lucky it had happened at the weekend, at least. She couldn't miss her first exam.

# 2026

Jude hums as the lift descends to the ground floor. It's only 8 a.m., but she's wearing full make-up and the too-expensive blouse she decided to treat herself to for filming last week. Her civic chain gives the bag in her lap a pleasing weight. She's in a good mood. She makes her way past the mailboxes, out of the building and around the corner to her parking spot. A few metres short of her car, she stops. There on the windshield, hooked beneath the driver's side wiper, is an envelope featuring a blue hotel logo. In scratchy handwriting she recognizes, it reads:

**WE NEED TO TALK**

She sighs. What does Kassia want now?

She snaps it from the windscreen and throws it on the passenger seat while she manoeuvres herself into the car. She's almost tempted to ignore it. To believe her luck has changed and things are finally coming together. She starts the car and pulls out of the car park in the direction of the castle, where she's agreed to meet the photographer from *KentOnline*. Her eyes keep flicking to the passenger seat, though, and by the time she arrives she's worked herself up into a state of panic about what's inside.

*It'll be nothing*, she tells herself as she parks. But whatever it is, she knows she must face it. Having her victory pasted to the homepage of *KentOnline* this afternoon won't mean much if everything else falls apart. She breaks the seal and reaches inside, removing a messy clutch of papers. On top is a yellow Post-it on which Kassia has written:

Tarek Zayat won't stop until he finds the truth.

Jude peels it off and looks at the light green certificate beneath. She reads the words *Certified Copy* and, lower down, Cali's name. Jude traces her fingers over the embossed paper, lingering beneath the *Cause of Death* box. Despite everything, she has not seen this before. She closes her eyes for a moment, willing away the images conjured by the words.

'Get a grip,' she says aloud, opening her eyes. She looks at Kassia's Post-it again. It's characteristically oblique, but she assumes the implication is that these papers are Tarek's. How Kassia came to have them, Jude doesn't want to know. But so what? Does Kassia want her to feel scared because Tarek has a copy of Cali's death certificate? It's hardly surprising that he does. She was happy to answer his questions about Cali's death. She told him exactly what she told Rose and the police ten years ago. She cried as she recalled the date on this certificate and the days that followed; not something she'd planned, but an honest reaction to his probing about the loss of her best friend. It had in fact felt cathartic to talk about it again after all this time, and she has no problem with him using that footage. It's Kassia who's making a drama out of this.

She moves the page aside to reveal another, almost identical certificate. Several of the boxes on this one, however, are stamped *UNKNOWN*. Jude purses her lips as she reads the date. Her eyes scan to the cause of death: *Thoracic spinal fracture and aortic rupture.* Perhaps she should not be shocked by this either, but she crumples a corner of the certificate in her

266

hand. That date and those injuries are too close to home. This could too easily have been her own fate.

Underneath the certificates, is a sheet of lined paper folded in half. Jude opens it to find it covered in biro notes. A small white rectangle is hidden in the crease. She lifts the rectangle. It is thicker and stiffer than the paper, crudely laminated by rows of overlapping Sellotape. She turns it over and a glint of light is reflected in the glossy sheen. Moving it slightly reveals the photocopied face below. A young girl in a hijab stares up at Jude, her features set in a serious passport pose. Jude's hand begins to tremble. She tries to picture the envelope of snapshots in the box beneath her bed. As far as she knows, those are the only photographs that exist. They've lived undisturbed alongside Cali's nail polishes and Pez for almost a decade. The police, the press, they never had photos, never knew what their nameless girl looked like alive.

Jude steadies her hand and focuses on the image. *It can't be*, she thinks, staring at the girl. She's too young. The eyes look different, and the face too full. Nevertheless, her gaze lingers on the mole above the girl's jawline and doubt creeps in.

'Mo,' she says to the silent car, then lets out a low, guttural moan. Everything that has ever gone wrong in her life can be traced back to Mo.

# THE SEARCH

## CONFERENCE ROOM

Rose drinks from a glass of water.

ROSE

My mum rang me on the way to work. I was late and hungover, I almost didn't pick up. Is your sister with you? she said straight away. I'd never heard panic in her voice like that. She told me the school had rung, Cali hadn't turned up for her first exam.

CUT TO.

## JUDE'S FLAT

Jude sits with hands in lap.

JUDE

Rose arrived and I did everything I could to help her out. It was scary, but what's awful is that I didn't really think anything was properly wrong until—

(wipes tear.)

I mean, I just thought Cali had gone off somewhere. I think we all did. None of us thought it was serious.

CUT TO.

ROSE

I knew right away that it was serious. The last time Cali hadn't returned my calls for this long was when she took Mum's lithium. And I know she'd been doing better, but there was no reason for her to miss that exam. I just knew in my bones that something wasn't right.

CUT TO.

JUDE

I thought maybe she didn't want to do the Biology exam, that was all. And she'd be back in a day or two and find the fuss hilarious.

But Rose was really worried. She called the police. I suppose that's when it started to feel real.

CUT TO.

ROSE

It's not like you think it'll be. That's the first thing I learnt.

I'd seen TV dramas where the whole town turned up to help with a search – where people cared about volunteering and helping out. There was a big one filmed around the corner at Broadstairs. I remember Cali wanted to get the train and see if she could be an extra. She had this idea about being spotted in the background and turned into a star.

(looks away.)

CUT TO.

JUDE

I don't think anything can ever prepare you for something like what happened that week. I don't think I'll ever stop processing it.

# THEN

Rose wasn't thinking about TV dramas as she hurried up the hill from the station that Tuesday afternoon. All she was thinking was that she needed to find her sister.

Jackie was dressed and sitting with an ashtray on the front step. Rose searched every room, unsure what exactly she was looking for. After grilling her mum about who she'd contacted, when she'd last seen Cali and what mood she'd been in, Rose crossed the rec and climbed Jude's porch. Her dad answered. He looked confused to see her, but covered with his usual politeness.

'Jude's not here,' he said. 'She's volunteering at the food bank at the church. She'll be back later if you want me to get her to call you.'

Rose shook her head and backed down the steps. Of course Jude was volunteering, she thought. Wouldn't that look perfect on her UCAS application?

'Can I help you?' a woman in a long cardigan asked as Rose pushed through the church doors.

'I'm looking for Jude Campbell.'

'She's out back. Shall I get her for you? Who shall I say it is?'

'A friend,' Rose said, aware she did not sound in the least bit friendly. She caught sight of Jude across the room and shouted her name, causing others to look.

Jude spun to face her. She had a large plaster covering her right cheek. Rose pushed past the woman in the cardigan and headed across the room. 'Have you seen Cali?'

'Excuse me,' a man said, stepping in her way. 'I'm not sure what you're doing, but it's not appropriate for you to come in here shouting.'

Rose tried to get past him, but he gripped her arms. She looked at his little moustache and round glasses. *I'll punch you*, she thought.

'It's okay, Brian,' Jude said, walking up, the half of her face not covered by the plaster smiling warmly at Rose. She led her to the doorway, shielding them from the stares. 'What's up?'

'Have you seen my sister?'

'Not since the weekend. We're on study leave.'

'She's not answering her phone.'

'Oh.' Jude frowned and glanced briefly at something over Rose's shoulder. 'She's probably with Goo—Kev. She asked me to stay over on Saturday and then she buggered off to—'

'She missed her Biology exam,' Rose interrupted.

'Oh.'

Rose narrowed her eyes, surprised that Cali's best friend didn't know she'd bunked an exam.

'I didn't see her,' Jude said quickly, 'but I had to leave straight away to get here.'

'Don't you go in together?'

Jude shrugged. 'Not always. Like I said, she ditched me on Saturday night and we haven't spoken since.'

'What happened to your face?'

Jude touched her fingers to the plaster. 'I fell. Stupid really, I was holding a glass and tripped over the cat and . . .' She trailed off.

Rose raised her eyebrows, but she didn't really care. 'Do you have Kev's number?'

Jude pulled her phone from her back pocket and Rose copied the number into her own. She dialled on the pavement outside the church. Kev picked up on the first ring. He told her he hadn't seen Cali since last Wednesday. He was on a seven-day stretch at work and she'd told him she had to revise, so he hadn't thought it weird that they hadn't spoken in a few days.

A few hours later, Rose sat in her mother's living room staring at two police officers. She hadn't wanted to call them and had been building up to dislike a couple of burly men. Instead, she found herself opposite a woman not much older than herself, with dark brown eyes and a powerful, gym-worked stance. Her partner was a little older, wore glasses and twisted her wedding ring as she spoke. It felt horrible, the four of them cramped in that stuffy room. Rose opened the curtains, but somehow that made it worse.

They asked the questions Rose expected them to ask – when was Cali last seen, her age, height, weight, whether she smoked, did drugs, if there was trouble at home. Rose looked at her mum to answer the last one and Jackie shook her head slowly. Rose wondered what the officers were making of them. Mother unresponsive, sister over-protective.

'Given Cali's recent mental health history, we're going to class her as high risk.'

Rose stared at the carpet.

'Have you checked to see if any of her belongings are missing?'

The younger officer followed Rose into Cali's room and they looked around.

'Her backpack's not here,' Rose said, unsure what she was meant to be looking for.

'How about clothes? Her hairbrush? Make-up?'

Rose opened Cali's wardrobe and scanned the mascaras and eyeliners littered at the base of the mirror propped against the wall. 'Maybe. I don't know.'

They checked in the bathroom. There was a mug by the sink with half a dozen splayed toothbrushes and three upturned, almost empty bottles of shampoo in the shower. Rose had no idea what was Cali's. 'I'm sorry.'

The officers said they'd talk to Cali's friends and put her details around the region.

After they left, Jackie retreated to the sofa bed. Rose heard the chatter of the TV through the walls. She poked around the kitchen to find something for them to eat and discovered two cans of lager she must have left last time. She'd been ignoring messages and calls from Diego all day, but finally braced herself to read them.

> Where are you?
>
> Claire is doing her nut. She's talking about a disciplinary if you don't get here in the next five minutes.
>
> Seriously, you've properly left us in the shit today.
>
> Are you okay?
>
> Call me.
>
> Fuck, Rose, you're really worrying me. Where are you?

*I'm fine*, she typed. *My sister is missing and I had to come back.* Diego replied immediately.

> Rose! I was so worried. ¡Dios mio! you should have called. Claire's taken you off the rota. She says

you're not allowed to work until
you've had a meeting with the
regional manager. She wants me to
get your keys off you.

Tell Claire to suck my dick.

You don't mean that.

I do actually. I quit.

Diego kept typing, asking her questions and pleading with
her to reconsider. He promised to help mediate, but Rose
closed the window and muted her notifications. She took a
plate of food in to her mum, then sat in the kitchen eating
her own. She'd lost both her girlfriend and her job now, but
she felt strangely free. Both were the right decision; the only
way she could be here for Cali.

She put on her jacket and headed out. She wasn't sure what
she was doing really, but she had to do something to help
look for Cali. She walked up to the Western Heights, then to
the bandstand in Pencester Gardens, then back round to the
harbour. Finally she ducked into one of the pubs she used to
drink at as a teenager. She remembered searching the walls
with her mates for weird-sounding names, daring each other
to sneak a cock and balls next to someone's world record.
Tonight, she pushed through to the bar and found herself
staring at Megan Sutcliffe, the clarinet player from two years
below that she'd seen on the app.

'What can I get—oh, I know you from somewhere, don't
I?' Megan gave a frown, clearly struggling to remember why
Rose seemed familiar.

'We went to the same school,' Rose supplied, wondering
which way Megan had swiped.

'Right, oh yeah,' Megan said, though she still looked confused. 'What can I get you?'

Rose ordered a pint of Grasshopper and settled on a bar stool. Megan set it before her, took the money and turned to serve someone else. The pub was quiet, and before long she drifted back to Rose's end of the bar.

'So you still here or just visiting?'

'Um,' Rose said, staring at the dregs of her pint. She didn't feel like making small talk. 'Visiting, I guess.'

'For anything nice?'

Rose hesitated. 'My sister's missing.'

Megan's smile vanished. 'Seriously? Like missing missing or run away?'

'I don't know. I spoke to the police today.'

'Fuck, I'm sorry.' Megan reached across the bar to touch Rose's wrist, holding on for a moment too long.

Rose looked up into her eyes. 'Thanks,' she said, feeling a rising of desire that was instantly replaced by a sick, guilty feeling.

She drained her pint and Megan offered her another on the house. A couple walked in and she left to serve them. After a while she came back to polish glasses. Rose's worry about Cali felt like a persistent drill in the back of her head; it couldn't be drowned out, but the numbing properties of alcohol and inconsequential chat did make it a little more bearable.

She'd just emptied her third glass when an old woman walked into the bar and asked if she wanted to buy a lucky charm. Rose shook her head.

'Come on, love,' the woman said. 'At least take a look.'

Rose looked at the rocks in her hand and chose a black one with a purplish hue. The woman told her they were five pounds each.

'Five pounds?' Rose said and Megan laughed, showing her teeth. The woman gazed at Rose with sad eyes. Rose gave her a note and she moved on to the table of women by the door.

'She got you,' Megan said, catching Rose's eye. 'In every day, she is, must make a fortune.'

Rose pressed the stone into her palm and wondered what it would be like to show that kind of desperation to strangers.

She kept drinking until Megan finished her shift, then followed her up to the staff area. They locked themselves in the stock room and Rose tugged down Megan's jeans. Megan leant up against a shelf of post-mix while Rose clutched her. It wasn't long before she was squeezing her thighs against Rose's ears and telling her she was close. Rose's heart started to pound and her breath caught in her throat. She tried to pull away but Megan pressed her hand against her head. Rose choked and spluttered.

'What the fuck?' Megan said, but Rose was scooting back against the cleaning products, clutching her chest.

'Are you all right?' Megan said, her pubic hair shining with spit.

Rose shook her head. She was gasping, her heart hammering. The drill was grinding into her temples.

'Shit. What do I do?'

Megan pulled up her jeans and fumbled with her zip. Rose tried to focus on her face as she struggled to help her up. Her limbs felt like weights but eventually she stumbled to her feet, leaning on Megan's shoulder as she unlocked the door and led her to the couch in the staff room.

Megan disappeared then and someone else came in to say they'd called an ambulance. Rose was given a paper bag to breathe into. The paramedics arrived and took her blood pressure. They sat with her while her breathing slowed.

'You've had a panic attack,' one of them said. 'Is there

anything you're feeling anxious about? Or something you were doing that could have brought it on?'

Rose shook her head and followed them downstairs, her face burning. They told her she was fine for now, but to get checked out by her GP and think about talking to someone if it happened again. Megan walked her outside and pressed her number into Rose's hand.

'Call me.'

\*

Jude was waiting outside the house when Rose got back. She didn't know if this was a good idea, but it was the best plan she'd managed to come up with.

'I have to show you something,' she said before Rose had even got to the door. Her hands were trembling as she followed Rose into the kitchen and pulled a pale paperback out of her bag. 'You have to see this.'

Rose read the title. 'Jude, I don't—' she slurred.

'It's Cali's copy,' Jude said, cutting her off. 'She left it at my house.'

'Okay,' Rose said. 'Thanks for returning it, but—'

Jude had to bite her tongue not to scream with impatience. She hadn't counted on Rose being wasted. 'Just look,' she said, picking up the book and thumbing through the annotated pages. She cracked the spine and laid it on the counter, pointing to the passage she'd highlighted in yellow earlier this evening.

Rose's eyes followed Jude's finger.

> *There is a cliff, whose high and bending head*
> *Looks fearfully in the confined deep:*
> *Bring me but to the very brim of it,*

282

*And I'll repair the misery thou dost bear*
*With something rich about me. From that place*
*I shall no leading need.*

'All right,' Rose said, clearly not following. She looked as if she might be sick.

'This character's had his eyes plucked out and he wants to die,' Jude said, pointing at the page. 'He's asking to be taken to a cliff so he can jump off.'

Rose frowned. 'So?'

Jude flicked forward a page and pointed to another two lines, this time circled by Cali's own pencil.

*GLOUCESTER: Dost thou know Dover?*
*EDGAR: Ay, master.*

Finally, Rose's expression changed. Jude felt a rush of sweat pool in her armpits.

'She's afraid of heights,' Rose said dumbly.

Jude tried to keep her face neutral. 'It's why it's called Shakespeare Cliff.'

Rose swallowed. 'What do we do?'

'We need to show the police.'

Jude knew she should have told someone earlier, that it was wrong that she hadn't. Each white lie had led to another and now she felt trapped in a sticky, suffocating web, but she was trying to make amends. Short of taking Rose's hand and leading her up to the cliff right now, she didn't know what else to do.

She stood by Rose's side as she made the call to the police, nodded and took the handset when DI Dixon asked to speak to her. She relayed what she'd rehearsed about Cali being obsessed with the play, always quoting lines and refusing to revise anything else. That bit, at least, was true. 'I don't know,' she said when DI Dixon asked if she believed her friend might have acted on the text. 'I'm scared she might have.'

She and Rose stood in silence after DI Dixon hung up, until Jude took charge and went in to tell Jackie.

She returned the next morning to help get them out of the house. In a strange way, now things were happening like this, she did feel a sense of purpose. Perhaps it was better that she hadn't told anyone immediately, that she'd had some time to process her own loss. This way she could fully support Rose and Jackie. Both were in such a state already that she couldn't imagine what the truth would bring.

Jude was expecting tape and cars and a little crowd, even a reporter or two, but when they arrived at Shakespeare Cliff all they found was one police car on the road at the top and two uniformed coppers on the water-side of the railway tracks at the base. The lack of drama felt awful. *Cali's down there!* she wanted to scream. *She deserves more than this!*

'We came to help,' Jackie said after they'd climbed down to join them on the rocky sea defence. It had been dry all morning, but the marbled sky promised another downpour.

'It's not necessary,' one of the officers said, looking at Rose as if she might be able to exert some influence over her mother. Rose stared back, her mouth hanging open like a goldfish. She really was useless, Jude thought.

'Have you found anything yet?' she said, her voice cracking.

The officer shook her head. 'It's cut off from here to Samphire Hoe right now. There's not much we can do on foot until the tide goes out.'

Jude felt a rush of nausea and looked away. Would Cali

even still be there? What if she'd washed out to sea? What if they never found her and Jude was the only one who knew for sure what she'd done? The only one able to grieve?

'You shouldn't be here,' the first officer said, glancing at Jackie who was wandering towards the water. 'If we find anything—'

Jude saw Rose take a breath before approaching her mum. Jackie had been teetering on the edge all morning. Now she called Rose a witch and ran down the concrete steps towards the sea. Water slopped over her shoes and she stopped. Jude felt the eyes of the officers on them. She looked at Jackie and Rose on the water's edge and suddenly it hit her what they were about to learn, what it was going to do to them.

'Come on,' she said, stepping past Rose and into the water. It was freezing, but she tried not to wince. This was the least she could do. She held her hand out to Jackie. 'We need to let them do their jobs. Let's go home.'

'It was awful,' Rose says. 'Not being able to help, not knowing what was to come. Minutes felt like hours, hours felt like years.'

She pauses and Tarek sneaks a look at Kassia, observing her neat greying bob and the crease between her eyebrows. He did a double-take when she walked in with Rose this morning, surprised to recognize the woman from the card shop and the council meeting. 'It's you,' he said and they had a polite laugh about the strangeness of him hearing about her for two days and not realizing they were circling each other's orbits. 'Were you there to support Jude?' he asked about last night's meeting.

'In a way,' Kassia said with a tight-lipped smile.

He isn't against Kassia's presence per se, but it would have been nice to have had some warning. Rose does seem quite animated with her here, though. He's only had to ask two prompt questions all morning, which is a relief because his mind keeps wandering to his trashed room. He should probably have marched down to reception as soon as he saw it, demanded a new room and an explanation as to how someone had been allowed to do that to his. But they would have called the police and he doesn't want them involved. If this was the same person who sent him those notes, then they're trying to scare him. The last thing he wants is to show that they have.

'All we could do was wait,' Rose says, glancing at Kassia. 'Imagining the worst.'

Tarek would be the first to admit he's unrecognizable from the boy he was ten years ago, but even so it's hard to picture this plump woman with her severe frown as the cool PhD student Rose first fell for. He'd like to ask if she'll let him interview her too. Professionally, this is meant to be a clean investigation, an in-depth focus on two perspectives rather than a canvas of everyone's opinions. Privately, however, this morning's events have convinced him he needs to chase all the leads he can find.

He sneaks another look at Kassia. She'd make a tricky interviewee, that's for sure. They made small talk while Gary got Rose mic-ed up, but Kassia was swift at batting his questions back, practised no doubt from her training as a therapist at revealing only what she chooses. In the five minutes they were talking, Tarek found himself discussing Helen and her new poetry collection, their plans for a nursery and his uncertainty about his next project, while Kassia did little more than listen and smile.

She gave no reaction either when Rose recounted the incident in the pub with this Megan woman. She must have known already, he decided, for Rose to have spoken so candidly. She would have had to confess as part of AA, of course. The fourth and ninth steps would have required her to admit the nature of her wrongs and to make amends. She and Kassia were on a break, he gathers, but still, it must have been hurtful. Maybe that's why Kassia's here today, in fact, because she knows the laundry her wife is airing. He glances at his notes, wondering if Megan's still in the area, and if she and Kassia ever met.

He turns his attention back to Rose. They're getting close to what he's here for now and he needs to pay attention. It's a long shot, he knows, but with Jude sticking to her story that she doesn't remember anything and no other witnesses, his last hope is that Rose might know more than she realizes about the night of her sister's funeral. He needs to know what happened that night in the Grand Shaft – why Jude fell, and the girl they knew as Mo lost her life. He's almost certain now that she was his sister. After seeing the lookout, sensing her presence, he can feel it in his soul. Maybe Rose saw or heard something earlier in the day, or maybe she discovered some detail later amongst Cali's things that will help him slot the pieces together. If she can shed any light at all on how and why Inji died, then this will all be worth it.

His phone vibrates against his thigh and Gary scowls at the noise. It'll be Helen asking how his day is, telling him she's looking forward to his return. He nods at what Rose is saying, but what he really wants is to withdraw to the small, comforting world of his wife. He's exhausted and disturbed by what happened in the night, but he knows that's not all that's going on. As much as he wants Rose to open up and tell him she knows exactly what happened, to answer every question he has about his sister's last hours and to disprove the ridiculous theories he knows can't be true that she was blackmailing and trying to kill Jude, a part of him is also terrified she might do exactly that. The loss and guilt and hope he has felt for Inji for the past ten years has been such a driving force, such a defining feature of his identity, that he doesn't know what will be left if he actually finds an answer.

'Can we take a break?' Rose says, answering his prayers. It's a request today rather than a demand like yesterday. She's like a child on best behaviour with Kassia here, he thinks.

'Twenty?'

Gary removes his headphones and goes to unclip Rose from her microphone. Kassia remains seated until Rose is sorted, then the two of them walk silently from the room.

'Wife's a bit of a cold fish, isn't she?' Gary says, laughing.

He checks if Tarek wants anything, then leaves in search of coffee.

Tarek wanders into the hallway too, making sure to lock up the room. He reads Helen's message and sends a reply, then heads through the lobby towards the back door. He nods at Gary waiting to order at the bar. Rose is scrolling through her phone in a chair by the window. Tarek thinks again of his trashed room. Who knows what he's doing here? The hotel staff, the Kent Police officers he first got in contact with, the people processing his application at the Missing Persons Unit, the volunteer who let them in to film at the Grand Shaft, Gary, Olga ... That's it, apart from anyone Rose and Jude might have told.

A couple hurries in from outside and Tarek holds the inner door for them before stepping through. The outer door is swinging shut behind them and he has his hand on the metal plate, ready to push it back open, when he hears a familiar voice outside. He lets the door fall not quite shut against his palm and looks through the gap. Kassia stands on the pavement with her back to him, her phone pressed to her ear.

'Jude, I told you I would look into it and that's what I did,' she says. 'Now what are we going to do?'

Tarek hears the crackle of the other voice, but not the words. He looks behind, feeling conspicuous, but no one is coming. He leans gently against the door. Kassia lets out a frustrated sigh and looks up and down the street while Jude continues to talk.

'There is one more thing I can try but—'

Tarek takes a step back and eases the door closed just as Kassia glances over her shoulder. After a moment he looks again. She's nodding.

'Okay, I have to go. But don't do anything stupid. Our deal still stands.'

Tarek turns to leave but isn't quite quick enough. Kassia pushes the door open and knocks into him.

'Oh,' she says, her eyebrows drawing together.

'Sorry, my fault,' Tarek says, fumbling to get out of her way.

She holds the door with her palm. 'On your way out?'

'Right, yes, thank you.' Tarek takes a step towards the street, then hesitates. *Fuck it*, he thinks. Who's he kidding that this has ever been a professional investigation? He turns, careful to maintain his characteristically nervous disposition and to flash a quick, ignorant smile before asking: 'Would you – I mean, can I ask – would you like to be part of the documentary too? Give your side of everything?'

Kassia laughs. 'I am okay, thank you.'

'I think it might really help,' he says, bobbing his head. 'Add balance to Rose's story.'

'Honestly, I barely knew Cali. I met her once.'

'But you knew—you *know* Jude, don't you?' Tarek glances pointedly at the phone in Kassia's hand.

Kassia frowns. When she replies, her voice is lower and crisper than before. 'Mr Zayat, I don't know what it's like for you in London, but Dover is a small place. It's hard enough being an outsider here. Running a business, trying to start a family, getting on with daily life – those things aren't easy for people like me and Rose. So, with all due respect, the last thing I need is to have my face on TV stirring up ancient history.'

Kassia blinks at him, surprised herself it seems by her outburst. She turns to leave, but hesitates and looks back over her shoulder.

'Honestly, I wish you might have thought more about the consequences before asking someone as vulnerable as Rose to relive all this.'

# THEN

Rose was making tea when they got the call. It was Thursday morning and Jude had just come over to see if there was anything she could do. Rose put the spoon down and looked at the number on her phone, trying to convince herself it could be good news. Cali might have come back. She could have turned up somewhere or got in touch. Rose had been telling herself she didn't believe Cali's annotations in a stupid school book meant anything important, that her sister had been doing better, that she was thinking about university, and that there was a world of difference between the 'provocative thinking' she'd been experiencing at the beginning of the year and what Jude had suggested she'd done.

A small part of Rose must have already known the truth, though. Because when she finally picked up and when DI Dixon said she was sorry, but they'd found a body and they needed Rose or her mother to identify it, she didn't react. Not properly. She nodded, then realized DI Dixon couldn't see her, so said yes, okay. DI Dixon said she'd pick her up. Rose didn't ask where they'd found the body. She didn't ask if they were sure it was Cali. She just hung up and stared at Jude, who was sitting at the table looking like she hadn't taken a breath since the phone had rung. Rose watched as fat tears rolled down her face and understood that was how she was meant to react too. She placed her phone on the counter and walked into the living room. Jackie was asleep, balled under the covers, so Rose turned away. She sat by the door, listening to Jude sobbing in the other room, waiting for DI Dixon to arrive. Later, she would wonder what had gone through her head in those minutes that felt like hours. Not anything important or useful or practical. Not anything that in any way prepared her for climbing into that patrol car and driving through the town she'd grown up in, being led into an office in the morgue and asked if she was ready.

Because Cali's body had lain amongst the rocks at the base of the cliff for a few days and because of the impact of the fall and the things water did to flesh, they wouldn't show her to Rose in full. She was shown partial photographs instead. First Cali's hair. Then her shoes. A swollen hand with chipped fuchsia streaks on the bitten-down nails. Finally, and only after Rose had assured them she'd be okay with it, a section of blue-grey skin with a long white scar.

'She got trapped under a roundabout,' Rose said, to no one in particular. 'When she was six. I was pushing it and she kept asking me to go faster and faster, so I did. The next thing I knew she was on the floor, her leg caught beneath the mechanisms, being dragged round and round.'

Nobody said anything.

'She had to have seven stitches.'

Rose had to sign to confirm she was sure the images were her sister. Even so, she found it hard to believe the days' old body the officers had poked and probed and taken pictures of could really be Cali. It couldn't be the girl who'd shrieked when Rose had pulled her hair, who'd woken her in the night to check for monsters, who'd cried because she'd realized one day everyone would die, including Rose and their mum and Jude and her. It couldn't be the person who'd written the messages Rose still had on her phone, who'd sent selfies with her nose pressed up like a pig's, who'd posted stories every day, documenting the minutiae of her life. It couldn't, Rose told herself, be the sister she'd promised to protect.

'. . . found at the base of the cliff . . . searched via helicopter . . . an alcove in the chalk debris . . .'

Rose heard only some of what DI Dixon said that day and had to piece the rest together later. Cali had been found almost directly beneath Shakespeare Cliff. There was a small section of beach down there only accessible at low tide. The Search and Rescue helicopter had scoured the area, but looking from the air, Cali had been difficult to see amongst the tumbled rocks.

'The path is set back, so she must have left it to get to the edge. It had been raining and it's uneven up there where she fell from.'

Fell. Jumped. Jumped. Fell. They chose their words carefully, but Rose knew what they were thinking.

'She's afraid of heights,' she kept repeating.

'We found her backpack on the cliff. There was a half-drunk bottle of wine in there. The post-mortem will check for other substances too.'

Rose didn't know what to say. Finally, she managed, 'Was it instant? Did she suffer?'

DI Dixon frowned. 'We're looking to determine a time of death, which will tell us more.'

She dropped Rose off at the house and offered to come in to help relay the news to her mother. Rose shook her head. Even with everything going on, she didn't want DI Dixon to see the state of her family. She wondered if they still counted as a family. For a brief moment years ago they'd been that advert-ready foursome, driving up to a restaurant or setting up windbreakers on the beach. They still got strange glances as people tried to figure out how Cali got her looks from blonde Jackie and ginger John and whether the older kid was a boy or a girl, but they were close enough to the mould to get by. It was almost ten years though since Cali and Rose had sat around a restaurant table and argued over what to order, begged to be allowed Cokes and promised they still had room for dessert. Now it was just Rose and her mum. And she had to be the one to tell her.

'Your wife didn't want to stay?' Tarek says as Rose re-enters the room alone. He has a strange expression on his face.

'She had stuff to do,' Rose says.

Gary clips the mic back to her shirt and she waits for them to get organized. Finally she decides to speak up. 'Is—is what I'm saying okay?'

Tarek stops what he's doing. 'So long as it's the truth.'

She sighs. Kassia gave another warning before she left, but back in this room with the camera lens winking before her it feels silly to imagine these men have come all this way and gone to this much trouble to entrap her. There's no way they can know what she did. No way unless she tells them, which she won't. So the best thing she can do is to tell as much of the truth as she's able. These were the worst weeks of her life, but if they can be turned into something positive, if the money can offer a new start for her and Kassia as a family, then it will be worth revisiting them.

'What I remember,' she says slowly, 'is the silence.'

She's aware of Tarek nodding to Gary to start rolling, but it's like they're far away. She stares, without focusing, into the lens. 'Mum stopped speaking. Even when I shouted at her, she just sat there.'

Passing on the way to the bathroom or hearing the other boiling the kettle in the kitchen felt like a fresh stab of pain, she remembers, another reminder of Cali's absence. Alone, Rose could cocoon herself inside her grief. It was terrible, obviously, but also somehow a comfort. *I've lost my sister*, she kept saying to herself, trying to make it sound real. But when confronted with her silent mother, all Rose's emotions tipped over. *She's lost Cali too* was not a thought she was ready or able to face.

In the two weeks between the discovery of Cali's body and her funeral, Rose didn't cry. She knew she should, but she couldn't. She slept and drank, smoked Cali's replenished weed stash and cut herself off from the world around her. At night she imagined Kassia's arms and her steady breaths beside her ear, but she couldn't bring herself to call. She didn't know what to say or how to reply to the long list of messages she'd been ignoring. A simple *Cali's dead* would have done the trick, but typing those words felt as impossible as saying them. And what would happen if she did? Kassia would jump on a train, Rose knew she would. She'd be with Rose in a matter of hours, holding her and caring for her and loving her in all the ways she wanted but none of the ways she deserved.

'And your mother hasn't spoken since?' Tarek prompts.

Rose returns her focus to the room. 'Not a word.'

'Did you blame her?'

She shifts in her seat. She'd been blaming her mum for things all of her life. For leaving. For coming back. For forcing her to live with John. For not standing up for her. But this was on a different scale.

'Cali's death was all of our faults,' she says. 'That's what I felt. To blame my mum would not have been to let myself off the hook. Because if she had somehow caused this, then I should have known, shouldn't I? I should have protected Cali.'

# 2026

They take another break and Tarek steps outside. There's a strong wind blowing off the sea and the sky behind Shakespeare Cliff is a deep grey. He stares at the jutting headland, trying to imagine what it must be like for Rose to see that every day.

He shakes his head, reminding himself she may not deserve his sympathy. Her wife certainly doesn't seem to. He selects a number and presses dial. It rings and rings. He pictures Jude in her flat, staring at his name and wondering whether or not to answer. The longer she doesn't, the more his suspicions grow. *Pick up*, he wills. Is he being paranoid? Or is it only common sense to wonder if the people you've deceived are also deceiving you?

He barely heard a word Rose said in that last session. All he could think about was that phone call and Kassia's response when she realized he'd overheard. Despite his training and awards, he's realized he's been approaching these women utterly naively. He's been looking for information about his sister's death, trying to prove her innocence, all the while barely contemplating the idea that Inji's innocence might mean someone else's guilt. All along he's treated Rose and Jude, as well as Kassia and everyone else involved, as witnesses rather than suspects.

Well, that changes now.

He hears Jude's syrupy sweet Cali Walker Foundation answer message, hangs up and opens a browser. If these women are keeping things from him, then he needs to find out what. *Megan Sutcliffe* brings up sixty-four results. On the second page he finds the one he's looking for. She's listed as Pub Landlady, Whitstable. He clicks to request a connection. He needs to talk to someone who knew these women back then. In the message window, he types out the most honest explanation he's given anyone yet:

Dear Megan
You don't know me, but I'm looking for information about my
sister. I'm desperate and I need to talk to you about anything
you know about the Dover Girls, Rose Walker or Kassia
Dąbrowski. My number is 07677 159285.
Please get in touch, this is urgent.
Tarek Zayat

There's a tap on the window. Gary waves to him from inside and makes a gesture against his wrist. Tarek turns back towards the main door, taking one last glance at the storm brewing over Shakespeare Cliff.

# THE FUNERAL

## CONFERENCE ROOM

Rose stares at the floor.

> ROSE
>
> Jude helped me organize everything. She con-
> tacted Cali's dad, invited people at school. She
> must have contacted John too, because I certainly
> didn't.
>
> (looks up.)
>
> I was a mess. I just—
>
> Fell apart.

CUT TO.


## JUDE'S FLAT

Jude straightens her jacket and tucks her hair behind her ear.

> JUDE
>
> I was glad to help Rose. She and Jackie needed
> me. With what they were going through – well, it
> was the least I could do.

CUT TO.

ROSE

We took Mum to different doctors, had all these tests. Selective mutism, the first one said. A freeze response, another told us. Somatic symptom disorder, they eventually changed it to. When a mental disorder manifests as a physical symptom.

(scratches behind ear.)

She can speak, she just won't. She hasn't said a word since the day I told her Cali was dead.

CUT TO.

## STILL: ORDER OF SERVICE

Light blue booklet with a smiling photograph of Cali on front.

CUT TO.

JUDE

(wipes tear.)

Emily Dickinson said it best: 'That it will never come again is what makes life so sweet.'

# THEN

The coroner's report came through the day before the funeral. It confirmed that Cali hadn't died immediately. The drop was not sheer and she'd likely crashed against the bracken and rock, slowing her fall. She'd broken both her arms, fractured her left femur and dislocated her shoulder. Remarkably, she'd only suffered a small head injury, but this led to a slow subdural haematoma. The report said this would have eventually caused a loss of consciousness and finally death, which was estimated to be around 11 p.m., Sunday 15th May. Jude had told Rose and the police that she and Cali had gone to sleep around 2 a.m. on Saturday night. Cali had been gone when she woke up in the morning, Jude said, so she must have left the house between 2 a.m. and 8 a.m. It was impossible to know exactly when Cali had fallen, but what the report meant was that it was likely she had lain at the base of that cliff with blood collecting between her skull and the surface of her brain for most of a day before she died. She may have been awake for some of it, feeling sick and confused, with a headache that kept getting worse, until an extreme drowsiness pulled her under. There was no telling, really, how her other injuries might have impacted the rest of her life, but if they'd known where to look, if they'd been alerted immediately, if Rose had worried sooner, if someone had seen her . . .

If . . . If . . . If . . .

If any number of things had been just slightly different,

there was a small but palpable chance that Cali could have survived.

Nearing the edge of her sanity, Rose opened a chat. Megan responded almost instantly.

> I heard what happened. Is there anything I can do?

> Can you get molly?

Rose had got to the end of Cali's weed and, anyway, it wasn't what she was after. She'd been thinking about Diego's claims about therapeutic trials. Anything was worth a shot.

Megan didn't reply for a long time. Rose imagined her staring at her phone in disgust or anger or hurt. She didn't really care either way. She knew she should be buttering Megan up, knew she could if she put her mind to it, but what was the point? For once Rose was simply asking for what she wanted. What she needed.

*Pills okay?* Megan finally replied.

It felt strange walking back into the White Horse. Under different circumstances, Rose might have blushed or found her eyes wandering to the door that led upstairs. But today she just made her way to the bar and stood waiting for Megan to finish serving.

'Want a pint?'

Rose shrugged, but sat on a stool. Megan placed a drink in front of her alongside a small white envelope.

'How much do I owe you?'

'It's on the house.'

Rose tried to object. She didn't want to be in Megan's debt. She didn't want to owe anyone in this town anything.

'Really, it's fine.'

She took the envelope and peered at the three yellow tablets inside. Each one had a tiny *FANTA* written on it. Rose thought of warm cans on hot summer days, Cali laughing by the sea. She pushed out her stool and headed to the bathroom. Megan said something, but Rose didn't want to listen. Inside the cubicle she bit one of the pills in half and winced at the taste. She swilled her mouth with tap water and returned to the bar.

'Careful of the comedown,' Megan said.

Rose left the pub and walked to the beach. The afternoon sun was warm against her face. When she started rushing she took her shoes off and dipped her feet in the icy water. She watched the ships and gulls bobbing on the glittering sea and thought about her sister with more clarity than she had in days. Even staring at the pictures of Cali's body in the police station, the situation hadn't felt as real as it did standing there on the beach. Her little sister was dead. She had jumped from a cliff.

Rose turned and there was that cliff, towering over the sea as if nothing had happened. How many had died at its feet, she wondered. Who had Cali shared her deathbed with? Tomorrow Cali would be cremated, burnt into ash. Rose thought about Sean and Jax and her room in their house, about pissing around with Diego at work and fighting with Kassia on the station platform. For the first time those things felt linked to the pebbles beneath her feet, to the buildings in the town behind her, to her mum and those long summers spent gauging John's mood. Rose had tried to compartmentalize her life, but now she saw the tiny threads connecting everything.

She walked along the beach, bending to pick and hold pebbles. She reached into her jacket pocket and found the purple stone she'd bought from the woman in the pub. The one that was meant to bring luck. She threw it as far as she could, then chased it a few steps into the water, drenching her jeans. She felt like drinking the whole ocean. She felt like dancing. She felt like lying down and sinking into the ground. She felt like talking to her sister. She got out her phone and was about to dial when she realized what she was doing. She laughed. The gulls cawed overhead and the waves crashed as they had for millennia and Rose laughed because what else was there to do?

Back at the house, Jackie was asleep, or pretending to be. She still hadn't said a word. Rose paced around Cali's room, touching her things, holding them close. She buried her face in the sheets and felt her chest tighten at the thought that this intensity of feeling would ever end. She reached in her pocket and touched the bag of pills. She'd rolled for three days at a festival once and paid for it dearly.

She was staring at the time on her phone, trying to work out when she'd taken the first half and how she should pace the rest of what she had to get through the funeral, wondering if Megan could get more if she needed it, or something else, something stronger, when the doorbell rang.

Rose didn't feel surprised to find Kassia on the doorstep. She hadn't expected her, but now she was here it made perfect sense. 'Baby!' she said with an easy smile.

'I went to your work,' Kassia said. Her face was blotchy, as if she'd been crying. 'Diego told me.'

Rose pulled her into a hug, wanting to comfort her.

'Why didn't you call me?'

'Shh. I'm so happy you're here.'

Kassia stiffened. She eased herself away and held Rose's shoulders. 'Your pupils are huge.'

Rose pulled a face.

'Oh God, are you high?'

She didn't reply.

'What are you thinking?'

'Everything.'

'That is such a stupid idea.'

'It feels okay.'

Kassia ushered Rose to her bedroom and made her give up the remaining pills. 'I know this is awful, but this is not the way to deal with it.'

They lay on the bed for a while, Kassia's arms wrapped around Rose's back. Rose could feel her heart beating in her ears, a rush of energy and peace. 'I love you,' she said.

'I am certain you do right now.'

Rose turned over. 'No, I mean it. I'm sorry I'm shit. I love you more than I've ever loved anyone. I'll do anything not to hurt you, not to lose you—'

'You will not lose me.'

'How can you know that? I lost Cali.'

'I am so sorry, Rose.'

And finally, for the first time since her sister's death, Rose began to cry.

'So yeah,' Rose says, making eye contact with Tarek, 'that's what I did the night before my sister's funeral.'

He nods. He's been trying to stay on his guard, to notice her tics and press for any details she's trying to avoid. In spite of his new resolve, though, and his growing certainty that Kassia and Jude's deal must have something to do with this investigation – otherwise why would Kassia have responded so defensively out by the back door? – he's finding it hard to maintain the same level of suspicion towards Rose. His instinct tells him to trust her. 'There's no judgement here,' he says truthfully.

She crosses her ankles and sits back in the chair. 'The thing is, I don't even think it was a particularly bad idea. I wouldn't recommend what I did, obviously, but I sometimes wonder what would have happened if I'd been sober when Kassia turned up. My life would be entirely different if I'd pushed her away that night.'

Tarek has three missed calls when they break for lunch. One from Helen, two from withheld numbers. He steps into the corridor to listen to their messages while Gary resets the equipment for the afternoon.

Helen wants to know what time he thinks he'll be back tomorrow. Her parents are in London and she wonders if she should invite them for dinner. Her mother is asking if they've chosen a name yet. Helen chuckles as she describes her mother's nagging and Tarek feels a sharp pang. He misses seeing her laugh.

The second message is from Dainah Thomas, manager of the south-east Missing Persons Unit. 'Mr Zayat, your case has been forwarded to me. I'm pleased to say your application and licence have been approved. I realize this is short notice, but I happen to be in Canterbury tomorrow, so if you are available I would be willing to meet you at the records office to access the file and conduct the DNA test. Alternatively, we can arrange a time for you to access the digital records at our London office and send off for the tests.'

Tarek replays the message and writes down Thomas's contact details. He shakes his head at Gary who's locking up and asking if he wants a sandwich.

'Don't forget to eat, boss.'

Tarek dials Thomas's number. A receptionist tells him she's in a meeting but he's been briefed that Tarek might call. Within a couple of minutes he's off the phone with an appointment for tomorrow and an address written on the back of a receipt. He calls Helen and breaks the news that he won't make dinner with her parents. She says she understands. Tarek feels his heart twist. It would be easier, he thinks sometimes, if Helen was the type of woman to get mad at him for always prioritizing work. Her endless understanding makes him feel worse. He makes a promise that after this – after tomorrow – he'll be a different man. He'll commit to his life with Helen, to their baby and to their marriage. He just needs to close this last door to his old life first. He needs to say goodbye.

Helen asks how filming went this morning and what he's feeling about the project as a whole. He murmurs some replies as he makes his way through the hotel. He hates lying to her, but if he tells her about the room and the letters she'll only worry. They hang up with the usual *I love you*s and Tarek listens to the third message.

'This is Megan Sutcliffe. I-I have nothing to say to you and I don't appreciate you contacting me.' There's a pause and the sound of choking, or maybe crying. Her voice is breathier when it returns. 'I don't want anything to do with Kassia or Rose or whatever your business is with them. After what they did to me—' She breaks off. A male voice can be heard in the background. 'What's going on?' followed by muffled sobs and a short conversation Tarek can't make out. Then the man comes on the line: 'I don't know who this is, but my wife hasn't spoken to anyone involved in all that in almost ten years and we'd like to keep it that way. Whatever this is, you need to keep her out of it, okay? Contact us again and I'll call the police.'

Tarek replays the message, trying to hear what Megan says before handing over the phone, but it's useless. He concentrates instead on her tone and choice of words. What *they* did – so she knew Kassia as well as Rose, then. Did Kassia find out what happened in the pub? Was there some kind of scene? What could have been so bad that Megan is still this upset? It's possible, Tarek muses as he exits the hotel and walks along the front, that she feels guilty about her involvement with Rose and supplying her the drugs, that she's cleaned herself up and doesn't want to be reminded of her past. It's also possible, he acknowledges, that she knows something and someone has warned her off.

# 2026

'I've been trying to warn him off all week,' Kassia says, following Jude into her flat. 'Now we know why it hasn't worked.'

'Yet you've left Rose on her own with him?' Jude says. 'What if she says something stupid?'

'Rose is fine,' Kassia snaps. 'She has no more desire to fuck things up than you do.' She looks around Jude's living room. She's always found something unsettlingly cold about minimalist homes, however tasteful their design. Jude has no nick-nacks or clutter, just clean monochrome lines and garish yellow appliances. 'He heard me on the phone to you earlier. I don't think he caught anything except your name, but God, what a mess this is.'

Jude stares at her blankly.

She may look like she's grown up, Kassia thinks, but she's just as wet and annoying as she was as a teenager.

'Do you understand what's going on?' she asks. 'This man's not interested in some puff piece for your mayorship. He knew Mo and he's going to keep digging until he finds out what happened to her.'

Jude's face turns red and she folds her arms. 'But if neither Rose nor I say anything then he won't, will he?'

'What if he does? What if he unearths something?'

Jude's nostrils flare. 'Well, what can we do?'

'We need to *make* him stop,' Kassia says.

'How?'

'I have an idea, but I'm not sure if it's enough.'

Jude touches her cheek. 'I need this to go away. I've come too far to let some nosy journalist fuck it up. And I've got enough on my plate. I had this email this morning – they're banging on about the detention centre once more. I can't deal with my name being used like that again. That was the point of doing all this in the first place, to get the truth out there so I don't need to rehash it over and over—'

'The truth?' Kassia says, raising her eyebrows.

Jude has the decency, at least, to look embarrassed. 'You know what I mean. I know you don't understand, but I'm trying to make things right.' She gestures to the robe draped over the back of the armchair. 'All this is to make up for— Well, you know what I'm trying to make up for.'

Kassia frowns. 'What email?'

She gets Jude to open her mayoral account and show her. It's from the New Nationalist Action Alliance, the same group whose literature someone has been pasting all over Kassia's waiting room. Their language is colourful, their message firm: that Jude has a duty to support their latest campaign, and if for any reason she doesn't feel able to, then she can expect to find herself on the receiving end of one against her. Kassia clicks the link and is directed to a petition titled *Justice For Mayor Jude: Tell the Government to Reopen Dover Immigration Removal Centre*. She scans the text. They are rehashing the case that Jude's accident would never have happened if the government had had tighter immigration policies to keep people like Mo out. In particular, they pinpoint the 2015 closure of the detention centre in the old citadel on Dover's Western Heights. They've included a link to a list of reported crimes by foreign nationals in the area over the past decade, with Mo's alleged assault against Jude the most serious. The petition is only a few hours old, but it already has six hundred signatures.

'This is good,' Kassia murmurs. 'We can use this.'

'I don't see how,' Jude snaps. 'I don't support this. I'm trying to distance myself from this kind of thing, to do something good in this town. This is exactly the sort of—'

'Oh God, calm down,' Kassia says. 'Think about it for a minute. What if we can harness these idiots and their anger to show Tarek Zayat just how unwelcome he is here? To scare him off once and for all? Christ, you might even get a chance to boost your precious public profile in the process.'

'What do you mean?'

'I need you to reply to this email.'

# THEN

Jude read a poem by Emily Dickinson. She stood up and opened her mouth, but was barely conscious of the words she was saying. She'd taken the plaster off her face and had spent the morning watching people's eyes drift to her wound.

Rose and Jackie sat in the front row. Jude had been next to her parents in the second, so standing up to read was the first time she saw the congregation as a whole. A couple of their teachers sat at the back and Cali's therapist had turned up, which Jude thought was rather bad taste considering. Goofy sat with Bobby, tears streaming down his face. She avoided Bobby's eye. The weirdest thing of all was seeing John sitting near the back. Rose had been useless, so Jude had made the bookings and organized everything for today, including the invite list, which meant sending out notices and tracking down Cali's dad and stepdad online. Even so, she hadn't seen John since she was ten years old and it was strange to see his face after all this time. She remembered how he used to squeeze her knee, right above the cap, supposedly as a joke or a sign of affection, but it had always actually properly hurt. Next to him but one sat a handsome older man who was greyer and more leathery than the photos in the albums Jackie kept hidden behind the sofa, but who Jude recognized instantly as Cali's father. Gabe met her eye and she stumbled over a line. Where had these two men been when Cali was alive?

Rose got up next. She faltered halfway through an anecdote about Cali getting her head stuck between the banisters and screaming and screaming until Jackie had been able to put enough washing-up liquid on her ears to set her free. Rose looked in an even worse state than usual, Jude noted. Her skin was all blotchy, her eyes sunken in shadow, and she kept twitching her shoulder like she was trying to shake something off it.

There was a murmur of polite not-quite laughter as she reached the end of the story and tried to compose herself. 'What happened to my sister was a tragedy,' she said. 'A tragedy in the sense that if we'd known where to look we might have found her in time—'

Jude pinched her tongue between her teeth to keep her features still. She had been trying not to think about the coroner's report. It wasn't her fault, she told herself again. She'd acted in the moment: panicked, heartbroken, abandoned. She couldn't have known that Cali wouldn't die instantly, that if she'd raised the alarm . . . She'd been waking every night with an image burnt to the backs of her eyelids: Cali lying like a broken doll, pleading for her help.

*Stop!* Jude told herself as her mind began to conjure the image again. *Cali got what she wanted. She chose to jump. It was* her *decision.*

Rose wiped her eyes and continued: '—but also a bigger tragedy in that this world failed to provide Cali a home. *We* failed to keep her safe.'

Rose looked straight ahead with an expression that made Jude shiver. She turned to see what Rose was staring at and realized it was John.

Rose said something else, but Jude's attention lingered on someone behind John. The skin on her arms prickled with goosebumps as she recognized the face she'd hoped never to see again. On the very edge of the back row, staring straight ahead, sat Mo.

Jude glanced at Rose. She was sobbing and making her way back to her seat. Jude looked at those around her, but no one else had noticed anything amiss. Slowly, she turned back to face Mo. What was she doing here? How on earth had she heard?

Mo sat still, gazing ahead as if she was meditating or in a trance. She looked tiny, Jude thought, like she'd lost even more weight. She was wearing a tatty grey jacket and had a scuffed black rucksack on her knees. Jude remembered the curl of Mo's documents as she fed them into the flames. For the first time, she found herself wondering what Mo had done after the fire, where she'd gone, what she'd found, how she'd survived.

The service ended and people started hugging each other. Jude's dad settled his arm over her shoulder before she could slip away. She felt trapped. She kept looking over the tops of people's heads, wanting to know where Mo was. The reception was being held at a hall at the bottom of the hill and the crowd began to move outside. By the time Jude got out to the car park she'd lost sight of her. John came up and held out his hand.

'I don't know if you recognize me,' he said.

'Of course I do.'

Jude noted the redness around his eyes. She tried to imagine what all this must be like for him.

'I wanted to say thank you for being such a good friend to Cali,' he said, dropping his hand. 'I loved her like a daughter. It broke my heart not to be able to keep in touch.'

Jude bit her bottom lip as he pressed her into his chest. *Help me*, Cali pleaded in her mind, *Jude, you're the only one that can help me.*

'I had no idea she was struggling this much,' John sobbed, his body shuddering against Jude's.

'Excuse me,' she murmured as he released her, 'I have to go.'

The crowd had thinned out and there were only a few people remaining outside the crematorium, the rest making their way down the hill. She spotted Mo, standing amongst the memorial stones in the large garden. She was looking right at her.

Jude crossed the car park and unlatched the gate leading to the garden. Mo stood with her hands in her pockets. She'd unzipped her jacket and, beneath, Jude saw she had on Cali's blue hoodie. It was weird, seeing her like that, wearing Cali's things. Jude wanted to ask her to take it off. If anyone should have Cali's stuff, it should be her. She swallowed the thought and gave Mo a hug. It was awkward, but the right thing to do.

'Where did you go? We were worried.'

Mo didn't respond. Jude stared at the mole on her face.

'Is it safe for you to have come back?'

'I had to,' Mo said finally.

Did she? Jude wondered. Did she have to come here at all? Jude had heard her parents talking recently about the difference between refugees and economic migrants, about how people came here and deliberately destroyed their papers so they couldn't be sent back. It had crossed Jude's mind that maybe she'd done Mo a favour. Even if not, the point was, what did she really know about this girl?

'Where are you staying?'

Mo shrugged. She too looked like she'd been crying. After everything she must have seen and experienced, everything she'd lost, Jude was surprised Mo could be so upset by this. Hadn't she lost her own family and friends? Shouldn't she be crying over them? Cali was Jude's to mourn, not Mo's. *She* was her best friend. If anyone had a right to weep today it was her.

Mo was looking at Jude's cheek, not even pretending to hide her curiosity.

'I fell down the stairs.'

Mo didn't reply.

Jude remembered the day they met her on the cliffs, how lost and desperate she'd seemed, and how unhesitating Cali had been about helping her. 'I know a place,' she found herself saying, 'if you need somewhere to crash for a night or two. Somewhere you won't be disturbed.'

Mo scratched her arm.

Jude almost told her to forget it. Why was she bothering to help Mo when she so clearly didn't like her? *I don't need you,* Jude wanted to say. *You're the one who's here without anything, without a plan, probably without even a single pound coin or anything to eat.*

Then she heard Cali's voice in her ear, asking why, when she lived in her big house and had so many things, she didn't want to help Mo.

*Because she's not even grateful,* Jude replied silently. *Look at her, standing here like she wishes it was me that had just been cremated and not you. She called me obsessed, but she's the one who's come back.*

'Okay,' Mo said. 'That will be nice.'

Jude smiled. Perhaps she was reading Mo wrong. She'd clearly returned because she needed help again. Maybe this was Jude's opportunity to make amends. To make Cali proud. She still had Bobby's money. Maybe if she gave it to Mo now, it would make up for everything else, set things right. Funerals were about saying goodbye and letting go, weren't they? Well perhaps the universe had sent Mo back to Jude so that she could do just that.

'We need to get you out of here,' she said, looking around at the last few people heading towards the reception. 'I don't want my parents or Cali's sister seeing you and asking who you are.'

'Rose,' Mo said.

'Yeah. Rose is acting weird, and I'm not doing that whole Ellie thing again, not with teachers around who are gonna know you don't go to our school. I need to go back to my house and get my dad's keys, then I can take you to the place. Are you okay to meet in half an hour?'

Mo nodded.

'Will you be okay? Stay away from the reception.'

'I manage this far,' Mo said shortly and again Jude almost withdrew her offer. Why did she have to be so ungrateful? Couldn't she see what Jude was trying to do for her?

'Do you have more stuff?'

'A bag.'

'Go get it and meet me on Snargate Street. Do you have a phone?'

Mo produced a cheap handset with a cracked screen. Jude grabbed it and opened a map. She dropped a flag where she needed to go. 'See you there, okay?'

'As you like.'

Jude looked around to check nobody had been watching, then snuck out the back of the memorial gardens and up the hill towards her house. She tapped out a message on the way telling her parents she had a headache and needed a walk before the reception. In spite of the circumstances of the day, she felt buoyed. This was a chance to prove that all those things Cali had said in the lookout were wrong. A chance to make things up to her.

# 2026

'What happened at the reception?' Tarek says, working to keep his face neutral. They've finally reached the day of Mo's death; the moment this has all been leading up to. Whether or not Rose is hiding something from him, though, he knows if he presses her too hard she'll shut down. 'What can you tell me about that evening?'

She crosses her arms. 'Not a lot, to be honest. I'd promised Kassia I would take it easy, but it was awful, you know? I hadn't expected to see John or Gabe, or for how weird it was going to feel with all those people offering their condolences.'

She pauses and Tarek waits, impatient for her to continue.

'Every time someone took my hand and said how sorry they were, I found myself wondering how well they'd known my sister and if they might have had the power to prevent what had happened. You know that saying "it takes a village to raise a child"? Well, it takes a town to destroy one. I felt like everyone in that room had let this happen.'

Rose's nostrils flare, but she stares directly at the camera. Her body language is neutral, feet flat on the ground, shoulders relaxed. She doesn't appear to be shying away from these memories.

'Kassia kept telling me to go easy on the wine,' she says. 'I insisted I was fine, but obviously I wasn't. I hadn't seen Jude since the service. I wasn't sure why it mattered, but it did. Out of everyone, surely she deserved some of the guilt. She had no right to skip out on this. I'd seen her talking to some-one in the gardens outside the crematorium—'

'Mo?' Tarek cuts in.

Rose frowns at his interruption. 'I guess, but I didn't know it at the time. She had her back to me and this big grey jacket on. I asked Cali's boyfriend who she was and he said some girl from school. I didn't think much of it.'

Rose shifts in her chair. Tarek notices his knee trembling and covers it with his palm.

'Should I go on?'

He nods. He needs to tread more carefully, to keep his head.

'I told Kassia I needed some air. She asked if I wanted her to come with me but I said no. I told her I loved her and made my way to the door, trying to avoid all the sympathetic eyes. I miscalculated with one pair and found myself face-to-face with Megan.'

Tarek thinks of the message on his answerphone. Perhaps he should go to Whitstable, find Megan's pub and demand she talks to him.

Rose carries on. 'She said she was sorry for my loss and all that, then reached out to touch me. I stepped away, worried about Kassia seeing us. I kept on walking, but she followed me outside. I headed past the smokers and down the alley-way towards the bins, where for some reason I stopped. Megan asked if I was okay and I don't know why, but I was so relieved to be out of that room and so messed up thinking about Cali and John and how to look after my mum and what was going on with Kassia that I burst into tears.

'Megan wrapped her arms around me and said all the things you think are completely pointless but you do actually need in those moments. It was so wrong, though, to be standing outside in an alleyway with her while Kassia was inside going crazy with worry.'

Tarek leans forward. He's seen enough pain and guilt in his lifetime to know that what's in front of him is genuine. He really doesn't believe Rose is hiding something from him, but he *is* starting to worry she won't tell him anything he doesn't already know. He needs to move her beyond this self-flagellation. 'What happened next?' he says. 'Did you find Jude?'

Rose scratches the back of her hand. 'I asked Megan if she had anything. She gave me this look like I was insane, but I told her Kassia had taken the pills off me. She smiled then, as if we were sharing a secret that my girlfriend was a bitch. I wanted to defend Kassia, but not as much as I wanted to escape. Megan said she didn't have any more pills, but she did have something that might chill me out, take the edge off. Whatever it was, I wanted it.'

She pauses to take a sip of water, her face flushed.

'And that's basically all I remember. I woke up the next morning with a raging headache and my girlfriend completely and understandably furious at me. She said I didn't come back to the reception at all. She found me and Megan off our faces, talking all sorts of shit, and took us home to sleep it off. I didn't know about any of the things that happened until the next day. It should have been when Cali died, or before even, but it took until that day for me to realize I'd hit rock bottom. I begged Kassia to give me another chance. I promised I'd give all of it up if she did – the booze, the drugs, everything.'

Tarek stares at her. This cannot be it. 'You don't remember *anything*?'

'Nothing.'

He shakes his head. The tremble is back in his knee. 'But

what about Mo?' he says, his voice catching. 'What about what happened?'

Gary glances at him.

'Nothing,' Rose repeats. 'Until the police arrived and told us what had happened, I had no idea she even existed.'

Tarek runs his hand through his hair. He takes a breath. 'Okay, well how about Jude?' Last week Jude too claimed to have no memory after the service. She told him that she remembers seeing Mo at the funeral, feeling relieved to know she was okay, but she has no recollection of how or why they ended up in the Grand Shaft. 'How did she seem before she disappeared from the funeral?'

Rose shakes her head. 'I don't know. I mean, it was my sister's funeral. None of us were acting normally. It was fucking awful.'

'But what do you remember about seeing Jude with Mo?' Tarek presses, his words running into one another. All this amnesia is too convenient; someone has to be hiding something. 'Were they arguing? Did they look like something was going on? What were they *doing*? Where was Kassia in all this?'

Rose gives him a confused look. 'Like I said, I didn't even know who Jude was talking to.' She shrugs. 'Maybe I felt like I'd seen her before, or maybe it crossed my mind that it was weird, seeing Jude with someone I didn't recognize, but Cali's boyfriend said she was some girl from school. And Christ, my stepdad was there, Cali's real dad too – it was weird seeing any of those people.'

'You have to remember *something*!' Tarek shouts, hitting the arm of the chair with his hand.

Both Gary and Rose gape at him. Tarek swallows, aware suddenly of the rapid rise and fall of his chest.

Rose narrows her eyes. 'Can we stop filming?'

He shakes his head. 'We just had lunch. Let's go a little longer.'

'I'd like to stop filming.' Rose looks at Gary. 'I am requesting you turn the camera off.'

Tarek makes a small, shaky gesture with his hand. Obediently, Gary presses pause and the red light on the front of the camera goes out. He doesn't touch the sound equipment.

'Fine,' Tarek says. 'You need another break?' He nods, making an effort to compose himself. 'I'm sorry, that was out of line. Let's take five and then dive back in.'

Rose stares at him. 'What's going on? Why are you being so insistent?'

Tarek runs his tongue beneath his lip. 'I'm sorry, it's just a tactic. All I'm trying to do is get to the heart of the story. Viewers are going to want to know who Mo was, what she was doing at your sister's funeral.'

'But I already told you, I don't know. I can't help you with that.'

'I'm just double-checking. Memory is a strange beast.'

Rose studies him. 'Why are you doing this project?'

'It's an interesting story. An unsolved mystery.'

'No,' Rose says levelly. 'That's not what I asked. Why are *you* doing this?'

Tarek shuffles the notes in his lap, measuring how to proceed. Gary coughs and they both turn to look at him. 'Think I'll get a coffee,' he says and clatters out of the room.

Rose folds her arms and glares at Tarek. 'Well?'

'I—' he stutters.

'Seriously. What is going on? Why are you so invested in this? Why are you asking questions I've already answered?'

Tarek feels a prickly heat creeping up his neck. 'I'm simply trying to establish the whole picture, investigating all avenues of enquiry and—'

'Bullshit. I may not have two A-levels to rub together, but I'm not an idiot, you know. I read the contract you gave me, and if you've been lying to me I'm within my rights to withdraw my permission for you to use these interviews.'

Tarek stares at her in surprise. 'Honestly,' he says weakly. 'It's essential to . . .' He trails off, unsure what it is he's trying to say. He slumps forward, realizing how exhausted he feels. He's tired of the pretence, tired of everything.

Rose stands, making her chair wobble on its back legs. 'If you don't tell me what's going on, I'm leaving.'

Tarek looks up and holds out one limp hand. 'I'm sorry. I really am.'

'For what?' Rose says, towering above him.

He takes a breath. 'For not being honest with you.'

She lets out a hiss. 'Kassia was right.'

Tarek sits up. 'Please don't go.'

'Are you kidding?'

'I haven't lied, but I haven't told you the truth either.'

Rose reaches for her jacket.

Tarek doesn't know if this is the right thing to do, but it feels like all he has left. 'You're not the only one. I haven't told my wife, my boss, Gary, anyone at all what this project means to me.' Rose pauses by the door, so he hurries on. 'I needed you and Jude to talk to me and I was worried you'd refuse if you knew.'

She turns back to face him. 'Knew what?'

'I think Mo was my sister.'

Rose's eyes widen a fraction but she works to keep her face impassive.

'We travelled from Aleppo to Calais together. I sent her on ahead because I thought it would be safer. She was meant to go straight to our father's cousin in Manchester, but she never arrived. I never saw her again. I've spent ten years trying to find out what happened to her. Ten years not knowing.'

Rose stares at him. 'You're Mo's brother?'

Tarek nods. 'I lost her like you lost Cali. That's what I meant when I said I understood. I wasn't lying when I said your story would have resonance with people. It resonates with me. I wasn't drinking and doing drugs, but I let Inji down. I was meant to protect her and I failed.'

'Inji?'

'That was her name. But she had a friend called Mo. A friend who died. The last time I saw her I told her not to tell anyone who she was, so I think she gave Mo's name instead of her own. She must have been so scared.'

'What happened?'

'I last saw her on 23rd January 2016. I put her on a truck with twenty other people. It was meant to go to Birmingham, but I've hunted and there's no trace of her arriving there. Four months ago I came across an article about the Dover Girls. I'd heard of the incident before, but I'd never seen the name Mo, never made the connection. I think Inji got off the truck in Dover. I think she was the girl your sister met on the cliffs on the day of the riot, the girl she tried to help.'

'Are you sure?'

'Not yet. But I will be. I'm going to Canterbury tomorrow afternoon. They have the original records there, of when they found—' He swallows. 'Of when they found both Jude and my sister.'

'Then you'll know for certain?'

'If it was her, yes. Which will tell me how she died. It won't tell me why. I need to know what happened on the day of your sister's funeral. Some of the things people said, some of the things that were written—I can't believe Inji was blackmailing Jude. Something else happened that night and I need to know the truth. I want to clear her name.'

Rose shakes her head. 'I'm sorry for you and I'm sorry for your sister, but I can't help. I told the police everything I knew. I don't know what happened. Only Jude was there.'

'And she claims she doesn't remember.'

Rose lets out a breath, holding Tarek's stare.

'Do you think she could have killed my sister?' he says, realizing as he does that this is the question at the heart of his whole investigation. Something has been bugging him since the moment he met Jude, and his thoughts have been swirling since this morning trying to piece together the connections between her and Kassia, Rose and Megan, but it is only in naming this suspicion now that he feels the full force of its possibility. He spent days in her apartment and more re-watching her on-screen. All this time, has he been staring into the face of the person who took Inji's life?

Rose looks away. 'The papers said—'

'That my sister tried to kill *her*,' Tarek says, sending his notes flying as he gets to his feet. How has it taken him so long to see this? How can he have been so blind? 'That makes no sense,' he says, taking a step towards Rose. 'Inji was gentle. She wouldn't let me kill a slug. She had a kind heart. She wasn't violent.'

Rose's nostrils quiver. 'I'm sorry,' she says softly. 'I can't help you.'

Listening back to the recording after she's gone, Tarek tries to remember the wobble of Rose's lip, the blush that crept up her neck.

'I think we're done here,' she said, her hand on the door. 'I truly am sorry for you, for what you've been through, but I don't appreciate being lied to. I trusted you to tell my sister's story, to do her justice, but all this time you've had your own agenda. You didn't care about Cali at all.'

Tarek shook his head. 'That's not true. She helped my sister.'

Rose nodded. 'While you and I were letting them down, it sounds like our sisters helped each other.' She tilted her head back and Tarek watched a tear crawl towards her jaw. Then she locked eyes with him again. 'But that doesn't mean I have anything left to say to you or your camera.'

She walked out, leaving Tarek in the empty conference room. Some time later Gary found him slumped against the wall, gazing fixedly at a spot on the carpet.

'We're done,' Tarek managed to say. 'I'll tell Olga this is my mistake, my mess. You'll still get paid, but it's over. There's nothing here. No story.'

# THE GRAND SHAFT

## SNARGATE STREET

Jude gestures to the entrance gates behind her.

> JUDE
>
> Despite what happened, I still think it's a stunning piece of architecture.

CUT TO.

## AERIAL VIEW OF THE SHAFT

Medium long shot from above. Concrete steps lead down a steep bank to a circular platform. The grated well in the centre is surrounded by three sets of steps leading into the ground.

> JUDE
> (off-screen)
>
> The Shaft is over two hundred years old. Its unique triple-helix staircase winds around a central light-well dug into the cliffs. It's 140 feet high and was built during the Napoleonic Wars to link the harbour to the barracks on the Western Heights.

CUT TO.

## BASE OF SHAFT

Victorian brickwork. Slow tracking shot through gate to courtyard and into a dark tunnel at the base of the cliff.

JUDE

(off-screen)

The idea was that the military could ascend and descend from the top of the cliffs to the beach below as quickly as possible.

CUT TO.

## CENTRAL LIGHT-WELL

Up shot from base, staircase windows spiral around to the sky at the top.

JUDE

(off-screen)

From the outside all you notice is the gate at the bottom of the cliffs. But inside, as you can see, there are these secret staircases.

Camera pans to bottom, where Jude waits in her wheelchair.

JUDE

In a way, I don't find it strange that such an essential part of Dover's history is also key to my own.

# THEN

Mo stood where Jude had dropped the flag, leaning against the wrought-iron fence. It felt like it might rain, so she took off the oversized jacket the woman on the tube had given her, folded it carefully inside a plastic bag and zipped it into the rucksack with the broken strap she'd found in a skip. She'd learnt to be careful with the belongings she had, especially in the rain. Surviving a night cold was one thing, but cold and damp was much more difficult.

'Sorry I'm late,' Jude said, hurrying up. 'My mum came home to check on me, I had to sneak out.'

Mo's eyes fell again on the long pink wound crossing her cheek.

'Come on.'

Jude led her into a small courtyard at the base of the cliff. She hooked her bag across her body and began to climb the fence to the left of the gates.

'You said you have a key,' Mo said from the ground.

'Yeah, my dad volunteers here. But we can't leave the front gate wide open, so you'll need to know how to get in and out. Come on, this bit's easy.'

Mo frowned but followed her over the fence. She watched as Jude found her footing in the crumbling side wall. Within a couple of minutes they were over that too and standing in a grassy inner courtyard. Jude headed for the entrance and fumbled to insert a key into the padlock.

'What is this place?' Mo said as she followed her down a

long corridor. Jude had a small camping torch that cast long, trembling shadows along the white walls.

'It might not be super comfortable, but it's dry and quiet and there's another exit at the top in case someone comes.'

At the end of the tunnel they met a gate leading into a round light-well. Mo peered through the bars, but Jude had already started up the staircase to the left. She followed her up and around the steep spiral. Jude kept the torch trained close to her feet so Mo could see the way.

'There are three staircases,' Jude said, flicking the beam of the torch through one of the windows, 'all twisted round each other.'

Mo followed the light. It looked as if they were doing repair works in one of the other staircases. Materials lay piled on steps and thick stretches of reflective hazard tape glinted where some of the window bars should have been. 'You are sure no one will come?'

'The work's on hold,' Jude said, following Mo's gaze, 'and they only open it to the public once a month.'

'You think of everything,' Mo said as they continued to climb. This was a horrible place. Dark and cold and spooky and much worse than the lookout on the cliff. It may be private, but she had no desire to sleep here.

They reached the top and had to squeeze around a red-and-white barrier blocking the way. It was twilight. Jude stepped onto the circular platform and Mo followed. It had started to rain now, in that light, persistent way she'd learnt could soak you right through. Still, after the claustrophobic staircase, she was relieved to be out in the open.

'I'll show you how to get out up here,' Jude was saying, 'then we'll go back down and find somewhere for you to rest.'

Jude shone the torch up a long, straight staircase. Mo

grasped the central handrail and followed her to the tall metal gate at the top.

'It's not hard to get over,' Jude said. 'We used to climb in here as kids. It leads out to the Western Heights. You remember we went there once with Cali?'

They stood at the top of the staircase, Cali's name hanging between them. Mo shivered, though she didn't feel cold. Now was her chance. She'd come all this way and risked her safety to return to this place. She studied what she could see of Jude's face in the shadows, the long, raw scar dissecting her cheek. What was she capable of, this strange, obsessive girl?

'Why did you do it?' she blurted at the same moment Jude reached into her pocket and said, 'I've got something for you.'

'What?'

Mo swallowed. 'I saw you.'

Jude shone the torch in Mo's eyes, blinding her. Mo tried to stay calm. She was stronger than this girl. She'd been through more than her.

'In the fields by the cliff on the day with the fire. You were taking a different path, not the usual one.'

Mo had thought it was strange. She'd wanted to call out, but the path they were on had veered closer to the edge and Cali had stumbled and cried out. When Mo turned back, Jude was gone. Then she'd noticed the smoke and broken into a run.

'So?'

Mo squinted, but all she could see was the light. 'You do not admit it? That you started the fire.'

Jude laughed, a hollow, scared little laugh. If Mo had had any doubts, that laugh banished them. An innocent person would not laugh like that.

'It is why I leave. I am not afraid of police. I am afraid of you. Did you want to kill me, Jude? Did you mean to hurt Cali?'

'Of course not,' Jude burst out, the torch trembling in her hand. 'How can you say that? I loved Cali. She was my best friend. Nobody understands how much I cared about her.'

'Why did you burn my things?'

'What things? All of your things were *my* things. You're still wearing Cali's jumper—'

Mo frowned. 'This is a gift.'

'That's what you say. I think you're a thief. You take, take, take. I read your messages to Cali. You weren't even grateful for everything I did for you. You're a leech.'

Mo wished she could see Jude's face. 'You do not understand the world, I think.'

'And you do?' Jude's voice sounded shrill, panicked.

Suddenly Mo felt exhausted, by this girl, this place, everything. 'No,' she said quietly. 'I understand nothing. I come here because I see people who want to die, people who beg for death and who truly want life to end. Cali was not like those people.' Tears welled in her eyes. She had seen death before. Bodies floating in the sea. Her friends covered in blood. She'd lain in a fruit truck for six hours without the refrigeration turned on, those at the edge banging for the driver's attention, begging to be set free. She'd spent those hours trying to come to terms with her own death, until finally the doors were opened and they were all slapped awake and told to get out of there before the authorities came. At home she'd seen bodies laid out on the pavement, apartment buildings turned to rubble. She'd known friends and friends of friends who'd disappeared. She hadn't been able to get through to her family in months. She'd learnt to fear the worst. But for some reason it was Cali's death that had broken her. She'd waited two weeks before returning to the coffee shop after that first visit, plucking up then losing the courage to tell Rose who she was, to ask for her help. Rose hadn't been in that day, though, or the day after, or the day after that. Mo had sat there every afternoon until they closed, wondering what to do, who to turn to. One afternoon she'd noticed another woman lingering like she was. Better dressed, cleaner, though also not English which was something they had in common. Mo had stood behind her in the queue and heard the fat man in the green apron say, 'Rose isn't here. Her sister died, she's taking some time.'

'We can't know what was in her head,' Jude said now, lowering the torch. 'Or why she did it.'

Mo choked back a sob. She'd run out of the café, through the crowds and tourists, bashing into people, pissing them off, running in no direction at all, but finally hitting the river. Her head spinning amongst the buskers and the people taking self-ies, she'd wanted to scream. Cali could not be dead. This was too much. Everything Mo touched turned to dust. She should have been the one to run into the fire. She should have let her own flesh burn. She had made it to England, but at what cost? What had happened to her family? To everyone she had loved? And now to the only friend she'd thought she had left?

'What happened?' Mo said, reaching for Jude. 'I do not understand.'

'Me neither,' Jude said. She too was crying. She took Mo's hand and squeezed, finding or giving comfort – it was unclear which. Mo found herself folding her into her arms. They'd never touched like this before. Mo still did not trust this girl and she did not forgive her for setting the fire, for chasing her away, but something was shifting inside her. Of all the losses she'd experienced in the past twelve months, this was the first she was able to share. Jude was the first person – the only person – who could understand this grief.

'I keep seeing her,' Jude hiccoughed into Mo's shoulder. She trembled in Mo's embrace. 'Asking for my help.'

'Me too,' Mo said. Since that day in the coffee shop, she'd been picturing Cali reaching out for her, telling her she shouldn't have run away. What Rose had said at the funeral felt true: they'd *all* failed to keep Cali safe.

'She just stepped out,' Jude murmured now. 'I didn't know what to do. She looked so peaceful. I didn't realize—I didn't know.'

Mo stiffened. Had she understood that correctly? She removed her hands from Jude's back and pushed her away. 'You were there?'

Jude wiped her face with her sleeve, but continued to weep.

'Jude,' Mo said. 'Did you see Cali die?'

\*

Jude lifted the torch again and watched Mo blink in the cold beam. The rain was coming down and they were getting wet. 'I-I didn't,' she stumbled. 'I mean, I—' She wiped her face and took a breath. 'That's not what I said.'

Fresh tears sprung to Mo's eyes. Jude watched one roll past the mole on her cheek. 'If you were there, you could have stopped her,' Mo whispered.

Jude shook her head, making the light from the torch wobble. 'It wasn't like that.'

She sniffed. She could feel her pulse thudding through the wound on her cheek again. She wanted to curl up. She wanted to be at home, in bed, with her parents knocking on the door offering comfort. Jude's best friend had been cremated today. She was in shock. She was grieving. She was fifteen and sitting her exams while trying to deal with the most complex and painful thing she'd ever been through.

Mo squinted through the light. 'At the funeral, Rose said Cali could have been saved.' Her voice was louder now, less controlled. '*You* could have saved her.'

Jude felt a pressure on her chest, something trying to crush her. She remembered the brush of Cali's lips that night, rough and uncaring. She remembered the split second between seeing her standing there and seeing the empty cliff. She had no words to explain these things to Mo. This girl couldn't understand what it was like to lose a best friend like that. She'd spent a few weeks hanging out on their cliffs, that was all. She had no idea what was between her and Cali. No idea at all.

'You let her die!' Mo shouted. 'You are crazy, you—'

Jude let the torch clatter to the floor. 'I am not crazy!' she screamed, remembering Cali whispering that to her after she sliced her cheek, but also something else. Something from years ago. Another time she was accused of being something she was not. A single word spat across the chlorine-soaked tiles, followed by the feeling of euphoria as she stepped forward and shoved Vicky Redcar off the edge and into the pool. Jude gripped Mo's hoodie and threw her whole weight behind an echo of that shove.

Mo screamed as she tumbled down the long, straight staircase, her limbs bumping concrete and bashing against the handrail until she came to a stop against the fence at the bottom. Jude listened to her whimpering, her heart pounding in her chest. Her fingers dropped to her pocket and felt the fifty-pound notes in there. She'd grabbed them when she went back to the house, along with the blanket and the food in her bag. Her mum had come home and she'd had to pretend she needed some space, that she'd meet her at the reception. How many times had she lied to her parents for Mo? How many times had she put herself at risk? And for what? For a stranger who stood at the top of these steps and accused her of betraying the person she'd loved most in the world.

She removed her hand from her pocket and looked at the money in the moonlight. She thought of what Cali and she could have done with five hundred pounds. This money would have lasted a while on their walk. Or just having fun. They could have gone out, bought things they liked, blown all of it on clothes and make-up. Even without this money she and Cali could have done some of that. They could have done anything if it hadn't been for the girl who'd turned up on their cliffs in January. If it hadn't been for her, Jude wouldn't be standing here panicking about what to do. If it hadn't been for Mo, she'd still have her best friend.

The sound of the wind and the patter of the rain fell away as she descended towards the snivelling girl. Jude had been shivering before, but now she felt the heat of adrenalin. She stopped on the bottom step, held out her hand and let the money fall to the wet concrete at Mo's feet. 'Leave,' she said, her voice almost level. 'I don't care where or how, but if you ever come back you will see just how crazy I am.'

# 2026

Rose stares ahead, her coffee going cold on the table in front of her. It's 8 a.m., but she's been awake for hours. Also on the table is the bottle she's just retrieved from the bottom of the bin outside. She had to split the bag and fish through Kassia's make-up wipes and dental floss to get it out. A crisp contact lens remains stuck above the captain's knee. For now, the lid is still on.

She hears Kassia's alarm from the bedroom, a groan, then silence as she hits snooze for the second time. She was out when Rose got back yesterday, and didn't return until late again. They haven't had a chance to speak, and in a way Rose is glad. Kassia was right, she should never have trusted Tarek. She put everything at risk, and for what? To ease her conscience? To feel close to Cali? How is she going to admit to Kassia that she got it wrong?

She keeps picturing Tarek yesterday, begging her to stay. There was something so desperate in his face. She knows she needs to think about herself and Kassia and the life they have, but she can't get his expression out of her head. As difficult as it was to come to terms with Cali's suicide, she cannot imagine what the last ten years would have been like if she hadn't known what had happened to her sister at all.

Kassia's alarm goes off again and this time Rose hears the sound of her padding to the bathroom. She gets up and places the bottle behind the bleach and dishwasher tablets beneath the sink. She refills the kettle and picks up her phone. A headline catches her eye and she clicks play on a video link. A local news report begins as she turns to retrieve the milk from the fridge.

'Kent Police have launched an investigation after various areas in Dover, including an historic site, were vandalized last night. The two-hundred-year-old building behind me was broken into and graffitied with racial slurs and the repeated phrase "Go Home". Similar messages were left beneath the Banksy mural on York Street, on properties around Market Square and on the pavement outside the Best Western Hotel.'

The kettle pings and Rose reaches for the yellow mug Kassia likes.

'Acts of vandalism, violence and racially motivated aggression in the county have doubled so far this year compared to the same period in 2025, confirming a decade-long year-on-year trend. Numbers obtained from Canterbury Magistrates' Court show that there have been 197 prosecutions, compared with 101 this time last year. Of the 2026 number, 41 of those were either arson or vandalism and 84 were threats of violence.

'Newly appointed Dover Mayor Jude Campbell spoke to us earlier about the incident.'

Rose twists the top back on the milk and looks at the screen. Wearing that ludicrous gold necklace, Jude appears on Snargate Street with a grave expression.

'This is an act of violence against not only the property and history of this town, but also the people living here. It is utterly despicable. Dover is a multicultural, diverse and welcoming town. I promise to make sure the individuals responsible are caught and face the full force of the law. In fact, I'd like to take the opportunity today to declare that, under my mayorship, Dover is *open*. I'm going to make it my personal mission to prove that these messages couldn't be further from the truth.'

The footage switches back to a reporter pointing out red graffiti on white brickwork. The camera scans over a swastika, before lingering on a large, dripping:

YOU DON'T
BELONG
HERE

# 2026

Tarek glances at the screen above the receptionist's head as he waits to be checked out, reading the subtitles. *The anonymous self-claimed Neo-Nazi organization New Nationalist Action Alliance have claimed responsibility for the actions in a statement on their website. Images of the vandalism were leaked online overnight and led to a brief trending of the hashtag #GOHOME.*

Tarek stares at the letters until they're replaced by the next line of speech. The story moves on and two women in a studio begin talking about the impact of the ever-weakening pound on holiday-makers. Tarek looks around, feeling as if he's being watched. He hasn't slept. He sat up all night watching footage of Jude, beginning to doubt his own sanity. He pulled his room apart looking for Inji's passport photo, which he was sure he'd left on the desk. He searched every crevice, but it was nowhere. When it got light, he looked out of the window and his knees buckled at the sight of the blood-red writing on the street. He knows he'll sound paranoid if he says it aloud, but he's certain the messages around town are for him. Whether or not he's right about Jude, someone wants him gone. If that means he's close, though, then all the more reason to continue – with or without a camera. His appointment is at eleven, so he'll go to Canterbury and see what the file says. Maybe there's something the police missed all those years ago, something he can use to confront Jude—

'There's a package for you, sir,' the receptionist says, handing over his bill along with a small parcel. There's a flurry of

344

activity in reception today. Porters ferry buckets of water outside to wash off the graffiti and guests linger on their way to breakfast to gossip about the drama. Tarek picks up the parcel and pulls at the tape covering the familiar mega-corporation logo. The cardboard flap opens to reveal a copy of Helen's most recent poetry collection.

'What—' Tarek says, but the receptionist has stepped to the side to serve someone else. He picks up the thin book and runs his thumb over his wife's name. Who would send him this? He flicks through the first few pages, but there is no inscription or note. He lingers on the dedication, staring at his own name, then turns the book over. There, on the back, beneath the impressive quotes and next to Helen's short bio, the eyes and mouth of her author's headshot have been scratched out.

Tarek drops the book. 'Who left this?' he shouts.

Both the receptionist and the other guest turn to him. 'Sir—'

'This is absurd! I need to speak to your manager. I want to know who left this and I want to see the CCTV from Wednesday night.'

He knows he's making a scene, but he does not care. This is too much now. Fucking with him was one thing, but involving his wife is quite another. He shouts at the receptionist and paces while the frightened kid radios his manager. When the suited woman finally appears, Tarek launches into her. He picks up the book and waves it in her face, ranting about his room, the notes, the message outside and everything he's been telling himself he hasn't let faze him. She manages to usher him into an office and, once he's calmed down enough to give a coherent explanation of what happened to his room two nights ago, she apologizes for the inconvenience and distress. He shakes his head when she asks if any of his property was taken and if he'd like her to contact the police. They will laugh at him if he tries to make a report about a photocopy of a passport photo, even if it means more to him than the most expensive possessions in the world. After some negotiation, the manager agrees to let him view the corridor CCTV from the night in question.

Tarek sits back in his chair, trying to regain his composure as she completes the paperwork and locates the file. A few moments later, in the stuffy, windowless office of the Best Western Hotel, he is staring at footage from just before midnight on Wednesday. A plump figure dressed in a black raincoat walks calmly down the hotel corridor and fishes for a keycard. They have a hood up and the face is in shadow, but Tarek recognizes the figure's build and movements and realizes just how stupid he's been. He asks for it to be rewound and watches again as Rose's wife lets herself into his room.

# THEN

Rose crouched against the wall. She could hear whimpering against the barrier at the bottom of the stairs above. Someone had fallen and Rose knew she should do something, but her limbs were stuck. Her tongue felt thick in her mouth and she had the sensation like she was floating.

After checking Rose was sure, Megan had looked up and down the alleyway, then fished a small baggie from her purse. She'd tipped a pyramid of powder onto the end of her fingernail and held it out. As soon as Rose had snorted it, she'd felt a rush of relief. She'd had enough of her own thoughts and emotions; what she wanted was to give herself over, to feel something – anything – that wasn't this.

She'd stood with Megan for a while, accepting a second and third hit, until Megan said she needed a drink. Rose told her she'd see her back inside. She watched Megan go, then walked the other way down the alleyway, towards the high street.

It had started to rain. The shops were closed and people were heading out for the night. Her phone buzzed in her pocket, but she ignored it. She passed the church where Jude volunteered and the pub where she'd had her first legal drink, wondering what was left for her in this place. She went into the pub and took her pint to a window seat. She shouldn't have left Kassia at the reception. She thought about going back, but knew Kassia would be mad at her. Right then, Rose felt truly certain that she loved her. All of her. Her strength and bossiness, her shyness and self-doubt. It almost made her laugh thinking about how much she felt for one simple, strange, imperfect woman who twice now had come uninvited to this crap port town to care for her. She looked around the bar, wondering if other people could tell what she was thinking. Then she glanced out the window and saw Jude hurrying along the opposite pavement.

Rose scraped back her chair and clattered outside. She could have called Jude's name. She could have asked her what she was doing. Instead, she followed her through the high street, past the closed-up shops with their desperate sale signs. Past the Wetherspoons pumping out Lady Gaga to old men drinking session ales. Jude turned right on Queen Street, then round the corner to Snargate Street, where she stopped outside the Grand Shaft. Rose crouched behind a parked car for cover and watched Jude greet someone. She recognized Cali's blue hoodie and bit back a cry.

'It's just a jumper,' she said aloud, her heart thudding against her ribs. Whatever Megan had given her was kicking in. It wasn't Cali, of course it wasn't. The person inside was too small, too skinny. She turned her head and Rose realized it was the same girl she'd seen talking to Jude in the gardens earlier. Suddenly, she also realized why she seemed so familiar; she was staring at the homeless hot chocolate kid from work.

'What the fuck?'

She watched the two of them climb the fence and the wall. Whatever she'd expected Jude to be up to, however much she distrusted her goody-two-shoes volunteering act, she hadn't had her down as the type to break in to private property.

Rose waited, but neither girl reappeared.

'Go on then,' she slurred. The sun had set, and by the time she'd clumsily followed them into the inner courtyard she could hardly see. 'Jude?' she hissed, but there was no reply.

They couldn't have actually broken in to the Shaft, she thought through her stupor. The thing was designed to withstand invasion. Still, she stumbled over to the entrance and placed her hand against the seam between the gates. The chain holding them together rattled and came away in her hand.

Whatever was going on now felt really wrong. Rose's fingertips tingled as she traced them along the cool stone. The tunnel was pitch black, but flickers of light danced in the corners of her vision. She had to restart her phone twice before it would work, but she finally got the torch on. She lurched to the end of the corridor and took the first staircase, remembering Kassia's laugh when she'd called this place the Grand Gash.

Halfway up, hearing only her own footsteps and panting, Rose began to wonder if Jude and the girl were here at all. She stopped and turned a full circle, her foot slipping on the narrow edge of the step. What if they'd climbed back over the opposite wall and returned to the reception? Or sprouted wings and flown away? Rose sniggered. What exactly had Megan given her anyway? Then she stopped laughing and felt a rush of panic. She imagined returning to the bottom and finding the gates locked. Her whole body started to tremble. Her thoughts turned to Kassia and she fumbled to open her messages. What could she say? *Please come, I need your help. I've done a stupid thing and now I'm afraid.* She stared at the empty text box, the blue light of the screen making her feel vaguely nauseous until it timed out and turned black. Rose dropped to her hands and knees and continued her way up.

At the top, she crawled under the barrier and began to breathe more easily. She remembered standing over there with Kassia, talking about home. She looked up and smiled with her tongue out. The rain felt incredible on her

349

burning skin. She tried to swallow, but her tongue was too large to put back in her mouth. She snorted. She felt properly fucked.

There was a little moonlight, so she switched her phone light off and blinked until her eyes readjusted. Her vision was flickering slightly, but mostly she felt okay. At the top of the long flight of steps she knew there was a big functional fence. It was more ominous-looking than the ornate ironwork at the bottom, but if she gave herself a minute to rest here and then took it slowly, she reckoned she could throw her jacket over the spikes and climb it. Then she'd make her way back to the reception. She'd admit to Kassia what she'd done and tell her she was sorry, but that now she felt sure. She was ready to dive in the deep end with her. She'd lost Cali; she couldn't lose her too.

That's when she'd heard the voices. Shouting at first, then one long, ear-piercing scream as someone crashed down the steps. Rose had dived against the wall beneath the staircase, where she was still cowering in the shadows.

She heard footsteps slapping against the concrete above her head.

'Leave,' she heard Jude say, then a rushing in her ears.

'Stay away,' came the other girl's voice. She sounded scared.

Rose was trembling again. She watched the reflections from Jude's torch on the wet stone. She needed to move, but her muscles had been replaced with cement.

'Cali made her choice,' Jude said.

Rose felt her eyes filling with tears. Cali *had* made her choice. Rose wished with all her might she could take that choice back. What she would give for one more day with her sister, one single chance to convince her to live. The voices continued, but they felt far away. Rose had the sensation like she was falling into herself, like she was drowning in thick oil. Repeatedly, she tried to pull herself to the surface, to concentrate on moving her lips, her tongue, anything.

'It's your fault,' she heard Jude say as she tuned back in. 'Everything would have been fine if you hadn't turned up. I was crying and bleeding and Cali walked away because of you.'

There was a thud, then a scuffle. Rose heard Jude scream and then shoes slapping down the final steps towards her. The girl in Cali's hoodie darted past her and down one of the staircases.

Rose felt like the sea was crashing in her ears. With a jolt she managed to rock herself forwards. Her eyes scanned the dark landing as she tried to stitch her thoughts together. *Come on!* she urged. With everything she had, she willed herself to her feet and stumbled after the girl.

'Stop!' she tried to shout. It came out thick and muffled, but it came out, which was something. She wasn't far ahead. Rose hurried as fast as she could. 'Wait. I want to help.'

The girl looked back, a flash of confusion on her face. She tripped and tumbled down half a dozen steps.

Rose caught up with her and crouched down. 'Are you okay?'

'Rose?' Jude said from above. 'What are you doing here?'

'Now we both hear what you said,' the girl said, her voice unsteady. 'We will tell people what you did.'

Rose stared dumbly up at Jude, trying to keep track of what was happening. What was she supposed to have heard? Something bad, clearly. Something that was making this girl afraid. She had no idea what the girl was talking about, but she understood that she needed help.

'Calm down,' Jude said, descending towards them. She studied Rose for a moment, her features easing in relief. 'Look at the state of her. I bet she doesn't even know where she is.'

Rose tried to stand up, but her left knee gave out and she had to hold the wall. 'Stay away from her,' she slurred.

Jude gave a nervous-sounding laugh. 'She's so fucked she can't even stand. Who's going to believe an undocumented immigrant and an off-her-face dropout?' She placed her hand in the middle of Rose's chest and pushed gently.

Rose fell down two steps before her arm responded to her brain and reached out for balance. 'Leave us alone,' she said with effort.

Jude's expression darkened. '*You* of all people are not going to ruin my life.'

She moved towards Rose, pressing her face close. 'Where the fuck were you when Cali needed you?'

Rose gazed at the pink wound on Jude's face, feeling the truth in what she said. She took a step down, then another.

'I used to think you were so cool,' Jude said, 'but you're just a waster. You and your snooty girlfriend, you think you're so much better than me. Telling Cali I'm a spoilt brat, how dare you? You were nothing to Cali. You weren't the person she turned to, you weren't the one she needed, you weren't the one she—'

Rose lunged at Jude, trying to grab at her clothing. 'Shut up!' she choked.

Jude's footing was firmer than Rose's and she pushed her away, cracking her head against the inner wall. Rose felt the air against the back of her neck and, distracted, turned to look at the window by her side. Then Jude's palm connected with her cheek and she stumbled on the narrow edge of the step. Hazard tape snapped in Rose's hands as she reached for the bars that weren't there. She regained her balance, but Jude was struggling with her now. Rose managed to grab her shoulders and attempted to thrust her off. She was bigger and stronger than Jude – it should have been an easy fight – but her reactions were slow, her body struggling to obey her brain. Jude screamed in her ear, and Rose twisted in her grip, dancing clumsily away from the window. With one final surge, she thrust Jude forwards.

If she'd pushed her slightly to the side, or if Mo hadn't chosen that moment to try to help, if Jude hadn't lost her footing on the edge of the step, or if Rose had used slightly less force, then it would have been different. But Jude crashed into Mo and they both fell against the edge of the window. Jude toppled first, losing her balance and reaching out for anything she could grab. Her fist closed around Cali's blue hoodie and dragged the girl inside it with her as she tumbled through the window.

They must have cried out. There must have been a noise when they hit the ground. But Rose heard none of it. She slid against the cool wall and slumped in the dark staircase, falling deep inside herself, only distantly aware of the gentle buzzing of her phone against her thigh.

# 2026

Tarek shakes Dainah Thomas's hand. He's held it together through their two-hour meeting, through a guided inspection of the file on Unidentified Death HY07541, through an examination of every statement and every detail, and through the technician's brusque DNA swab and stern explanation that the new INSTA-technology is fast but not accredited for prosecution purposes. He can't keep it together much longer. His brain is swirling from everything he's learnt today. He remembers the painted pony in the museum, galloping round and round the old zoetrope, never reaching its destination. He is like that pony, he thinks. His chest aches. He needs to get outside.

'Goodbye, Mr Zayat,' Ms Thomas says. 'It was a pleasure to meet you and I hope this was of help.'

'Thank you,' Tarek manages to say. 'I appreciate your time.'

He pushes open the first, then the second door and finally he's out, back in the bustle of traffic and tourists. All he has to do is make it to the station. He doesn't care about Jude or Kassia or Rose any more; all he wants right now is to sleep. In a few hours he'll be back with Helen, back in his life. This doesn't have to be the end. It doesn't mean he has to give up. But it's time to go home.

He begins down the short flight of steps, raising his head only as he reaches the bottom. There, waiting for him with her hands thrust into her jacket pockets, her weight on one hip, is Rose.

'Can we talk?'

Tarek sighs.

'Is Gary here?' she says, looking behind him. 'Do you have the camera?'

He frowns. An hour ago he read her police statement from 4th June 2016. The file contained almost identical ones from Kassia, Megan and Jackie, confirming that the night before – on the evening of Cali's funeral – the four of them left the reception together and returned to the house, that they remained there until the police arrived in the morning. Confirming, in other words, that none of them were anywhere near the Shaft on the night Mo died and that all along Tarek has been barking up entirely the wrong tree. 'No,' he says. 'Filming's over.'

She looks disappointed. 'I need to tell you something,' she says. 'About that night.' She glances at the file in his hand. 'You can record it if you want. I don't know, on your phone or something. I've been thinking and it's important you know the truth. More important than my reasons for not telling it.'

Tarek stares at her. In spite of everything he's just learnt inside, his interest is stirred. 'I have something to tell you too, actually,' he says. If nothing else, he'd like to see how she responds to the information that her wife has been harassing him. 'Shall we find somewhere quiet?'

They come across a small park. They walk a little way in and find a sheltered wooden bench. Rose insists again that she wants Tarek to film her, so to humour her he gets out his phone and the mic adaptor he always carries.

'Whenever you're ready,' he says wearily.

Rose places her hands in her lap. 'What I told you yesterday wasn't true. There are black spots and what Megan gave me was definitely cut with something strong, but I do remember some of what happened.'

355

She looks up from the lens of Tarek's phone and locks eyes with him.

'I followed them. I followed Jude and your sister into the Shaft and I was the reason they fell. I'm so sorry, but it was me. I killed your sister.'

# THE TRUTH

## ABBOTS MILL GARDEN, CANTERBURY

Rose sits on a bench.

> ROSE
>
> I woke up on the Western Heights the next morn-
> ing and the first face I saw was Kassia's. Megan
> was there too. Kassia said she'd traced my phone.
> She'd put this thing on it ages ago, apparently,
> when I was working a lot and she was worried I'd
> lied to her.

> CUT TO.

## SMALL THERAPY ROOM

Kassia sits with arms folded.

> KASSIA
>
> I want your viewers to know I'm not talking to
> you by choice.

> INTERVIEWER
> (off-screen)
>
> How did you find Rose?

> KASSIA
>
> (sighs.)

I bumped into Megan in the bathrooms at the reception. It didn't take a genius to put things together. I asked her what she had given Rose. Ketamine. The stupid girl. Then she started blathering about a stock room.

(looks away.)

I returned to the main room, looking for a way out, but Rose's mother had collapsed. I tried calling Rose, but she wouldn't pick up, so I took Jackie home. Megan followed us, gurning and blathering about wanting to find Rose. I was scared for Rose and also angry at her. I'm not proud of having enabled her location sharing – I was working on my feelings of insecurity. But after what Megan had just told me—

CUT TO.

ROSE

I should have gone straight to the police, but Kassia convinced me not to, that nothing good would come of it. When they came to us, we told them we'd been home all night.

(rubs face.)

When Jude woke from her coma I was convinced she'd tell everyone what I'd done. But she didn't remember.

CUT TO.

### KASSIA

I traced Rose to the Shaft and Megan showed me a way to get in from above. I told her to wait outside. I wanted to talk to Rose alone.

When I found her, Rose was entirely still. She couldn't speak, couldn't say anything. I saw the broken tape hanging from the window. I didn't know what I would find, but I looked out and down.

(inhales.)

That was when I understood I had to get her out of there.

CUT TO.

### ROSE

I should have thought about Mo's family and the consequences of what I'd done. All I thought about was myself and what I still had to lose. Cali would be ashamed of me. Like you said yesterday, she tried to help your sister. And I think, in a way, your sister tried to help her. I realized this morning that I've spent ten years betraying them both. You of all people have a right to know the truth. You need to know who to blame. Who to hate. I've been a coward, but I'm finally ready to face the consequences of my actions. I want you to tell the world that I pushed Jude and I killed Mo.

CUT TO.

KASSIA

(shakes head.)

Rose doesn't know the whole story.

INTERVIEWER

(off-screen)

But you do?

KASSIA

(sighs.)

Look, the only reason I'm telling you any of this is because Rose doesn't deserve the blame here. She's carried her guilt for all this time, but it's not her fault. She was in a state and her memory of that night is incomplete – which isn't a bad thing. There are some parts I'm glad she's forgotten. That I hope she never has to know.

All I've ever done is try to protect her. It was working until you came along.

INTERVIEWER

(off-screen)

Is that why you tried to scare me off?

KASSIA

(shifts position.)

Do you want to know what happened that night or not?

# THEN

Kassia looped her arm around Rose's waist and pulled her to her feet. 'Come on, baby,' she urged.

Rose's eyes drooped and she was murmuring things Kassia couldn't make out, but after some encouragement she did manage to lift her foot onto the next step.

'That's it, you're doing well,' Kassia said, half-balancing, half-pushing her up the tight staircase. Kassia's heart pounded in her chest and her mind whirred with what she'd just seen at the bottom of the Shaft. She needed to get Rose to safety, then she'd figure out what to do.

At the top, they still had the long, straight staircase to navigate. Reluctantly, Kassia shouted for Megan to come and help. She balanced Rose against her shoulder as she waited for the awful woman to climb over the gate and skip down to meet them.

'What's going on?' Megan said with a grin. Her enormous pupils looked like bullets in the moonlight.

'She's messed up,' Kassia said. 'Help me get her out of here.'

Together they guided Rose to the top of the stairs where, with a lot of encouragement and a few firm slaps, they convinced her to hold her own weight as they helped her climb over the fence.

'I left something in there,' Kassia said once Megan and Rose were both on the other side. 'Take her somewhere safe – I'll catch up with you.' She was trying to sound casual, but could hear the strain in her own voice.

Megan gave an over-exaggerated shrug. Kassia watched her take Rose's arm and stumble towards the path, no part of her wanting to leave the two of them together. She had no choice, though; she couldn't just leave what she'd seen. She turned and hurried back down the stairs, back towards the bottom of the Shaft.

# 2026

The receptionist eyes Tarek as he waits. She's not happy that he's insisted on staying. Dr Dąbrowski is with a client, she's told him.

'I only want a few minutes of her time,' he said. 'I think she'll want to speak to me.'

'I don't know about that,' the woman muttered, but agreed to let her know he's here when the session ends. 'You still might have to come back another day,' she added with pursed lips.

Tarek sits patiently in the padded wicker chair, knowing he will not come back another day. This is it. All the way on the train from Canterbury he questioned what he was doing and why he was still choosing to do it. This project is over. He has his answers. Thanks to Rose, he may even still have a salvageable documentary to present to Olga. He should be getting into St Pancras by now, making his way home to Helen. Instead, he is back in Dover. He had to walk past three of those '#GOHOME' tags to get here. This will be the last time, he tells himself. After today, he never wants to set foot in this town again.

He looks around the bland waiting room. A man with a greying beard sits on the far end of the tired leather sofa reading a leaflet. There are three therapists who operate out of this clinic, Tarek read on his way here, taking a mixture of private and NHS clients. He clicked on Dr Kassia Dąbrowski's BACP profile and read her specialisms: psychoanalytic psychotherapy; group analytic psychotherapy;

long-term treatment for trauma, abuse and PTSD; and recovered and unreliable memory therapy. There was a list of her qualifications and links to papers she's published. In another town, Tarek has no doubt, she'd have a higher hourly rate and be working out of somewhere rather more impressive than this.

'Mr Zayat.'

Kassia is standing in the doorway of her small practice room, wearing a black button-down dress. The client who has just emerged with her steps over to the receptionist, who begins to blather an apology about his presence. Kassia waves a hand. 'It's fine, Cherise.' She turns to Tarek. 'You had better come in.'

He follows her into her room and takes one of the two low comfortable chairs.

'I do not have long,' she says, sitting opposite him. 'How can I help?'

Tarek leans forwards, his knees high and in the way. Kassia's seat is the exact same as his, but she looks at ease, upright against the chair back, legs crossed at the ankles. He clears his throat. 'I know it was you who trashed my room and sent those letters.'

Kassia's lips pinch together slightly, but otherwise she doesn't react.

'And I know why. Rose told me what happened.'

Kassia narrows her eyes, but still doesn't say anything. Unsure what else to do, Tarek reaches for his phone and swipes through to the footage he took earlier. He watched it twice on the train here. He taps a place near the end of the timeline and props the phone against a plant pot so Kassia can see.

Tarek watches the steely professionalism drain from her face as Rose talks.

'Please don't use this,' she whispers when it's over. 'Rose

doesn't understand what she's saying. She doesn't know the whole story.'

Tarek looks at the tears welling in her eyes, weighing his options. 'Will you talk to me on the record?'

He knows from the look she gives him that she truly hates him. But he also knows he's close to something.

Kassia wipes her eyes. 'If that's what it takes.'


'Why didn't you just go to the police?' he says after she's recounted how she got Rose out of the Shaft.

'And tell them what?' Kassia says. 'That I'd found my girl-friend inside a k-hole with two bodies?'

'It was an accident.'

She looks at him coldly. 'You are very naive for someone who has been through what you have. Do you think people like Rose get believed in a place like this? People like you or me? Who is it that sits in our parliament? Who is it that's just been made mayor? That's the sort of question only someone who's never had reason to wonder if the police are there to protect or prosecute them asks.'

Tarek thinks of his own justifications for not reporting the vandalism to his room. He feels chastened by the truth. 'So what did you do?'

'I thought fast. I had to. I found Mo's phone and called the emergency services from that. I muffled my voice with my hand and said I'd seen two teenagers breaking into the Shaft, that they needed to come quick. I kept the phone to dispose of later and followed Megan and Rose on the map. They were in the old gun battery at the top of the Heights. Megan was crouched beside Rose, giggling in her ear. I screamed at her and she let out another burst of laughter. Rose was slumped against a wall, her eyes half closed. I looked at Megan's enormous pupils and I didn't know what to do. I realized she was the only other person who knew Rose had been in the Shaft.'

Tarek remembers the statements he read earlier. 'You needed her to give Rose an alibi.'

Kassia nods. 'I had an idea. I didn't know if it would be possible, but Rose was passed out and Megan kept grinning and wiggling her tongue between her lips like a grotesque schoolchild. It made me feel sick what she'd told me about her and Rose. I knew I couldn't trust her.'

Tarek watches Kassia press her fingernails into her palm. 'What did you do?'

'I took her outside and sat up all night telling her stories. When she came round in the morning I worked on convincing her we'd been in that same gun battery all night, that everything else was just the workings of her imagination and the drugs. That it would be best if we all said we'd stayed with Jackie.'

Tarek frowns. 'What do you mean, you told her stories?'

Kassia's gaze settles on the waxy plant to his left. 'Ketamine is a dissociative drug. It cuts you off from your surroundings, detaching you from your bodily experience. A k-hole is like being halfway to a coma. While the real world recedes, your imagination can take over, drawing you into a world of delusions and hallucinations. I sat beside Megan and tried to help her imagination along. I recalled the very worst things I had read. Stories from abusive childhoods, women who'd fled their husbands. Every case study that had ever disturbed me.'

Tarek takes a sharp breath. 'Why?'

Kassia folds her hands in her lap and locks eyes with him. 'I wanted to confuse her. I thought if I could instill other people's trauma in her head then she wouldn't be able to tell what had really happened that night. I wanted her to wake up confused and scared and to assume it was all the result of the drugs. Or that she was going mad. I didn't care what it did to her, as long as she kept quiet about Rose.'

Tarek swallows. 'Did it work?'

Kassia breaks their gaze, her eyes glazing with tears. 'I don't know for certain. It wasn't exactly a controlled experiment. Regular ketamine users have been known to show ongoing dissociative and psychotic symptoms after the drug has worn off, so what she was going through was not necessarily unusual. She was very upset, I know, but she told the police what we agreed. A few months later, she moved away.'

Tarek shakes his head. 'How could you do that to someone?'

'I did it to protect the person I love.'

'But you're a practitioner. You're bound by a code of ethics. If your patients knew—'

Kassia blinks, allowing her tears to fall. 'None of us knows what we will do for love until it is tested. This is what I risked that night and this is what I have continued to risk for my wife.' She wipes her eyes. 'Look, I agreed to let you film me because you already have Rose confessing on camera and I can't undo that. But there is something Rose still doesn't know and, whatever you do with any of this footage, I am begging you, for her sake, not to tell her.'

Tarek feels the prickle of adrenalin. 'About your deal with Jude?' he guesses.

Kassia nods at his phone. 'Can we turn the camera off now? All your viewers need to know is that Rose is not to blame, that Jude deserved what happened to her and that Mo sadly got caught up in it.'

Tarek leans forward. 'Why did Jude deserve it? What did she do?'

Kassia stares at him for a moment, then stands up, shaking her head. 'This was a mistake.'

'Wait!' Tarek says, standing up too. 'I have something to show you.'

He grabs his computer from his bag and fumbles to open the folder of Cali's stories. He scrolls down to the last file, presses play and turns it to face Kassia.

'If you're out there,' Cali says, her voice crackly with tears, 'I'm sorry.'

'This was Cali's last communication,' Tarek says. 'Posted at 10.41 on the 14th May 2016.'

Kassia stares at him. 'So what?' she says, though Tarek can see she's shaken.

He taps at the screen again. 'And this is what Jude wrote in response.' He turns it so they can both read the text.

| | |
|---|---|
| 22.47<br>jude_campbell<3<br>commented on your story: | Do you think she cares? Do you think Mo gives a shit about you? Nobody does. That's why they leave. Your dad, John, Rose. |
| 22.48<br>jude_campbell<3<br>commented on your story: | Mo's long gone, just like everyone else. |
| 22.48<br>jude_campbell<3<br>commented on your story: | I'm glad I set the fire and I'm glad she ran away. |
| 22.48<br>jude_campbell<3<br>commented on your story: | I hope she's been deported. |

370

22.48                          I hope she's drowned.
jude_campbell<3
commented on your story:


22.49                          I hope you both drop dead.
jude_campbell<3
commented on your story:


'Did you know Jude sent these?' he asks as Kassia sits back
down, her face frozen in horror. He glances at his phone,
still propped against the plant pot, still recording. 'Is that
why she deserved what Rose did to her?'

Kassia shakes her head slowly. 'All I knew was that she
was there.'

# THEN

Kassia stood on the doorstep with flowers in her hand. These houses were large and grand, but they reminded her of something from a horror movie. The porch and the chipped balcony above her head didn't look quaint to her, but ominous.

'Hello?' Sandra said, opening the door. Her eyes drifted to the flowers. 'Can I help?'

'I'm here to see Jude,' Kassia said as sweetly as she could. 'I'm Rose's girlfriend.'

Sandra looked tired. 'Right, sorry, we've met once, haven't we? Come in.' She stepped out of the doorway and ushered Kassia inside.

'I don't mean to intrude, but it would be lovely to talk to her if she's up for a visitor?'

Sandra nodded. 'Let me see if she's awake. Do you mind taking your shoes off?'

Kassia did as she was told and placed the flowers on the edge of a bookshelf. All the way from London she had been wondering what she would say. She'd told Rose she was at a conference and that she would be back this evening. She'd been observing over the past couple of months how small lies grew into big ones, but she couldn't have told her the truth. Rose was still barely sleeping. She'd completed a four-week rehab programme and had been going to regular meetings, but Kassia knew it was more than the normal effects of withdrawal that were keeping her up. Their relationship was stronger than ever and Kassia felt certain finally of Rose's commitment, but that hadn't stopped her feeling scared that Rose would relapse. Especially when they heard the news that Jude had woken from her coma.

They'd waited for the knock on the door, but it hadn't come. *Finally, we are lucky*, Kassia thought when she heard Jude had told the police she remembered nothing. It had felt like a miracle. The more she thought about this luck, though, the less convinced she became. What were the chances, she wondered, of Jude's amnesia coinciding with the very thing they needed her to forget? She began to question whether Jude was lying and, if so, why? What would possess her to protect Rose? Kassia thought about how cloying Jude had been that weekend they'd visited. There was something about her that Kassia hadn't been able to place. She'd hung around like she couldn't let Cali out of her sight. And the questions she'd asked, like Kassia was both someone to be impressed and an alien to be inspected. At the funeral too, Kassia had watched how Jude held herself as she read the poem. She hadn't felt like she was looking at someone who had lost her best friend, more like someone on a stage, stepping into the limelight. There was that gruesome cut on her cheek, which she seemed to turn towards people as she spoke, daring them to look. Maybe Kassia was judging Jude unfairly. Maybe there was nothing she was hiding and she really had lost her memory of that night. But she needed to be sure. She remembered well enough her own adolescence. She remembered the bitchiness and betrayals. She remembered feeling like nothing was in her control and the only peace she could find was in a moment of pain. If she was going to protect Rose, she had to find out exactly what Jude knew.

'Do you want to come up?' Sandra said from the top of the stairs.

Kassia smiled and picked up the flowers. On the landing Sandra told her she couldn't stay long, that Jude needed her rest, but that she was pleased to have a visitor. Sandra opened the door to let her in, then retreated back down the stairs.

'Hello,' Jude said with a weak smile. She was propped on a stack of pillows, a small pile of newspapers beside her on the bed. There were three vases of flowers on the chest of drawers and another on the mantelpiece.

'I guess you don't need these,' Kassia said.

'Thank you anyway.' Jude watched in silence as Kassia set the flowers down and turned to shut the door. 'To what do I owe the pleasure?'

Kassia glanced around the room, her eyes landing on a headline on top of the pile of papers. More gloomy uncertainty about the consequences of last month's vote. She felt unnerved by Jude's persistent smile. 'I wanted to see how you are.'

Jude gave a small shrug. 'Some days are good, some days are bad.'

Kassia stepped over to the desk chair and sat down.

'I'm not going to walk again, if that's what you're asking.'

'I'm sorry.'

'It could be worse. I wouldn't be alive, apparently, if someone hadn't called an ambulance.'

Kassia dug a fingernail into the flesh between her thumb and forefinger. 'And you – have you remembered anything else about that night?'

Jude looked at her for a long moment. 'Is there something you want, Kassia?'

Kassia felt her pulse quicken and the deep, sickening sensation of being right about something you've hoped isn't true. Jude's hard expression told her that she did remember Rose's presence in the Shaft, that she was daring Kassia to press her on it. But why was she covering for Rose? What was Jude worried about?

'Why are you really here?' Jude said, cocking her head.

'You're protecting Rose.'

Jude blinked. 'Why would I do that?'

Kassia studied her face. She looked paler than normal, tired. The wound on her cheek had healed, but left a long, raw scar. 'Because of what she knows,' she said slowly, taking a guess.

Jude looked away and Kassia felt a surge of adrenalin.

'You are worried what she will tell people.'

Jude snapped her head back to Kassia, every ounce of sweetness drained from her face. 'What do you want?'

'I want you to tell me what happened.'

Jude let out a frustrated sigh. 'Why? Rose has told you what she heard, right? That I saw Cali jump. So what? I couldn't have stopped her. I wasn't in her brain. It *wasn't* my fault!' Jude took a breath, her cheeks flushed.

Kassia stared at Jude, her mind racing. Jude lowered her eyes. There were fish on the pattern of the duvet covering her legs. A tear dropped into their ocean.

'What happened?' Kassia whispered.

'We had a fight and she ran off. Then—' Jude cut herself off.

'Then what?'

Jude sniffed. 'I saw her on the edge.'

Kassia bit down on her bottom lip. 'And you watched her jump?'

Jude wiped at her face with her sleeve. She looked up at Kassia with a hard expression. 'It's not as bad as what Rose did.'

Kassia held her gaze. She understood what this meant. How could she not with Rose wailing in the middle of each night about the coroner's report and what might have been different if they'd known to look earlier? What Kassia had done for Jude in calling that ambulance, in giving her a chance at life, Jude had denied for her best friend.

'I'm not going to go to the police, if that's what you're here to ask,' Jude said. 'I could – Rose is lucky – I'm the one they'd believe. But I won't, okay?' Jude smoothed the duvet covering her legs. Her hands trembled.

Slowly, Kassia was beginning to understand something else: what this knowledge would do to Rose. 'Listen to me carefully,' she said in a low voice.

Jude looked up, her face pale.

'Rose didn't hear you admit that in the Shaft. If she had, I don't think you would be here right now.'

Jude shrank into the pillows, fresh tears filming her eyes. Kassia knew she was scaring her. She knew Jude was just a frightened little teenager who'd made a big mistake, but she had to get through to her. '*You* are the one who is lucky, Jude. If Rose knew what you've just told me, she wouldn't care what happened to her. She would shove you down that shaft a thousand times over.'

Kassia paused, taking in Jude's wide-eyed fear.

'But I know now and that's what you need to worry about. Because *I* care what happens to Rose, even if she doesn't. So you and I are going to make a deal. You will not do anything to harm Rose and she will not do anything to harm you. Do you understand? You keep quiet and so will I.'

Jude let out a sob.

'And I don't want you talking to her. Ever again. If you need something, you come to me. Are we clear?'

# 2026

Rose looks at her wife, curled foetally towards her. She places a kiss on her forehead and slips from the sheets. The sun is pouring through the kitchen blinds. She's not used to sleeping this late. She wonders how many more mornings she'll have in this house.

She'd expected to feel panic after returning from Canterbury, but it still hasn't arrived. The bottle of Captain Morgan's sits unopened beneath the sink where she left it. The sense of relief at finally telling the truth, she's found, is too great to be crushed by a fear of the future. For the first time in ages, she feels at ease. What will happen will happen, she tells herself. This isn't the worst, after all. She's been visiting her mother every day and done what she can to sort out her finances, but the rest is out of her hands. Kassia, thankfully, has a lot going on at work and agreed to postpone their next round of fertility treatments without question.

She turns on the radio and pulls out a pan to make breakfast. The DJ tells her it's Sentimental Saturday and asks her to call in with her favourite nostalgic hit. He waffles about his first radio gig, a 2 a.m. slot, and plays a track Rose remembers from her childhood. The next reminds her of the only school disco she ever attended. The one after that she doesn't know, but a few minutes later she finds herself moving to the opening bars of a dance track she used to love. She pictures Diego for a second, his arms in the air and his hip thrust out, gyrating with some nameless stranger. Rose smiles as she cracks the eggs.

The nine o'clock news comes on and the presenters list the local headlines. Rose only half listens as they run through reports of tailbacks after an accident on the A20, four new drug-charge arrests at the port and another scandal hitting Dover council, this time in the form of a leaked email from the new mayor to members of the far-right hate-group New Nationalist Action Alliance, implicating her in the acts of vandalism carried out across the town last month. 'She could face criminal charges,' the presenter concludes.

There's a clatter in the hallway as something falls through the letterbox. Rose wipes her hands on a tea-towel and goes to see. A padded brown envelope lies on the mat. She picks it up, expecting it to be a book for Kassia, but in neat black print she reads:

## FAO: ROSE WALKER

She returns to the kitchen and slides her finger under the flap. Inside is a small storage drive and two sheets of paper.

*Dear Rose*

*Enclosed is the final cut of the documentary. Please watch it.*

*My producer has booked it to air from 11th July, but what I haven't told her is that I have wiped my hard drives and am sending you the only copy. The station address is below if you want it to be shown.*

*I thought this was my story, but for a while now I've known it is yours. If you read the next page, you will understand. I'm sorry it has taken me this long to admit.*

*It is up to you what you want to do with this. I have built my career on the premise that the truth is the only thing that counts. Those that keep us from it, I believe, keep us from ourselves. You*

*may or may not agree, but as it looks increasingly likely I will never*
*know what happened to my sister, I take comfort in being able to offer*
*you certainty about yours.*
  *Whatever you decide, I wish you peace.*
  *You deserve it.*
  *Tarek*

---

The second page is a DNA report. Rose scans the disclaimers telling her this technology is not approved for prosecution purposes and the report can only be used to detain someone for a maximum of thirty-six hours before acquiring a full clinical test. Then she reads the result.

| **ID number:** | Subject A | Subject B |
| --- | --- | --- |
| **Name:** | Tarek Zayat | Unknown Female |
| **Item:** | cheek swab | hair sample |
| | | |
| **Relationship:** | Alleged sibling | Alleged sibling |
| | | |
| **Date tested:** | 28th May 2026 | |
| **Facility:** | Canterbury Records Office | |
| **Results:** | Combined Full Sibling Index: 0.00001899 | |
| | Combined Half Sibling Index: 0.0163 | |

**Interpretation of Results:** Subject A is excluded as the biological sibling of Subject B. This conclusion is based on the non-matching alleles observed at the STR loci listed above with a DI equal to 0.
The probability of fraternity is 0%.

Rose stares at the final line. She remembers Tarek's face in the park as she told him the truth. It did not crumple as she'd expected with sorrow or pain or anger. He remained impassive as she spoke, holding his phone out as if all she was telling him was what she'd had for breakfast. She told him she was the one that killed his sister and he didn't react. Now she knows why. Mo was not Inji after all. The girl who fell to her death with Jude when Rose pushed her was not Tarek's sister. But that also means he has not found her. His search must continue.

'Baby?' Kassia calls from the bedroom. 'Is there coffee?'

'One minute,' Rose shouts.

For a split second, she is transported back to the Shaft, back to that night. She is staring at the skinny girl in Cali's jumper crouched and shaking on the stairs. Who was she if she wasn't Tarek's sister? Someone else's? Their daughter, niece, granddaughter. A child who once had a family and a home, then got lost halfway around the world. A stranger whose life Rose ended.

She glances at the handle of the cupboard beneath the sink. She's been meaning to get rid of the bottle before Kassia finds it – to open and empty it down the plughole so she has no chance of retrieving it again – but each day she has hesitated. There is something comforting about its presence. She does not need it, she's been telling herself, but she likes that it is there, waiting like a faithful lover in case one day she does.

She pulls her eyes away and returns her attention to the envelope. She slips her fingers inside and removes a small, thumb-sized storage drive. The label reads:

DOVER GIRLS.
WATCH ALONE.

# Acknowledgements

I've been told second-book syndrome is entirely common, but I was not in any way prepared for how difficult extracting this novel would be. It would not exist without the professional and personal support of some truly wonderful people.

My editors, Jess Leeke and Clio Cornish, have been masters at guiding me towards coherence. I cannot overstate how lucky I feel to work with them and the whole team at Michael Joseph. Special thanks also go to Clare Bowron, Sarah Bance, Emma Henderson and Laura Nicol.

My agent, Marilia Savvides, is brilliant, not least for her patience when I got stuck on a mantra of 'I can't do this!'

The only thing that balances the solitude of writing is the warmth and comradeship of workshops. I couldn't have finished this book without excellent feedback and critiques from the North London Writers' Group (especially Emma Flint, Caroline McCarthy, Cathy DeFretas, Marianne Levy, Alix Christie and Adi Bloom), from Stef Radu, Maria Thomas and Nina Reece, and from Cath Walsh, Heather Binney, Sam Priddle, Emily Tempest and Lisa Smith.

For help with research, I am eternally grateful to Liza Frank, Lucy Bryson and Nina Emett for talking to me early on about refugee experiences in Brighton. I'd also like to thank Mohib, Emmanuel and the other friends I've made through Refugee Tales (www.refugeetales.org – please check them out, get involved, and go on a walk!). Mohib, Alicia Lopez Rios, Miguel Ferreira and Reem Al-Awadhi have all been endlessly patient with my cultural and linguistic queries, while Mandy from the Western Heights Preservation Society was kind enough to give up her time to let me nosy around the Grand Shaft.

For propping me up through various crises of confidence, I need to thank my friend Nikolaus Morris, my housemates Oli and Geelia, and my mum, who has always been my rock, my sounding board and my biggest cheerleader. And for lending me her roof terrace to write a first draft on, I will always adore Amy Vlastelica.

My partner Lucy, I have to thank for everything, from supporting me through frantic plot meltdowns to agreeing to spend a rather unromantic Valentine's Day in Dover. I truly couldn't have written this book without you.

And, finally, to every best friend I have ever had:

Hannah
Ruth
Kayleigh
Steph
Abigail
Becci
Vicky
Vickie
Bethan
Rose
Gemma
Lizzie
Lizzi
Nat
Trev
Jen
Laura

Kristin
Kate
Fran
Bryony
Varsha
Emma
Alicia
xx

# A Note on Writing
# Other People's Stories

I struggled to write this book partly because of an awareness of the dangers of writing about experiences so different from my own. I am not arrogant enough to believe I have done anything like justice to the refugee experience, and would encourage readers to seek out those who do. Some books I recommend are:

*Butterfly*, Yusra Mardini
*The Pianist of Yarmouk*, Aeham Ahmad
*Refugee Tales, Vol 1, 2 & 3*
*Lights in the Distance*, Daniel Trilling
*The Displaced: Refugee Writers on Refugee Lives*, edited by
    Viet Thanh Nguyen
*The Girl Who Smiled Beads*, Clemantine Wamariya and
    Elizabeth Weil
*We Are Displaced*, Malala Yousafzai